Waiting
for the
Miracle

ANNA MCPARTLIN is a novelist and scriptwriter from Dublin, who has written for TV serial dramas featured on BBC UK, RTE Ireland and A&E America. She has been writing adult fiction for over ten years, and also writes for children under the name Bannie McPartlin. She lives with her husband Donal and their four dogs.

www.annamcpartlin.com

@mcpartlin.anna
@annamcpartlin

Waiting
for the
Miracle

Anna McPartlin

ZAFFRE

First published in the UK in 2021 by
ZAFFRE
An imprint of Bonnier Books UK
80–81 Wimpole St, London W1G 9RE
Owned by Bonnier Books
Sveavägen 56, Stockholm, Sweden

This is a work of fiction. Names, places, events and
incidents are either the products of the author's
imagination or used fictitiously. Any resemblance to
actual persons, living or dead, or actual
events is purely coincidental.

A CIP catalogue record for this book is
available from the British Library.

Hardback ISBN: 978–1–83877–388–5
Export ISBN: 978–1–83877–389–2
Special edition ISBN: 978–1–83877–581–0

Also available as an ebook and an audiobook

1 3 5 7 9 10 8 6 4 2

Typeset by IDSUK (Data Connection) Ltd
Printed and bound in Great Britain by Clays Ltd, Elcograf S.p.A.

Zaffre is an imprint of Bonnier Books UK
www.bonnierbooks.co.uk

To every woman out there struggling. You're not alone.
It will get better. Hang in there.

Prologue

May 2010

CAROLINE WAS DOUBLED OVER in the front seat of her car. Pain seared through her.

No big deal.

She was pretty much bathing in her own blood by now but not panicking.

Everything's A-OK.

Her hands were shaking and her legs weak. She gripped the steering wheel to steel herself for the big one, the one that would feel like a knife or skewer being shoved up her arse.

Could be worse, could be on fire.

She began breathing in and out slowly and with her eyes closed.

Here we go . . .

FUCKKKKKKKKKK.

Yip, there it went.

She was glad she was parked in her driveway. The last one happened while she was on the M50 – she had nearly driven into the back of a truck with a chemical warning sign and taken out half the motorway. She could see the headline blazed across the front page of a national newspaper: Woman on Her Period Blows Up Dublin.

She continued to breathe through the dull, sickening, unrelenting pain, waiting for the next short, sharp knifing before even

1

attempting to get into the house. Dave's car wasn't in the driveway. That was unusual; he was normally home before her. He was probably in the pub having one stiff drink before walking through the front door. *Fair enough*. She had a bottle of wine in the boot of the car. She planned to drink every night for the foreseeable.

Caroline wasn't a weeknight drinker normally, but aside from the monthly evisceration, there were extenuating circumstances. Their beloved dog, Bruno, had died at exactly 7 p.m. the previous night. She read the time on the clock on the car: six forty-five. *This time last night he was alive. He was snuggled into my chest and I was softly caressing his little ears just the way he liked. He seemed calm.*

She waited and watched for the car digital clock to hit seven – the moment her little boy died. In chronic pain and with an apocalypse in her pants, she whispered to him, 'One day anniversary today, buddy. I hope you're at peace. Mammy loves you.'

Once inside, Caroline made her way upstairs. She stripped off and got into the shower, watching the red water turn to pink and then clear while she sat in a ball with her back against the cold tiles, the full force of the water pouring down on her. She was bone tired. Her scorched insides burned and she ached all over. She just wanted to sit for a while.

Eventually, she stood up. When she was dry and dressed in a loose top and another soft pair of elasticated black trousers that she kept for days like these, she worried a little because Dave still wasn't home. *Problem at work? Delay on M50? OMG! Crash?*

As soon as she opened the kitchen door, she forgot her momentary fears when she laid eyes on Bruno's bed in the corner of the room, his toys placed neatly inside. She felt the urge to kneel down and take a sniff of it, to remind her of Bruno's smell, and suddenly she was on her knees, inhaling the dog's scent. *My little boy*. She was on the floor hugging and kissing Bruno's bed for a minute, maybe a little more, before coming to her senses, wiping his stray hair from her mouth and struggling to stand.

She was holding her stomach with one hand and clutching her lower back with her other, moving towards the kettle to boil water for a hot-water bottle, when she saw the note on the fridge door. She walked towards it, not expecting it to be life-changing.

It was folded over, with her name scribbled in big letters on the front and held onto the fridge by a magnet with the picture of a sheep and the words 'thinking of ewe' on it. She pulled it and the magnet dropped to the floor. She stooped painfully to pick it up. As she rose, slowly, she glimpsed those first few words:

I'm sorry, Caroline.

What the . . . ? She dropped the magnet, her full attention now focused on the note:

I can't do this anymore.
I love you, but we're done.
  Dave.
  XXX

Justin O'Halloran Knows My Name

Catherine

I WAS BORN IN 1959 AND Ireland was a very different place when I was growing up. I came from a small rural town – a pig farmer's daughter. We weren't rich but we weren't poor, either. I knew what it was to work, but I never wanted for food in my belly or clothes on my back. There were five of us – four boys and me.

The oldest, Charles, I barely remember. He was born with mental and physical disabilities so severe that my parents were encouraged to place him in a home. There was one photograph of him, a baby in my mother's arms, over the fireplace in the sitting room of our home.

I came after Charles, followed by Mickey, who was big and strong and nearly six foot aged fourteen. Next came Ronan – there wasn't a year between them but they were very different. He wasn't as big or strong as Mickey, which was unlucky for him because they fought all the time. My father didn't stop them. He liked a fight. He used to say, 'If you don't want to get beat, get better.' A year and a half after Ronan came Tim.

My mother's womb came out after Tim; it had been battered to bits by then. We were hard babies to carry; the doctor said it was a miracle she survived having us. Physically she did – I'm not sure about mentally. She wasn't the warmest woman in the world, but she could be kind when she put her mind to it. And my dad . . . well, when I remember him, mostly I just recall him working on the farm.

I don't remember when I first started watching Justin O'Halloran. The boys' school was next door to the girls' and we could see them play hurling through gaps in the mesh that covered the fence. Justin was so handsome – broad-shouldered with black hair and big brown eyes. He was fit, too, and such a fine player. He wore his hair like Elvis and he was definitely the best looking boy on the team – and in the school, even in the whole town. I think I loved him long before I knew him. I definitely dreamed about him, probably from about the age of thirteen. I won't say what we were doing, but I always said a Hail Mary as penance as soon as I woke.

I was beautiful back then. Of course I didn't know it, but looking back, it makes me sad to think I didn't embrace it while I could. My mother was a redhead; my father once had a head of black hair, but that was gone by the time he was twenty-five. My brothers were all sandy and freckle-faced, but I was like my mum – a traditional red-haired, pale-skinned, green-eyed girl. Even though I was tall and lean like my dad, I had a fine set of boobs on me and a good set of childbearing hips – at least that's how my doctor described me during a check-up that left my mother red-faced and fuming. I was fourteen at the time.

'Don't be listening to that man's talk of boobs and bearing anything, do you hear me?' she'd said as we left his office.

The first time Justin and I talked, I was coming out of a shop with a bag of bullseye boiled sweets and he was leaning on a car bonnet outside. He was looking my way and said, 'Hello, Catherine.'

Mary Mother of God. I thought I'd die there and then – and I nearly did.

I tried to wave, utter the word 'hello' and inhale all at the same time, causing the bullseye I'd popped into my mouth to shoot down my throat and stick halfway, immediately obstructing necessary airflow. I turned as red as a beetroot and, with no air reaching my lungs, I started to choke to death, right there and then.

But Justin was quick on his feet and in a matter of seconds, he was banging the back of me with his fist. As quick as lightning, the bullseye flew out and hit the shopkeeper's dog in the face. He barked fiercely and Justin stood between us, protecting me in case he pounced. To be fair, he was a geriatric Jack Russell, but between the lack of oxygen and Justin's heroism, I was swooning.

With legs made out of rubber, and with Justin's help, I managed to sit down on the car bonnet. He rested his hand on my shoulder. I was wearing three layers, including a duffle coat, and I could still feel his strong grip.

Justin O'Halloran is touching me!! Holy Mary, Mother of God, pray for me.

'You all right?' he asked when my breathing stabilised enough to answer.

'Yes . . . Thanks . . . for s-saving my life,' I stammered.

'I did, didn't I?' He grinned.

Then he leaned over and grabbed one of my sweets out of the brown paper bag and popped it in his mouth. I thought that was really cool.

'I've seen you before,' he said.

'I've seen you before, too.' *Every day since we were six.*

'Your name is Catherine Sullivan,' he said.

I nodded, chuffed to bits he actually knew my name. *Justin O'Halloran knows my name! Oh, thank you, Saint Jude of desperate cases and lost causes.*

'Your dad has a pig farm.'

I nodded shyly, embarrassed; his dad was a judge.

'I'm Justin O'Halloran,' he said, and he offered me his hand. 'Nice to meet you.'

As our bare hands clasped, a mind-altering and stomach-churning electricity sparked between us. I just couldn't answer. I felt faint, my stomach was doing the cha-cha, and I feared I'd gone and wet myself.

He walked me home, just to be sure that I was OK. At the gate at the end of the lane, nestled between acres of fields and grazing pigs, we stood together and said our goodbyes.

'Can we talk again?' he asked.

I nodded so vigorously he laughed at me. I was embarrassed and felt a little silly.

'OK, then, come up to the mesh tomorrow after the match and we'll talk.'

I nodded less enthusiastically and then I was off, running down the long, winding path home. When I hit the farmyard, I navigated around the pigs, even stopping to pet one or three of them.

'Hello, Marilyn Monroe. Hello, Neil Diamond. Hello, John Wayne.'

'You look happy,' Dad said as he walked out of the shed with a large bucket of feed.

'I am happy, Dad,' I said, and blew him a kiss like I'd seen Marilyn Monroe (the actress, not the pig) do from the steps of a plane on my best friend Rose's black-and-white TV.

Dad just laughed at me.

'I don't know where we got you from,' he said.

I wasn't really sure where they'd got me from either. No one had really bothered to explain.

Chapter One

Caroline

THE GROUP MEETINGS ALWAYS started at 8 p.m. on the dot and no messing. Tonight, Caroline sneaked in at three minutes past, which meant she missed the opportunity of grabbing a coffee and/or one of the dry biscuits left out in a round tin with a picture of a crying child on the top. She didn't want biscuits anyway. Her dog had died, her husband had just walked out on her and her womb was still trying to make a break for it, wearing her stomach as a backpack.

Only an hour and a half had passed since her life had been shattered. She had thought about skipping the meeting and staying instead on her kitchen floor in a small ball for eternity – but instead she'd stood up, boiled the kettle, filled a hot-water bottle, got in her car, placed it on her lap and driven to the meeting.

And here she was. She waved the hot-water bottle and sneaked into her seat, bowing her head to acknowledge her tardiness. Sheena, a no-nonsense countrywoman in her early fifties, standing at the top of the room, nodded to show she accepted the gestured apology. Caroline knew that Sheena was very strict on timing and it was her who wielded the power.

Sheena's eyes softened as she looked towards the woman who was speaking. The woman's name was Janet, a girl-next-door type cum Rose-of-Tralee type. She was what Caroline's dad would describe as a low-talker. When Janet spoke, everyone was forced to lean in.

'The doctor says I'm ready to try again . . .'

'What?'

A woman standing at the back of the room strode purposely forwards. She was tall, lean, muscular, built like an athlete. Her long dark hair was tied into a messy bun. She wasn't pretty. She was striking. Caroline couldn't put an age on her.

'The doctor says I'm ready to try again,' Janet said.

'I can't hear you.' The woman grabbed a chair and pulled it along the floor so that it made a terrible scraping sound.

Who the hell is this?

She seemed aggressive, despite the smile on her face. She was acting with the confidence that comes with familiarity, but Caroline had never seen her before and she'd been going to the meetings for two years.

Janet inhaled and raised her head a little. 'I said, the doctor says I'm ready to try again!'

'Oh, good for you.' The woman was sitting among the group now.

'What does Jim say?' Sheena asked. She didn't give the new woman so much as a dirty look for her disruptive behaviour. Instead, she smiled and nodded to her.

Caroline frowned. *Seriously?*

'Jim says he's not ready, not after what happened last time . . .'

The room became very silent. The women who knew Janet's story bowed their heads. The one who didn't, Rude Newbie, sniffed and asked, 'What happened last time?'

Oh crap, Caroline thought. *Here we go again.* Caroline was expecting a torrent of tears from Janet, but instead Janet answered the woman, talking even more quietly than usual.

'I had a molar pregnancy.'

'What's that?' the woman asked.

'The fertilised egg was non-viable.'

'And?'

The woman was really starting to get on Caroline's nerves now.

'It's described as a gestational trophoblastic disease,' Janet said in almost a whisper.

'Like one of those tumours with hair and teeth?'

'That's a teratoma,' Natalie said.

Natalie was the resident know-it-all. Not in a bad way – Caroline liked her – but she was just one of those people who collected and retained information. She was a small, petite woman who worked in a stockbrokerage by day and spent her evenings cleaning up at pub quizzes around the Dublin, Kildare and Meath areas. She was a shark.

'No hair, no teeth, just a clump of tissue really, like a bunch of grapes.' Janet sighed more loudly than she spoke. 'We called him Derek.'

'How did you know it was a him?' the new woman asked.

'We didn't, but Jim's father comes from a long line of Dereks. His older siblings all had girls, so if we had a boy there would be an expectation. He's a dickhead though, so, you know . . . Every cloud.'

Rude Newbie started to laugh. And then she really laughed. Out of nowhere, Janet joined in. Caroline wasn't sure why, but suddenly she was laughing, too. It could have been hysteria, but it didn't matter – her life was in tatters and if she didn't laugh, she'd just cry again. She guessed Janet felt the same.

Woman after woman started to giggle. Caroline wasn't sure if it was because Janet had named her gestational trophoblastic disease Derek just to piss off her father-in-law or whether it was Rude Newbie's contagious laughter that did it, but in the end, even Sheena joined in.

Sheena was usually much better at tea and sympathy than seeing the funny side of life. She was a serious woman, but also incredibly kind. She'd lived every loss and disappointment with each woman in the infertility group. She was well past having a baby now, but she'd started the group years before when she was desperate to have a child and no one could explain why she and her husband couldn't conceive. Unexplained infertility. It was a cruel and isolating diagnosis that threatened to destroy them – but it didn't. Sheena had set up the group to help others like her.

When finally the laughter stopped, Sheena invited Rude Newbie to tell the group a little about herself.

'I'm Veronica – thirty-five years old, a pilot and a speed freak . . .'

'The drug?' Sheena asked with some concern.

'No, fast cars on tracks.'

'Oh.'

'People call me Ronnie.'

'Are you married, Ronnie?' Sheena asked.

'No.'

'But you would like kids?'

'Yes.'

'But you are finding getting pregnant difficult?'

'Impossible.'

'Nothing's impossible,' Sheena said, which was ironic because for her, it had been just that.

'Would you mind if I just listened tonight?' Ronnie asked.

'No problem at all,' Sheena said. 'You are welcome here.' She encouraged the others to applaud Ronnie, then turned to Caroline, nodding at the hot-water bottle she was hugging. 'Caroline, how are you feeling?'

'How do I look?' She attempted to smile, but her eyes filled at the same time. *Shite.*

'Terrible,' Sheena said.

Caroline sighed. 'Bruno died,' she said, and the tears coursed down her cheeks before she could stop them.

Bruno had been diagnosed with dementia three years ago. Looking back, it had started at the age of thirteen, when Caroline's placid little terrier decided to take out joggers with a great vengeance as they ran past. Everyone else in the park was safe – kids, walkers, cyclists, all fine – but then a jogger would pass and Bruno would shake his head from side to side and growl. Then he went for it, running at them as fast as his tired old legs would let him, trying to sink his teeth into the nearest shin. So he went on the lead after that and it was a concern but not a huge deal. Joggers always got on Caroline's nerves a little anyway.

After about a year of terrorising joggers, Bruno began to find his way into corners, where he'd stay staring at the wall for hours on end. He became a little more distant, a little less friendly.

He used to be Caroline's best buddy, waiting for her by the window when she left the house, snuggling beside her when he knew she was too sore to sit on; he always knew just where to place himself to give her the best comfort and warmth. He was her pal, her shadow, ever since he was six weeks old, and she was his everything. Of course he loved Dave, too, but not like he loved her. Bruno knew she needed him more. He made the unbearable bearable.

Slowly, her loving little dog disappeared before her eyes. He became aggressive when touched, scared all the time, dazed and aggravated. In the end, he would spend his evenings walking around her kitchen in circles until he finally collapsed. She knew it was cruel to keep him alive, but she loved him and she didn't want to let him go. And more than that – she didn't want to be the one to make the decision.

She'd hoped his weary heart would just stop on its own. On the odd days when he would allow her to hold him, she used to whisper, 'It's OK to go, you know. Your mammy loves you. I'm so grateful for you. You've been my best pal ever. Couldn't have hoped for a better dog than you.' She'd given him permission – but he still wasn't leaving her. Even in his weakened, desperate state, he remained. Every now and again, she'd pick him up just to stop him from walking into walls and she'd hug him close. For a split second, he'd recognise her and rest his weary head on her shoulder. She'd kiss his furry face. *I love you.* Then he'd pull away and jump down and walk into another wall.

Dave couldn't bear to talk about it. The vet gave them a prescription of benzodiazepines to calm him and help him sleep (the dog, not Dave). They worked a little but not a lot. Six months later he was just as bad and now possibly addicted to benzos. It was far from ideal. Caroline had to summon all of her courage and talk to Dave.

'Please, Dave, we have to let him go.'

'Ah, no. It's not right. He'll go his own way.'

'Please don't make me beg to put my own dog down.'

'He wants to live.'

'He wants to walk through a fucking wall.'

'I can't, Caroline.'

'Please, Dave.'

'Shit.' He had looked down at Bruno asleep in a corner, twisted and shallow breathing. 'He's our boy,' he whispered, and she nodded.

'That's why. He's suffering, Dave. Please.'

Twenty-six hours ago they were sitting in Dave's car outside the vet's and Bruno was still and calm, as though he knew and he was prepared, as though he wanted to go. Caroline smelled him and to be fair, he was really old and he smelled a bit like a scented shit stick, but she didn't care, she inhaled him anyway.

'Mammy loves you.'

Dave had just looked forwards. He couldn't speak.

They had made an appointment and the vet knew why they were coming. They sat in the waiting room alone, Caroline holding Bruno close to her and Dave rubbing the dog's head.

'You're OK, boy, you're doing great. Everything's fine.' He kept saying it over and over.

When the vet walked into the waiting room, Caroline's heart started to race and she clung to her dog a little tighter, her eyes burning and lip trembling. Dave looked like he was about to bolt out of the door.

The vet, a kind man named Harry, had kneeled down in front of them and ruffled Bruno's fur.

'You're doing the right thing,' he said.

Caroline and Dave couldn't speak. They were both battling tears and snorting snot bubbles.

Harry escorted Caroline and Dave into an examination room. He took Bruno from them to put a cannula in his front leg to administer the drug that would stop his heart and they waited for him to return.

'I'm in bits here,' Dave said.

'I know, love.'

They hugged one another tight and she could feel his wet cheek on hers. She wasn't sure whose tears were running down her neck, but it felt cold and uncomfortable.

When Harry came back in, Bruno had a cannula inserted and it was secured to his leg by a red plaster. Red was always Caroline's favourite colour on him. That nearly sent her over the edge, but then he was in her arms again, still calm and just waiting. The vet had the drugs ready to go on a metal tray on the counter and

Caroline watched him move towards them, all the while hugging and kissing her dog and thanking him for not trying to make a break for it.

'Thank you, Bruno. Thanks for everything. Mammy loves you.'

She knew calling herself mammy to a dog made her sound ridiculous, but she didn't care. *I am his mammy and I do love him, and it is what it is.*

Harry snapped his gloves on. 'Are we ready?' he asked.

And of course they weren't ready, but Caroline slowly nodded her head.

Dave quickly kissed the top of Bruno's head. 'You're such a good boy, Bruno.'

'Now, folks, don't be scared – when the needle goes in, Bruno might fight it a little. As he's going, he might make a sound, a gurgle or a jerk, and he might even let his bowels and bladder go.'

Dave stood back.

'Are you sure you want to hold him?' Harry asked.

'Yes,' Caroline said with her face snuggled into him, crying all over him. 'I'm here, Bruno.'

He didn't move a muscle. He just stared straight ahead. As soon as the needle hit the vein, he was gone – no gurgle or jerk. He just died, quickly and so quietly.

'He was exhausted, the poor mite,' Harry said. 'Take a few minutes. You did good.' Then he left them alone in the room.

There was stunned silence, followed by a torrent of tears.

'We should say something,' Caroline whispered, throat sore and eyes burning.

Dave sniffed. 'Like what?'

'I don't know . . . What he meant to us.'

'OK.' He cleared his throat. 'Dear Bruno . . .'

'It's not a fucking letter, Dave!'

'Well what am I supposed to say? You're so smart, you do it.'

15

'You're right. Sorry. Just be natural.'

He straightened his back and shifted his weight from one foot to the other. He cleared his throat.

'Right, then . . . We loved ya, boy. Still do. Always will. Yours very sincerely, Daddy Dave.' He looked towards his wife with tears in his eyes. 'That all right?'

'That's lovely.' She was blubbing again. 'There's nothing else to say, is there, Dave?'

'No, love.'

'Except that I'll be lost without ya, buddy.'

'He knows.'

'He used to,' she said, and they both cried and rubbed Bruno.

Dave held her hand and kissed it. 'We're OK, Caroline, we've got each other.'

'I know,' she said, and she wished it were enough.

In the car on the way home, Caroline blurted that she wanted to try for kids again.

'I know I promised. I know we said we'd been through enough. I know it's hard and I know it's expensive and heartbreaking, but I want to try again.'

Dave was quiet. She could see he was getting angry; when he spoke it was almost through gritted teeth.

'You promised.'

'And now I renege.'

'You're thirty-eight! Your eggs are fucked and you're in bits. We tried so many times. We failed. The end.'

'This could be our chance, Dave.'

He pulled the car into the hard shoulder.

'There's still time. One more, please.' She wasn't sure anymore if she was crying more over their dead dog or their non-existent baby.

'We've just lost the dog and you're getting your period, so we'll discuss this when you're done with that.'

She really hated it when he did that. 'What kind of bullshit thing is that to say?'

'You see – you're getting snotty.'

'I'm getting snotty because you are suggesting that because I'm due my period, I'm not being reasonable . . .'

'And as a result, you get snotty.'

'Well, you involuntarily shit an iron brick and see how snotty you get!'

'We agreed we'd move on with our lives and we'd be happy. I'm happy, Caroline.' He looked her right in the eye. 'Are you?'

And maybe it was because she'd left Bruno dead on a steel table in the vet's or because she was due her period, but she couldn't answer him. Dave silently turned on the engine and put the car back in gear. They drove home without a word.

The next evening, he'd pinned a note to the fridge door and left.

'I'm so sorry about Bruno,' Sheena said now, and all of the others joined in to offer their sympathy. They all knew about her Bruno. Caroline spoke of him often.

'Who's Bruno?' Ronnie asked.

'Her dog,' Natalie said. 'A terrier, sixteen years together. He was her rock.'

Ronnie seemed unimpressed. 'Oh.'

Caroline wiped her tears. 'I'm fine. I'll be fine. It was for the best.'

'Get a new one,' Ronnie said.

Caroline felt the overwhelming desire to physically hurt her.

'That's the thing about animals – they're replaceable. People aren't. At least most of them . . . Men, they're replaceable – or is that just me?' Ronnie looked around the group. 'What do you think?'

Caroline began to sob, not because Ronnie had dismissed her dead dog but because her husband of eighteen years was gone too and he was not replaceable. Eighteen years together, filled with love, loss, joy, sadness, hope, heartbreak, laughter – and her marriage was ended in a fifteen-word note the day after her dog died. One question kept popping into her head. *Who the fuck leaves their wife on a Wednesday?*

She didn't ask herself why. She knew why.

'It's a bit soon for a debate on replacement,' Sheena said delicately, pulling a fresh tissue from the box she kept on a small table beside her. She passed it via Janet and Natalie to Caroline. 'It's going to be all right,' Sheena said, 'and when it's not, call me.'

Caroline nodded as she blew her nose. She didn't mention Dave's departure. She couldn't bring herself to – it was too fresh, too surreal.

'I'm fine, really,' she said, and thankfully, the group moved on.

After her, it was Mary's turn. Mary was from the inner city. She had just finished her first round of IVF and her blood test was scheduled for three days' time.

'I'm sick with nerves. I keep thinking, I am! No, I'm not! Then I am! Then no, I'm not. Me fuckin' nerves are gone. My Pete thinks I'm having a breakdown.'

'It's perfectly natural,' Sheena said.

'Maybe,' Mary said, 'but I'm telling yis, if I'm not, I'll fuck myself in the River Liffey.'

'Ah now, none of that talk,' Sheena said. 'And anyway, it's much harder to drown yourself than you'd think – and the Liffey is filthy. You don't want to die in filth, do you, Mary?'

'No. Not really. I'm not great with smells. Maybe I'll just throw meself off a building.'

'You won't do that, either.' Everyone leaned in to hear Janet's low voice. 'I heard of a woman in Cork who threw herself out of her second-floor window. She's a paraplegic now. Couldn't even try again if she wanted to.'

'Jesus!' Mary said. 'All I'm saying is if I'm not pregnant, I'll want to die.'

'Yeah, well, you won't.' Caroline shifted in her seat. 'You'll be devastated and angry and bitter as fuck, but you won't want to die. You'll just want to put yourself through it all over again.'

Eight years, four operations and six IVFs, a dead dog and a husband who just left, and I still want to do it all over again. Pain ripped through her. She felt a little queasy. *What's wrong with me?*

'Do you want us to pray with you?' Sheena asked.

'You're either pregnant or you're not, Mary,' Ronnie said.

Caroline couldn't work out where her accent was from.

'Four Hail Marys and a bloody Our Father isn't going to change that,' Ronnie said.

'Thank you for your input, Ronnie, but although prayer may or may not affect the outcome, it might help the soul,' Sheena said in her most pious tone.

Ronnie sniffed and belched. Sheena made a face you'd expect from a startled four-year-old.

'Excuse me,' Ronnie said and then winked at no one in particular.

The praying was the only element of the group meetings Caroline couldn't handle.

'Mary, a prayer?' Sheena said.

'You're grand, thanks,' Mary replied, and Ronnie gave her the thumbs up.

After the meeting, Caroline made her way to the coffee counter. She was in the queue just behind Ronnie.

'You want milk in yours?' Ronnie asked, turning to her.

'No, thanks.'

Ronnie made them both coffees and handed Caroline hers.

'I'm sorry about your dog. I've never had one, so they always seemed a bit annoying to me. Then again, so did kids until . . .' She trailed off.

Caroline relaxed a little. 'I know what you mean. I wasn't sure I wanted them either, and then I did. And when I couldn't it became all I wanted.'

'That's shit.'

'Yeah, it is.'

'I don't want to be insensitive and I know I can be, so forgive me, but one day when you're ready, there's loads of dogs out there that need rescuing. You look like you've a lot of love to give.'

Caroline bit back tears. 'You're not the insensitive arsehole I thought you were.'

Ronnie looked a little shocked, but then she grinned.

'Thanks. And aside from whinging over a dead dog in front of a woman who lost a mole called Derek, you're not such a dick, either.'

Caroline giggled. 'Good point.'

Ronnie held out her cup to clink, and Caroline accepted.

'Anyone else a bit of craic in this place?'

'Not that you'd notice.'

'I bet Janet has a bit of go in her. If only she'd speak up.'

Caroline tried to smile. She found herself warming to Ronnie, but she needed to go. Her hands were starting to shake and her knees were about to give up.

Ronnie looked her up and down. 'Go home,' she said, 'before you collapse on us.'

Caroline nodded. She placed the half-full coffee cup back on the catering table. 'It was nice meeting you.'

'You too.'

At home in the bath, Caroline lay quietly in the dark, focused on a flickering candle. She'd taken pain medication so that she could attend the meeting. She wasn't pain-free but she was comfortable, and reality seemed a little frayed around the edges. Her face felt tight – the facemask she'd slathered on was hardening – and her bobbed black hair was thick with conditioner. She listened to the silence and absorbed the emptiness of the room.

Dave's gone.

She'd promised – after multiple operations, after IVF rounds, after all the hormones and heartbreak, she'd promised she was done. That together they would find a way of being enough.

She'd lied.

Caroline had tried hard to let go of motherhood, and maybe if she and Dave lived in a bubble, everything would have been fine. But with each happy announcement from friends and family, it became harder to smile. Without hope, she isolated herself from the many new mothers in her life. Their endless baby talk and repeating the funny things their kids said made her want to scream. After one kids story too many, it began to dawn on her that she didn't give a fuck if little Tommy could go potty and she wondered why it took ten minutes to tell a story that ended with a toddler taking a shit in a plastic box. Over the years, jealousy turned into boredom or antipathy and she could no longer relate to her peers. Many of her friendships just faded away.

Worse than that were her siblings, who decided the way to go was to hide their pregnancies from her for as long as possible. When it was completely unavoidable, they'd reveal what was already obvious to every dog on the street. This big announcement usually took place over Sunday lunch in her mother's house, and always with a patronising, 'We just didn't know how to break it to you . . .'

Her younger sister, Michelle, had got nervous and blurted, 'I mean, we literally only started trying. I've been on the pill for years and . . .' before their mother coughed loudly and shook her head.

That pissed Caroline off. It shouldn't have, but it did. Instead of being happy for her sister, she'd only felt fury, while Michelle felt unnecessary guilt. It made things awkward between them. They drifted further apart after the baby was born. She barely saw her nephew, now four. She had a slightly better relationship with her other sister, Lisa. She had three kids and lived in Cork, so it was easier to have a phone conversation every now and again and press 'like' once in a while on the endless stream of family photos.

In the end, aside from her parents and her work colleagues, all she had in this world was Dave and Bruno. Attending the group meetings helped. Those women weren't a replacement for friends, but it was nice having people to talk to who understood.

Despite Caroline's condition, she was managing to hold down a good job as a litigation solicitor for a large firm, specialising in contract disputes. Her employer gave her the option of working remotely when she needed to and with the help of her lovely personal assistant, Nuala, she managed. No matter how bad the pain was, once she was propped up in the safety of her own bed, hopped up on meds and surrounded by hot-water bottles, she could work through anything. In fifteen years at the firm, she had missed only one arbitration meeting and had never missed a court date. She no longer enjoyed her job, but the salary and perks were undeniable.

She should have respected Dave's position. They had been through enough.

But she couldn't. Because, what if . . . *What if this is our time? What if our baby is just waiting to be born? What if . . .*

But her husband had had enough of what if, and she had promised and she had lied.

He's had enough . . .

The air in the room felt dense and heavy.

She didn't make a sound, but a torrent of tears loosened the mud mask on her face.

Finally . . .

She stayed in the bath until the water was so cold that it made the myriad of scars and burn marks on her swollen stomach stand out, red and angry. Her body ached and her extremities were turning blue.

What have I done?

The Tale of Sad Siobhan

Catherine

JUSTIN AND I TALKED through the gaps in the mesh that covered the school fence most of that week. They were short conversations, but enough to convince me that he was the most important person in the world. We sat on either side of the fence; I imagined our backs were touching and, despite the fence between us, my insides fizzed with excitement. We talked for hours. He wanted to study law in Trinity and be a judge like his dad. I wanted to have three kids.

'I'd like you to have three kids, too,' he said, and I nearly died with happiness.

After that first week we met face to face in an old cinema. It was really just a dark and freezing-cold broken-down building, but we sat together and held hands. Despite the damp smell and the possibility of rats, I was in heaven.

'Can I kiss you?' Justin asked.

Thank you, Saint Jude of desperate cases and lost causes . . .

I nodded and my insides fluttered as he kissed me softly. It felt so nice I thought I might vomit.

Don't vomit, please don't vomit.

We kissed a lot after that and one day he placed his hand on my boob – over my vest, my knitted jumper and my stupid bulky duffle coat, but I definitely felt it. I kissed him deeper, and then he was on top of me and I got a bit of a fright, him being so broad and heavy, so I pushed him off.

'Sorry,' he said, brushing himself down, 'I got a bit carried away is all.'

'I know,' I said, pulling at my clothes. 'Me too.'

I smiled at him just to let him know that I was OK and that everything was great. I didn't want him thinking bad of me, that I was some sort of tease. I wanted him to feel for me the way I did for him. Pure love.

'Doesn't matter. We'll get married as soon as we're done with school,' he said, and I thought I might have a heart attack there and then and die of fright.

I was very dramatic in those days. *Justin O'Halloran's wife. Catherine O'Halloran! No, Mrs Catherine O'Halloran or Mrs Justin O'Halloran. Mother to the three O'Halloran children!* I was glad I was sitting down, because my knees felt terribly weak.

I gathered my thoughts together before they all blew out of the top of my head, and reality dawned on me. He was seventeen and he was in his Leaving Cert year. I was fifteen and would be in school for two more years.

'But you're going to college to study law and I'll be working on a pig farm.'

'I'll be home some weekends and anyway, I'm turning eighteen in six months and then no one can tell me what to do.'

He sounded so sure of himself, I believed him.

'I love you, Justin,' I said. I really meant it.

'I love you, Catherine.'

And maybe he meant it, too – in that moment, at least.

My best friend, Rose, was nervous about him. 'Don't get too carried away, Catherine,' she told me, but I just wasn't capable of listening. She didn't ever talk badly about him because she knew how I felt, but she warned me to be careful. She didn't tell me that we were no match or that I was living in a dream. She wanted me to be happy – but she also saw what I couldn't see: that I'd never be enough for Justin O'Halloran.

She patiently listened to my daydreams about our future and the stupid stories I'd tell about innocuous things he'd say and do. In her bedroom and with music on loud so her mother couldn't hear, I'd tell her about the kissing and the touching. She wanted to hear every detail, but she was scared, too.

'Don't do anything you'll regret, Catherine.'

'I won't.'

'You have to say no.' She whispered it, even though Eric Clapton's 'I Shot The Sheriff' was blasting.

'I'm fifteen!' I said.

I'm not sure either of us really knew what we were talking about. There was also a part of me that knew I'd do whatever he asked. I was scared of that. I couldn't risk losing him and I knew I had to walk a very fine line. I just wasn't sure where that line began or ended.

'You don't want to end up like Sad Siobhan,' Rose said.

We'd all heard the stories about young girls who disappeared from towns and suburbs all over Ireland, with no real explanation, leaving behind a trail of whispered gossip and fear. There was one such girl from our hometown. She had disappeared one day, twenty years before, when she was sixteen. She was one of the Burke family and her name was Siobhan.

Her family never spoke of where she had gone, but the rumours were that she'd gotten herself pregnant – that's how they said it back then, she'd gotten herself pregnant, like that was even possible. When it came to sex, women were sinners and men were not only absolved from sin, but they were also omitted from the narrative completely. *She'd gotten herself pregnant.* They said that Siobhan's parents had sent her away to a mother-and-baby home.

Nobody really knew much about what went on in those places, but theories were rife and all were laced in horror. All we knew for sure is that the girls who ended up in those places were girls to be shunned. Once inside those walls, they disappeared from view, and so they should. They were fallen women, a stain on society. We never questioned it any more than we questioned the sun rising or setting. It was what it was.

Poor Siobhan returned home a decade later and according to those who knew her, she was a very different girl. She was skin and bone and walked with a stoop, head down, facing the ground, her gnarled hands always knotted in front of her. She refrained from making eye contact and rarely spoke. Her mother spoke for her. She was always neat and tidy, in clothes too old for her. She'd been home at least ten years by the time I was old enough to notice her. She was always called Sad Siobhan. She wasn't yet forty but she might as well have been a hundred. To us, she didn't seem like a person at all, just her mother's broken doll.

I turned sixteen two days before the New Year's Eve dance. Mammy had bought the most beautiful cream silk and she pulled out her sewing machine and followed the pattern we'd both picked out together. In the space of a week, she'd made the prettiest dress I'd ever seen. The hemline was a little crooked and the neckline a little snug, but it was still the most precious thing I owned. I looked at myself in the mirror and I imagined myself as his bride. *Mrs Justin O'Halloran.*

Our school held a New Year's Eve dance every year and I had been to just one before. I had loved it. It went on until the stroke of midnight, when everyone would holler and cheer and stand for the national anthem before the nuns blew whistles and escorted us from the building. Some went into buses, others into the cars of parents who had missed out on their own celebrations to drive their children home. The townies always walked. That was usually even more fun than the dance itself, walking home in the middle of the night, talking under the stars.

I spent the whole of my sixteenth birthday wishing the day away while my family made a fuss of me. As I ate my mother's chocolate cake, I just kept thinking in two days' time, I'd been in Justin's arms, dancing in front of my friends and the whole school.

That night I wore my perfectly wonky dress and when he saw me, he smiled his lovely big smile and my heart melted. I was dancing in his arms and within moments, the hall and everyone in it faded away.

'Justin O'Halloran, step back from that girl!' Sister Joan interrupted. 'I want to see at least three inches between you at all times.'

She roughly pulled us apart, but as soon as she turned her back, we were glued to one another again, linked by hips, chests and cheeks, dancing to Frankie Valli's 'Can't Take My Eyes Off You' and Etta James's 'At Last'. When the fast songs played, like the Beatles' 'Help' or The Rolling Stones' 'Satisfaction', Justin and I sat on two wooden chairs, drinking orange and holding hands. When the nuns weren't watching, I rested my head on his shoulder.

Mrs Justin O'Halloran.

I watched Rose with my other friends, dancing together, giggling and laughing. At one point, Rose came over to ask me to join them.

'Go,' Justin said, and I really didn't want to, but he moved away to talk to his friends.

I danced with Rose and the other girls for two songs, constantly watching him over her shoulder, missing him despite the fact he was only a few feet away.

'I miss you,' Rose shouted in my ear.

'I'm still here!'

'Are you?' she said, and the question stung me.

'I'm doing my best.' I felt suddenly annoyed. *Why can't she just be happy for me?*

'He's not the centre of the universe,' she said, and I walked away from her because, to me, he was.

While my friends danced, gossiped and giggled, I sat with Justin, watching the swirling lights as the DJ spun the tracks on the stage of the school hall.

Afterwards, as the nuns attempted to disperse us, we started on the road home. First we were part of a gang, Justin's friends and mine, all talking and making jokes. Some were sharing cigarettes and others were swigging from bottles of contraband alcohol they'd hidden along the way, but little by little, they all peeled off until finally we were alone.

Arm in arm, we walked on, hugging one another tightly and battling the biting cold. The stars were hiding the night behind a heavy fog.

Half frozen, we stopped outside his granny's house. It was a grand place, on a hill looking over the town. His granny had died of old age four months earlier.

'It's just gorgeous,' I said. I'd always loved that house.

'It's nice enough.'

'It's better than nice – it's the dream.' I grinned.

It had magnificent stone walls, a massive front door and big wooden windows. It was perfectly square, and detached. It was beautiful.

'Do you want to see the inside?' he asked.

I hesitated. I had always wondered what the inside of that house looked like, but of course I was scared. It was night-time. We were alone. I was desperate for a break from the cold and excited too, but I knew I should get home. *What if Mammy and Daddy are still awake? They'll be missing me.*

'Come on,' he said, fishing for the key under a plant pot. 'I'll probably get it in the will anyway, so one day it might be yours, after all.'

Holy Saint Jude!

That swung it. I followed him into the grand hall. He grabbed some matches out of his pocket and lit a candle.

'The electricity was shut off a while ago.'

'I like it. It's romantic.'

And it was romantic. It was two horny teenagers alone in a dimly lit grand old house, loved up and with our nethers on fire. One lit match in a bat cave would have felt romantic.

He started to show me round. First, the big old sitting room with sheets covering the furniture. Next, the kitchen – which wasn't as nice as I'd expected, but I immediately knew what I could do to make it homely. Then he moved to walk up the grand staircase and I stalled for a moment. Just a moment. *Can I trust him? Can I trust me?* I didn't even really know what would be asked of me or what could happen. I only knew when two people 'loved one another', they had babies.

Justin turned to me and his eyes seemed to twinkle in the candlelight. When he held out his hand, I let go of my worries and reached for him.

He led me to a big bedroom at the top of the stairs. It had a large bed in it, covered in pillows and blankets.

He sat down. 'Do you like it?'

'It's everything I thought it would be.'

'Good.' He smiled. 'You deserve the best.'

Then he took me in his arms and we started to kiss. It felt so good. The soft bed underneath us seemed to envelop us whole. He unzipped my dress and pulled at the straps of my slip and bra. Suddenly, I felt the sting of cold on my breasts – but not for long, because they were in his hands, and it felt weird but also fantastic.

He moved underneath, rubbing himself against me, and the friction did something to me – it was thrilling, electrifying even, and I swear I didn't want it to stop. I writhed on his bulging pants and then instinctively, I unzipped him, freeing the bulge. And honestly, it seemed to spring out of nowhere. It frightened the life out of me, but Justin pulled at my pants and before I knew it, it just slipped in. No fiddling or fecking around – one minute it was bulldozing its way out of his pants and the next it was inside me.

It hurt a little at first, like a sharp pinch, and then I felt a trickle and hoped I hadn't just peed on him. That would have been terribly embarrassing. I forgot that worry quickly enough as he moved inside me. It hurt a little more and then it stopped. All of a sudden, I was sitting on him and riding him like a prize pony. And it felt so good, I didn't want it to stop.

It did, very quickly. He spewed something hot and sticky inside me and his bulge collapsed like a wet rag. *Oh!* I remained sitting on him for a moment or two, unsure what to do and conscious my breasts were on show. I folded my arms to cover them and looked around the room, waiting for the right moment to extricate myself.

31

He looked up at me and laughed. 'What are you doing?'

'Admiring the room,' I said, and I was only half lying. I was admiring the room, but I was also battling the urge to cry. I didn't know why.

'Do you want to lie down beside me?'

'Yes, please.'

I dismounted him and lay there looking up at the ceiling. He grabbed a cigarette from his jacket and lit it and inhaled. I liked the smell of a burning cigarette, although I'd never tried one. Daddy believed that smoking cigarettes was just a way to burn money.

Thoughts of my father tied my stomach in a knot. I needed to go home but I wanted to stay.

'Did you like it?' he said after a few drags of the cigarette.

'Yeah. You?'

'Yeah. Can we do it again?'

'I don't know,' I said. 'We have to be careful.'

He turned to face me. 'We're getting married anyway, aren't we, Catherine?'

'Yeah, I know, but . . .'

'As soon as I graduate from Trinity, we'll marry.'

'But that's three and a half years away.'

He smiled. 'I'll come home every weekend and you'll come to visit me. I'll be staying with my aunt. She lives in a huge house on the South Circular Road with a big red door. You can't miss it.'

'As if your aunt would have me.'

'She won't even know you're there – I can sneak you in and out whenever I want.'

'How do you know?'

'Because my brother, David, did it for the entire three years he lived with her. The house is so big he barely saw her once a week.'

'But what about my parents? They won't like me going to Dublin.'

'It'll be fine, I promise.' He kissed me deeply, and I believed every word he said.

Chapter Two

Natalie

Natalie always enjoyed the meetings. She loved a laugh and 'Derek' would make her smile for a while. Still, on the bus home, she mused on what poor Janet had gone through and shuddered at the thought.

Natalie wasn't like the others in the group. She had no fertility problems; in fact, her consultant said her bloods were excellent and no stimulation was required. The issue was that her partner was a woman.

Natalie had always wanted children. She wanted a big family, and when she found Linda and love, she was in her late twenties. Now, aged thirty-two, it was time.

Linda had never really thought about kids. 'I mean, why would I?' she'd said the first night Natalie mentioned it, over cheese and wine in a basement just off South Wicklow Street.

'Why would you not?' Natalie asked. 'Look, I'm not suggesting either one of us gets with a man – I'm suggesting sperm donation.'

Linda needed time to think. It was a big ask. *Kids!* Natalie knew Linda hadn't pictured her life with kids; she had pictured excelling in her career, taking big expensive, adventurous holidays, retiring by the sea – not crying babies, snot and attitude.

It took a year to talk Linda round and another year to research. Natalie was all about research; the more information she had, the more likely they were to succeed.

Natalie had joined the group at first for that reason and though it had been helpful, after a few weeks she began to feel like a fraud. The other women were so honest, but she was wary of speaking too openly. It was 2010 and though Ireland had come a long way, there was still so much further to go. Family was deemed off the table for most gay couples.

One night, she finally opened up.

'I can have kids – at least, I think I can. I'm healthy and all the numbers look good. I'm sorry.' She heard herself apologise, which she hadn't meant to do. 'Not sorry I can have a baby, but sorry I'm a lesbian.' That is not what she meant at all. *What the hell is wrong with me?* 'Not sorry I'm a lesbian either, obviously, just . . .'

'Stop talking,' Caroline had said. 'We know what you mean.'

Natalie smiled.

'Besides, you're not our first lesbian,' Sheena said. 'There was Christie and Georgia and that tiny woman, Edna.'

'Edna wasn't a lesbian,' Caroline said. 'She was asexual.'

'Oh, that's right. She ended up with triplets.' Sheena nodded to herself. 'I don't know how that tiny woman carried three babies without buckling.'

And that was it, Natalie was embraced by the group and it felt really good.

She read every book on home insemination using a known donor and hospital insemination using an unknown donor. She inhaled all of her fellow group members' stories, committing each and every outcome to memory. She spent her Saturdays online seeking information on practices all over the world. As an actuary, she was good with numbers – she played the numbers game a lot – but in the end, listening to the women in the group, she realised numbers meant nothing. *It will either work or it won't.*

After much deliberation, they decided to ask Linda's twin brother, Paul, to donate.

It had sounded icky to Natalie when Linda first brought it up. 'Seriously? Your brother, *Paul*?'

'If the baby is from your egg and growing in you, I want some of me in the mix. Paul is the next best thing to me.'

'But *Paul*?'

Linda might never be called a beauty, but she was fit and strong. Aside from her penchant for multiple earrings, she had a softness to her face and the most beautiful big brown eyes. She was special. She was bright and articulate. She was a human rights solicitor, making an actual difference in the world.

Paul was balding and doughy with a paunch. He was the manager of his local grocery shop, having started there part-time aged sixteen. He was a bachelor who hated everyone and everything, and who loved to complain while bathing in his own misery. Paul was not special. Paul was *Paul*.

'I want the baby to be part of me,' Linda said. 'If I'm doing this, I need some assurance that this child will be my family no matter what.'

Natalie saw what she meant. If their relationship were to end, Linda would have no legal rights – but Paul, as the biological father, would, and ultimately, Paul would do anything Linda asked. In a way, it was perfect – except for . . . well . . . It was Paul.

Fucking Paul.

They asked him over for Sunday lunch. Natalie made a pasta dish. He announced he was gluten intolerant.

'Since when?' Natalie said.

'Since Tuesday when I did the test.'

'Fuck off, Paul,' Linda said.

It was not a good start.

Over a dessert of lemon tart and cream – which was not gluten-free, but Paul said he'd chance it – Linda broached the matter of him being their sperm donor. He was shocked. So shocked a little tart fell out of his gaping mouth.

Natalie's stomach turned a little. *Fucking Paul.*

'Is this a joke?'

'No,' Linda said firmly. 'We want a baby. Natalie will carry it and you will provide the genetic material so that I'll be related to my own child.'

'If you're so worried about genetic material, why don't you carry it?'

'I'm forty-four, Paul.'

'So?'

'So, my eggs are fried. Natalie's thirty-two and she's always wanted to have a baby.'

He sat back, thinking things over, and a few seconds of a heavy kind of silence followed before he piped up, 'So, do I have to ride her?'

'No you do *not*!' Natalie almost screamed.

Paul put his hands in the air. 'Eh, you're the one looking for my swimmers. I'm not sure you are aware of it, but they live inside my knob.' He pointed to his penis.

'That's not technically true, Paul,' Linda said calmly. 'Look, we'll wait until Natalie is ovulating and then we'll ask you to cum into a cup and we'll take it from there.'

'What do you mean?'

'I mean, you toss off in the bathroom and I'll insert it into my girlfriend's vagina using a home insemination kit in the bedroom.'

Natalie winced. Linda was often described as not being one to beat around the bush and never had it been more true. Paul's face was a picture and Natalie felt a pang of pity. Linda would get what she wanted, because even if Paul had the personality of a brick, his love for his sister was undeniable.

'God Almighty.' He was wearing a look of genuine horror. He sat in silence for what seemed like a very long time. 'And then what?' he finally asked.

'And then, hopefully, a baby.'

'And what about me?'

'What about you?'

'I'll be a dad?' He emphasised the silent question mark.

'Well, technically,' Linda said, 'but the baby will be ours.'

'So what about me?'

There was a moment's pause.

'What do you want, Paul?' Linda asked. As his twin sister, she knew him better than anyone in the world. He would do it because it was for her and she would pay because it was him.

He folded his arms. 'All that anyone wants is to be appreciated, Linda.'

'How does ten grand sound?'

He smiled. 'Appreciative.'

'For that amount, I want you to see a doctor and get tested. We need to make sure your sperm is good.'

'Fine – but for the record, my sperm are great.'

They shook on it before Linda hugged her brother tightly. Natalie heard her whisper in his ear, 'I would have gone to fifteen.'

He pulled back and grinned. 'I would have taken two.'

She hugged him again. 'Thanks.'

It turned out Paul's sperm were not great. A semen analysis revealed Paul was suffering with low motility and after questioning, he admitted he'd received a very serious kick to the balls three years earlier from a woman in a bar, for reasons he refused to specify. It resulted in testicular torsion and a night in A & E, and he was forced to wear a cup for two weeks. That fact combined with a lifetime of smoking dope and wearing briefs tight enough to cut circulation made it a perfect storm for slow sperm.

Linda was devastated. If Natalie had been honest, it felt like a relief. Maybe they could move on to someone who wasn't *Paul*. Then the doctor told them how changes in lifestyle could help with motility and Natalie saw how quickly Linda picked up.

Damn it.

Six months later, Paul had given up smoking dope and had lost two stone. Following a second test, his motility had increased, but not so much to recommend home insemination. The consultant felt an intrauterine insemination in hospital would work best.

'It won't be a home conception,' Natalie said.

'No, but if you want, we can try for a home birth?' Linda sounded almost excited.

Natalie grinned. 'I love you.'

'I love you, too.'

Paul raised his eyes to heaven. He looked like a different person now. He seemed happier too, and gradually, Natalie realised she no longer minded that Paul would be the father of her child. Everything had clicked into place. It all made sense.

Natalie's transvaginal scan revealed she had an ovary reserve of fifteen, which meant she was in good shape. All she needed to do was wait for day fourteen of her natural cycle the following month and Paul's slightly sluggish sperm would be inserted inside her. Hopefully, all being well, she would soon be baking a baby.

Sitting on a bus on the way home from the infertility group, Natalie daydreamed about all that lay ahead. She wondered if they'd have twins. After all, Paul was a twin. Two for the price of one – she liked those numbers. Soon, she'd be inseminated . . . with Paul's sperm. *Don't think about that. Focus on the baby.*

She spent the whole ride home thinking about baby names with a huge grin on her face.

Pig Girl

Catherine

JUSTIN AND I HAD sex twice after the New Year's Eve ball, once in February and again in early March. It was 1976. Justin was working hard to get into college and his dad was on his back about wasting time with 'the pig girl' – that's what he called me. Once, in the middle of March, he stopped his fancy car and made Justin call me over.

'Who are you?'

'Where are you from?'

'Your father, is he the pig farmer?'

'What are you doing with my son?'

I answered all of his questions but that one. I wasn't sure he'd like the answer.

He told me to go home and made Justin get into the car. As he drove away, I heard him calling me a bloody 'pig girl'. Justin just bowed his head.

I told myself that Justin wasn't his father. Besides, he loved me.

After that, we saw each other less and less. There was always an excuse not to meet. He was studying hard. His exams were only three months away. He had expectations to succeed that I didn't understand. He told me I didn't understand a lot. I wanted to, but it's hard to understand something unspoken. Even when we did spend time together, he was sulky and distant. I, too, was behaving differently. I was more emotional, less rational. I tried to hold on to the old me, but I found it hard.

'I can't have you crying,' he told me once. 'I'm too busy for tears.'

'I'm sorry.'

I said 'I'm sorry' a lot. He never did.

It wasn't just my personality that was changing little by little. My body was changing, too. Slowly at first and then all of a sudden it just ran off on me, doing its own thing. I hadn't bled for a while and then I did and then I didn't again. I really didn't know where I was. I hadn't felt sick like my friend Nora's mother, who used to walk round town with a bucket round her neck. I had been tired, but I thought that was mostly down to me being so sad because I didn't see much of Justin anymore. Weeks went by and then that belly of mine just popped out. I didn't know what to make of it.

At first I thought stress eating was making me fat. Rose noticed it and I told her it was nothing. 'I'm eating too much,' I said. And she believed me because I was. Every time I saw her I was scoffing sweets.

I cried myself to sleep every night, tossing, turning and not really sure what was happening. I was fighting my own suspicion and frightened to face the possibilities. If Justin noticed, he never said. He pretended he was too busy studying to see me, promising everything would go back to normal after his Leaving Cert exams.

I pretended I believed him, and maybe I did. I wasn't prepared to let go of the dream life he had promised.

Chapter Three

Janet

JANET ARRIVED HOME TO find her husband, Jim, with his head stuck in the washing machine.

'What are you doing?'

'I'm building a bridge – what does it look like I'm doing?'

'It looks like you've stuck your head in the washing machine.'

He came out, red-faced and hassled. 'I swear I put a load in with a pair of my favourite red argyle socks and only one's come out. It disappeared one of the grey one's last week and a yellow one a month ago. That machine has it in for me.' He pulled his leg back as though he were about to kick it.

'Don't kick it.'

'Kick it? I'm going to tear it apart, babe.'

'No you're not,' she said. She sat down at their kitchen table. 'Sit down, Jim.'

'No.'

'Why?'

'Because you're going to start . . .' He trailed off.

'It's time.'

'It's only been a year.'

'Exactly,' she said. 'It's been a year. It's time.'

'Can't.' He looked like he was going to cry. 'Not now.'

'Why not now?' she asked, and maybe it was because she talked softly, but she always sounded so calm. Jim never did.

'Because . . .'

'I know it's hard after what happened, but we want a family, remember?'

Jim was pacing now. 'That was before the clusterfuck that was Derek.'

'Please don't call Derek a clusterfuck.'

Jim pulled a chair out from the table and leaned on it. He had tears in his eyes. 'Three early miscarriages before Derek. All that hope and disappointment . . . And you heard the doctor – if you have one complete molar pregnancy, the chances of a second are increased.'

'So?'

'So?' he repeated. 'So you took to your bed for three months. I had to clean you, feed you and dress you. I thought you were going to die on me.'

'I know I took it badly, but that was before I found the group. They've really helped, Jim. I won't do that to you again. I swear.'

Jim put his face in his hands. For a while he sat in silence, thinking. After five minutes, he lifted his head and he looked at her.

'We'll try,' he said, 'but no matter what happens, we're done. I'm getting the fuckin' snip.'

She smiled and nodded. 'Absolutely,' she said, and then she was on her feet and hugging him tightly. 'I love you, Jim.'

'I love you too, babe.'

She moved to leave the room.

'Babe,' he said, and she turned back. 'You wanna start tonight?'

She grinned. 'That was a quick turnaround.'

'Yeah, well, if we're doing it, might as well do it. Besides, my balls are bursting.'

'I'm not ovulating till next week, so save them till then.'

He sighed. 'Right, then.'

Janet took the stairs two at a time.

'I hired *Tropic Thunder* from Chartbusters,' Jim called after her.

'I'll get my jammies on,' she said.

Although Jim had been the only person in Janet's life to hear her without using the words 'what', 'pardon' or 'for God's sake, speak up, love', the distance of a room, hall and fourteen steps was probably too great even for him.

Janet stripped off and as she did, she patted her belly. Her pregnancies hadn't left any signs; it had been too early for stretch marks. She looked in the long mirror that was part of her wardrobe, turned side on and pushed out her slim tummy, arching her back. She wanted a big belly, full with child. She wanted morning sickness and exhaustion and to fart at inappropriate moments. She wanted to be swollen. And she'd happily trace every stretch mark that came with getting bigger. After seven years of marriage, three years of trying, two cycles of IVF, three early miscarriages and Derek, she was ready for what would come.

This time I'll be better. This time it will work. This time . . .

The Bull Priest

Catherine

IT WAS LATE JUNE and with his Leaving Cert behind him and a new life in Dublin beckoning, Justin was all but gone out of my life by the time my mother dragged me by the hair up the stairs and stripped me of my clothes to reveal my growing belly. She slapped my face and spat on me.

'How dare you!' she screamed and slapped me again.

That was the moment my pregnancy was confirmed.

'Who did this?' she roared. 'Who did this to you?'

I was so shocked and scared I blurted his name. 'Justin O'Halloran.'

Mrs Justin O'Halloran.

'The judge's son?' she asked, stepping back from me, her voice high-pitched and almost squealing.

'Yes.' I was crying and shaking with the cold, covering my naked bulging belly with my hands.

'And he loves you?' she asked.

'Yes,' I said, although I wasn't so sure anymore.

My mother nodded. 'Fine then, get dressed and go for a long walk. Don't come home until it gets dark.'

'Why?'

'Because I have to tell your father and it's better that you're not here.'

She walked out of the room, and I dressed and left as quickly as I could. I didn't know where to go, so I went to Justin's grandmother's house and fished the key from under the plant pot. I spent hours lying flat on his grandmother's bed, the place the baby was made. I was alone. He never came. I didn't expect him to. I knew he was in Dublin taking extra classes before the exams began in two weeks, but still, as I lay there, I dreamed he would save me.

As day turned to night, I walked the lonely winding path to the farmyard and to the house. My father was waiting by the door in his best suit, my mother standing by his side wearing her only fancy dress. He didn't look at me when he instructed me to get in the van.

'Where are we going?' I asked, though I suppose I already knew.

'The O'Hallorans.'

My brothers Mickey and Ronan were standing behind the front door, both staring at me like I were some sort of exotic beast. Neither spoke. As the van took off, they just shut the door. No one spoke in the car, either. The silence was as thick as gone-off cream, and the stench of anger and disappointment was sour. We stopped outside the judge's house; the lights were on in all eight windows and there were two cars parked in the large driveway. Daddy got out and walked to the front door while my mother and I waited in the van.

It was Mrs O'Halloran who answered the door. She was wearing a black velvet dressing gown.

'I'm sorry to disturb you, but I need to speak with your husband urgently,' Daddy said.

Mammy just looked straight ahead towards the mountains fading to black.

'He has office hours.'

'This is personal.'

'It's after ten. I'm sure it can wait till morning.'

'It can't.' He placed his foot in the door so that she couldn't close it.

She called out for her husband. 'Jeffery,' she said, and she repeated the name again and again, getting a little louder and more hysterical with every call. She wasn't moving. She probably thought Daddy was some kind of vagrant. She kept herself firmly between him and her posh antique telephone table.

Finally, Jeffery O'Halloran appeared, looking flustered, in a shirt, waistcoat and jacket paired with wide pyjama bottoms.

'What is it, woman?' He stopped and took a look at my father. 'What do you want?'

'I need to speak to you.'

Are you there, Saint Jude? I wondered.

'So speak.' He looked out at me and at my mother in the van, and I knew what he was thinking. *The pig girl.* He didn't move a muscle.

Please, Saint Jude. Help me.

'Fine. If it has to be here, then it has to be here.' Daddy looked briefly into the van.

My eyes were glued to him and the O'Hallorans. He turned back round to face them.

'Your son has gotten my daughter pregnant,' he said, and Mrs O'Halloran nearly collapsed.

'Oh my God!'

'Who says?' the judge said.

'I say.'

'And what proof do you have?'

'My daughter's word.'

'And what good is the word of a pregnant harlot? For all I know, she could have been with half the boys in town . . .'

'Jeffery, please . . .'

'I'll handle this, Imelda,' he said, pushing his wife back. 'I will speak to my son and if he tells me he is not the father, I will take you to court and I will sue you for slander.'

'My daughter is not a liar.'

'Really? And before today would you have said she was a whore?'

Then the judge slammed the door on my father.

I heard my mother make an almost imperceptible whimper. Daddy stood looking at the door for a moment or two, not really sure what to do. Then he turned and walked to the van before screeching out of their big driveway and hurtling through the town like a tornado. He didn't speak except to say four words: 'If you are lying . . .'

I prayed Justin would do the right thing and tell the truth. I prayed. *Oh, Saint Jude, please . . .*

Three nights later, I woke in my bed to find a bull of a priest standing over me with his hand covering my mouth.

'It's time to go, Catherine,' he said.

The room was dark, but I saw the silhouettes of my parents standing under the light in the hallway. He dragged me to my feet and instructed me to put on my dressing gown. I didn't own a set of slippers. I looked for something to put on my feet, but he was already shoving me down the stairs.

Mammy was crying. She was holding my daddy's old suitcase.

'Mammy?' I asked, and I was crying now, too.

'It's for the best,' she said, handing it to the bull priest before looking away.

'Mammy? Mam! Mammy?'

She refused to meet my gaze.

'Mammy, please.'

The priest almost had me to the door. I looked back to my father.

'Daddy?'

'I warned you about lying,' he said, and he stepped into the kitchen and slammed the door.

'But I'm not,' I screamed, trying to pull away from the bull priest. 'It's him who's lying. It's not me. I swear, Daddy.'

I could hear my three brothers walk onto the landing. I briefly glimpsed Tim, crying and waving to me as I was being dragged out of the door.

'I'm not lying,' I screamed as loud as I could, so that half the county would hear me and maybe someone, anyone, would believe me.

The wind was whistling and we were remote. No one was coming to save me. My love was a liar and I was a fool. I looked for a car, but all I saw was a bicycle. The bull priest tied the case to the back of it and forced me on.

It was 30th June, 1976 and I was facing the long, winding pathway, five months pregnant. I was barefoot and on the side-bar of the bicycle of a priest who smelled of old whiskey, leaving behind my home and family for the last time.

Chapter Four

Caroline

TWO DAYS PASSED AND there was no word from Dave. Caroline knew he'd be hiding out in his mother's house. She desperately wanted to see him, but there was no way in hell she was going there.

Well played, Dave!

Jean, his mother, was a big woman with a huge presence and an odd world view. She'd never really warmed to Caroline and she'd overheard her one Christmas complaining that while Caroline was pleasant enough most of the time, she didn't half go on about her lady bits.

'I mean, if I wanted to talk about fannies, I'd go and get my own sorted, but I don't, so I won't.'

Jean suffered from a prolapsed womb, which she ignored for five years until eventually she began to walk around as though she were carrying a ball between her legs. At last she went, she talked; she got her fanny sorted. If only life were that simple for Caroline. Having had a very successful operation, Jean was so pleased that she snapped and told every female and gay male she could find. She didn't bring it up with heterosexual men, because she didn't want to be raped – she actually said that one night after one too many wines: 'I mean, you mention your fanny to one of those fellas and you're asking for trouble.'

Caroline tried to keep out of her way as much as possible on account of her being a mad yoke. Jean always had an opinion on what Caroline should do to sort herself out and every time they spent longer than five minutes in one another's company, she'd lament that it was such a crying shame that her only son wouldn't be passing the name down to a new generation. Caroline invariably reminded her mother-in-law that with a surname like Stroker that was never going to happen anyway. In the early years, Jean had defended the name vehemently, especially when Caroline refused to change from her maiden name of Murphy.

Over the years, Caroline and Jean built up a mild tolerance for one another, but there was no love lost. Caroline couldn't face her now, not while Jean's son was back in his old room, which she kept exactly as he'd left it aged twenty-one. *He just moved out. He didn't die.*

Caroline tried to call him on his mobile phone – four times the first day and then three the second. She wondered how many unanswered calls from a wife to her husband it would take for her to look crazy. She figured less than five would be the appropriate amount. She didn't text. She hated texting and anyway, what would she say? *Please come home?* She'd already said that on his answer service seven times in two days. There was nothing else to add. Nothing had changed.

She made a private appointment with her specialist for the following Friday. After one more day of hell, she returned to work in the office and stayed late to avoid her empty, soulless house.

Later that week, she closed a big case at work successfully and was taken to lunch by the two partners. Over pan-fried scallops, they asked her if she would consider a partnership. It came as a shock. It was recognition for her accomplishments and lovely to be considered, but she just couldn't imagine it. And besides, with a baby coming . . . She had a habit of doing that, pretending to herself that just because she was trying for a baby meant that she'd have one. Even without the prospect of another round of IVF, she was barely managing to cope with her endometriosis as it was. Partnership would mean more time in the office; and it just wasn't practical.

She asked for some time to think. Susan Clarke told her to take her time, but Elizabeth Wylie wasn't as cool about hanging around. The two women were strikingly similar – both tall, thin blondes, both single, strong, focused, academic. The only real difference was that Susan had a life outside the office and Elizabeth didn't.

'Look, Caroline, we've got an opportunity here to be the best and brightest all-female partnership in Dublin. Snoozing is for losing.'

'I think you mean, if you snooze, you lose,' Susan said.

'Same thing.'

'I disagree.'

Elizabeth ignored her. 'Big picture, Caroline – your name on the wall: Clarke, Wylie and Murphy.'

Caroline was even more relieved than ever that she hadn't changed her name to Stroker. *Clarke, Wylie, Stroker!* Within five minutes of the sign going up over the door, they'd be known as Clarke's Willie Wankers.

'Give me a week to think it over,' she said.

Days passed and there was still no sign of Dave. Caroline was sitting in front of her consultant, Lucy Belton, wondering where he was or what he was doing.

I'm here, back in this place, missing you.

The walls were white, unadorned by prints or posters. The table was pushed up against a window that looked down on a car park, and the only thing to suggest that she'd gone private was the upholstered chair she sat on and size of the bill she'd pay on the way out.

Lucy Belton was a small, fit woman in her sixties with short grey hair. She was reading Caroline's file when she entered. She looked up and smiled at Caroline as she sat on the comfy chair. She offered to shake hands.

'How are you, Caroline?'

'Good, thanks.'

'What can I do for you?'

'I'd like to try another round of IVF,' she said, and she noticed the look that crossed Lucy Belton's face – a mixture of confusion and pity.

'Oh, Caroline, I thought we'd agreed . . .'

'We did,' she said, 'but I changed my mind.'

Lucy purposefully looked around the room to make a point. 'And where's Dave?'

'He didn't change his mind,' she said, and she could feel the weight of Lucy's gaze upon her. 'I'm doing it alone.'

'I'm sorry.'

'It's fine,' she said.

They both knew it wasn't fine.

'What are my options?' she asked. 'Regarding sperm?'

'We have a partnership with the European Sperm Bank. You have access to a wide choice and once you choose, it will be exported here in time for your treatment.'

'Brilliant. I presume there's a menu.'

'Of course. Look, Caroline, sperm donation is the easy bit. We need to discuss your egg quality.'

'Well, if you're not happy with the quality, we can use a donor egg, too.'

'So you want to go through another round of IVF to stimulate your own eggs first?'

'Yes.'

Lucy flipped the pages over. 'Despite our last attempt?'

'We had two good embryos to implant.'

'The word "good" is a stretch.'

'Fine, viable.'

'Just about – neither resulted in a pregnancy and we had zero embryos to freeze.'

'I want to try.'

'And my advice is that you have put your body through enough, but if this is really what you want . . .'

Caroline nodded. 'It is.'

'I'll get you booked in.'

Lucy didn't need to explain the process. They both knew what lay ahead. After discussing the dates of Caroline's last period and agreeing a start date, she headed home.

It's good. It's going to be good. Dave will see that. He'll get on board and if he doesn't, I'll have the European Sperm Bank . . . But he will . . . He will.

Dave's car was in the driveway when Caroline got home. Her heart skipped a beat. *He's home!* She sprang out of the car, unlocked the front door and dropped her briefcase in the hallway. He was in the kitchen, making a cup of tea.

'Are you back?' she asked.

'Yeah.'

She moved towards him, but he stopped her by raising his hand.

'I'm here because my mother treats me like I'm fourteen years old and I've nowhere else to go.'

'Oh.'

'I'm moving into the spare room, Caroline, and after some time to think, we'll need to work out our next steps.'

The mortgage was paid for. She knew the next steps he meant were divorce and selling the house. It felt like a slap to the face.

'Oh, right.' She felt sick and disappointed – and responsible. It was her fault.

Was he really serious? He looked serious. *Couldn't be. Could he?* She'd make him see sense. At least now he was home, she could work on him.

'There's fresh sheets on the bed.'

'Thanks.'

'You're welcome.'

He's back! You're mine now, Dave Stroker!

He went into the sitting room and turned on the TV. He sat there staring through it. She went upstairs and had a shower. Then she slipped into bed and, after reading the same page of her book four times, she gave up, turned the light out and lay in the dark, thinking. She thought about what she was doing. She knew how much she'd hurt Dave, that he was mentally and emotionally disengaging. Even her consultant had all but cried when she said she was going for another round. She knew she was being selfish and maybe even foolish, but she had to give it another try. She was sorry but not sorry.

I have to try. Just once more.

The next group meeting Caroline attended, Ronnie caught up to her in the car park.

'You look better,' Ronnie said.

'I feel better,' Caroline admitted. She had been pain-free for over a week.

'You weren't here last week.'

'I had to work late.'

'Oh yeah. What do you do?'

'I'm a solicitor.'

Ronnie recoiled a little and even scrunched up her face.

'What's wrong with that?'

'Nothing really, except what's the difference between a solicitor and God . . . ? God doesn't think He's a solicitor.'

Caroline laughed. 'That's a shit joke.'

'But is it a joke?'

'Do you know, I instantly disliked you, then I liked you and now I'm not sure.'

Ronnie chuckled and slapped her on the back. 'Not the first time I've heard that.'

Sheena was in a tizzy when they got inside. The floors had been waxed and Mary had slipped. She was lying on her back, crying, refusing to get up.

'This is better than the soaps,' Ronnie whispered into Caroline's ear.

Sheena paled when she saw Caroline. 'She didn't land on her back, she just slipped and steadied herself and then she lay on her back, I swear to God above.'

'What's going on, then?' Caroline asked.

'I'm not pregnant,' Mary said just as Natalie and a few others walked through the door.

Caroline and Sheena sat down on the freshly waxed floor beside Mary. Caroline took her hand.

'I'm sick for you,' she said.

'We all are,' Sheena said.

Mary sat up and wiped the tears from her eyes. 'I thought . . . this time . . . this is it . . . I'll be a mother and we'll have our family. And it was a hard round, you know . . .'

And the women nodded. They knew.

'I thought it would be worth it, but it wasn't and now there's nothing.'

Sheena hugged her. Ronnie went to the catering table and came back with a cup of tea for Mary.

'There is something. There's you. You have you. That's something,' Ronnie said.

Mary stood up with Sheena and Caroline's help. She looked at Ronnie. 'Yeah, well,' she said. 'I'm sick of me.'

'Don't be. In the end, you are all you have.'

Caroline saw a flash of pain cross Ronnie's face as she spoke. She recognised it instantly.

Mary took the tea. 'Thanks.'

'I put two sugars in,' Ronnie said as Mary took a sip.

'Oh Jesus! I'm allergic to sugar – anaphylactic shock! You're after killing me!'

Ronnie looked like she might run, but the others were well used to Mary.

'Only messing, two sugars are fine,' she said after a moment and moved to her chair.

She cried quietly through the meeting, but she smiled, too.

When no one else was talking, she looked to Caroline. 'How many rounds did you say you had?'

'Six,' she said.

'Jesus Christ.' Mary was crying again. 'I'm not able for that.'

'You're able for more than you know,' Caroline said. 'And I'm going again.'

Sheena nearly dropped her teacup. 'I thought you'd come to terms with moving on.'

'I thought I had, but then why am I still coming here for the past few years?'

'Because it's good to talk.'

'I want more than talk. I want a baby.'

'Good for you,' Janet said, 'and Dave.'

Caroline paused. 'I might be doing it on my own.'

Mary bowed her head. 'He left you?'

'More like a fork in the road – he's on one path, I'm on another,' she said.

She didn't really believe it. Caroline was a 'prepare for the worst, hope for the best' kind of person.

'That's shit,' Ronnie said. 'I'm really sorry.'

'Thanks, girls.'

Another few women spoke after that. One, a girl who'd only been to a meeting a handful of times, stopped by to tell them all she was fifteen weeks pregnant. Mary cried again.

'It will happen for you, too,' she said before she got up and left midway through the meeting.

Mary looked like she wanted to punch something or someone.

'She's just trying to be supportive,' Caroline said.

'She's gloating.'

'She's happy.' Everyone leaned in to hear Janet. 'She's just happy.'

'How are you getting on, Janet?' Sheena asked.

'All good. We've got an appointment with the consultant next month.'

'Good for you.'

After the meeting, Ronnie suggested to some of the ladies that they go for a drink in the pub across the road.

'I can't,' Mary said.

'Why not?' Ronnie asked.

'Because if I drink any alcohol, I'll drink all the alcohol, and if I do that I'll get into a car and drive into a wall.'

'Ah! But if you're that drunk you'll probably miss the wall.'

Mary was not impressed. 'No thanks.'

Ronnie turned to Caroline, Janet and Natalie. 'What about you three?'

Caroline would usually have made excuses, but she didn't want to return to her divided house. 'I'm in.'

'Fuck it,' Natalie said and it was the first thing she'd said all night.

Janet nodded. 'OK.'

'Great.' Ronnie clapped her hands together. 'Let's do this.'

Caroline had never had a drink with the ladies before and she was looking forward to a large one.

The Pitiful Whore

Catherine

I MET MY BROTHER, CHARLES, just once. I was seven and he was nine. I don't remember much more than that old hospital disinfectant smell. It was so strong it burned the insides of my nostrils. I remember mustard yellow walls and cracked black-and-red tiles under my feet and the sounds of crying, wailing, giggling, shouting and excitement all at once. I felt my mother squeeze my hand tightly – so tight, it hurt – but I didn't make a sound.

He was in a cot, my nine-year-old brother. He was staring at the wall, his limbs twisted, his mouth gaping, dribble snaking down his raw red chin into the folds of skin and lines that etched around his neck. He didn't look like anyone I'd ever seen before and of course he terrified me. My mother spoke kindly to him.

'There's my boy. Oh! Charles, look who I've brought to see you.' She pulled me closer. 'This is Catherine. She's your sister.'

He didn't look our way but he made a sound, like a gurgle and a groan all at the same time. His eyes never left the wall. My mother sat and placed me on her knee. She spoke to him about the farm and all the work that had to be done. She talked about my father and how Charles looked so like him.

'He's so sorry he can't come to see you – he just can't leave the farm. Charles, you understand, don't you?'

He groaned and kicked, and I suppose she took that as an answer in the affirmative, because she beamed at him.

'Course you do. You're such a good boy.'

Then she spoke about my brothers. Mickey had just turned five, but he was a big and strong child, so different from the fragile state I found my older brother lying in, there in front of me in a steel cot.

'Mickey's asking for you, and so is Ronan. They send all their love.'

I knew it wasn't true. Mickey and Ronan hadn't asked her to pass any messages on because they didn't know him. Like me, they had barely registered his existence.

'Oh, and the weather outside, Charles, can you feel the light breeze coming in through the window? Can you smell the sweet honeysuckle climbing the walls outside? Oh, and I brought strawberries and that nice Sister Bridget will make sure you have some for your tea.'

As she talked on, her voice faded and instead I focused on this twisted boy, my eldest brother, Charles, in a steel cot staring at the wall. I thought about what it would be like to be in his head and body and I wanted to cry. He never stopped dribbling and his face, chin and neck were raised and sore. I wondered why with all her talking she didn't lean over and wipe him. She didn't touch him the whole time we were there. As we left, she leaned over and grabbed his blanket, pulling it up and over him before blowing him a kiss.

My brothers never met Charles. I have no idea why she decided to bring me just once. She visited the hospital once a month, on her own. My father never went.

I thought about Charles often after that – how gentle and sad his eyes were, staring at the wall. Charles was just a boy who needed love and I was sorry I hadn't had the courage to touch him that day in the hospital.

I had hoped that the nuns had been gentle and kind to him, but now I knew better.

I remember the long road beyond the big steel gates. The path seemed to go on forever before it eventually opened up onto a courtyard, facing the largest house I'd ever seen. It had maybe forty windows within imposing old grey stone. I couldn't take my eyes off the big red door, just like the one Justin's aunt had on the South Circular Road.

I knew it was what they called a mother-and-baby home. Of course, it wasn't a house and it definitely wasn't a home.

It had started to rain at some point on our journey, and my hands and feet were blue with the cold. Although I'd just travelled ten miles on a cross bar I didn't feel any pain. My mind was too clouded by fear and confusion.

But then I saw a grotto in the grounds, the Virgin Mary holding the baby Jesus, and I saw Sad Siobhan's face looking right at me as clearly as though she were standing in front of me. I felt something inside me collapse. I knew there was no escape and it terrified me.

The priest pulled me towards the red door. He rang the bell, once, twice, three times. We waited, both soaked to the skin, him carrying my father's suitcase. I was standing in nothing but my nightie, so wet from the rain that it was stuck to my protruding belly.

The door opened to reveal a nun and she was the scariest-looking woman I'd ever seen. Her expression was formidable and she smelled strongly of bleach. The priest pushed in past her, dragging me along, and the nun shut the heavy red door behind us. I stood on the hard, cold, intricate mosaic tiles, staring down at blood flowing from my right foot, tracing the trickle as it inched along the tile, making its own design. I hadn't been aware I'd cut myself, but I was dragged barefoot, kicking and screaming, across a farmyard, so it must have happened then.

They didn't speak to me, only to each other. The priest dropped the case onto the floor.

'That's some night out there. I'm soaked through.'

'So you are, Father. It's a bit late for intake.'

She attempted a smile. It was chilling.

Saint Jude, are you there?

'When God calls,' he said and he winked at her.

'You should get warm – there's some scones left over from tea. I'll deal with this.'

He didn't look at me. Instead, he leaned in to her.

'She doesn't have a medical file – she's not seen a doctor.'

The nun stared my way, disgust written all over her face.

'By the look of her, she's at least four months gone, if not five.'

'The parents only just found out.' He sighed deeply. 'Heartbroken.'

'What else would they be? It's not every day you find out your own daughter is a fallen woman.' She looked at her watch. 'If you hurry, you'll catch the second half of *The Late Late Show*.'

'Well now, how well you know me. It's my very favourite. Scones, tea by the fire with *The Late Late* and the lovely Sister Mary Frances – sure, this isn't turning out to be a half-bad night at all.'

'You'll have to do without me. I believe in God the Almighty in heaven and not in Gay Byrne on *The Late Late Show* with his feminist agenda.'

The priest chuckled to himself. 'Live a little, Sister.'

'I'll do it my way and you do it yours.'

She attempted a frosty smile again before they both walked off in different directions, leaving me to stand on the cold tiles, alone.

I didn't move. Not an inch. I don't know why I didn't open that big door and run. But I was freezing, exhausted and terrified. To my left was a giant wooden staircase and beyond that a fireplace, a piano and a few chairs. To my right was a long corridor lined with doors. One of them was slightly ajar and light streamed into the otherwise dark hallway.

I waited, sick with fear, shaking violently with my teeth rattling so hard that I feared I'd break them. I thought about lying down on the cold tiles, but I'd seized into one pathetic position, hunched over, hugging my protruding belly. I felt like one of the many statues that stood on plinths, gazing down on me. If I had turned to stone, they'd probably have called me the Pitiful Whore.

Eventually, Sister Mary Frances reappeared.

'What are you doing still standing there? Stupid girl!'

'I don't understand,' I said, and my voice sounded different, like it came from somebody else.

She pointed to the open door. 'Knock, wait to hear the word "enter" and walk inside.'

She tutted and I moved to walk towards the door.

'Excuse me?'

I turned to face her.

'What did your last slave die of?'

I didn't understand until she pointed to my father's case. *Oh.* I slowly picked it up and I walked to the room indicated, knocking on the door.

When I heard a voice say the word 'Enter,' I walked inside, to be greeted by a thin rake of a woman with a long face and teeth too big for her tiny mouth. She was staring at me with contempt.

'Dear God, look at the state of you.'

I stood shivering and shaking. I was bursting for the toilet and scared I'd make more mess on the clean floor. There was a chair in front of me, but I wasn't invited to sit down.

'I'm Sister Joanna. What's your name?'

'Catherine,' I said.

'Not anymore. From now on, you will be Katie.'

'But that's not my name.'

'It is here.' She handed me a piece of paper with a number written on it. 'That's your work number. Memorise it.'

I looked at it. My number was 10078.

'How far along are you?'

I wasn't sure. I'd only had sex three times.

'Is this your first offence?' she asked.

'I don't understand.'

'Have you been pregnant before?'

'No.'

'You have no shoes.'

'No.'

'No, what?'

'No, I don't.'

'No, Sister Joanna.'

'No, Sister Joanna. I left in a bit of a rush.'

She looked to my suitcase. 'Well, I hope someone thought to pack you a pair, because otherwise you'll be stuck. I have no medical files for you.'

'No.'

'No, what?'

'No, Sister Joanna.'

'How did you know you were pregnant?'

'Because my mammy slapped me.'

Sister Joanna thought about that for a moment or so, and I thought I noticed the smallest hint of a grin.

'Can you feel it move?'

'I think so.'

'You think so, what?'

66

'I think so, Sister Joanna.'

She scribbled something down and then rang the bell. She continued to write as I stood there, waiting, until Sister Mary Frances entered the room and suddenly I remembered why Sister Joanna looked familiar. My brother Tim got a game of Buckaroo for Christmas and she was the spitting image of the plastic bucking horse.

'Time to go,' she said, and she looked at the case that I had unwittingly dropped to the floor.'

'Yes, Sister . . .'

'. . . Mary Frances.'

'Yes, Sister Mary Frances.'

I picked up my father's suitcase and followed her out into the hallway, up two floors to a large doorway.

'It's lights out. The girls are sleeping. Don't speak to them – not tonight, not any day or night. They are *not* your friends. Take this time to be silent and penitent for your mortal sin, and hope to God that with hard labour and prayer, we can still salvage your soul.'

She closed her eyes and blessed herself before she opened the door.

I could see sleeping mounds, twenty deep, in steel cots. The room felt even colder than me and I was colder than the dead. Sister Mary Frances pointed towards a bed at the end of the room; it was the only one free. Then she walked out. The door clicked closed and I made my way to it in the dark.

The room was silent save for gentle breathing. There was a small locker beside the bed and a cross hanging on the wall just above it. Jesus was nailed to it, the painted blood trickling down his feet. There was a small rail beside it and a few dangling empty hangers. I opened the case and searched for shoes to put on my bloodied feet. There was one pair of runners, four pairs of knickers, four pairs of socks, three of my mother's maternity dresses and my grandmother's light blue wool cardigan. My mother had packed a bra that was already too small for me, two old vests, a bath towel, a face flannel, one tube of toothpaste and rosary beads. That was all.

I moved towards the window and looked out. I could see the grotto under the moonlight and the grounds seemed to go on for miles. Somewhere behind me I heard a girl quietly sobbing. I got into the hard bed and wrapped myself up in the rough old bedclothes that smelled musty. I didn't cry that night; I was too shocked, hurt and frightened.

But I cried every night after that.

Chapter Five

Natalie

THE DATE WAS SET and Paul's sperm were ready. Natalie wondered if she was. Of course she wanted to be pregnant and a mother to a child, but *Paul's* child? Even with the haircut and the change to his usual grey pallor, his personality hadn't changed. He was still *Paul*. He'd insisted on being paid a grand a month for the six months he was getting his sperm in shape, explaining to his sister that it was the least she could do.

'I mean, Linda, no one's asking you to freeze your balls.'

'I don't have balls, Paul.'

'Well, your overines . . .'

'What the hell is an overine?'

'You know what I mean.'

So they paid him – six grand over six months. Linda agreed to pay him the balance of four grand for the sample. Natalie and Linda's solicitor wrote up the contract and Paul had his stoner friend, Robbie, look through it because he'd worked in a bank for six months before he was fired for only turning up when he felt like it. Paul was too cheap to get a solicitor, but he also knew that Linda would do the right thing by him anyway.

'After all, I'll be the father of your lover's child,' Paul said over coffee.

Natalie's skin crawled.

She and Linda had a fight as soon as he walked out of the door.

'You're not scared that he's too close to this?' Natalie asked.

'He's just close enough.'

'Linda, what if he wants to be in the baby's life?'

'Natalie, he'll be in the baby's life as Uncle Paul.'

'What if he bonds with it? And wants more?'

'It's Paul. He hates people and he despises kids – if anything, we'll see him less. Besides, the only thing Paul's ever bonded with is his own hand.'

That wasn't true. Linda didn't mean that. The one person Paul did love was Linda, and if he only loved his flesh and blood . . .

'You're just being difficult,' said Linda. 'I know you don't like him, but he would never deliberately hurt me.'

'You hope,' Natalie muttered.

'I *know*!'

They were shouting, not screaming. They were both frustrated, but it didn't go beyond that. Linda was good at avoiding an all-out row. She would place her hands on Natalie's cheeks, hold her face gently and look into her eyes.

'You worry too much.'

'You don't worry enough.'

Linda smiled. 'It's going to be great.'

Natalie nodded in the affirmative, but she wasn't so sure. Something had started to bother her recently. Paul was never around. Before she was pinning her hopes on his donation, it would have been a blessing, but now it raised her hackles. He'd turned down dinner three times in two weeks; that was unheard of – he never turned down free food.

Linda brushed it off. 'He's fine. Probably out with his friends.'

'Well, I hope he's not smoking dope.'

'He's not. He knows. Relax.'

But Natalie couldn't relax.

One day, Natalie stopped by Paul's house to drop off some left-overs before attending the infertility group. He answered the door in a towel. *Oh God, my eyes.*

'What's this? You finally looking for a bit of this?' He shook his lower half and laughed.

Dirty pig.

She smiled politely. 'No, just here to feed you something healthy.'

It was then that a woman in a dressing grown came to the door. She looked like Harry Potter with tits.

'Who's this, Paul?' she asked.

I could say the same, Natalie thought.

'This is my sister-in-law. Well, my sister's missus.'

'Oh! The lesbian?' the woman said, fixing her round spectacles so she could have a good look. 'You don't look like one, if you don't mind me saying.'

'I do mind you saying, and what are we supposed to look like?'

She pointed to a photograph of Paul and Linda standing side by side at a wedding. He was in a suit that was too large for him and she had half her head shaved, wearing a pair of dungarees and half a dozen earrings.

'Like that,' she said.

'This is Sylvia,' Paul said, looking very happy with himself. 'My girlfriend.'

'Jesus!' Natalie said under her breath.

Sylvia glared at her. 'Excuse me?'

'Nothing. I'm just shocked. Paul never mentioned you.'

'Well, we've only been seeing each other a few weeks. We've just made it Facebook official. Went live five minutes ago. So, you're the first actual human we've told in person.'

'I'm honoured.'

Sylvia's phone was vibrating in the pocket of her dressing gown. She plucked it out and looked at it.

'Seven messages!' she said, shaking her phone. 'I'm just going to deal with this. Nice meeting you. My first lesbian . . . Well, that I know of.' She beamed. Then she was gone.

Natalie looked at Paul. 'Seriously? Who is this woman?'

'Don't start. Not everyone is exposed to rampant lesbians the way I am.'

'Rampant lesbians? Don't make me hurt you.'

'It's a joke. Relax, for fuck's sake.'

'Forget jokes, who is she?'

'Sylvia, my girlfriend. What are you missing here?'

'How? Where? And since when?'

'Is that any of your business, Natalie?'

'We're paying you a grand a month for your sperm, so yeah, it is.'

'Don't worry, there's plenty to go round.'

Natalie made a gagging sound.

'Sometimes you make me feel bad about myself,' he said. 'It's not cool.'

She ignored him. 'Does she know?'

'It's not the kind of thing you mention on a blind date.'

'So, when are you telling her, now that you're *Facebook official*?'

'Soon,' he said, and slammed the door in her face.

In the pub after the meeting, Natalie drank only half a glass of beer because she was driving. She would never normally have agreed to drink with a bunch of mere acquaintances, but she needed time to think before she went home and told Linda about the new woman in their lives. *Bloody Sylvia.*

Ronnie made a toast as soon as the drinks were served.

'To all of you – I hope you're up the pole in no time.'

They raised their glasses.

Janet said, 'Me too,' before downing her vodka in one.

'Jesus, Janet, what's the story here?'

'No story,' she said. 'Just really needed a drink.'

'Nervous?' Caroline asked her.

'Yeah.'

'Me too.'

'How about you, Natalie?' Ronnie said. 'You nervous?'

'A bit. I'm ovulating in two weeks, so that'll be our first attempt. I know it's not the same. I don't have to go through what you all go through, but still, it's a big deal.'

'Yeah, of course it is,' Caroline said, nursing her gin and tonic.

'So, you're the first out of the gate, so to speak?' Ronnie said to Janet.

'Well, if you mean we'll be trying from now on, yes.'

'And then Natalie's intrauterine insemination in two weeks,' Ronnie said. 'Then two weeks later Caroline's getting started. Right?'

They all looked around at one another.

Natalie nodded. 'Right. Well, you know what they say, success rates are one out of three. So here we go.' Ronnie raised her glass again.

The other women just drank. Janet drained her already empty glass.

Natalie drank deeply. *Well then . . . Sorry, ladies, but screw you. I'm in it to win it.*

She left after one glass of beer.

Natalie found Linda in the utility room, folding warm clothes straight out of the dryer.

'We may have a problem,' Natalie said.

'It's not a problem. Paul rang me. He told me all about Sylvia and we're still on.'

'And you don't think she'll have a problem with his sister's girlfriend hijacking his sperm?'

'She's not even going to know.'

'Seriously?'

'Oh, Natalie, relax! Paul's longest relationship has lasted two months. Sylvia's not going to be a problem.'

'You haven't met her. She's just as fucking annoying as he is. This could be real.'

'And if it is, the deed will be done and she'll just have to live with it.' Linda sniffed one of her favourite fleece hoodies. 'Yum,' she murmured.

Natalie left her to her sniffing and sat on the sofa, staring out of the window. She looked at the small buds that seemed to have appeared overnight on the blossoming tree that took up half the garden. It absorbed all the sunlight, making the front room darker than it should have been, but still the tree was lovely, even if pink wasn't exactly her colour. She looked at it for a long time.

She had a bad feeling that she couldn't shake. She prayed her dream wasn't about to fall apart.

Sister Buckaroo and the Vicious Ones

Catherine

THAT FIRST MORNING, I WOKE to a bell. Bleary-eyed, I spied girls of different shapes and sizes jumping out of bed and dressing as quickly as if their lives depended on it. Aside from some whispers, no one really spoke or looked my way, except for one slight girl with a big bump and long black hair, tied up in a loose bun. She smiled at me before scurrying away. She looked no more than twelve.

I was filthy and still really cold. I put on an old vest and my own knickers and my mother's blue maternity dress, because it was the only one with long sleeves. I wore my grandmother's light blue wool cardigan, and a pair of socks and runners. My bones ached, but I no longer felt like I was going to die.

I followed the last girl out of the room and down the staircase to the dining room. Some girls served the food while others cleaned up; most queued and then sat and ate. Nuns were omnipresent, parading the dining hall, at least three at any one time. I took my bowl of porridge to a long table, where a few girls sat together at one end, but as no one joined me at the other, I was alone. I wasn't hungry at all. I needed the toilet – the urgency had passed overnight, but now it was strong. A girl passed me, collecting empty bowls.

'Excuse me?' I said, and she glared at me. 'I just need the toilet.'

'What is that you are saying?' Sister Mary Frances asked from behind my back.

'I just need the toilet.'

'You just need the toilet, what?'

'Sister Mary Frances.'

'And why didn't you go with the rest of the girls before breakfast?'

'Because I didn't know where it was.'

'Get up,' she said.

When I stood, she balled her fist and stuck out her knuckles, pushing them into my back.

'Move.'

She marched me through the dining hall and then through the hallway and up the first staircase and then the second, her knuckles digging deeper and deeper, until we came to a door on the opposite side of the corridor to the room I'd slept in.

'What does that say?'

'Toilets,' I said.

She dug her knuckles in further.

'Toilets, Sister Mary Frances.'

'Are you blind, Katie?'

For a second I'd forgotten I was no longer Catherine and I looked around for a Katie.

'Don't look so gormless.' She shoved her knuckles so far between my ribs I wondered if she'd end up inside me.

'Sorry, Sister Mary Frances,' I said.

'Move.'

She waited for me as I walked into the bathroom stalls. I faced twelve toilets and behind me were twelve sinks, no mirrors. At the end of the room was a window with bars on it. That was the first time I understood I was in prison.

Help me Saint Jude. Help me Justin. Help me Mammy. Help me Daddy. Somebody please help me.

And then the baby kicked for the first time, just like that, a little kick to tell me that I wasn't alone. *It's OK,* I soothed. *We'll be OK. I swear.*

It was just us together against the world.

When I emerged from the room marked 'Toilets', Sister Mary Frances stared at me as though she were looking right through me.

'You'll need to be sharper and smarter if you want to get through this,' she said, and then she walked away to the sound of her rosary beads banging against her leather sash.

Because I was a farmer's daughter, I was assigned to work in the vegetable garden. They were having trouble with their tomato crop. Sister Agatha, a quiet, small woman, escorted me into the greenhouse. I could see instantly that they were dying on the vine, and she was at her wits' end. She'd just transferred from a convent and didn't know a thing about fallen women or vegetables. Neither did I, but I pretended I did because it was nice out in the gardens and in the greenhouse. Most of the nuns stayed away – even Sister Agatha most of the time; she was a nervous creature who didn't like the sun or the cold, rain or wind. She wasn't a fan of any kind of weather really. So the girls who worked outside were mostly left alone.

It meant that we could talk to one another if we wanted to. Some didn't want to talk at all, but I would talk to anyone who would let me. I wanted to know everything about the place so that I could plan my escape.

I'm not sure at what moment I decided to escape, but I knew I wasn't going to stay. *No way.* I had no idea where I'd go, but that was a thought for another day.

I was bullshitting Sister Agatha about why the tomato crop was failing when I first met Marian. She was older than me, although I don't know by how much. She had short blonde hair, with delicate features and pale pink lips.

'It starts with the soil, Sister Agatha,' I said. I'd heard my dad say something like that once.

'Really? It's the same soil they've always used, I'm sure.'

'It's the drainage.' I honestly don't know where that came from.

'Oh,' she said. 'Well, can you fix it?'

'I'll do my best.'

'Good.'

I realised I hadn't said 'I'll do my best, Sister Agatha,' but she had moved off before I corrected myself. She wasn't as stuck on being addressed by her full name as the others. I picked up a container of tomatoes and checked to make sure there were holes in the bottom. There were. *Damn.*

For some reason, I shook it. Marian laughed.

'Well, aren't you full of shit?' she said and I turned to look at her. She was smiling wide.

I like her.

The baby kicked. *Baby likes her, too.*

'I am,' I said. 'I want to stay here. It's better out here.'

She nodded. 'A taste of freedom.'

'Something like that.'

'They need more water and less of that south-facing sunlight in the afternoons,' Marian said. 'Move 'em round and they'll do fine.'

'Why didn't you tell her?'

'She didn't ask me. I don't talk to them unless they talk to me.'

'That's good advice,' I said. 'Any more of it?'

'Don't tell anyone your real name, no matter what. When you leave here, you have to leave it all behind.'

I nodded. 'OK,' I said, but tears were forming in my eyes. 'But not the baby, not if I don't want to?'

She looked at me with pity. 'You'll want to,' she said, and she picked up a shovel and went outside.

I got busy watering the tomatoes and working out the trajectory of the sun and the timings to move and shield the tomatoes. She was right; I could see the plants that were most affected were the ones directly inside the window in the afternoon sun. Marian had saved me, and I in turn would save the tomatoes. Despite everything, it felt good.

It was Marian who introduced me to swearing. She liked to swear a lot, especially within those walls.

'Fuck them, anyway,' she'd say. 'At least we get to leave. They have to stay and they deserve it, the miserable bitches.'

Sister Agatha wasn't so bad really; she was one of the nuns who ignored us and that was a kindness. It was the ones who didn't ignore you that you had to be careful of. Sister Mary Frances was a tyrant. I called her Sister Vicious because she'd left bruises on my back. Marian laughed. 'We call her Knuckles,' she said, and I laughed at that, because although she was vicious, the name Knuckles just suited her better.

After that, I called her Sister Knuckles. Then there was Sister Joanna. Marian and some of the girls had called her Sister Horseface, but once Marian heard my Sister Buckaroo, they changed over.

'That's brilliant – Sister Buckaroo! I love it. We'll keep it! Do you hear, girls?' she said to some of the girls picking potatoes. 'Horseface is now Buckaroo.'

She laughed again and some of the girls smiled and whispered. Others just got on with their jobs, disinclined to join in. For most of us, having been stripped of our own identities and free will, our only rebellious act was in nicknaming the women who terrorised us. Of course it was childish, but then some of us were still children.

Marian was my first friend. Maria was my second. There were loads of Marians, Marias and Marys in that place. My Marian was known as Marian 2. Maria was Maria 3. I think I was the only Katie.

Maria was the little one in my dorm, with the long black hair tied up into a loose bun. She looked about twelve and slept in the bed next to mine. She was dying to talk to someone. No one really talked to her because she was so young.

'Why is it always so cold in this room?' I asked her three nights into my stay. 'It's July!'

She seemed so thrilled that I had spoken to her and a little unsure as to whether it was actually happening. She pointed to herself and I nodded.

'We're north-facing and in an alcove – you see, the building juts out, leaving us in a shadow.'

She walked to the window and pointed to the grey building obscuring our view. I looked up at it and saw that there were at least another two floors. At the top there was a large window; I saw a girl standing there, looking down to the ground far below.

'That's the attic room and below it, there's a stone yard. A girl jumped a month ago, just before I got here.'

'Was she all right?'

'God no! She was as dead as a doornail.'

'That's awful.'

'She wasn't the first,' Maria said. She looked at the girl staring down towards the ground. 'She won't be the last.'

I immediately backed away from the window. 'Why don't they put bars on it like on our floor?'

'Dunno.'

'Money,' one of the other girls said. She was a big girl, with freckles and a kind face. 'They only started using the attic recently, piling us all in, to make as much money as they can. See, first they make us work our fingers to the bone, then they sell the babies, then they charge our parents to get us out of here. They barely feed us – they certainly don't clothe us.'

She looked at me when she said that and I was mortified; the dress I was wearing was a putrid green with big collars and puffed sleeves.

'No sanitary supplies,' she went on. 'You see Deirdre or Denise or whatever her name is, over there?' She pointed to a girl kneeling by her bed, saying her prayers. 'She arrived with no toothpaste – she spends her days cleaning her teeth and tongue with her flannel and her breath stinks of carbolic soap.' She looked over to the girl. 'No offence.'

The girl started to cry. Maria went to her locker and grabbed her toothpaste. She walked over to the girl on her knees, holding it out.

'You can share mine,' she said, handing it to her.

The girl took it and hugged it to her chest. 'Thank you. Thank you so much.' She ran out to the toilets, tears flowing.

It was such a simple gesture, I wished I'd done it.

'I hope you get it back, or you'll be the one flannelling your gob from now till the time you deliver,' the other girl said.

'What's your name?' I asked.

'Doesn't matter,' she replied. I found out later that it was Bernice.

'What do you mean, we have to pay to get out?'

'Don't you know? If your family doesn't pay to release you, you get to work here for three years after you give birth.'

'No, that's not true. It can't be.' In all the years of gossip and rumour about Sad Siobhan and girls like her, I'd never heard that.

'No? Just ask the girls who work the laundry – or have you not noticed those poor skinny, sweaty cows who are queuing up for the dining hall as you're leaving?'

I had noticed them, but it didn't compute. I didn't understand, so I unsaw it.

But there was no unseeing it after that. I looked at those girls and wondered how many months or years of their lives they had lost to this terrible place. Not every girl whose parents couldn't or refused to pay for their release was sent to the laundry – just the trouble-makers, second-time offenders, or the plain unlucky ones.

I started to notice the others, now that my eyes were open: no pregnant bellies, no babies, just work. Some cooked; others cleaned; some even painted and decorated. The nuns didn't pay for staff. We *were* the staff. They made an industry out of selling fresh fruit and veg, the laundry picking up the slack for local hotels and restaurants, and by making and selling rosary beads, knitwear and linen. Everyone had a job that either saved the nuns money or made them money. The only reason that there weren't bars on the window of the attic room is because none of the girls had arrived with soldering skills.

It was another shock. My parents weren't poor, but how much money would those nuns want to release me? And after what I'd done, even if my parents had the money, would they pay?

I hugged my belly. *We're leaving here anyway, kiddo. Just got to work out how, when and where we go. Don't worry about it. We'll find a way.*

Bernice didn't speak to me after that. She kept to herself, but every now and again I'd see her around. One day she disappeared for a day and a night and then she returned, a ghost of a thing, shaken and sad.

There were two nurseries on the third floor. One was for the normal babies, the other was for the sick or disabled ones. Nursery One was where you prayed your baby would end up, because Nursery Two was a nightmare. Without family support, the girls couldn't take their babies out of Nursery Two and give them the care they needed, even if they wanted to. Those babies were kept for seven years, until the State stopped paying the nuns for their keep. After that, they were shipped off to industrial schools.

I learned that after Bernice returned and the word spread that her baby was in Nursery Two. She stayed for two months after that and I never saw her speak a word to anyone again. We all felt a little scared of her, like bad luck was contagious. Then one day she was there, and the next she was gone. Her family must have paid for her release. The baby remained behind.

I thought about Justin all the time. *Does he know about us? Does he care? Is he trying to find us?* I wanted to believe he'd looked up from his books after he was done with the Leaving Cert and realised I was gone, that he was desperate to find me so we could begin the life he'd promised. *I'm here,* I'd call to him in the darkness. *We're here.*

Maria and I talked every night.

'I'm scared,' she told me.

'Me too.'

'My daddy comes to see me. He brings me things all the time, so if you need anything, just say.'

'Thanks,' I said. I would have loved some custard creams, but I didn't dare ask.

My parents didn't come to see me at all. I thought at first that my mother might come once a month, like she did so many years before with my brother Charles. But he didn't get himself locked up, I suppose. I thought about him a lot in that place. I cried for him because he had been at the mercy of the nuns and now I knew what that felt like. No wonder all he could do was stare at the wall. *I'm so sorry, Charles.*

Maria wanted to tell me her real name.

'Don't,' I said. 'No names.'

'But we're friends.'

'No names.'

'Will I ever see you again?' she asked.

'I hope not.'

She started to cry.

'I don't mean it badly. I just mean, once we leave, we can't look back.'

She nodded. 'You're my best friend.'

'And you're mine.'

I thought about Rose. I wondered what she was doing and if she knew where I was. The rumour mill would be working overtime. She'd be worried about me. *I'm not Sad Siobhan, Rose. I'll never be Sad Siobhan.*

'I want to go home,' Maria said after the longest time.

'And you will.'

'I don't know how this happened.'

'Just stay away from boys,' I told her.

'But I don't know any boys.'

My heart skipped a beat and my head whizzed around as I tried to connect the dots. She had to know a boy to get pregnant. She had to have been with a boy – or a man.

Then I thought about her dad always coming alone, always with a gift of whatever she wanted. *Ah no. That couldn't be right.* I didn't dwell on it. It made no sense, so I packed it away.

'You need to stay away from men,' I said.

Her eyes filled. 'What if I can't?'

'Then you have to run.'

'Where to?'

I didn't know the answer. 'I'll think about it,' I said. Then I fell asleep.

When I woke, it was to the sound of Maria's screams.

'Help me,' she said.

I jumped up and one of the other girls turned on the light. I pulled the rough blanket away, to find Maria's sheets stained with blood.

'Call the nuns,' I screamed, and I held her to me.

'Don't let me die. I don't want to die.'

I told her of course she wouldn't. 'You're only having a baby.'

Sister Mary Frances tramped in, her veil off, her head wrapped in something that looked like it was a stocking. She was wearing a brown dressing gown.

'What is wrong with you, girl?' she shouted – then she stopped when she saw the blood. 'Lift her. Help me get her to the delivery room.'

That was on the third floor next to the maternity ward and opposite the nurseries. Sister Knuckles and I held Maria between us, hauling her up the stairs. She was crying all the way. When we reached the room, another nun I'd only seen in the corridors was waiting for us.

'Get her on the bed.'

We lifted Maria onto the bed. She held on to me.

'Stay.'

'Go,' Sister Knuckles said.

I looked up at her. 'Please.'

'Now.'

85

'I'm sorry,' I told Maria, and Sister Mary Frances stuck out her fist and knuckled me out of the door.

'Please, please, please, Katie,' came Maria's terrible screams.

But the door slammed and I stood in the hallway, stuck to the floor, listening to my young friend crying her eyes out and begging the nuns to be kind to her.

The last thing I heard was her saying the word 'no', over and over, and then a scream that was loud enough to tear a hole in the world.

After that, my legs just started moving. I was walking and then I was running and running with nowhere to go, down the corridor then the stairs, past the dorm and into the main reception. It was in pitch-black darkness, but I felt my way towards the mighty red door until my eyes adjusted and I pulled and pulled on it. I was only short of pounding, but even in my despair I knew that no one waited outside.

I crawled back up the stairs, exhausted and scared for my friend. I climbed into my hard, unwelcoming bed and hugged my baby tight. Maria's screams ran around my head. *It will be OK*, I said. *We're leaving this place. Do you hear me? They won't get us. I'm not Sad Siobhan and I'm not poor Maria.*

I didn't sleep at all that night. I lay awake listening to the world around me. Hours later, I heard an ambulance siren pealing and I prayed to Saint Jude. *Save her.*

Chapter Six

Janet

JANET STARTED HER MORNING off in Zumba class. She had the rhythmic capabilities of a donkey, but she enjoyed dancing so she kept going, no matter how bad she was. She never showered in the gym, always drove straight home and showered there, safe from chatty auld ones, the young ones prancing around with their knickers off, away from the smell of mould. She spent her afternoon cleaning the bathrooms and then browsing through old magazines before driving to the recycling centre and binning them, along with a ton of plastic water bottles and Jim's beer cans.

She had a bath around 4 p.m. and started reading a crime novel about a serial killer being hunted by another serial killer. She loved a crime novel, but even by her standards, this one was pretty grim. A page-turner nevertheless. She felt bad about feeling sorry for the serial killer who was now being serial killed and then wondered what the fuck was wrong with her. She read till the water turned cold, then she cooked Jim his dinner and left it in the microwave. She knew he'd be working late. He was always working late, at his pest control company, saving her and the planet from the great pest invasion.

Janet spent a lot of time alone these days. Before Derek, Janet had run her own business for five years, but that felt an age ago now. She'd kept working at her shop throughout her early miscarriages. After the third one, she'd been diagnosed with antiphospholipid syndrome, an autoimmune disease that produced antibodies that attacked her own body. The solution was to take an aspirin every day and when she finally managed to get pregnant with Derek, she had to inject herself twice a day with a blood thinner called Fragmin. It was painful but necessary, and at first it seemed to be working.

She had miscarried two of her other babies at six weeks and one at seven. On week six with Derek, she confined herself to bed. On week seven, she only got out of bed to do a stock take at her shop. Week eight she went back to work part-time. Week nine she was back full-time. Week ten she even went for a swim. Week eleven she and Jim went out to dinner and they stayed out walking along the beach till two in the morning, talking about the future. Jim was so excited, jumping like a child. Week twelve passed like a blur and the announcement was made to family and friends, and the cards came flooding through the door. Week thirteen she was floating on air, picking out maternity wear. She bought two babygrows, one in pink and one in blue. The phone never stopped ringing. Everyone was so excited to share in their joy.

Then on week fourteen, the scan happened and all that joy turned to dust. The injections had done what they needed to do. The molar pregnancy – that was a whole different problem.

Janet lay there on a table with jelly on her stomach, her hand in Jim's. His firm grip had weakened and suddenly, he wasn't standing anymore, he was sitting. And she was looking at a screen and she couldn't see the curves of a baby, little fingers and little toes. She couldn't see anything really – nothing her eyes made sense of. Just a snowstorm.

So she stared and kept staring as the words spilled out of her consultant's mouth. Jim let go and rested his face in his hands.

'I don't understand,' Janet had said, her hands on her swollen stomach. 'I'm pregnant.'

'You're not,' the consultant said softly. 'That's due to the rapid proliferation of trophoblastic tissue inside the uterine cavity.'

'Please, for fuck's sake, speak English,' Jim said, his head still buried in his hands.

'There is no heartbeat. There is no baby.'

It had to be removed by a D & C followed by suction. It felt like an abortion. It was one, except the baby wasn't a baby – except, it was to her. She cried the whole way through.

Janet didn't return to her little second-hand vintage shop in Clontarf village after Derek. Before that, Janet had loved all things vintage, although she never wore her own stock. Instead, she favoured skinny jeans and jersey tops. She had a wardrobe full of them. She'd put a lot of effort into keeping the shop afloat, but after Derek, she plunged into a dark depression, hibernating in bed for months on end. And without her, there was no shop.

By the time she was back on her feet, the premises was rented to a pizza takeaway and all she could do was either sell off her stock to a rival shop or try to hawk it on the internet. So she set up a new Facebook page and Twitter account. She modelled the pieces herself in her own bedroom and put them online, selling bits and pieces. It wasn't enough. She didn't know what she was doing on the World Wide Web and it was time to admit her business had failed.

Jim didn't mind her not working. His pest control business was booming.

'Rats are everywhere! I'm talking end of days, the size of cats rats! There aren't enough hours in the day to take on all the work.'

'That's great, love.'

'And as for cockroaches, those little bastards are trying to take over the world. Not on my watch, Janet. I'm saving the planet here, babe.'

'My hero.'

'And it's not the end of the world if you don't go back to work. It's nice to come home to dinner after what I go through on a daily basis.'

Janet was torn. She liked her independence but her beloved little shop was gone. She didn't have the energy, the will or the capital to start over. She wanted to keep trying for a baby and there was no point in looking for work while she was trying to get pregnant – and, if she did become pregnant, what then? *Is that it? Rearing a child, cleaning the house and making dinner? And if so, what was wrong with that?* After what she'd lost, wouldn't that be enough?

She didn't know. It was confusing.

One step at a time, Janet. Get pregnant and then we'll take it from there.

She felt excited but also scared about the prospect of trying again. She hadn't told her parents or her sister or her friends. They had all been there for the fallout; they would not be on board, having watched her lie in her own dirt. No, she would wait until she had a viable and healthy pregnancy to declare. It would be lonely going through all that business on her own, but the last time everyone had been part of the pain as well as the joy and it sucked. *Never again.* And anyway, she wasn't alone. She had the group, and when he wasn't going toe to toe with a rat or a bat, she had Jim to lean on.

The group meeting was the first time Janet had spoken to anyone that day. Jim had left for work early and she'd been on her own all day. It felt good to talk, even if she didn't say much. When the offer came for a drink after the meeting, she realised how thirsty she was. *Absolutely.* She hadn't expected to down her vodka in one, but it had happened and there was nothing she could do to take it back. She felt instantly sick, and Ronnie announcing their odds didn't help.

One in three? Natalie or Caroline or me?

It was Natalie's first go. Caroline would be after Janet. Caroline had been through more than anyone, six IVFs, multiple ops, a life peppered by pain, but Janet had lost four children, who for the short time they had lived inside her, had been her world.

Sorry, Caroline. Please let it be me.

Janet only lived round the corner from the meetings and the pub they were drinking in was nearby. Natalie left first, then Caroline. Janet sat at the table, drinking a glass of water.

Ronnie looked over. 'Are you OK?'

'I feel a bit dizzy.'

'Do you want me to wait with you till you are fit to drive?'

'Oh no, thanks, I'm walking home.'

'Not on your own, you're not,' Ronnie said and she placed her arms on Janet's shoulders. 'Come on, I'll get you where you need to go.'

'Are you sure?'

Ronnie grinned at her. 'I'm never unsure.'

They walked from the pub to Janet's house arm in arm and it felt strange, but there was also something warm and comforting about Ronnie. Janet couldn't put her finger on it. They talked about Ronnie's job as a pilot. Janet was impressed when she talked of her love of the sky.

'I feel at home up there, above it all. That's my happy place.'

'Sounds lovely.'

'It's like being in a warm bubble most of the time. Every now and then it gets hairy, but that's when it's really fun.'

Janet nodded. 'I used to own a shop,' she said.

'And now?'

'Nothing.'

Ronnie smiled. 'Maybe a baby.'

'Maybe, and till then, the highlight of my day is reading a crime novel in a bath at four o'clock in the afternoon.'

'Could be worse.'

'Like what?'

'Like a million things.'

'Like a serial killer being killed by a serial killer,' Janet said.

'Exactly.' Ronnie laughed. 'You could always look for something part-time.'

'Yeah, I suppose I could.'

Ronnie dropped Janet to her door.

'Would you like to come in?'

'Nah, I'm going to walk for a while,' Ronnie said.

'Where? It'll be dark soon.'

'I'm a big girl.'

'OK, mind yourself.'

'Will you be there next week?' Ronnie asked.

'Yeah. Should be. You?'

'If my flight lands on time.'

'OK, see you then.'

Janet closed the door behind her. Jim was walking down the stairs, freshly showered and wearing his favourite tracksuit bottoms and a T-shirt that was four thousand years old with the words 'Frankie Say RELAX' on the front.

'Who's the tall one?' he asked.

'That's Ronnie,' she said, following him into the kitchen. 'She's from the group.'

He switched on the microwave. 'Yeah? And what's her story?'

'No idea. She hasn't said anything yet.' Janet took out a knife and fork and poured herself a glass of water. 'Maybe she'll talk next week.'

After dinner, Janet headed into the utility room to put on a wash. Jim had thrown his overalls into the wash basket.

'I think we should start trying tonight,' she said through the open door.

'Maybe tomorrow night, babe. I've been up to my neck in rat shit all day.'

'Tomorrow then,' she said as she riffled through the pockets for the usual cash and tissues.

'Great, I'll bring home a bottle of wine,' he called through.

She pulled out a tissue, a chocolate bar wrapper and a piece of paper with a phone number. The words 'when you need to talk' were written on it and the imprint of a lipstick kiss.

WTF . . . Is this a joke? Am I living in a 1980s soap opera? Who does this? And why? And what the fucking fuck?

She didn't say anything. She just pocketed the number and put on the wash.

A Time to Mourn and a Time to Run

Catherine

NO ONE EVER SAW MARIA or her baby after that night. In the days and weeks afterwards, I waited for sight of her or word of her baby, but I was met with a wall of silence. Life went on as though she'd never been there; a new girl cried herself to sleep in Maria's bed and our twisted little world kept turning.

I'd like to think she was taken to a hospital in time, that she had her baby where she was surrounded by proper doctors and kind nurses. I'd like to think she survived the birth and had the strength to keep away from the man who put a baby in her. But by then I knew better. My friend and her baby were likely dead, and I could feel myself falling apart piece by piece. I wished I'd let her tell me her name, so that one day I could try to find her.

I needed to move fast before there was nothing of me left.

Marian was shocked about Maria. She didn't know her like I knew her, but her loss was still unnerving.

'I'm sorry,' she said.

I was tending to my recovering tomatoes while she messed around with some compost.

'This place is hell – we just gotta get through it as best we can.'

'I'm leaving here,' I said.

'Yeah, you and me both.' She chuckled and sang John Denver's 'Leaving on a Jet Plane' softly to herself.

94

'I mean it,' I said. 'I'm making a break for it. You can come if you want.'

Marian looked round at me. 'Don't be silly.'

'I'll need your help,' I said. I had thought about nothing else but escaping since the night Maria disappeared.

'No.'

'Marian, I'm not giving up my baby and I'm not staying here three fucking years.'

I think that was the first time I'd used the word 'fucking'.

Marian was momentarily impressed. 'Good for you . . .' But then she thought about it. 'If they catch you, you'll end up on the laundry and if you end up there, you are *fucked*.'

'I have a plan,' I said. 'The side door, there's only a heavy bolt on the bottom. I'm going out of that door – I'm going to see how long it takes to walk down that avenue and find out if those gates are even locked. I need you to be there to open the door when I come back.'

'You want me to leave my room and sit by a door for hours and not get caught? Yeah, absolutely no problem. I mean, if James Bond can do it . . .'

I'd never seen a James Bond film, but I figured it would be a little more exciting than him sitting by a door.

'I'll leave after lights out. At one in the morning, just come down and open the door.'

'What if I can't stay awake?'

'Then I am *fucked*.'

'What if someone sees me?'

'It's the back corridor – no one even uses it.'

'And what are you hoping to do?'

'If I can make it to that gate and somehow get through it or over it, then I'm going.'

'And *where* are you going?'

95

'Dublin.'

'And then what?'

I'd been thinking about Justin a lot recently. I had started to wonder if his father had even spoken to him about me. Justin might not know at all – and then, if he did know, if I found him and told him, things would be different. He might be trying to find me but have no idea where to look. Once he saw me and he felt the baby, he would save us. I believed that. I still loved him, and in the absence of my parents or the clergy, I needed to believe in him.

'I'm going to find Justin.'

I'd told her about Justin over the course of our many days working together. She'd warned me not to use his surname or tell me anything about his family, so I didn't. I only told her about his aunt's house on the South Circular Road, the one with the big red door. I was going to leave this place and I was going to catch a train and I was going to find him. It was early October by then, so I knew he'd be in college in Dublin.

'You need a ticket for a train.'

'I'll hide.'

She looked at me. I was bigger now, more obvious than ever.

'I'd like to see you try.'

'I'll find my way to the South Circular Road and I'll tell him.'

'And what if he already knows and he's a lying bastard?'

I sighed heavily. My heart felt as empty as it did full. 'Then I'll move on.'

'And the baby?'

'I told you – I'm keeping it.'

'You're sixteen with no Leaving Cert.'

'I'm a hard worker.'

'And who's going to take care of the baby while you work?'

'I'll sort it out.'

'You're dreaming,' she said.

'So let me dream.'

Marian sighed. 'Fine. Go on your goose chase. I'll let you back in.'

There wasn't time to waste, so I let myself out that same night, just past midnight. I got dressed and crept out of the room and down the stairs, past the atrium and into that back hall that nobody used. Opening the bolt took all of my reserves of energy, heavy and rusted as it was. The door opened onto the stone yard where those poor girls had taken their own lives. I ran across the hard ground as fast as I could, trying not to think of them. Then I ran round the side and past that awful grotto, down the avenue. I kept going and going.

I stopped running when I got a bad stitch, but I kept walking, at first fast but then I slowed down. *Come on, kiddo, help me out.* I kept going, puffing and panting and squeezing the pain out of my side until I finally made it to the gates. The main vehicular entrance was locked and way too high to climb, but I searched along it both sides, only to find a slimmer, smaller gate meant for pedestrians. It was open. I couldn't believe it. I stepped through it and I nearly ran then and there – but I had no clothes. I needed to take what little I had in case Justin let me down. I couldn't go in just a nightie and old woman's cardigan and a pair of runners.

So I stepped back in and, with wind under my wings, I ran all the way back. I waited for maybe an hour, worried that Marian had fallen asleep, until at last I heard the click of the door opening and saw Marian's face.

'I'm leaving,' I said and she nodded.

We walked back silently together. She went to her room and I went to mine. No one was awake. I slipped into my hard, rough bed and half an hour later, the morning bell rang.

Marian and I said our goodbyes in the vegetable patch. I asked her to come with me again, but she had resigned herself to letting her baby go. She had a job to go to and a family willing to pay to have her back. I understood. I wished her luck.

'Mind yourself, Katie,' she said.

'If I don't, no one else will.' I tried to laugh. I don't know why; just because it was true, didn't make it funny.

I waited till the lights went out and all the girls were asleep. Then I packed my suitcase. I didn't have much, so it didn't take long. I made my way out of the room and down the stairs, through the atrium and into the back hall. Then I opened the bolt. I ran across the stone yard and round to the front, past the grotto. I kept going and going until I saw the big gate.

I made my way to the smaller pedestrian gate, half hidden among the bushes, and reached to pull it open. To my horror, it was locked. I screamed and screamed and I prayed. *Please, Saint Jude, patron saint of desperate cases and lost causes. Help me. Help me. Please.* I pushed and pulled at the gate. I kicked it. I rammed it. By the end, I was covered head to toe in bruises from fighting a bloody iron gate.

It was too late to go back and even if I did, Marian wouldn't be waiting to open the door today. They were going to find me. *So let them.*

I sat on my father's suitcase and waited in the bushes with my head in my hands.

That's when I saw the laundry truck heading my way. The vehicular gate opened and the truck rolled by me. I sprang up and ran through it as fast as my legs could carry me. I had been locked up in that place for just over three months and it had felt like a lifetime. It didn't matter that I was heavy with child – I felt as light as a feather.

I don't know if the driver even saw me. I didn't care.

I was free.

We did it, kiddo.

Chapter Seven

Caroline

CAROLINE USUALLY SPOKE TO DAVE about everything, but they weren't talking now. She missed it. She missed him.

She cornered him in the kitchen one evening when he was heating up a ready meal for one. She used the time he was stuck waiting for the microwave to tell him about the offer of a job promotion.

'That would have been good.'

'What do you mean?'

'You're going to say no.'

Caroline looked at him. 'I haven't thought it through yet.'

'Well, let me assure you. When you do, you'll turn them down, so you can try for the baby you're never going to have.'

'You don't know that.'

'Everyone knows that but you.'

'Why are you being so cruel?' she asked.

'I'm just being real, Caroline. The world doesn't just revolve around you and what you want. I live in it, too, and I'm done pretending that everything is going to be OK.'

The microwaved pinged. He pulled out his food, put it on a tray, went into the sitting room and shut the door. She could hear the TV blaring and she just stood in the middle of her kitchen, a little paralysed.

He was right. She was never going to take that promotion, so that she could selfishly pursue a baby who might never be hers. She was willingly risking their marriage for a pipe dream. She knew she was devastating him and he didn't deserve it. He had been there for her through thick and thin. They were best pals and he was the love of her life. And yet, with every miserable and failed attempt to conceive, she was telling him that he would never be enough. Dave understood that as long as Caroline had even the tiniest chance of conceiving, she'd keep going and to hell with him.

She knew that if she did proceed using another man's sperm, there would be no going back. It was slowly dawning on her that Dave wasn't pretending, wasn't trying to shock her or shake sense into her – he was giving up on her and he was right to. She was a lost cause. *I'm sorry, love.*

She was slowly walking their marriage over a cliff and if she didn't conceive, she'd end up utterly alone. The pain of losing her husband seared through her and she wanted to raise her voice above the football commenters shouting through the TV screen next door. *I pick us, Dave.*

But she couldn't, because she didn't.

Caroline told her employers that she refused their offer of partnership. They were in Susan Clarke's smart glass box of an office. Elizabeth seemed shocked, Susan not so much.

'I don't understand,' Elizabeth said.

'It's just not for me.'

'But have you looked at the offer? At the figures?'

'Of course she has,' Susan said.

Caroline looked away. 'I'm happy with what I'm doing now.'

'Are you? Because I don't believe it,' Susan said.

It came out of nowhere. *Am I?* Caroline didn't know. She wasn't really sure. *What is happy, really?* She was sorry she'd brought it up.

'Of course.'

'You don't look happy – and I'm not talking about your medical condition. Even when you're well, you don't seem content. I thought a stake in the company might change that.'

'I'm fine,' Caroline said.

'Clearly, you're not fine. Caroline,' Elizabeth said, 'you're demented if you think turning down this kind of offer is acceptable. You're a litigator, for fuck's sake . . .'

'Elizabeth . . .' Susan began.

'She knows a good deal when she sees it. You aren't going to get anything better anywhere else, if that's what you think.'

'I'm not looking to leave,' Caroline said. 'I just want to do my job.'

'OK,' said Elizabeth. 'Thanks, Caroline.'

It was a curt ending to the meeting and as Caroline was leaving, she spotted the unopened champagne on the side table. *Sorry, ladies.*

She was getting sick of saying sorry, even if it was in her own head.

Caroline had to wait until day three of her menstrual cycle to have her blood tests for follicle-stimulating hormone, estradiol and anti-mullerian hormone to assess the health of her pituitary gland and ovaries. They also needed to test her thyroid and prolactin hormones. It included genetic tests, a blood count, vitamin D levels, blood type and infectious disease status. She sat in a padded chair in the phlebotomist's office with a needle in her arm, focusing on a poster of a uterus in watercolour. The needle had slipped in easily and without any fuss; now, the nurse was taking vial after vial of blood.

'You're doing great,' she said gently.

'This is nothing.'

'There, all done,' the nurse said, removing the needle and placing a thick cotton ball on the site.

Caroline automatically pressed down on it, and the nurse nodded and smiled.

'An old pro . . .'

Less of the old . . .

She bagged and tagged the blood, then put a plaster on Caroline's arm.

'There you go,' she said. 'The hospital will alert you with results.'

'I know,' Caroline said as she closed the door behind her.

Caroline arrived at the hall early. Sheena was alone, setting out the chairs. She pointed to the water boiler.

'Ah, great, you can fill that and put it on for me.'

Caroline did as she was told. When it was full and on the boil, she cut and plated up a cake she'd bought in the supermarket.

'Looks good,' Sheena said.

'Shop-bought, I'm afraid.'

'How's everything going?' Sheena asked when she was finished creating the perfect semicircle with folding chairs.

'I'm good. Pain is reasonable this month. Just did my bloods today.'

'Fingers crossed.'

The light flicked on, to indicate the water had boiled.

'Coffee?' Sheena asked while digging a teaspoon into an industrial-sized can of instant ground coffee.

'No. I'm off all caffeine, carbs and sugar for the foreseeable.'

'You're not going to have a slice of this lovely cake?'

'Nope.'

Sheena poured herself a coffee. She grabbed a slice of the cake and took a chunk out of it.

'It's very good,' she said, and Caroline smiled at her.

The two women sat, waiting for the others. There was still ten minutes to go.

'And Dave?' Sheena asked.

'Still the same.'

'You know, I don't have any children, but I have my husband and honestly, without him I'd be lost.'

'I know where you're going, Sheena . . .'

'No, you don't. I understand why you feel the need to keep going and I support you, but at some point we have to take stock in life. Sometimes we need to focus on what we have as opposed to what we don't have.'

Caroline shifted in her seat. 'I'm doing this.'

'I know.'

'I want to be a mother more than I've wanted anything in my life.'

'Me too.'

'There's still time for me, Sheena.'

'I know.'

'I've been so miserable these last few years. I've tried to enjoy the freedom everyone keeps saying they are so envious of. The trips abroad and the lifestyle Dave celebrates. But nothing fills the hole. I just want to feel whole again.'

'And a baby is the only solution?'

'The only one that feels right.'

Sheena patted Caroline on the hand. 'Sometimes we don't get what we want or what we need. Sometimes we have to find a way to find peace regardless.'

'Is that what you've done?' Caroline asked.

'Yes.'

'And are you at peace?'

Sheena pursed her lips. 'Depends on the day.'

'Why did you never adopt?'

'We looked into it, but I don't know . . . it just never felt right.' Sheena's eyes shone. 'I don't know why. Maybe there's something wrong with us, that we couldn't see our way to giving a poor child a home.' She sounded sad but also resigned. 'You?'

'Dave and I looked into it after the second IVF. We went to one of those meetings with all the social workers giving one speech after another and everything they said scared us. They spoke at length about the legal difficulties and the cultural issues. Domestic adoption is almost impossible these days. Girls have choices.'

'Good for them.'

'Yeah, good for them,' Caroline said. 'Inter-country is like climbing Everest. At least that's what they say. The prospect of years of vetting for us, our family and friends just seemed so invasive – and God only knows what Dave's mother would have said. We'd probably get fucking arrested on the back of her testimony.

'The real stickler was that we had to provide proof that we'd stopped IVF treatments for six months before we began the process. I wasn't willing to give up on having my own child for the prospect of waiting years to adopt. So we thought, *fuck it, sounds too hard*. We just had no idea how hard it would actually get.'

Sheena placed her hand on Caroline's. 'Don't lose him, Caroline.'

She looked past Caroline to see Ronnie approaching. She was wearing her pilot's uniform.

'Apologies, I came straight here.'

'No need to apologise at all,' Sheena said. 'Tea? Coffee?'

'Oh, I'd murder a coffee.' Ronnie plonked herself on the chair beside Caroline.

Sheena moved to make the coffee. 'Milk, sugar?'

'Milk, no sugar, thanks . . . Sweet enough.'

Caroline looked across at her new friend. 'You're not married, are you, Ronnie?'

'God no,' Ronnie said.

Caroline wasn't sure if Ronnie was straight or gay or anything else, but Ronnie had a way of shutting down conversation that intrigued Caroline. She didn't push. This wasn't work. She wasn't being paid to interrogate anyone. It was interesting to her that Ronnie could seem so open and yet so secretive all at the same time.

'Anyone in your life at all, then?' Sheena asked, handing Ronnie a coffee.

'Nah, just me, all alone in the world.' She pulled a sad face.

Sheena handed her a slice of Caroline's shop-bought cake. 'I'm so sorry.'

Ronnie laughed. 'Don't be sad about that.' She glanced around as several other women began to come through the door. 'Trust me, it's better this way,' she said before taking a large bite from the cake.

Who are you, Ronnie? Caroline wondered.

Another Big Red Door

Catherine

THE PRISON GATES WERE FAR behind me and I wasn't sure where I was, so after running with a suitcase for as long and as far as I could, I slowed to a stop and asked an old woman walking her dog where I was.

'What? What do you mean?'

'Where is this?'

She stared at me. It must have been early in the morning; it was only just light.

'Are you joking?'

'Is it Cork city?'

'Course it is – where else would it be?'

'Do you know where the train station is?'

'I do.'

'Well, could you tell me – please?'

She pointed. 'Straight ahead, about a mile or two. You can't miss it.'

'Thank you.'

Tired and sore as I was, I went on running, keeping an eye on the road to see if I was being followed. I hurried when I could and took breaks when I had to. *Stay with me, kiddo. We're nearly there.* I saw the sign for the station and it was like a dream come true. *Nearly there.*

I hadn't a penny in my pocket, but I read the board and saw that a train was due in less than half an hour. I hid in a toilet cubicle, counting down the minutes in my mind and listening for the announcement. *The train to Dublin is due on platform one. Please stand back from the platform and take care when alighting the train.*

This was it. I was nearly home free.

I counted in my head to eighty then sneaked out onto the platform, keeping my eye out for any nuns, priests or railway guards. I was lucky – the platform was busy, with plenty people to hide behind, so when the doors opened, I just moved with the crowd.

Inside the carriage, I made sure to sit on the aisle seat and waited for the train to depart. *Please, Saint Jude, let's get this thing moving.* Once we pulled away from the station, I kept my eye on the aisle, waiting for the conductor to check everyone's tickets.

It was then I saw the nun. She was approaching slowly and I wanted to run, but my legs were jelly and I had nowhere to go. She looked at me and smiled.

'Is anyone sitting here?' She pointed to the seat opposite.

'No,' I croaked.

'Is it all right if I join you?'

'Fine.'

She sat down and I held my breath. She was polite – too polite to be one of those nuns. But then, maybe she was playing games, pretending to be something she wasn't. Isn't that what they all did on the outside?

'You're travelling alone, dear?' she said after a few minutes had passed.

'My husband's waiting for me in Dublin,' I blurted out. I saw her looking at my hands, or maybe I imagined it. I couldn't tell. My heart was racing. My breath hitched and for a second I thought I was dying. 'My hands are swollen,' I said, to address why I wasn't wearing a ring.

'I hear that happens.' She nodded. 'Don't worry, it will all be over soon.'

Oh God. Is that a threat?

I looked around, desperately trying to see if she was really alone, but everyone looked so normal, chatting together, eating ham sandwiches and crisps and drinking tea. I was so hungry I thought I was going to faint.

'You don't look so well,' she said, and it sounded like she was concerned, but I couldn't trust her.

'I'm too hot,' I said. 'I have something lighter in the case. I think I'll change.'

'Now?'

'Yes, now.'

I stood up and walked away, sweat dripping down my back. At the end of the carriage, I wrestled with the case. It was lodged behind two others crammed into the hold. A young fella enjoying a smoke with a few friends between the carriages helped me to secure it. I took it into the toilet and placed it against the locked door. I sat there for an hour, bobbing up and down on the hard toilet seat with an empty stomach and a rapid heartbeat. *We're OK, kiddo. We're nearly there now. Next stop Dublin.*

About two hours into the journey, there was a knock on the door.

'Excuse me, this is the conductor. I have to check all tickets.'

'I'm not well.'

'I'm sorry, ma'am, but you've been in there a very long time. I'll need to check on you and your ticket.'

Shit! Just stay calm, kiddo.

I opened the door just a crack, letting him see my pregnant belly.

'I'm fine, but my ticket is with my friend in my seat and I can't leave right now.'

He looked at me, then down the aisle. 'Which seat?'

'I don't know, two or three carriages down. Her name is Mary and she's wearing blue.'

I closed the door, sat back down and held my breath.

I waited, and when no other knock came, I relaxed, but only a little. There were still two hours to go, still time to get caught. I don't know if the conductor was lazy and didn't want to bother finding a Mary in blue, or if he saw the terror in my eyes and took pity on me. Either way, he never came back.

When the announcer heralded our arrival into Heuston Station, Dublin, I started to breathe easier. I was finally free. *You see, kiddo. I told you. You can count on me.* A kick came in reply.

Dublin was loud and busy. I asked one of the railwaymen how far it was to walk to the South Circular Road. He thought about it for a minute and called to his friend.

'Buster, how far to walk to the South Circular Road?'

'From here?'

'Well, hardly from fuckin' Japan . . . Sorry, love.'

Buster thought about it. 'I'd say you'd do it in less than half an hour on a good day.'

'That's what I thought,' the man said. 'Course, you might take a little longer,' he said, looking me up and down.

It was a big relief. I was beginning to fade fast. My legs were shaking; my mouth and lips were dry.

They drew me a makeshift map and as luck would have it, the South Circular Road was pretty much in a straight line from the station. I took a minute to thank Saint Jude, then began to walk.

After three stops for a quick sit down, I made it in just over an hour. The street was longer than I had imagined and there was more than one red door, so I just starting knocking on every house with a basement and a big red door. I knew Justin's aunt was his father's sister; she was a teacher who never married, who lived in their family home. Justin said that's why she felt obliged to allow him and his brothers to live with her during their college years. He didn't describe her as a particularly warm or friendly person, but he said she liked to keep to herself. I was hoping he was right.

'Excuse me, Miss O'Halloran?'

'No.'

Doors slammed in my face again and again until I was midway down the road. Then I climbed the steps of an imposing red brick building with another big red door and rang the bell.

A woman answered, but she was too young to be Justin's aunt.

'Sorry to disturb you,' I said.

'It's no problem. I was just going.'

I moved to leave.

'What can I do for you?'

'It's nothing. Wrong house.'

'You sure?'

'I'm just looking for Miss O'Halloran.'

'Oh, she's inside.'

'Really?'

'You're a friend?' She looked at me, a little puzzled.

I was a pregnant teenager, wearing a pink corduroy maternity dress, a pale blue granny cardigan, a pair of pop socks and filthy trainers.

'I know the family,' I said.

She nodded. 'She's just in the kitchen. I'm sorry. I have to run or I'm going to be late for my lecture.'

'OK,' I said and she skipped down the steps, grabbed her bike and cycled away.

She left the door swinging open and I pushed it with my hand.

'Hello?'

I walked into the hall.

'Hello?'

A woman appeared and I knew at once she was Justin's aunt. She looked just like his dad, except a little fiercer.

'Yes? What can I do for you?'

'I'm here to see Justin.'

'And you are?'

'An old friend.'

'I see,' she said.

'I could wait for him in his room downstairs. I really don't want to bother you.'

'No. It's no bother. Why don't you stay here with me?'

It wasn't an invitation, it was an order.

I said, 'OK,' and suddenly I felt a little faint, and then everything faded to black.

When I came to, Aunt Martha was holding me.

'My God, you gave me a fright.'

'I'm so sorry,' I said, struggling to rise. 'Please don't fuss. I just haven't eaten.'

'Well, why didn't you say so?'

'I'd only just walked through the door.'

'For the love of God, come on.' She helped me up. 'I have a kitchen full of food.'

It was such a relief to eat. The cold-fish aunt who Justin had described to me was far kinder than her face or features suggested. She made me roast chicken sandwiches with butter and salad cream.

'How is that?'

'I think it's the nicest thing I've ever eaten.'

She laughed. 'Well, leave some room for cake. I have a nice chocolate one in a tin.'

'Oh, I love chocolate cake. It's my favourite thing in the world.'

She smiled as she reached for the tin. 'My name is Martha,' she said, offering me her hand.

'Katie,' I said, and then I heard myself and I shook my head. 'No, not Katie, I'm Catherine. I'm sorry. I don't know why I said that.'

'Don't be. We all make mistakes.'

I wondered if she thought I was as odd as my socks. We talked about general things like the weather and gardening and whether I liked school. We didn't mention my pregnant belly, or what I was doing here.

An hour later, we could hear a door bang downstairs.

'That's him, he's home. I'll show you down the stairs.'

We walked together to a small door and she knocked, opened it and shouted down the narrow staircase.

'Justin, it's your auntie Martha. I have a visitor here for you.'

I heard him before I saw him. 'I thought Jen left ages ago – what are you two planning, anyway?'

Then he appeared, looking up the stairs. He saw me and I took in the look of horror on his face. I hoped it was just the puke pink maternity dress, the pale blue granny cardigan, the pop socks and the filthy trainers.

'Hi,' I gulped.

He looked so smart, in trousers, a shirt and a blazer. He backed away like I was something to avoid.

'Go on, my dear,' Justin's aunt said, and she closed the door behind me.

I walked down the steps slowly and carefully. *We're OK, kiddo. We're going to be fine, no matter what.*

Chapter Eight

Natalie

NATALIE ARRIVED AT THE MEETING just before it started. It was a full house, with only one chair left to sit on. It was next to Ronnie.

'Saved it for you,' she said, and Natalie nodded her thanks.

Mary told everyone herself and her husband were going on holiday to Vegas to forget their troubles. Everyone thought that was a brilliant idea.

'Might even tie the knot again in one of those drive-through chapels. Why not?' She was upbeat, masking her disappointment. 'No baby doesn't mean no party. Means the absolute opposite, in fact. We can party for the whole week if we want to.' The smile didn't reach her eyes.

Natalie noticed Caroline shuffling in her chair. She had often talked about the trips she and Dave took. They had always seemed to be off somewhere in the past.

'Anyone else want to share?' Sheena asked, taking a sneaky glance at her watch.

Natalie raised her hand. 'I do.' She didn't wait for permission. 'We have the insemination tomorrow. I'm really nervous. My consultant broke her wrist last Tuesday, so one of her team is going to do the deed. A bloke, something Smith, I think his name is.' She laughed. 'Never had a bloke between my legs before.'

'You could always ask for a woman if you're not comfortable,' Caroline said.

'Ah no, it's fine. Who cares, right?'

Ronnie leaned forwards. 'But that's not what's bothering you?'

Natalie sighed and nodded. 'I thought I'd be more excited. This is all I've wanted for a really long time and now it's here, I don't feel the way I thought I would.'

'Nerves can get the better of all of us,' Sheena said.

'I'm not nervous, either. I'm just . . . numb.'

'It's the procedure,' Caroline said. 'I hate them – everything they do, it makes you feel less, no matter how kind or chatty they are while elbow deep in your uterus. It's degrading. But afterwards, when the procedures are done with and you're home alone, lying flat on your bed, then a little joy creeps inside you. From there, hope and excitement springs, and the wonder of what if . . .' Caroline trailed off, and Natalie could see she was battling not to cry.

'Did Dave get excited?' she asked.

Caroline nodded and smiled. 'Oh yeah. The first few times, he was fit to burst. Then, you know, less and less.'

'Linda's not excited. We don't even really talk about it except to fight about her brother.'

'Everybody's different,' Janet said. 'Jim cried for a week every time I got pregnant.'

'Yeah, maybe.' Natalie sighed. 'I just thought it would be different.'

Afterwards, when Natalie said goodbye to everyone and headed out to the car park, Ronnie followed her.

'Where you off to now?' she asked as Natalie unlocked the door.

'A pub quiz.'

116

'I love pub quizzes. Stuck for a teammate?'

'Always,' Natalie said.

Ronnie sat in the passenger seat and put her belt on before Natalie had a chance to argue. They took off down the road, in silence at first, with Ronnie looking out of the passenger window at the world as it passed them by. Natalie kept her eyes on the road ahead, wondering how exactly it came to pass that this stranger had landed in her car.

After a while, Ronnie reached into her pocket and pulled out a handful of crystals. 'Oh, damn, I forgot to hand these out at the meeting.'

'What are they?' Natalie said, looking at a bunch of white crystals with one black one rolling around in the centre of her palm.

'The moonstone is the divine feminine stone. It shifts energies from fertility to conception right through to pregnancy, child-birth and even breastfeeding. Well, that's what it said on the leaflet, anyway.'

'I didn't peg you for a person who believes in all that stuff,' Natalie said.

Ronnie shook her head. 'I'm not. I think it's utter bullshit.'

'I don't get it.'

'What if it's not? What if I'm wrong? What if I know nothing at all?' Ronnie asked.

Natalie thought about that for a moment while Ronnie focused on the crystals in her hand.

'Do you think there is something better than this?'

'Than life?' Natalie said. 'I don't know.'

'Do you hope?'

'I've never really given it much thought,' Natalie said, and she was being honest. She was a facts-and-figures girl. Spiritual stuff just felt a little fudgy or pie in the sky to her.

'I used to be you,' Ronnie said. 'I never gave it a second thought.'

'And now?'

'Now I do, so fuck it, why not give it a whirl?' She handed a crystal to Natalie.

'What's the black one?'

'Ah, that's for me.'

'How come it's different?'

'I'm special.'

You are that, Natalie thought.

When they arrived at the pub, it was populated by round tables and people standing around chatting, while a man with a curly perm, a dickie bow and a shiny blue jacket and black trousers tested the mic.

'One . . . Two . . . One-two . . . One-two, one-two . . . Can you hear me there, Sophia?'

'Loud and clear, Bennie.'

'Nice one, Soph,' he said into the mic before placing it on a small makeshift stage.

Natalie waved to her friends sitting in the corner of the room.

'These are friends from work,' she said to Ronnie quietly. 'They don't know that I'm trying for a baby.'

'I'll say nothing.'

They reached the table and Natalie made the introductions. 'Triona and Liam, this is Ronnie.'

'Fantastic! Good to meet you, Ronnie. How are you on arts and science?'

Liam was a man in his late sixties with a head of white hair and a beard that he'd dyed pink.

'Not too bad, Liam,' Ronnie said.

'Great, that's our one weakness.'

'Speak for yourself,' Natalie said, half joking, half insulted.

I'm fuckin' amazing at arts and science.

'Well, anyway, welcome to Team Winner-All-Right,' Triona said.

She was a woman in her mid-forties who could fit into a child's tracksuit. She made Natalie feel oversized – never mind how the gazelle that was Ronnie must feel.

Bennie got the ball rolling soon after.

'Right now, lads, welcome one and all. We're running late, so let's just get started before Sophia here gets all arsey on us. We don't want that, do we, lads?'

The crowd murmured and Sophia wagged her finger at everyone.

'We'll start with some general knowledge. Sophia will hand around five questions. Take your time, lads – as long as you're done in three minutes, we're golden.'

Natalie grabbed the questions from Sophia.

'Has everyone got their sheets?' Bennie said.

The crowd murmured, 'Yes.'

'Good stuff. Question one: what is the common name for aurora borealis?'

Natalie had the answer written down before consulting anyone.

'Question two: Afrikaans was developed from what European language?'

'Dutch,' Ronnie whispered.

'Are you sure it's not French?' Triona asked.

'I thought it sounded a little German,' Liam said.

'It's Dutch,' Natalie said. 'I've written Dutch.'

'Ah, hold on now, Natalie,' Triona said.

'It's definitely Dutch,' Ronnie said. 'I lived there for a while; my first job was with South African Airlines. Best time I ever had. Really wish I'd stayed there.'

'Question three . . .'

'You're an airhostess?' Liam asked.

'. . . What poisonous, oily liquid occurs naturally in tobacco leaves?'

'A pilot,' Ronnie said.

Natalie was focusing on the quiz. 'Nicotine.'

'Well done, young lady,' Liam said.

Natalie looked round. 'Wha'?'

'I was talking to Ronnie. A pilot. Very fancy.'

'Can we just focus on the quiz?'

'Poisonous?' Triona repeated. 'Are you sure that's not a trick question?'

'Nicotine is poison,' Natalie said.

Ronnie nodded.

'Yeah, but it's only a little bit. Not really,' Triona said, fingering her box of cigarettes. 'I mean, ricin is a poison. You wouldn't catch anyone smoking that.'

'Ricin is in the beans of a castor oil plant, Triona. Ever had castor oil?' Natalie said.

Triona looked to Liam, who bit his lip and kept his head down.

Natalie look across at her. 'The answer is nicotine, Triona.'

'Right, Jesus, who shoved a poker up your arse?'

Ronnie laughed. 'She's just stressed. Doing sums all day can be very stressful.'

'I'm not stressed, thank you. I just want to win.'

'Why?' Ronnie said.

'Why not?' Natalie shook her head. 'The top prize is four tickets to Beyoncé. We can sell those tickets for a small fortune.'

'You stuck for money?' Ronnie asked.

'No.'

'Well then, relax, and let's enjoy ourselves.'

Liam and Triona grinned.

'I like her,' Liam said.

'Me too,' Triona said.

Natalie wished she'd slammed the car door in Ronnie's face.

But then the strangest thing happened: she did relax. She forgot all of her anxieties about the next day's procedure and she started to enjoy herself. Ronnie told stories about her exotic life, but not in a boasting way; she was funny and down to earth, and her stories were often self-deprecating. Between messing around and laughing, they managed to miss some questions, and for the first time in a long time, Natalie and her team came second, winning four bottles of cheap whiskey.

They left through a side door.

'Sorry if messing around made you lose first place,' Ronnie said.

Natalie smiled. 'I had a good time.'

'Me too. Thanks.' Ronnie waved her bottle of whiskey in the air and started to walk into the night.

'Hold on, where are you off to?'

'Home.'

'I'll give you a lift.'

'I'll get a taxi.'

'Sure?'

But Ronnie was so far down the road she didn't hear her, or if she did, she just kept on walking.

The Girl in the Pastel Pink Corduroy

Catherine

JUSTIN WAS WAITING FOR ME in a small sitting room area. I looked around; there was a kitchen and a toilet off to the side. 'You never said it was a flat on its own. If I'd known, I would have knocked on your door.' I don't know why that seemed important to say at the time.

'What are you doing here?' Justin asked in a voice that simmered with anger.

'I've come to see you,' I said, and although my insides twisted, the baby didn't move a muscle.

'Why?' He made it sound like I was some stranger appearing at his door. That really pissed me off.

'Oh, I don't know, Justin – maybe because you told me we'd be married, I got pregnant and then you left me.'

He was staring at my pregnant stomach. I placed my hands over it, protecting the baby from his vicious gaze. I saw the way his lips curled and I could tell he was disgusted by me.

'I didn't know,' he said. It wasn't defensive, it was accusatory.

Well, two can play at that game.

'Did your dad ask you if you were the father of this child?'

'I don't know what you are talking about.'

I knew he was dismissing me.

'Did you lie?' I asked in an even tone, even though I wanted to scream and roar. *Don't scream,* I told myself. *Don't shout.*

Don't act out. Just hold his gaze. Hold him to account. It's OK, kiddo. We're not done for. Not yet.

I was searching for the old Justin, the sweet boy who'd saved my life from a bullseye and an angry ancient dog, the boy who told me he loved me.

'No,' he said. 'I didn't lie.'

'So he's the liar,' I said. 'He said you denied getting me pregnant. They dragged me to one of those places that everyone whispers about.' I couldn't hold it anymore; the dam burst and tears flowed down my cheeks. 'No matter how bad they say it is, it's worse.' I held on to my stomach and stood there, hunched over, crying my eyes out.

He slumped onto his armchair, his head in his hands. 'This is my fault.'

'Yes,' I said between sobs. 'It is.'

'What can I do?' he asked. 'How can I fix this?'

'You can do what you said you would do,' I shouted. *What a stupid fucking question.*

'It's not that simple.'

'It all sounded so simple when you were inside me.' I had no idea where that came from.

It shocked him, too. He seemed to take me more seriously after that.

'Sit down,' he said.

I sat.

'Do you have anywhere to go?'

I shook my head. 'No.' Although I'd stopped sobbing, unbridled tears rolled down my face.

'You'll stay here. We'll work it out,' he said, and although he didn't look happy about it, he didn't seem as angry.

I almost couldn't believe it. 'Really?'

'Yes,' he said. 'You should have a bath.'

The way he said it made me feel dirty. Of course I'd run for my life, spent hours in a tiny public toilet on a train, walked for miles and all in a cord maternity dress two sizes too big for me, so I probably wasn't smelling of roses.

'I'd like that,' I said.

His little apartment was really quite nice. He even had a bath in his bathroom. I hadn't had a bath since I'd been ripped from my home; there were only semi-cold showers in the institution. A silent nun called Sister Joan would stand in the doorway with her back to us, praying for our souls as twelve girls showered side by side, everyone minding their modesty and washing as quickly as they could. The water was at best barely warm and at worst freezing cold.

'Have you any other clothes?' he asked while he was running the bath.

'The others are worse again,' I said.

'My brother left some stuff here. He's a big fella; I can see if anything fits.'

It was a small act of kindness, but after months with the nuns, I was unused to it.

'Oh, that would be amazing. I feel so foolish in these horrible clothes,' I said, letting my guard down.

He nodded. 'Have a bath and relax. I'll get you some clothes.'

I waited till he left the bathroom to disrobe. I didn't have to wait long; he was in a fierce hurry to leave. I closed the door and locked it. It was lovely to be able to lock a door, although I was careful to unlock it, just to make sure I could. I did that a couple of times as the bath filled.

There was a small mirror over the sink; it was the first mirror I'd looked into since I'd been taken, and it was a shock. My face looked so different: round and puffy and fat. Aside from my red hair, I didn't look like myself at all. My hand involuntarily rose to my mouth and that was even chubbier in the mirror than it was when I looked down on it. My fingers ached, but then everything did. I couldn't look at myself anymore. No wonder Justin had viewed me with disgust.

Exhausted, I slid into the bath, surrounded by bubbles, warm and cosy and a million miles away from the misery of a Cork institution. I'd done it. I'd escaped. And though I knew that Justin didn't feel the same for me – and honestly, after what I'd been through, I really didn't feel the same for him either – he was going to help me. With the haze of love cleared, what was left was a different girl – not so romantic and silly or dreamy. Love felt like an illusion, not just because Justin had failed me, but also because of what my parents had done. That was the greatest betrayal of all.

I thought about Charles and the love that was denied to him. *I'm sorry, Charles. I'm so sorry.* I thought about my child and I swore I would love him or her no matter what.

I lay there with no dreams of being Mrs O'Halloran. All I cared about was my baby. Now that I was here, now that Justin had admitted the truth, maybe he'd be willing to do the right thing. I wasn't sure what that would look like, but he had money and a place to stay, and a responsibility that could no longer be denied.

We're safe, kiddo. You and me.

Justin called through the door. 'I've left a few shirts and some long johns outside. It's not ideal but it's something.'

'Thanks.'

I stepped out of the bath nearly an hour later. I opened the door a crack and pulled on the clothes he'd left. Justin's brother's white shirt looked like a dress on me and his long johns were too long but they were cosy. Even in men's clothes I felt more like myself than I had in my mother and grandmother's awful clothes.

125

I stepped into the sitting room, looking for Justin, but he wasn't there. I called out to him, but there was no answer. I went into the small galley kitchen to find a note on the counter: *Gone to get food.*

I relaxed. *OK.* I sat on one of his armchairs, reading a *Reader's Digest* magazine from the bookcase. It was full of books on law.

Evening had turned to night by the time he returned, holding up a bag of fish and chips.

'I thought you weren't coming back,' I said.

'Sorry, I got caught up.' He grabbed plates and dished out the fish and chips, then passed me a knife and fork. 'Get stuck in.'

I put a chip doused in salt and vinegar in my mouth, and after the plain and limited food in the institution, it was magic.

'Ahh! That's amazing,' I said.

Justin beamed. 'Good. It's nice to see you smile.'

I really looked at him for the first time; he seemed more like his old self.

'You look good in my brother's shirt,' he said.

'Anything is better than pastel pink corduroy.'

'That's true.'

We both chuckled and the anger I held inside me ebbed away a little – not because I forgave him, but because for the first time in a long time, I felt like myself.

After the food, fatigue took hold and I just wanted to sleep. Justin showed me to his room.

'Take my bed,' he said. 'I'll sleep on the sofa.'

I was glad he said that. I needed to be alone. I was so tired. He held the door open for a moment.

'I'm so sorry, Catherine,' he said. 'I never meant to hurt you.'

I didn't say anything beyond, 'Goodnight,' because sorry didn't help me and I didn't care if he hadn't meant to hurt me, because some things you just can't take back.

I thought about Maria screaming *No. No. No.* I could hear her calling for me and begging for someone, anyone at all, to show her some kindness. I thought about the girls who'd jumped and died in the stone yard I'd escaped from. The skinny girls lining up by the wall, silent, desperate, so broken they seemed held up by string. He was *sorry*. He had no fucking idea what sorry was.

I cried, quietly, into the pillow that smelled of him, for all the girls I'd left behind.

Chapter Nine

Janet

JANET HAD OBSESSED ABOUT the note she'd found in her husband's pocket since the first moment she clapped eyes on it. The old Janet, before the three miscarriages, the termination of Derek and the closure of her shop, would have run from the utility room with the note in the air, question after question tripping from her tongue. Now, Janet was not as quick to rush into anything. *What if I don't like what I hear? I won't survive it. I can't lose Jim, too.*

So instead she kept all of her fears and anxiety balled up inside her. *I'll just be better and sweeter and kinder and nicer and I'll really make an effort in the bedroom. I want a baby. I'll do what I have to.*

She shopped for new lingerie. She tried on something that was made of leather and lace and she didn't even know where to start with the straps. She felt stupid, standing in front of a mirror, one tit out and one in before realising it was back to front and having to start all over again. It did not look good and it felt horrendous. She tried on a little red basque number, which reminded her of something Doris Day would have worn if she were playing a Texas whore back in the day. Eventually, she bought what she always bought, lacy black knickers and a bra. Jim wouldn't even notice the difference. Still, she'd know.

She made him a special dinner. His favourite: beef and Guinness stew with colcannon.

'Oh, babe! You've outdone yourself.'

Have I? And what have you done?

She smiled. 'Nothing but the best for you, love.'

She showered and slipped into her new lingerie while he ate. She put on her silk dressing gown. *Oh, fuck, when did that hole appear?* She tucked the hole under the belt of the dressing gown, tying it in the front and then leaving it open enough to reveal her new bra. She put on a pair of high heels. She hadn't worn high heels since Derek.

She tried to walk on the carpet and needed to balance by holding her hands out. *You're not skywalking, Janet, get a grip.* She looked at herself in the mirror. *You've seen better days, haven't you, J?* She fixed her hair and refreshed her lipstick. She wondered what the woman who had put her lips to paper looked like. Did she wear leather and lace with buckles in ridiculous places? Maybe she did. Had he seen her in that stupid underwear? Had he touched her? Had he had sex with the woman who was available to listen to him anytime? *And what about? What did he have to say to this bitch?*

Janet noticed her face and neck were flushing red. It wasn't a good look. She breathed in and out deeply.

Calm down. You don't want to have angry sex.

Then she thought about that. *Maybe I do. Maybe that's exactly what I want.*

'Jim!' she shouted, but of course he didn't hear her. She moved towards the stairs, holding onto the banister. *I used to walk through town in these . . .*

'Jim,' she shouted again, but he still didn't answer.

Balls.

She took the shoes off and walked down the stairs, pushing the door open with such force it slammed.

'Jesus,' he shouted, knocking his fork off his front teeth. 'Ouch . . . What the . . .' He turned to face her. 'Oh, wow . . .'

His aching tooth seemed momentarily forgotten.

She pointed her high-heeled shoe at him. 'Move.'

'Wha'?'

'Upstairs. Now.'

'But I'm not finished my dinner.'

'You want to make this easy or hard?'

'Is that a trick question?' He stood up with his pants bulging and his balls on fire.

'Run,' Janet said, and he looked a little scared, but he went with it.

He ran up the stairs and she followed, heels in hand.

When Jim hit the bedroom, he started to strip off.

'I don't know what's going on here, but I like it.'

Really, would you like it if I plough this nine-inch heel through the back of your neck?

He was grinning. She grabbed him and she kissed him hard on the mouth. A little too hard – she felt her lips bruise, but he didn't seem to mind at all.

Does she kiss like this?

Then she pushed him onto the bed.

'Ah no, let's go against the wall.'

You don't want to be anywhere near a wall, mate.

She was on top of him before he could do anything.

'Ah, take it easy, I'm not a prized bull!'

But you are a prized bullshitter.

Suddenly, he was inside her and she was moving on top of him, and she had her hands around his neck.

'This is getting weird.' He looked slightly perturbed.

'Sorry.'

'No, don't be. It's cool and freaky. But I don't want to end up in the hospital.'

'OK, sorry.'

What the hell am I doing?

He grabbed her and kissed her and she melted into him.

Love you. Missed you. Who the fuck is she?

What is happening to us, Jim?

They had sex every night while she was ovulating. It started off angry. Janet couldn't switch the accuser off in her head until she relaxed and forgot about the woman's lips on the note in his pocket and focused. Then she'd remember how much she loved this man, how he'd taken care of her when she was so low she couldn't care for herself.

They'd lie awake together afterwards, him getting his breath back and her with her legs in the air, her back still firmly planted on the bed like a kid in a gymnastics class.

'Did I tell you I missed you?' Jim said the third time they'd had sex in one week.

'Yeah. Don't know why. I was here all the time.'

'No, you weren't.'

'That was a while ago now, Jim,' she said. She'd been coping well for at least six months.

'How will the drugs affect the baby?' he asked.

'The one I'm on is generally considered safe.'

'Generally?'

'I'll come off it if I get pregnant.'

'And then what?'

'I'll be fine.'

'Will you?'

'I'll be pregnant. I'll be fine.'

'Don't disappear on me again, love,' he said.

She felt like shit after that. *Is Paper Lips my fault? Did I leave him?*

Janet enjoyed the meeting. It was nice being with all the ladies; listening to their problems made less of her own and silenced her mind, if only for a while.

She had decided that she was going to ignore Paper Lips and move on. No point in digging up dirt. They were starting afresh and she would put her fear and frustration behind her. She needed to focus on her mental health. She needed to focus on getting pregnant and healing the wounds in her marriage. *You want my man, Paper Lips? You're going to have to fight me for him.*

She left the meeting as soon as it ended, wearing a purple basque and fishnet stockings under her jersey jumper and tight black jeans. They were cutting off her circulation and she needed to get home, get on Jim and get them off, or vice versa, which-ever came first. *Let's do this.*

Betrayal

Catherine

I WOKE UP TO THE HUSHED sounds of familiar voices outside the room and the hair on the back of my neck rose.

They're here.

I knew I was in trouble. I had made a huge mistake. I could sense them. Like prey sense the hunter. I could smell them and their carbolic soap. I could hear the gentle jangle of their rosary beads hanging from their belts and the sickly-sweet whispers.

I saw a key in the lock, so I ran to it and turned it over. They heard that. I sat on the bed hugging my stomach. *What to do? What to do? What to do?* There was a window in the bedroom, but it was too small to fit through. I could hear coughing and whispers, louder now.

A hand rattled the doorknob.

'Catherine, we're here to take you home,' a voice leaked under the door. It was Sister Knuckles.

It's nothing like home, you lying fucking bitch.

'Catherine, you have nowhere to go.'

True. So just a fucking bitch, then.

'We can stay here all day. We can have the door removed.'

'Catherine, stop this,' Justin said in a whining tone, and I wanted to slap him silly, maybe even punch him in his stupid face.

Stop what? Stop fighting them? Stop being me? What exactly did he want me to stop? I wanted to scream at him, but what was the point? He had made a mistake and he was determined I'd pay for it. He didn't just want me to stop, he wanted me gone – and they would happily see to that.

He was on their side now and I was trapped in a tiny room in a basement apartment on a long road in the middle of Dublin city. Even if I fought them off and escaped and ran so fast that they couldn't catch me, I was lost.

I had lost, and they had won.

And then I felt a little kick. *I'm sorry, kiddo. I had to try, right?* A kick said yes. *We just have to be strong. You and me. OK, kiddo?* I felt a little flutter. *Yes.*

I took off the white shirt and the cosy long johns and put back on the putrid green dress and my grandmother's light blue cardigan. Case in hand, I unlocked the door and walked out of the bedroom, to be greeted by the sight of sisters Knuckles and Buckaroo, a pale-faced Justin and his stoic auntie Martha.

'There she is,' Buckaroo said with a pretend smile.

'Safe and sound. Thank God,' Knuckles said.

They spoke to me softly and both were smiling sweetly. They were good actors.

Auntie Martha was silent and stood apart from the others.

I didn't wait for a speech or any more pretence.

'I'm ready,' I said, and I looked straight at Justin.

He couldn't meet my eyes.

'Rose told me about karma once,' I said to him. 'It means your fate is determined by your actions. I hope that's true. I hope whatever they do to me will be done tenfold to you.'

'Stop that vicious talk,' Sister Joanna said, and I wanted to tell her to go fuck herself, but I couldn't risk what she'd do.

I had to protect my baby. I just smiled sweetly and said, 'Of course, Sister Joanna.'

She took me by the arm and this time, I didn't leave kicking and screaming. I didn't call for my mammy or daddy, or beg Justin or his aunt to do the right thing. I just walked by the nuns' side, willingly, compliantly following their lead. I didn't try to run. There was nowhere to run to.

There was a small car parked outside. I was put into the back of it with my father's suitcase. There were no goodbyes. Justin didn't venture outside. His auntie Martha tried to give me one of her roast chicken sandwiches, insisting on the nuns opening the back window so she could shove it through. She dropped it on the seat beside me.

'You'll be OK. I promise,' she said.

They drove me through the streets of Dublin, out onto the motorways and through the towns between Dublin and Cork. I just sat there, not moving, soaking in betrayal. The people I trusted most had deserted me. I could feel myself breaking apart and I knew I couldn't let that happen. *I won't fail you, kiddo. No way. I may be forsaken, but I will not forsake. You've just got to give me a minute to find a way. OK, kiddo?*

I watched the world go by, absent-mindedly listening to the radio in the background. A male DJ was speaking about the politics of the day. He was laughing about how ludicrous the notion was that a woman would ever be president of Ireland. I stared out of the window and it felt like just another oppressive brick slathered in the wall. Ireland and the world were built for men and men only. I always knew it deep down. I just didn't know I knew it, not until that day when the boy who got me pregnant sold me down the river to the nuns, who both shook his hand and thanked him as they shoved me out of the door. *Good boy. You'll make a fine solicitor and an even better judge.*

Oh! And by the way, fuck you. I hope you die in a fucking fire. And, God, if you're listening, fuck you, too. The baby kicked. I worried it might be a warning. *I take that back.*

I saw the gates of the place from the main road. My stomach lurched, my head spun and I felt sick. The ache inside me turned to a piercing pain.

'You won't be escaping again,' Buckaroo said, and of course that sweet tone she'd offered Auntie Martha and Justin was all gone.

I was ushered inside. It was still morning. In the hallway, I passed some girls on their hands and knees, polishing the parquet flooring.

'Take your suitcase to your dorm, 10078,' Knuckles said. 'Then report to the doctor.'

The doctor told me I had high blood pressure and asked me how I felt.

'Fine,' I lied.

I felt excruciating pain, but I was afraid to tell him. *It will pass. Just hang in there, please.*

He pointed to my ankles. 'Did you notice how swollen they are?'

'I thought it was normal.'

'What about your face?'

'It's ugly,' I said.

'It's just very swollen. Any headaches?'

'Sometimes.'

'Bad?'

'A lot.'

'Nausea?'

'No.'

'Shortness of breath?'

'In here, no one breathes easy,' I said, and he sat back.

'We'll have to keep an eye on you.'

I was taken to the shower by Sister Angeline and Sister Peter. They watched me strip off, a slight smile on their lips. They didn't speak to me, they didn't touch me, but they tore into me with their eyes. I felt sickened and desperate, trying to wash myself clean while guarding myself and my baby from their dirty looks. They told me that I was sullied, unclean – and all the while I tried to hold on, but the baby was coming.

When the blood pooled under me, I couldn't hide it anymore.

Chapter Ten

Caroline

CAROLINE GOT HER BLOOD RESULTS a week later in her consultant's office. Lucy Belton pushed her glasses up onto the bridge of her nose and held them to her face, squinting a little.

'Well, the good news is you're free of STDs,' she said, and she wasn't making a joke.

'If I wasn't, that would make for an interesting conversation with Dave,' Caroline mumbled.

'You're talking, then?'

Caroline didn't expect that question. 'Sometimes,' she said.

Lucy sighed and refocused on the document in hand. 'Your AMH is coming in around 1 nanogram per millimetre, which is what we expected and it's OK. Your FSH is 8-ish IUs per litre.'

Caroline moved a little in her seat. 'That's the follicle-stimulating hormone. It's the important one.'

'It's low, but there's still hope. The good news is your oestrogen levels are coming in around 210 picograms per millilitre, which is perfect.'

'So we can move forwards?'

'We can.'

Caroline was so relieved, she raised her arms in the air and stamped her feet. 'Yes!' She laughed to herself. 'Yes! Yes! Yes!'

Lucy Belton even smiled a little. 'I'm happy for you, Caroline.'

Lucy had witnessed a similar celebration eight years before, when Dave received his results. Although it was obvious that the fertility issues lay with Caroline, the hospital needed to check the quality of her husband's sperm. It had never occurred to Caroline that he'd be nervous of the results, but when he aced it, he was so relieved he celebrated by punching the air, jumping up and doing a little victory dance, crying out, 'Yes, yes, yes, who's got it? I've got it.' Caroline had been mortified. Lucy had burst out laughing.

Things had been so different then. They had been excited, hopeful, bonded together and on a mission. Now she was screaming 'yes' on her own and it wasn't the same, but it was something.

The next test was the transvaginal scan. It was undignified and invasive, and Caroline had more of them than she'd had hot dinners. She was as familiar with her radiographer as she was with her hairdresser. Still, it didn't make taking off her knickers and parting her legs any easier. She was behind the blue paper curtain, removing clothes from her lower half and contemplating whether or not to keep her socks on, when Amelia, the radiographer, asked her how Dave was getting on with his new job.

The last time she was there, Dave had just left his IT job in the bank and moved into the gas company; the pay was better, the hours were shorter and it was less stressful. He'd been so content since the move.

'Good,' she said.

'Oh, I'm glad.'

'Still got the travel bug?' Amelia asked.

'Nah, I'd rather be at home these days.'

Now naked from the waist down, Caroline plonked herself on the bed and covered herself with a heavy paper blanket.

'Ready,' Caroline said.

Amelia pulled the curtain.

139

'I still want to go to Peru,' Amelia said as she placed herself between Caroline's legs.

'Yeah, it's nice.'

'Nice!' Amelia chuckled to herself. 'You raved about it the last time.'

'The food's amazing,' Caroline said as Amelia placed gel on the probe.

'Scooch down for me.'

Caroline scooched towards the end of the bed.

Amelia lifted the blanket back. Caroline could feel the air hit her.

'Now, a little cold.'

Caroline closed her eyes as the probe entered her.

'I love my food. What was your favourite meal there?' Amelia said.

'I don't know. Everything was good.'

Amelia was looking at the screen. 'Right ovary looks good.'

'What about the left?' Caroline asked.

'Can't find it. You sure you didn't get it taken out at some point?'

'What?' Caroline sat up a little. *Jesus Christ! Did I? No! Surely to shit I'd remember that!* Panic rose inside her.

'Ah, there it is. All good.'

Caroline relaxed. *Jesus Christ!* She lay back down.

'Ah, what's this?'

'What's what?' *What's what?*

'Just relax, lie back down.' Amelia was looking at the screen. 'OK, we have something here, but when do we not, right?'

Caroline's heart sank. 'I'm going to need a procedure, aren't I?'

Amelia covered Caroline with the paper blanket and snapped off her gloves. 'I'll pass this on to Lucy Belton. Try not to worry.'

For fuck's sake . . .

Back in Lucy's office, Caroline noticed a painting hanging on the wall. It comprised a dramatic blob of bubble pink pierced with spikes of red against a black background. It was striking in an unpleasant kind of way.

'That's new.'

'It was a present to Gerry,' Lucy said, leafing through her file. Gerry was another consultant in the practice.

'What's it supposed to be?'

'A troubled womb, apparently.'

'Looks like mine feels.'

'It's bloody awful,' Lucy said.

'Why do people think that the art on the walls of gynae always has to be impressions of wombs, ovaries or vaginas?'

'That's what I said.' Lucy flicked over a page. 'What's wrong with a pleasant landscape?' She looked up from the file and met Caroline's eyes. She sighed. 'Caroline, you have an endometrioma.'

'OK.' *Not the first time, won't be the last . . .*

'It's big.'

'How big?'

'Fifteen centimetres.'

'Doesn't sound that big.'

'Your previous ones were no bigger than nine and they were big.'

'Right.'

'We have to remove it before attempting IVF.'

'You sure we can't just ignore it?'

'Absolutely positive.'

'Fine. We'll remove it.'

Lucy wrote something down on the file. 'I can give you a date in three months.'

'No! Please, that delays everything.'

141

'I'll put you in for a cancellation in the meantime. That's all I can do.'

It was a setback, but not the end of the world. They would operate, remove it and she'd be back on track.

Everything will be fine.

The heater was broken at the group meeting that evening, but it was so packed, the small hall didn't feel cold. They cupped their hands around hot teas and coffees and they kept their coats on.

Caroline was the first to speak.

'They've found another endometrioma. It has to go before I can do another round.'

'Oh, shit, sorry,' Natalie said.

Ronnie looked round. 'What's an endometrioma?'

'It's a cyst on my ovary.'

'Bad luck.'

'My luck,' Caroline said.

'But they still believe you can move forwards?' Sheena asked.

'Yes, it's just another hurdle.'

She hadn't spoken to Dave about it. He didn't want to know. They barely spoke at all. He lived between the sitting room and his bedroom. She lived in the kitchen and her bedroom.

The house and her heart were halved in two, and as a room full of women clapped for her and wished her well, she thought only of him.

A Slap, a Baby and a Bar of Carbolic Soap

Catherine

I WOKE UP WITH MY LEGS in stirrups. Buckaroo and a nun who identified herself as Sister Theresa were standing over me.

'She's back,' I heard Sister Theresa say.

I tried to struggle to put my legs together, but they were tied and the pain I felt was so intense. Sister Theresa's hand was pushing down on my stomach. *Oh God. Please. Stop!* She had her hand halfway up my vagina.

'The baby has turned,' she said, pulling her hand out.

I was dizzy with the pain.

I remembered Maria's cries. *No! No! No!* I wouldn't give them the satisfaction. They were determined I would suffer for my sins – no medicine for me, no painkillers or gas and air. I'd be offered nothing that would help me and everything that would be done would be done to hurt me.

'Let her rip,' I heard Sister Buckaroo say. 'Let her tear. Maybe she'll think twice the next time she contemplates tempting a man.'

They had broken me and rebuilt me and broken me again. My body was ragged and raw and everything inside me screamed, but no matter how hard they seemed to try, they couldn't make me cry. I was too busy talking to my baby. *So, you're early, kiddo. That's OK. Doesn't matter. I'm here. I'm sorry. I shouldn't have trusted him. I won't make that mistake again. OK? Don't worry,*

143

they think they've torn me down and maybe they have. But you, my love, are the bloom among rubble, my miracle, and I will rebuild us.

I could feel myself slipping away.

'You have to push, do you hear me? We need to get this baby out of you.' Buckaroo suddenly sounded worried.

Oh no.

A sudden pain tore through me. I screamed.

'Stop that,' she said. She slapped me across the face. 'Stop that at once.'

Sister Theresa was elbow deep in me, pulling. I could feel myself tearing.

Oh, Saint Jude, I'm sorry for all I said. Please save me.

Sister Theresa was shouting. 'Her blood pressure's too high – she needs a doctor.'

'Calm down, Sister Theresa, we are way past that.' Buckaroo looked at me. 'Your contractions came on quick and strong and the baby's head is crowning. It's time to push.'

'I can't.' I didn't want to let go of my baby. *What if she hurts you, kiddo?*

'Stop this messing. Push and push now,' Buckaroo shouted.

'The baby needs you to push,' Sister Theresa said.

OK, kiddo, this is it.

So I pushed and she pulled, and I screamed and I cried. My body ripped apart and my heart rate soared, and the world went black.

The next thing I was aware of was a male voice.

'My God, what's wrong with you?'

'I really don't know what you mean, Doctor.'

Buckaroo. I recognised her voice.

'This was totally avoidable. I am sick of coming to this place and fixing up girls who should have been cared for properly.'

'How dare you!' I heard her say, and then she saw my eyes opening and she stormed out.

'Don't worry,' the doctor said gently. 'I've injected the area. No more pain for you today.'

The next time I woke, I was in a bed in a small room. I knew I was torn to pieces. There was blood and pus on the sheets, and I had a vague memory of being stitched up. There was no one around now. I was alone. To one side of the bed was a locker with a brand-new bar of carbolic soap resting on it; to the other I could see a baby in a steel crib.

Kiddo.

I peered into the crib and I knew instantly that the child was mine. Before I had a chance to pick the baby up and hold it, Sister Theresa came in.

'You need to lie down.'

'I'm fine.'

'You could have died. Lie down. You've been out for two days.'

I was so shocked, I lay down.

'What sex is it?'

'A girl.'

Ahhh, a girl. It's a girl. Oh, thank you, Saint Jude. I have a little girl.

'Is that black hair on her head?'

'A fine head of it.'

I held my breath. *OK, kiddo, you might look a little like your daddy, but I refuse to hold that against you.*

'Why is she here, with me?' I asked. None of the other girls got to stay in a room alone with their babies.

'Because she might die.'

'What?'

I tried to leap out of the bed, but I couldn't. It felt like my downstairs area had been sawn in two. I didn't know how to ask about all that and even if I did, I knew I probably wouldn't be told. *I hope I'm not ruined forever. I've only had sex three times. I really like it. Yeah, I said it. Fuck you, God.* Then I thought about the baby and how I needed Saint Jude on side at the very least. He wouldn't like me telling God to fuck off. *Sorry, Saint Jude.*

'She's premature and not thriving. She can't keep the formula down, so breast milk is her only option of survival.'

'She's not going into Nursery Two, is she?' I asked.

'Not if she starts to thrive, so I suppose that's up to you and your milk.'

'Oh God.' My heart felt like it might beat out of my chest.

'You'll have plenty of time for praying. Now, let's get you sorted.'

She grabbed at my breasts and exposed them before turning away to pluck the baby out of the crib. I could feel the cool air on my chest and at the same time a warm tear trickled down my face. Sister Theresa unwrapped the baby and picked her up, and before giving us even a second to say hello, she starting trying to attach us. The baby was still asleep. Sister Theresa flicked her arm, quick and sharp, to wake her and I had to call on all of my strength not to punch her in her face.

'Time to wake up now.'

After much fussing, my baby attached, and after a few terrifying minutes, she began to suckle.

Sister Theresa seemed happy. She sat and watched us.

I stared at her, this beautiful creature, this miracle, my miracle. *Oh, wow! Look at you.* I wanted to hug and kiss her and hold her on my shoulder and inhale the top of her head and count all of her fingers and toes. I wanted to be left in peace to love her.

'I'm fine by myself,' I mumbled. *Just give me one minute!*

'We stopped permitting girls to feed the babies a good while ago. It's cost-effective, but it causes confusion and their real mothers don't like it. It's best I supervise.'

'I am her real mother,' I said. 'I'm keeping my baby.'

It was the first time I'd verbalised my intention to a nun. Sister Theresa's lip curled, but she said nothing. Instead, she just waited and watched, so I did my best to ignore her and just focus on my little girl.

She curled her little fingers around my index finger and I couldn't have described all the wonder I felt. *You're here, kiddo. Look at us. We made it. Can you believe it?* I was awestruck. Her little face, with two brown eyes . . . *Just like her daddy . . . Damn it. Let it go, Katie . . . I mean, Catherine. My name is Catherine.* She had tiny ears, one perfect little nose and pretty pink lips that parted to reveal gums and a little tongue. I looked down her long neck, her thin arms and legs and her little tummy. Her ribs were showing – that was not cute – but then five fingers, five toes . . .

'You're a scrawny little yoke, aren't you?' I murmured. 'We'll see to that.'

'Don't talk to the baby,' Sister Theresa said.

'She's my baby, I'll talk to her if I want.' I don't know how I got the guts to say it.

Sister Theresa grabbed her from me within a moment. 'In that case, it's Nursery Two for this little one. Say goodbye.'

'I'm sorry. I'm sorry. Please, please. I won't talk to her. I won't even look at her. Please.'

She handed her back and the relief washed through me. *Oh God. Oh God. Oh God. Stay quiet, Katie. Stay quiet.*

After that, Sister Theresa just watched and waited. When the feed was done, she took my baby away.

Chapter Eleven

Natalie

ON DAY FOURTEEN OF NATALIE'S cycle, she and Linda drove to the clinic. Linda waited outside the room while the radiographer completed a transvaginal scan to ensure Natalie was good to go. Natalie was not a fan of the gel-covered probe entering her nunny, but it was for a good cause, so she exhaled, dropped her legs apart, stared at the ceiling and pictured what her child would look like. *The genes on my mother's side are strong . . . Come on!*

'Well, it looks like lefty's got it.'

'What?'

The radiographer turned the screen to show her. 'There it is – the follicle that's going to ovulate.'

'Wow.'

'Yeah, fascinating, isn't it?'

Once it was confirmed that Natalie's body was ready, the sperm was prepared in the lab. Her consultant's replacement was a man called Christopher Smith. He explained that an embryologist was washing the sperm, preparing the sample.

'So we can load the best ones into the test tube.'

'Right,' Natalie said, and her stomach knotted a little.

'So weird.' Linda was shaking her head from side to side.

The consultant smiled. 'It's pretty special.'

'Tell that to my girlfriend in stirrups,' Linda quipped before looking Natalie in the eye. 'Do you feel special, honey?'

Christopher Smith didn't know where to look. Natalie was lying on a bed and while she wasn't in stirrups and she was covered with a small blanket, she was naked from the waist down. She felt like crying. *Why is Linda acting like this? Why is it a joke to her? Why isn't she excited or at the very least full of fucking wonder?*

Christopher Smith pointed to the hatch in the wall. 'That's where the sperm will come from. As soon as it's prepared, the embryologist will pass it through the hatch. Then I'll put the sample into the catheter and we are good to go.'

Natalie looked across at the hatch. *Mad.*

Linda took her phone out to take a photo.

'Ah, please don't do that,' Christopher said. 'Actually, could you turn it off?'

So there Natalie was, in a small clinical room, legs akimbo, while her girlfriend messed around trying to turn off her phone and a stenographer placed jelly on her stomach, watching for Paul's sperm to appear through a hatch in the wall. *You couldn't make it up.*

Natalie saw the sample appear, then she braced herself.

'Just relax,' Christopher said.

Natalie didn't know what she was feeling – a tiny tug of the catheter, maybe – but then the stenographer was holding the probe over her fallopian tube and he pointed to the screen.

'Can you see?'

She could.

'The sperm in the catheter will be deployed at the opening of the left fallopian tube, placed right where they need to be.'

Just then, she saw a flash as Paul's sperm dashed towards her waiting egg.

'Wow. Did you see that, Linda?'

'See what?' Linda looked up from her phone. 'Are we done?'

'Yes.'

'That was quick.' She laughed to herself. 'I bet even Paul isn't that quick.'

Really, Linda? What the hell?

Once everything was detached from Natalie and her legs were closed and her bottom half covered, Christopher explained what would happen next.

'Wait two weeks before taking a test – not a day before two weeks. The reading will be incorrect if you try early, do you hear me?'

They both nodded.

'Will Monica be back by then?' Natalie asked.

'No. It's a bad break and that woman hasn't had a holiday in five years.'

'OK. Thanks,' Natalie said.

She felt funny walking out the door, almost afraid that Paul's sperm would fall out of her.

'It's not going to fall out,' Linda said, and she laughed to herself again!

What's so funny, Linda? Like, really? What is so bloody funny? Natalie was annoyed, but she said nothing. What could she say? *You aren't behaving the way I think you should?* It sounded a little controlling and weird, but something was eating at her.

Paul rang later that night. Natalie was on the sofa, lying with her legs elevated on cushions. Linda put him on speaker.

'Well?'

'It's done,' Linda said.

'So is she pregnant?'

151

Natalie winced. *Fucking Paul!*

'We won't know for two weeks.'

'Right, well, say nothing to Sylvia.'

'I don't know Sylvia, Paul,' Linda said.

'Well, you will. We're getting married.'

'Shut up!' Linda said.

'No, I'm serious.'

'You've known her five minutes,' Natalie said.

'Yeah, well, when you know, you know.'

'Paul, this is stupid,' Linda said.

'Who are you to tell me what's stupid?'

'What's that supposed to mean?' she said, and Natalie could hear the hurt and anger in Linda's voice.

'You know very fucking well.'

He hung up.

'What's he talking about, Linda?' Natalie asked, struggling to sit up.

'No idea,' she said, and Natalie knew she was lying.

Later that week, Natalie told the group about the insemination, but not about the knot that had remained in her stomach since then.

'Another nine days before we can do a pregnancy test. Feels like nine years.'

'Keep busy,' Sheena said.

'I'm just trying not to think about it.'

'How's that working for you?' Ronnie asked.

'Not great.'

'I know the feeling.' Ronnie sat back in the chair. 'I can't stop thinking. All I do is think.'

Her eyes shone and her lip trembled. Everyone stopped for a second and looked at her.

She raised her hand. 'I'm so sorry, Natalie, go on.'

'No. You go on,' Natalie said. Ronnie so rarely spoke.

She bowed her head and sighed long and heavy, emptying her lungs of air before shaking her head.

'Everything was great. I had lovely parents, an exciting life and a promising future.'

She shook her head from side to side. She tried to speak, but words failed her. A tear streaked her face. She wiped it with the back of her hand.

'What happened, Ronnie?' Sheena asked gently.

'They died.'

Ronnie's face crumpled and she sobbed into her hands. She was sitting between Caroline and Natalie, so they both wrapped an arm around her, holding her tight to them keeping her upright.

'I'm so sorry,' Ronnie said. 'I don't know where this is coming from. It was over a year ago now.'

Sheena soothed her. 'It's not easy.'

'Please, please – someone else talk.'

Ronnie looked so desperate that Janet spoke up.

'I can't stop thinking,' she said, and the other women leaned in. 'I'm thinking all the time.'

'It's hard not to when you're trying,' Caroline said.

A few other women nodded.

'Not about getting pregnant,' Janet said.

'Then what?' Sheena said.

'I think Jim might be having it off with someone.'

'No!' Natalie momentarily forgot about Ronnie. Surely it wasn't possible. *Not Jim!*

'I found a note in his overalls. A phone number, a note that said "you can talk to me anytime" and a lipstick kiss.'

'Do you think he travelled back in time to have an affair?' Mary said, scoffing.

'Exactly! Who leaves mystery notes in 2010?' Natalie said.

'Someone who wants to get caught,' Ronnie said, and everyone turned to her.

She straightened, and Natalie and Caroline removed their arms from around her shoulders. Her eyes were red, but she seemed more like herself again.

'What are the chances his wife does the washing? What are the chances she goes through his pockets?'

Sheena nodded. 'Ronnie has a point.'

Janet frowned. 'So, he's having it off and the woman wants me to know about it?'

'Maybe,' Ronnie said, 'but maybe something else.'

'Like what?'

'A crazy stalker,' Natalie said.

'We're trying for a baby!' Janet said.

Caroline looked aghast. 'You're still having sex with him?'

'Now, Caroline, there is no judgment here,' Sheena said.

Janet shrugged. 'You can't have a baby without sex.'

Natalie put up her hand. 'I disagree.'

'Oh, you know what I mean.'

'You still want a baby, even if your husband is cheating?' Ronnie asked before quickly adding, 'No judgment.'

Janet thought about it for a second. 'What I want are the babies I lost back.'

Although she spoke even quieter than usual, everyone heard her.

Natalie wasn't sure where to put herself. Then Ronnie piped up.

'Let's find out who she is.'

'Ah no,' Janet said.

'Is not knowing destroying your peace of mind?' Ronnie asked.

Janet nodded.

'So let's find out,' Ronnie said. She glanced at Natalie and Caroline. 'Are you two in or what?'

Natalie looked to Caroline and Caroline nodded. 'OK, if that's what Janet wants?'

Janet looked between them. 'Yeah. I think I need to know.'

Natalie nodded. 'OK then.'

'Please be careful, ladies,' Sheena said. 'This isn't an episode of Agatha Christie.'

'I bloody hope not,' Ronnie said. 'No one's looking to murder anyone.'

Natalie sighed. She wondered what she was doing getting involved in a near-stranger's mini drama, but if it was distracting Ronnie from her own pain and Natalie from her worries about Linda, then perhaps it wasn't so bad, after all.

Where Are You Now, Saint Jude?

Catherine

THEY KEPT ME IN THAT room for just one day. After that, I was sent back to my own bed. My breasts were so swollen they ached all the time. I was sore all over and I didn't know what I'd find in my downstairs area. I was afraid to touch it, in case I'd damage myself more, but I knew I couldn't allow infection to set in, so I used the carbolic soap. It was a whole new kind of torture, supervised by Sister Angeline and Sister Peter. They watched me wash myself and cry out in pain and allowed themselves slight smiles.

As soon as I was up and around, I worked in Nursery One, and thankfully, I found my baby there. She was in the corner of the room, a little away from the other babies. I bottle-fed and washed other girls' babies. I wasn't allowed to touch my own except when they took me into the side room to feed her. I didn't tell the other girls about it – not just because the nuns warned me not to, but because I didn't want them to be jealous or hurt. I didn't want it to make them any sadder or angrier than they already felt.

I didn't see Marian, but I watched out for her, because I figured she'd be due any day. The other girls were polite to me, but we were all going through our own little piece of hell, so near our own flesh and blood and yet so far. I caught one brushing against the baby in my arms that belonged to her. Another girl stood near her boy's crib and sobbed for a second or two before she went back to buffing the floor. One nun or another was always watching.

I breastfed for three weeks, always watched by one of the nuns. Sister Angeline always insisted on attaching the baby to me, even though we didn't need her help. It felt natural. Sister Angeline was always rough, pulling at me, pinching me. I said and did nothing. All I wanted to do was save my child from Nursery Two.

I could see that she was starting to thrive. Her skinny little arms and legs filled out and I could barely see her ribs. By the third week I could see a little pudgy tummy starting to form. I was overjoyed at first, and then the sadness took over; I knew it meant that our time together was coming to an end, at least until we got out of this place.

I wasn't absolutely sure what they'd do to me. I'd told them I was keeping her, but they insisted on keeping us apart. Could that really go on for three years? I didn't know, because none of the girls I knew and trusted in the place had dared to keep their babies. They'd never challenged the idea that they were unfit mothers. That didn't make it any easier. It changed every single one of them.

We were all caught between an unsupportive society and unsupportive parents, a church that deemed us filthy and indecent, and a corporation funnelling kids to adoptive parents both home and abroad in exchange for donations. The whole system felt unbreakable and maybe I was the only stupid one of the lot who thought that if I held my ground, I could beat them.

I talked to my baby in my head while the nuns watched us. I explained the whole thing. That life would be difficult for a while but that I'd find a way of talking to her and holding her and loving her and being there. That even when she was in one part of the building and I was in a whole different part, she had to know that I loved her, that we belonged together. She'd burp and fart, and every now and again take a shit on me. But she'd also yawn and stretch her arm right over her head, and she'd stare up at me with those big brown eyes. I loved every bit of it.

I called her Daisy, because she was a bloom in the rubble, my very own miracle.

One day when she was watching over us, Sister Angeline didn't try to attach us.

'This is your last day,' she said. 'The baby's fine – she's holding formula now. She'll stay in the nursery until you sign her over.'

I inhaled Daisy's sweet, intoxicating smell and placed her on my shoulder, our cheeks touching.

Sister Angeline pulled the chair that was usually near the bed towards the window and she sat down. Instead of watching me, she looked away, out of the window, to give me a moment in peace with my daughter.

It was the closest thing to kindness I'd ever experienced in that place and maybe that emboldened me.

'I'm not signing her over,' I said in a loud and clear voice.

'You can't raise this child,' Sister Angeline said. 'Deep down, I think you know that.'

'I'm not signing her over.'

She said nothing in reply to that. She didn't turn round, so I focused on my little girl.

'Your name is Daisy and you're my whole world,' I whispered to her.

Tears streamed down my face and onto Daisy. She scrunched her nose because she didn't like that at all. She wriggled and wrestled, so I rubbed her back and then she cried. Sister Angeline turned round.

'That will do,' she said, and she took her out of my arms. 'Go back to work.'

'Outside?'

'In the kitchen, where we can keep an eye on you.'

And that was it. I went to the kitchen.

Three weeks passed. I caught glimpses of Marian every now and then, from behind the kitchen counter where I served breakfast, lunch and dinner. She was visibly shaken the first time she saw me. I tried to smile at her to tell her I was OK, but she paled and looked away. We spoke only once after that, when passing in the hallway.

'Don't fight them, Katie. You won't win,' she said before shuffling on.

She was overdue by then and a few days later, she gave birth. The rumour was that she signed the papers that day and her parents paid for her to leave within the week.

I didn't make any new friends. I had Daisy now. I didn't need anyone else.

I tried to visit her, but nobody who wasn't assigned to the nursery was allowed entry.

'Number 10078, you are assigned for kitchen work, not nursery duty,' Sister Angeline said when I stood at the nursery door, and I begged her to let me see my baby.

'I'm keeping her, you know. She's mine.'

She closed the door in my face.

An hour later, I was called out of the kitchen to speak to Buckaroo. I was escorted to her office; it was the first time I'd seen her since before I'd given birth. A typewriter sat on the table in front of her as she talked. It looked out of place and so modern against all the Catholic iconography. She invited me to sit, which was new. I decided to remain standing.

'Katie, I know this is difficult for you, but I can't have you making trouble . . .' She waited for a moment or two before adding the word '. . . again.'

Her glare was intimidating, but I wasn't the girl she'd met the first night I was here. I wasn't the Pitiful Whore anymore; I was Daisy's mother. I made sure I was standing straight. Shoulders back, my eyes meeting hers.

'I don't want to make trouble, Sister,' I said calmly. 'I just want to see my baby.'

'The child is not yours.'

'She is mine. She will always be mine. She came from me.'

She didn't like that. She flinched. She folded her hands in her lap.

'I have some papers for you to sign.'

'I'm not signing anything and you can't make me.'

'Do you like working in the kitchen, Katie?'

'Not really.'

'Would you like to be moved?'

'I don't care.'

She stared into my eyes.

My hands were shaking, so I clasped them behind my back, squeezing my fingers together tightly. *You will not break me.*

'Go back to work,' she said, and I ran out of there.

Did we just win, Daisy?

A week after my meeting with Buckaroo, I was cleaning out a cupboard, when Sister Knuckles appeared in the doorway.

'You have a phone call.'

She escorted me to the office. Buckaroo was typing on her typewriter, clacking away as though I wasn't even in the room.

I picked up the receiver. 'Hello?'

'Catherine, this is your mammy.'

'Hi, Mammy,' I said, and I think I stammered. Hearing her voice shook me.

'You need to sign those papers.'

My heart stopped. I thought I might pass out. I sat down on the chair with my head in my hands.

'No.'

'Don't you say no to me, young lady.' She sounded panicked and strained.

'No,' I said.

'This will not end well for you, Catherine.'

'My name is Katie now and my number is 10078. You don't know anything about me.'

I could hear the clicks of the coins that she was feeding into the telephone box. I pictured her on Main Street, in her coat and hat, stuffed into that small glass-windowed box, popping her small change into the coin collector, hoping not to run out before she changed my mind.

'Stop that cheek right now. Sign those bloody papers, Catherine, or you will not have a home to return to.'

She hung up the phone. I placed the receiver down.

'Thank you, Sister Joanna,' I said.

I walked out of the door and instead of going back into the kitchen, I ran up the stairs two at a time and into the first toilet I saw. There I hid, hugging my knees to my chest, breathing in and out. I cried till there was nothing left.

What do we do now, Saint Jude?

I'd lost all respect for God and Mary and the lot of them by now. If they were going to stand over the evil I'd witnessed in their name, to hell with them. But I still had some hope for Saint Jude. He was instrumental in my escape from Cork. I'd prayed to him and then a laundry truck had arrived. I'd prayed to him from that cramped toilet in the train and the conductor went away and never came back. Saint Jude was on my side.

Now, sitting on that toilet, I prayed to Saint Jude.

We're really on our own now. We need your help more than ever, OK? They're not going to release me now. I know that. Three years isn't a long time. We can do it and by then, I'll be nineteen and Daisy will be three. I'll be old enough to find a little job and she won't be a baby anymore. I could take her with me. I could sell fruit in the stalls. I had seen those women as the nuns drove me through the streets of Dublin. They had babies strapped to them. I could do that. Daisy could help me. I bet she's going to be smart. Her granddad's a judge. Help us get through this. Please.

Chapter Twelve

Janet

JIM WAS STILL AT WORK when Janet arrived home, accompanied by Caroline, Natalie and Ronnie. She felt a mixture of relief and guilt to have told them. She had been mulling over her husband's possible infidelity for weeks and angry sex had only got her so far. She'd been snapping at him and he hadn't challenged her. She wondered about that – a guilty conscience, maybe. Or maybe his head was so full of Paper Lips, he didn't even notice.

Of course, it could just be that they were trying again and he assumed she was stressed about that, and of course she was. How could she not be? She carried a graveyard inside her.

In the last few weeks, she'd looked at the note again and again, if only to convince herself she wasn't going mad. This was Jim. He was hard-working, the salt of the earth. She knew him inside and out. They'd been together since they were teenagers. She'd never been with anyone else and neither had he . . . *until now?* He would never have cheated on her before the babies, but now, after everything they'd been through . . . could she even blame him? There had been some very dark days.

She couldn't bear to ask him about it. She was terrified he'd admit he was cheating and then what? Divorce? How could she function in this world without him? They were fourteen when they met. She didn't know life without him. Would he take the chance to run from her into the arms of a woman who could bring a baby to term? They had been through so much and, yes, that had bonded them in one way, but space had grown between them, too. There was so much unsaid.

You can always talk to me. That's what Paper Lips had said. *You can always talk to me.*

What did they talk about? The conversations almost scared her more than anything. Did he talk about her? How unhappy he was, what a disappointment she was.

She hadn't meant to bring up her concerns about her husband's cheating in the group. It wasn't that sort of group. But then Ronnie had looked so sad, so desperate for the group to move on, and it just fell out of her mouth before she even really registered saying it.

Then Ronnie asked her that question: Is not knowing destroying your peace of mind? And she realised it was. She needed to know. If she asked Jim and he answered yes, then she would have a choice to blow up her entire life or give her husband permission to carry on with another woman. But if she uncovered his deceit without his knowledge, she would have time to decide what kind of wife and woman she wanted to be. She needed to make a plan.

She popped the kettle on and switched on the Nespresso coffee machine as the ladies made themselves comfortable on high stools around her island. She ran up the stairs and pulled down the small box containing the two babygrows she'd bought prematurely. She kept the note in there, knowing it was the last place her husband would ever find it. She was back down the stairs in time for the whistle of a boiled kettle, and she made teas and coffees for everyone while Ronnie read the note.

'So what now?' Caroline asked.

'Now I call the number,' Ronnie said.

'And?'

'And watch this space.' She waved her phone. 'Janet, are you sure? Some things are worse than not knowing.'

Janet joined the other women sitting at the island. 'I'm sure.'

'Do you have a landline?'

'Yeah, it's just for the Sky box, though; we don't use it.'

'Great, write down that number for me.'

Janet scrolled through her phone for her house number and she wrote it down on a note pad. Then Ronnie picked up her phone and dialled the number on the note. Janet could hear the dial tone beeping and then the click of an answer machine. She inhaled.

'You have reached the phone of . . .'

It was an automated response. *Damn it!*

Ronnie held the phone closer to her ear and walked over to the window. 'Hello, this is Sarah Sullivan,' she said. 'I work with the Irish Prize Bonds. Apologies for the late call. We currently have twenty-two million in unclaimed prizes with tickets bought in the 1980s. If you believe it's possible that you bought Prize Bonds or received gifts of Prize Bonds, all we ask is you return this call to our Dublin office on 01-4444637 and provide us with your full name and address and date of birth. Thank you and good luck.' She hung up.

'She'll think it's a scam,' Natalie said, sipping from her cup of tea.

'I agree,' Caroline said. 'No way I'd fall for that.'

'Maybe,' Ronnie said, and then Janet's house phone started to ring. 'Or maybe she's a more trusting soul than us.' She turned her back and answered the phone while staring out at Janet's perfectly manicured garden. 'Hello, Prize Bonds Clearing House, how can I help you?'

'Hello, I'm looking for Sarah Sullivan.'

'Can I say who's calling, please?' Ronnie said. 'Tina . . . Can you spell that, please? . . . T-I-N-A. And your surname? R-O-S-S-I . . . Rossi. Is that correct? Hold the line, please . . .' She pressed the hold button.

'You can hang up,' Janet said quietly. 'I know who it is.'

Ronnie hung up. Everyone looked at Janet.

'She's the receptionist in my husband's business.'

'Always the poxy secretary,' Ronnie said, and the phone started ringing again. She didn't answer.

'What does she look like?' Natalie asked.

'Brown hair, good figure,' Janet said. 'She's young, twenty-two at most.'

'Maybe they're just friends,' Caroline said. 'Look, Janet, this is what we know: Jim's receptionist has a crush on him. That's all the evidence we have. It doesn't mean he's doing anything about it.'

'I vote on a little surveillance,' Ronnie said.

Caroline shook her head. 'We all have jobs.'

'Except for me,' Janet said. 'I have nothing.'

Ronnie looked across at her. 'You have us.'

'I don't even know you,' Janet said.

'I know you.' For a split second, it looked like Ronnie might cry.

'You lot know me better than anyone else in my life,' Caroline said.

'Me too,' Natalie said. 'I'm ashamed to say I kinda let my friends go when I got together with Linda.'

'After everything that happened when we lost Derek, I pushed everyone away. I felt so stupid and guilty and ashamed.'

'Why?' Ronnie asked.

'I don't know. Stupid because I should have known it was too good to be true. Guilty because my body keeps attacking my children in one way or another, and ashamed because I look at all the people in my life with kids and I resent them. I mean, I *really* fucking hate them for it.'

'Me too!' Caroline put up her hand. 'Women who push their prams into the back of your legs, screaming *"excuse me"* like they own the earth.'

'Men in suits who park in mother-and-baby bays just because they have an empty baby seat in the car and a sticker with "baby on board" on the back window,' Natalie said.

'Seriously, it happens all the time,' Janet said. 'I just want to scream, "You actually have to have a baby with you to park there!"'

'Yummy mummies,' Caroline said, covering her mouth conspiratorially.

Natalie nodded. 'And the breastfeeding or bust brigade. Like if you don't breastfeed, you're a bad mother somehow.'

'Women who can't talk about anything other than their kids,' Ronnie said.

There was a moment's pause and Caroline looked over at Ronnie.

'Can I ask you a question?'

Ronnie nodded.

'What *is* your story?'

Everyone stopped. The room grew silent. They waited for an answer. Ronnie fidgeted a little.

'I'm no longer a daughter and I'll never be a mother . . .' She trailed off. Tears collected in her eyes. She turned away, facing Janet's perfect garden as she wiped them away.

'And there's no hope?' Janet asked.

'No,' Ronnie said. 'Hope is lost.' She turned back to face everyone. 'So, what are we doing about Jim?' she said.

Everyone looked towards Janet.

'Well, I'm not working, so I suppose I'll just stake out his office, night, noon and morning, for the next week.'

'You want some company?' Natalie said. 'I'm off Friday afternoons and I can miss a few pub quizzes.'

'Put me in for a few evenings,' Caroline said.

Ronnie moved towards Janet and squeezed her shoulders. 'I'm not flying again till next week.'

As Janet showed the women to the door, she asked them outright, 'Are we friends now?'

They all looked around at one another.

'I suppose we are,' Caroline said.

Ronnie took down everyone's number.

Janet went to bed thinking about her husband and what he might or might not be doing with Tina Rossi. *You can talk to me anytime*. It still bothered her – of course it did – but at least now she had people to talk to.

You Have to Fix Yourself

Catherine

DAISY WAS TWO MONTHS OLD when the fire alarm went off. I'd never taken part in a fire drill. No one in the kitchen knew what to do. Sister Imelda just shouted at us all to run, so we did. We ran out into the hallway, and all I could see were nuns and pregnant girls scampering around wildly.

'To the front wall, girls. *Outside*!' Buckaroo was shouting.

Everyone was all over the place and all I could think about was Daisy. I headed up the stairs and down the corridor to Nursery One. Nuns were shouting at the girls to pick up the babies and head to the grotto.

'Which one?' one of the girls cried.

'There's only one bloody grotto,' Sister Theresa said, and then she blessed herself, asking for forgiveness, as though using the word 'bloody' was what she needed forgiving for.

Girls were moving quickly, picking up babies. I ran from cot to cot looking for Daisy.

'What are you doing here?' Sister Theresa asked.

'I'm looking for Daisy.'

'Who's Daisy?'

'My child.'

'Get out. Go to the grotto.'

Some of the girls tried to leave, but I blocked the door.

169

'Where is she?' All I could think of was seeing and saving my girl. 'No one is getting out of here until I see my child.'

Sister Theresa knew I meant business. She looked scared.

She paused, then said, 'She's gone.'

She can't be.

'You're a liar,' I screamed.

'She is gone, Katie, now stop this.'

No. No. No. I didn't sign anything.

'Where?' I looked around the room, searching for her. It was clear she wasn't here. I could feel the emptiness creep inside me.

'They took her three days ago.'

'Who?' I roared.

'Her new parents.'

My legs went from under me and it gave the others a chance to run with the babies. When the room was finally empty, Sister Theresa told me to get to my feet, but I couldn't. So she left me there.

I waited for the smoke and the fire, and more than that, I welcomed it. Nothing mattered anymore if Daisy was gone.

Of course, it didn't come. It was a false alarm. When the fuss was over, Buckaroo walked into the room, flanked by two other nuns.

'Get up,' she said in a stern voice.

So I got up – and I went for her.

I lashed out with my hands and my legs. I screamed and I shouted, and I pulled at her fucking veil. The other nuns didn't know what to do. They tried to pull me off, but they were no match for a wild woman. Another one of them appeared and she was on it. She filled a syringe and stuck it in me. All the fight faded and I hit the ground hard.

I woke up in a small dark room. No windows, one door. Just a wall. It was locked. The bed was small. No locker, no blanket. I remembered my child had been taken. I hadn't signed anything, but she was gone. I didn't give her up. I didn't let her go. She was taken. She was stolen. I didn't know what to do.

I couldn't think. I couldn't breathe. It felt like the world had fallen in on me. I cried and I cried and I cried and I cried, but I didn't thump the door or kick it or scream. It seemed too late for that now.

I don't know how long I was there. A few days, I think, but not more than a week. My heart was broken, my mind shattered. I spent most of the time just looking at the wall. I thought of my brother Charles in his cot in that home run by nuns. I understood the comfort he found now in staring at the wall.

They stuck needles in me to keep me quiet. Everything was foggy and felt far away, even my thoughts. My mind ebbed and flowed on a sea of drugs. My chin was raw from dribble, just like Charles.

That's when I heard him, calling to me. I'd never heard his real voice, because he couldn't speak, but I knew at once that it was him. I turned from the wall and he was sitting by the bed.

'Charles?'

'You have to be OK to get out of this place.'

'I can't be OK. They took her.'

'You have to fix yourself, or they'll put you in a mental home and they'll keep you there till you die. You don't want that.'

'I'm sorry, Charles.'

'Don't be sorry. Just sit up and act nice and be polite and do what you have to do to get out.'

'Are you out?' I asked.

'I'm gone,' he said. 'They've done it to other girls, Catherine, they'll do it to you.'

And then he was gone.

171

It took a few minutes or maybe an hour or a day, but at last I sat up. I fixed my hair the best way I could and I breathed in and out. Then I built myself back up one brick at a time.

One of them knocked at the door. I didn't know her, but I welcomed her in.

'Do you feel any better?' she asked.

'Yes, Sister . . .'

'. . . Theresa,' she said.

'Yes, Sister Theresa. Thank you, Sister Theresa,' I said.

'And you are ready to go back to work?'

'I'd love that, Sister Theresa.'

'You have some apologies to make.'

I made myself nod. 'Yes, I do. I'm so very sorry. I really don't know what came over me, Sister Theresa.'

She smiled. 'We all make mistakes. To err is human, to forgive is divine. God is watching.'

'I hope so, Sister Theresa,' I said.

They let me out of the room later that day. I apologised to Buckaroo for attempting to kick the shit out of her. I didn't put it that way, of course. I returned to the kitchen, kept my head down, and three weeks later I was called to the office.

Buckaroo handed me an envelope. When I opened it, I found a ticket for the boat to England, a piece of paper with an address and phone number on it, and just enough money to get me there.

'Your debt has been paid, Katie. You'll leave in the morning.'

'To England?' I asked, looking at the ticket.

'There will be a job waiting for you, as a domestic in a hospital in Manchester. Room and board will be provided. Good luck to you.' Then she began typing on her stupid typewriter again.

I put the money in my mother's blue maternity dress with long sleeves and I walked out.

I finished doing dinner that evening and the next morning, I packed my daddy's suitcase full of tat and Sister Knuckles drove me to the port. She waited and watched as I handed in my ticket, queued with all the other pedestrians and walked onto the boat. I went inside so that she couldn't see me anymore, and after five or ten minutes, I watched her leave through a porthole.

Then I picked up my daddy's suitcase and I walked off that boat. I was seventeen years old and I was ready to fight them all.

Chapter Thirteen

Caroline

ONE DAY, DAVE ASKED CAROLINE about taking away Bruno's bed while she was poring over a shopping list and he was clearing out the fridge.

'I could put it in the attic with his toys,' he said.

She looked at it. It sat in the corner by the window where Bruno used to spend his time watching and waiting for unsuspecting foxes before his mind blurred and he lost all appetite for life.

'Just another week,' she said.

'I nearly broke my neck tripping over it last week.'

'Turn on a light.'

'He's dead, Caroline. Why can't you just accept reality?'

Dave left the room after that. She knew he was talking about the dog, but he was also talking about her campaign to get pregnant. She could see the hurt and anger building in him, and she wanted to fix it but she couldn't. As each day passed, she wasn't sure if he even wanted her to.

Everything seemed to be falling apart. The climate at work had felt strained since she'd turned down the offer of a partnership. She was steering clear of all family because she couldn't face telling her parents that she was trying again. They had made their feelings quite clear about it the last time she ended fertility treatment.

'Thanks be to fuck,' her dad had said.

'George!' her mother had roared.

'Bring out the champagne, Claire. We're going to celebrate this.' He'd hugged his daughter tight. 'Enough. You've so much going for you, love.'

'I know, Dad. I feel good about it,' she had said, but she was lying. She was just tired of it all, and too sore and too sad to keep going.

'You should plan a trip,' her mother had said while pouring out some sparkling wine.

Dave had smiled. 'That's a brilliant idea.'

That was when the trips away started. European city breaks at first and then sun and snow holidays and big once-in-a-lifetime trips. She'd experienced so many cultures and so much life in the three years that had passed since they'd given up trying for a baby. She took all the holidays she'd never taken before. They'd had four once-in-a-lifetime trips before she actually began to lose the will to live.

She didn't tell her family about the disintegration of her marriage. She was sleepwalking through it, hoping it wasn't really happening, because it couldn't be. *Could it?* She didn't want to upset them and if she kept it all to herself, maybe it wouldn't happen. Life without Dave seemed impossible. But still she sat in her bedroom looking at a menu of sperm from men who weren't Dave. She even left it on the kitchen counter to see if he'd have some sort of reaction. He didn't. He just threw it in the bin and poured the leftovers of a chicken curry over it. She isolated herself, away from anyone who would burst her little bubble.

One evening, Caroline's sister Lisa called to discuss their mother's birthday lunch the following Sunday.

'Best behaviour, Caroline.'

'I don't know what you mean.'

'Look, Michelle is going to be there and you might as well know, she's pregnant.'

That was a punch to the gut. 'Good for her,' Caroline said.

'Do you mean that? Because when she told you about being pregnant with Tommy, you freaked out and you haven't spoken to her since.'

'That's not true. And I was going through a particularly difficult IVF at the time. I was fucking bananas on hormones.'

'Tommy is four. You've seen him less than I've seen my dentist.'

'Well, I'm busy.'

'You live half an hour from her door.'

'I don't want her rubbing my face in it, Lisa.'

'Oh, for fuck's sake, that's not what she's doing.'

'Why don't you let me decide what's happening to me?'

'Fine,' Lisa said. She hung up.

It was one of two unpleasant conversations Caroline had that week. The second came when she received an unexpected visit from her mother-in-law, Jean.

'Dave's not here,' she said on opening her front door.

Jean barrelled past her. Caroline closed the door and followed her into the kitchen. Jean made herself at home, boiling the kettle as though she owned the place.

'So, you're just going to throw my son away for a pipe dream?' she asked, opening the fridge and grabbing some milk.

'Yeah,' Caroline said. 'I am.'

'That's cold.'

'I want to try again. Dave doesn't. I can't give up. It's what's known as an impasse.'

'I know what an impasse is, you cheeky cow! And I also know what reneging is. You agreed it was over.'

'And I was miserable.'

'Oh, for God's sake, look at your life.' She waved a hand around Caroline's beautiful home.

'It's a house, Jean.'

'And you're telling me that's it? Just because you don't have children, it's empty. What about my son?'

'I love him. I want him to be a part of this.'

'You selfish bitch! He was a part of it, again and again, and it nearly destroyed him. He made peace with it. He got on with it. He made the best of a bad lot . . .'

'Is that what I am?'

'I was referring to your situation, but if you want to act the bollocks about it . . .'

'I want . . .' Caroline said, and her voice was shaking.

'I want. I want. I want. We all want, Caroline, but we can't always have. Dave knows that. He's a grown-up.'

'What if he's wrong?' She heard the desperation clear in her own voice. 'What if we have a chance? What if we could have what you have? Can you even imagine what life would be like without your kids?'

Jean shook her head from side to side and she mellowed. 'Six IVFs and you didn't even come close. It's not going to be different this time, Caroline. You know it's going to be more pain and suffering and sadness.'

'I have to try.'

'And he will leave.'

'Will he?'

'I suppose we'll wait and see.'

Jean didn't stay to drink the cup of tea she'd made.

Dave didn't come home until well after eleven that night. Caroline heard the door closing to his bedroom and she knew that even though Jean was like a bull in a china shop, she had a point.

Having cut herself off from her real life, Caroline joined Janet and Ronnie on a stake-out. Janet was sitting in a rental car wearing a wig her mother had from the sixties, with a pair of her dad's binoculars around her neck. After three days of parking outside her husband's office, the findings so far had been inconclusive. Tina Rossi's reception area was glass-fronted, so it was easy to watch her, but all that Janet had observed was that Tina didn't really leave the desk unless it was lunchtime. And then she either went to a sandwich shop two streets down or she brought sandwiches with her and ate them in the canteen. Janet couldn't see the canteen from her car. Her husband had so far not been in reception at lunchtime, though she had seen him stop to talk to her as he entered and exited the building. She told them she had witnessed some mild flirting between Jim and Tina. She flicked her hair and laughed at everything he said, but that was all.

So today Janet was parked outside Tina's house. She'd followed her home yesterday.

Ronnie was drinking from one of the takeaway coffees she'd bought. Caroline took one, but Janet refused.

'I'm off it while I'm trying to get pregnant,' she said.

The irony that she was in a rental car wearing a wig while surveilling her husband did not go unnoticed.

Natalie parked behind them and got into the car. She'd brought coffees too, but everyone already had one. She handed a tea to Janet, then dumped the other two coffees out of the window, having remembered that Janet was only drinking tea.

'Oh, so sweet,' Janet said, taking it from her. 'Thanks for remembering.'

'What are we doing?' Natalie said.

'Watching to see if Tina goes out tonight.'

'You know, to meet anyone,' Ronnie said. 'Primarily Janet's husband.'

Caroline sipped her coffee. 'It was my idea. The day surveillance was going nowhere, and they're hardly going to go at it in a glass-fronted reception area.'

'And why not just follow Jim?' Natalie asked.

'Because Jim is in and out of houses all over Dublin with work,' Janet said. 'I'd never keep up.'

It was just after 8 p.m. when the door opened and Tina walked out of her house. Janet nearly dropped her tea.

'It's her! It's her!'

'Get after her,' Ronnie said, and Natalie and Caroline strapped into the back seat.

'We didn't think this through,' Janet said, crawling along as Tina continued to walk. 'She'll see us.'

Ronnie shrugged. 'She's on her phone; she'll see nothing.'

Caroline was beginning to feel a little uncomfortable. 'Are we just going to kerb-crawl her?'

Tina stopped at a bus stop and Janet parked across the street. They waited.

'So now what?' Caroline said. 'We're going to follow the bus?'

'It'll be fine,' Natalie said.

The bus arrived. Tina got on and Janet followed the bus.

A few moments later, her phone rang. She answered on speaker.

'Jim?'

'Hi, babe. Listen, I'm going to grab a drink with a few of the lads from work.'

Natalie hit the back of Janet's chair. Caroline held her breath.

'OK, good. Have a lovely time.'

'Where are you?'

'Nowhere.'

'Wha'?'

'I'm home. I'm home.'

'You sound like you're in the car.'

'Nope, in the bath.'

'OK. Enjoy your bath.'

'Will do. Enjoy . . . the lads.'

He hung up. Janet started to cry.

'It doesn't mean anything,' Caroline said.

They watched Tina disembark from the bus and followed her towards Jim's favourite pub. Janet was shaking.

'She's right, it doesn't mean anything.' Natalie didn't sound so sure.

Janet parked across the street. She pulled off her stupid wig and wiped her nose with it, then sat in the car and wept.

'I'm pregnant,' she said at last.

'*What?*' Caroline said. 'You've only been trying for a few weeks!'

'Turns out I was pregnant when I was trying to get pregnant. I just didn't know it.'

'How?' Caroline asked.

'Never mind how, we know how,' said Ronnie. 'How long?'

'The doctor thinks twelve weeks!' Janet burst into tears. 'I just found out today and I couldn't really get my head around it. I think I just needed to say it out loud for it to be real.'

'Jesus, Janet!' Caroline said. 'That's really good news.'

'Is it? I'm on meds for depression. I need injections to keep the baby and I didn't know I was pregnant. I'll start them tomorrow, but what if it's too late?'

'But the baby is fine,' Natalie said.

'Yeah, but for how long?' Janet said. 'And this stress. I mean, what the hell am I doing here?'

'I'm really excited for you,' Ronnie said.

'Yeah, go Janet,' Natalie said.

Janet allowed herself a slight smile before wiping her eyes and refocusing on the door of the pub.

'Do you want answers?' Ronnie asked.

'Yeah.'

'Stay here,' Ronnie said. 'Caroline, let's go inside.'

Natalie nodded. 'I'll stay with Janet.'

'What does Jim look like?' Ronnie asked.

Janet showed them a photo of him, one of hundreds on her phone.

Caroline followed Ronnie into the pub. Ronnie ordered two G & Ts at the bar.

'Ah no,' Caroline said.

'Do you like G & Ts?'

'Yeah.'

'Well then, neither of us is pregnant. Let's drink.'

Ronnie made a good point.

The pub was dark, the light coming mostly from lamps and candles. It was pleasant and warm with a fire lit in the corner. There was a match featuring on the flat screen, but the sound was turned down. A man in his sixties was playing the guitar and singing old Irish songs, accompanied by a girl on the fiddle.

Caroline watched Tina. She was talking to a few men, but none of them were Jim. *A good sign.*

And then Jim stepped through the door and Caroline recognised him instantly. He joined the group. *Shit.*

'Maybe it's a work night out?' Ronnie said.

'But why didn't he mention the receptionist was going?'

'Maybe he doesn't care if she's here or not,' Ronnie said. 'Maybe it's OK.'

Caroline realised Ronnie was willing it to be OK. It wasn't such a jaunt now that Janet was pregnant and crying in the car.

Jim was still wearing his overalls. He pulled them off his shoulders and knotted them at his waist, revealing a tight T-shirt. There was a dartboard near where the group stood and after a few minutes of chatter, they started a game. Ronnie and Caroline sipped on their drinks, watching. Jim was mostly talking to the lads, laughing and joking, but then he sat beside Tina.

They started talking, heads close together. When he wasn't throwing darts, he was back sitting beside her. And despite the match on the TV, the work lads playing darts and the music playing, they seemed lost in their own little world. At one point, she touched his hand and he squeezed hers.

Caroline had seen enough. She drained her glass. 'Let's go.'

Ronnie followed suit and led Caroline through the pub.

'What will we say?' Ronnie asked.

'Exactly what we saw.'

'I saw a man cheating on his wife.'

'It's not like they were having sex,' Caroline said as they reached the pub door and burst out into the cold night air.

Ronnie sighed. 'There are lots of ways to cheat that don't involve sex.'

Stick With Me, Kid

Catherine

IWALKED OFF THE BOAT with a ten-pound sterling note in my pocket, meant for a train fare to Manchester, and little spare change. I kept going until I found a bank, then I went up to the counter and asked the girl standing behind it to change the money for me. She smiled at me and said, 'Certainly,' and I hadn't expected that. I thought she'd make a fuss and call the manager, and maybe somehow a nun would appear and take me away.

'Thank you,' I said, a little too gratefully.

She handed me fifteen Irish pounds and ten pence. It was the most money I'd ever had in my pocket.

I knew there was only one place I needed to go, and that was home. I had to see my family. I had to tell them what was done to me. I knew that my mother had thought it best that I leave that place without a baby, but now that they'd paid to release me, maybe if I told her about Daisy and when we were in each other's arms, she'd change her mind. Stealing was wrong. She'd told me that all of my life. Surely she'd help me right that terrible wrong.

I knew it was a long shot, but I had to try. Besides, I had nowhere else to go.

I took a bus from the port to town and then I asked people for directions, following signposts that led me to the bus station. The fare was four pounds return.

The girl at the ticket counter said, 'Ya might as well, love. It's three pounds fifty single.'

Because I didn't really know if I'd stay at home or not, I took the girl's advice and covered my bases.

I walked down the length of the bus and even though there were some double empty seats, I sat down beside an elderly woman. I was scared that if I picked two empty seats, a nun would come from nowhere and sit next to me the whole way to Cork.

The old woman sighed and grumbled under her breath. 'The bus is half empty.'

'Sorry, I'm just a bit scared on my own.'

'Scared? A big girl like you, what's there to be scared of?'

'Nuns,' I said.

She looked at me and then she looked around furtively to make sure there were no nuns on board.

'Fair enough. Stick with me, kid. I'll see ya right.'

'Thanks.'

After that, we talked about her kids, who all lived abroad, and her dead husband, who was a prick, God rest him. It was my first time hearing the word 'prick', and I liked it.

'Prick,' I repeated, and it felt good to say.

'He was, but sure, aren't most men? Except for me da. He was a walking saint.'

'I know a lot of pricks, but they're mostly women,' I said.

She looked at my putrid green maternity dress. 'You're out now.'

My eyes filled with tears. I didn't need to say anything else.

'Never look back, do ya hear me? Never.'

'They took my baby,' I said to the stranger.

'Love, ya have to let it go.'

'I can't.'

'Then it won't just haunt ya for the rest of your days, it will ruin you.'

After that, she fed me toffees and half of her egg and cress sandwich. We talked about her trip to Clonakilty to visit her best friend.

'I heard Clonakilty is lovely,' I said.

She smiled. 'Nowhere outside Dublin is lovely. People just say that to be nice.'

'I used to love where I lived,' I said.

'Maybe you will again.'

'Dunno, it seems so small and . . .'

'. . . Parochial.'

'What does that mean?'

'Small-minded,' she said.

'Yeah, small-minded.'

'You'll find your way.'

After that, I fell asleep on her shoulder and slept the rest of the way. When we parted, I hugged her. She hugged me back and kissed me on my forehead.

'You mind yourself,' she said, and then she was gone, mixed in with the crowd.

She had been genuinely kind, and no one had been kind to me for a long time. I didn't even know her name.

Another short trip later, I stepped off a bus on the main street of my small town. It was after 8 p.m. on a cold and wet night. I was about to walk towards the farm, when I heard a familiar voice.

'Catherine?'

I kept walking.

'Catherine? Is that you?'

Oh, that is *me!* I'm *Catherine.* I turned round and stared.

'Rose?'

185

'Jesus Christ! We thought you'd up and died.'

She ran over to me, hugging me tightly. 'Where've you been?'

I shrugged.

'They said you went to England to mind your sick aunt.'

'That's right.'

'I didn't know you had an aunt over there.'

Me neither.

'And is she all right now?'

'She's grand, thanks.'

'What about school? You've missed half of Leaving Cert year.'

'Don't know, really.'

'Right . . .'

We stood looking at one another. I could tell she didn't believe me, but she was polite enough not to say.

'I was hoping you'd write,' she said.

I bit my lip. I didn't want to cry. 'Sorry.'

It was all a bit awkward. I knew I looked mad in my mother's old worn-out maternity dress and I was clearly biting back tears. I didn't know what to say, but I knew that I had missed her.

'Do you want to come to mine and we can catch up?'

I did, but things were different now. 'I should go home.'

'Are they expecting you?'

'No.'

'So come to mine. My mam and dad are staying at Auntie Bridie's on account of Uncle Dick being an awful man . . . It's a long story. Anyway, I'm on my own.'

I managed to smile. 'OK.'

Rose lived in town and her house was small but it was pretty, and it always smelled of flowers. I followed her into the kitchen.

'You hungry?'

'I had half an egg sandwich and some toffees on the bus.'

'So you're starving?'

'I wouldn't say starving.'

'Would you eat some chocolate cake?' She opened the fridge and took it out. 'I know it's your favourite.'

'Oh God, I love chocolate cake.'

'Well then, today is your lucky day. Mam made it for Auntie Bridie and forgot to take it.' She handed me a spoon. 'Dig in.'

We sat at her kitchen table tucking into chocolate cake, listening to the songs playing on the radio. It had been so long since I'd heard music. I hadn't realised how much I missed it. Rose filled me in on all the local gossip, but there wasn't much in all the time since I'd left. She told me she'd decided to be an air hostess when the final exams were done.

'You could be one, too. I'm not even sure you need a Leaving Cert for it, if you're pretty enough, and you are.'

I said I'd think about it, but I knew it would be impractical when I got Daisy back. I couldn't imagine they'd let me do a safety demo with a baby on my back.

When we were full of cake and both lying on the sofa foot to head, she grabbed at my hand and held it.

'Are we going to talk about what you're wearing?'

'No,' I said.

'OK.'

We were both silent for a while.

'But you're all right now?'

'I am,' I said, and I wiped away a stray tear.

'I'll find some of my clothes later. You can have them.'

'No. It's fine.'

'You're not walking through this town first thing tomorrow morning in that,' she said, and that was the end of the discussion.

We lay there together listening to 'Bohemian Rhapsody' on Rose's record player.

'Do you like it?'

'It's the best thing I ever heard,' I said, and suddenly I was crying.

Then we listened to it ten more times and finished off the entire chocolate cake.

'You should know,' Rose said. 'He's seeing someone. A posh girl from Dublin.'

I knew at once she was talking about Justin.

'Her name is Jennifer. I saw her at Mass with him. She stays in the house.'

Jen from Auntie Martha's doorway. Of course.

'Good for him.' I found it hard to conceal my bitterness.

'You're better off without him. He was never good enough for you.'

I squeezed her hand. 'You're a good friend, Rose.'

'Good friend? I'm your best friend.'

I nodded. I thought about Marian and poor Maria and all the other girls I'd met behind those terrible grey walls. I wondered where they were now and hoped they were with people as lovely as Rose.

I slept with her in her bed that night and when I woke up, it was to the sound of her singing to the radio and I could smell bacon frying. I dressed in the clothes she'd left me – a pair of flared jeans and a plain white T-shirt a little too big. She'd even left a bra out for me, which was a little tight, but it was the first time I'd worn a bra since I left home. In Rose's clothes, I felt a little more like me.

She fed me a big Irish fry, telling me that she was jealous I was so skinny. The weight had fallen off me after Daisy was born. Between breastfeeding, too little food and too much work, I had become one of those skinny, miserable girls who lined up against the wall. I hadn't even noticed.

'You're so pretty,' she said.

I didn't feel pretty; I felt old and broken.

She said goodbye to me at the door when I left to see my parents.

'It was great seeing you, Catherine. Don't be a stranger, OK?'

'I won't.'

'And, Catherine?'

'Yeah?'

'I'm really sorry about your dad.'

'What about him?' I said.

Her face fell. 'Oh, Jesus. Nothing. I'm sure he'll be grand.'

I don't know if she said anything after that. I was halfway down the road by the time the word grand flew out of her mouth.

Chapter Fourteen

Natalie

NATALIE CLIMBED INTO THE CAR and scooched over in the seat to let Caroline in. Janet was waiting anxiously for the debrief.

'We saw him go in,' Janet said. She was as white as a ghost.

'He was there all right, but so are the other lads from work,' Caroline said. 'They're playing darts.'

'And?' Janet said, and her lip trembled.

'And he was talking intimately with Tina,' Ronnie said.

'Intimately?'

'On their own, face to face, he touched her hand.'

Natalie felt her stomach turn. *Anxiety or pregnancy?* It was hard to tell. She had one more day to go before she took the test. It was unbearable.

Worse still, Linda's behaviour was becoming more and more weird. She was working on a very difficult case involving a refugee family who were seeking asylum and it was not going well. Whenever Natalie asked Linda about the case, all she got in response was 'It's complicated.' Linda's moods were often affected by cases, but there was something else going on with her and Natalie knew it. *It's not the baby. Is it?*

A week earlier, Paul had come over unannounced one night when Natalie was home alone. Her car was in the driveway and the lights were on, so she couldn't pretend she wasn't there. She couldn't hide. *Fuck!* She had opened the door and smiled.

'Hello, Paul.'

'Hello, Natalie.' He walked inside, heading into the sitting room and plonking himself down on the sofa. 'What's cooking?' he said, looking at her stomach.

She wanted to take a golf club to him.

'Waiting on the test.'

'Well, fingers crossed,' he said, and she wasn't sure which way he wanted it to go.

'Linda's not here.'

'I know.'

'So why are you here?'

'Thought we should spend more time together.'

The hairs on the back of her neck electrified. *Why? WHY?* 'I don't follow you.'

'We could be parents of a child.'

'Linda and I will be the parents.'

'Yes, but so will I.'

'But not really.'

'But yeah really.'

'But we agreed.'

'And that agreement stands. Still, biologically I will be the father of your child.'

'Who have you been talking to?'

'Does it matter?'

'Oh my God, it's your stupid banker stoner friend.'

He grimaced. 'He's not stupid.'

'The baby is mine and Linda's. You are the uncle. Tell your banker friend to re-read the contract. The End.'

'But is it Linda's?'

Natalie felt sick. 'Yes.'

'Is it?'

'Get out,' Natalie said. 'Get out before I end up doing time for you.'

He had obviously believed her, because he left quickly. She sat and thought about what he'd said. *It is Linda's. It is.*

And yet Linda was avoiding her, working late nights and barely speaking when she got in.

Natalie told herself she was being paranoid, about Linda, about Paul. She was nearly as bad as Janet. *I'm just a wig and a rental car away from madness.*

Janet wanted to go home.

'Shouldn't we wait to see what happens next?' Caroline suggested, but Janet didn't want to see.

She was done stalking. She needed to think about things.

Natalie was glad. She just wanted to go home, too.

Ronnie hugged Janet and the hug seemed to catch her by surprise, but she was grateful.

'You've all been so good to me,' Janet said. 'Thank you.'

As Natalie left to get her car, Ronnie remembered to wish her luck for her pregnancy test in the consultant's office the next day. Caroline and Janet chimed in with best wishes.

One in three. That was what Ronnie said. Janet was already pregnant. Clearly she was the one, but maybe ... *And then what? Will Linda have time for me then?*

Natalie's consultant had warned them at the very start of the process that home pregnancy tests were not to be trusted.

'You do not do it. You come into the office and we will take a blood test to check your HCG levels. That is how we know. Understand?'

Natalie did understand, and it had seemed easy to follow her consultant's advice when she was at the beginning of the process, but the last two weeks had been hell. She bought three tests. She toyed with peeing on a stick every minute of the day. Whenever Linda was home, she was disinterested.

'They said wait. So wait.'

Natalie had refrained, not just because she had unusually strong willpower, but also because Linda's distance was worrying her. She spent much of her time trying to quieten or deny her concerns, but they were ever-present, gnawing at her.

When the morning of the blood test arrived, Linda was due in court.

'You can text me,' she said, flying out of the door.

Natalie felt sick. She knew that Linda's job was important and lives were on the line and it was just a blood test, but it was also huge and possibly life-changing.

She didn't make a fuss. The nurse would take the blood and then she'd get the call a few hours later. It was fine. She didn't need her hand held.

'Good luck,' she said.

'Thanks,' Linda called, and she was in her car and driving down the road before Natalie slammed the door shut.

She schlepped into the phlebotomist's office. It was a young man in his mid-twenties, with thick brown hair parted to the side and big blue eyes peeping out through frameless glasses. He seemed delicate, nice.

'You must be so excited,' he said, and he seemed genuinely happy for her. 'There is nothing more incredible than life.'

'I know.'

'I shouldn't say it, but I have a good feeling about you.'

'Do you?'

'I really do.'

'Why?'

'You're glowing.'

'I ran here,' Natalie admitted. 'Had to park the car five miles away!'

He smiled. 'Ah! It could be that, then.'

'I'm scared.'

'Don't be. What will be will be.'

When he touched her lightly on her shoulder, it reminded her how long it had been since Linda had touched her.

Natalie left the office and walked through Dublin city, taking a shortcut through Trinity College, surrounding herself with young students. She tried to distract herself. She watched them talking animatedly, smoking, drinking coffees, laughing and shouting out greetings as others passed. She felt like an alien.

She exited the archway and headed towards Dawson Street, stopping for tea and a cupcake in the coffee shop next door to Viva Hair. Afterwards, with time to kill and still waiting on the call, she went into the salon. The owner, a handsome grey-haired man named Tony, gave her a blow-dry. When she mentioned she was gay, they chit-chatted about the scene.

'A lot's changed,' he said.

'For the better.'

'A lot done. More to do.' He sighed. 'It's 2010 and I want more than just mere tolerance. I'm hanging in there for marriage.'

'My girlfriend and I might be having a baby,' she said.

'Good for you.'

'I'm waiting on the pregnancy test results.'

'Whoa,' he said.

The phone rang a few minutes later.

'Oh, fuck. It's them.'

Tony blanched a little. 'I'll give you your space,' he said and he slunk away.

She picked up the phone.

'Hello, Natalie, it's . . .'

'I know who it is.'

'I'm sorry, but I'm afraid it's negative this time.'

Her heart seemed to cave a little. She needed to catch her breath. Her ears were suddenly red-hot and her neck flushed.

'No?'

'I'm sorry,' the nurse said.

'Are you sure?' she asked. *Stupid question, Natalie. Stupid fucking question.*

'I am, but this is by no means over. I'm sure Monica made you aware that the chances of getting pregnant this time were low, but because of your age and health, it was the best way to go. But we can move on. I can make an appointment for you for a date when Monica returns and she can go through the next steps.'

'What are they?'

'I can't say for sure, but they will probably include a stimulated cycle, which would involve Clomid fertility drugs.'

'Is that it?'

'You'll have a trigger injection of HCG and then we'll bring you into hospital to inseminate within thirty-six hours.'

'I hate needles.'

'Me too.'

Natalie breathed out. 'And it's definitely negative?'

'Absolutely 100 per cent. I am sorry. So, should I make that appointment for you?'

'Yes. Thanks.'

Natalie's hair wasn't finished, but she wanted to leave.

'I totally understand,' Tony said.

'How much do I owe you?' she asked.

'For that mess' – he waved a hand at her hair and winked – 'nothing.'

'I'm sorry,' she said, and she wasn't sure if she was talking to Tony or to herself.

'Don't be. Life has a way of kicking you in the arse, but . . .'

'But?'

He shrugged. 'But we endure.'

And suddenly he seemed even sadder than she did.

She left Viva Hair with half a blow-dry and a feeling of great despair.

I Wish Things Were Different

Catherine

IDIDN'T TAKE IN THE TOWN as I ran through it. I stopped to take my first breath when I reached the gates of the farm, needing to get some air into my lungs and take a moment to steel myself for what was to come. Then I walked down the long, winding path that separated the fields my father spent his life wandering, past the pig sheds and into the yard. I knocked on the brown mud-splattered, splintered door, even though I knew it was always left unlatched. I stood waiting.

My mother opened it and stared. The look on her face was like she'd seen a ghost.

'What are you doing here?' she asked urgently, looking around to see if there were any witnesses.

I didn't understand. I couldn't take it in.

'You shouldn't be here,' she hissed.

She pulled me inside and slammed the door.

I stood on the creaking old floorboards, ruined by years of trampling and treading, rainwater, mud, kids, dogs and even a few pigs. The colour on the hall wall was a musty yellow. I hadn't noticed how godawful it was when I lived here; it made the place darker than it should have been.

'This is my home,' I said, looking towards the old green carpet that covered the rickety staircase.

'Not anymore, Catherine. You can't stay here.'

'So I make one mistake and I'm out?'

She'd paid to release me. That must mean something, surely?

'It's not that simple.'

'Well then, explain it to me.'

I wasn't used to being so forceful with my mother; even though I had changed a lot, it still somehow felt wrong.

'I can't. You have to leave this town and never come back.'

My knees buckled. 'I'm being banished?'

My mother was upset. She wasn't crying, but she faced the wall and placed her hand gently on it to steady herself. I was familiar with the trick by now.

'Things have changed here. You're better off going.'

'What's wrong with Daddy?' I asked.

I heard her gulp. 'He's not well, Catherine. He's not able for farm work anymore.'

'And the boys?'

'Mickey left last summer after Daddy got sick. I suppose he was afraid he'd be stuck with the farm. He's in London working on the buildings. He sends home a few pounds every now and then. Ronan is doing his best. Tim tries to help, but he's still only a small thing.'

'I could help,' I said. 'I'm better than the boys with the pigs. I always was.'

She leaned a little heavier on the wall. 'You can't stay here.'

'Why?' I shouted.

As she turned to face me, she almost collapsed back and leaned her full body weight on the hallway wall. She didn't answer; instead, her eyes were drawn to a large black-and-white photo on the wall opposite, of my father in his youth, surrounded by other young men from the town, all sitting on a trailer, caps on, smoking, mouths wide open, glee in their eyes. It was taken when he was about eighteen, two years after his parents had died in a car crash, not long before he met my mother. It was the only photo that was on any wall in the house. My parents' wedding photographs were in a book in a box under the coffee table. We children were featured in a few albums, with more gaps for photos than actual photos, hidden away on the top shelf of my parents' wardrobe. That was the photo that made it to the wall: my father, when he was young, free, handsome and single. No woman or children to hold him down.

'Mammy? Why can't I come home?' I said.

My mother slid down the wall and sat on the dirty floor with her legs stretched out in front of her before looking me right in the eye. She spoke so softly it was hard to hear her.

'Because the judge provides us with a monthly income and in return, you can never come home.'

Breathing felt almost impossible. I couldn't believe it. My thoughts unravelled. *Daddy's sick. They need money. The judge is paying them.*

I have to disappear forever.

'I have no choice,' she said.

But she did have a choice. It wasn't an easy one, but it was a choice. My choice had been ignored. My child had been stolen. I would never have abandoned Daisy for any reason, anything or anyone. Not like my mother was abandoning me.

'Why?' I asked quietly.

'Because we'll be destitute without it.'

'Not you. The judge! Why?'

'He doesn't want trouble for his son.' She broke eye contact, because she knew I hadn't lied to her; she knew that Justin O'Halloran was the father of my baby. Worse than that, she didn't care.

199

The next thing I remember is sitting at the kitchen table and my mother pouring tea. Her hands were shaking.

'Am I ever going to see you again?' I asked.

'I'll come and see you when you're settled.'

'And Daddy?'

'He can't travel.'

'And the boys?'

'They are so busy on the farm.'

'I feel just like Charles,' I said, and she rubbed her face with her hands. 'It won't be once a month, though – maybe once a year if I'm lucky.'

'Life is complicated, Catherine,' she said.

She looked as old and decrepit as the house that was no longer my home.

'Oh, I know,' I said. 'Trust me, I fucking know.'

'Your mouth!'

She sounded alarmed, as though a simple word was more shocking than anything else that had happened today.

'Yeah, the nuns are whores for the language.'

I said it to hurt her and it was a shock when she laughed. I laughed too, and then we were both crying.

'I'm sorry,' she said.

'Me too, Mammy.'

And angry and bitter, too, but what else could I say? We lived in a world that was unfair and full of pain and despair, and I wanted more for my little girl. My Daisy. So I stood up and I shook off my sorrow. I told myself that I would overcome it. My girl would never suffer as I had done.

I asked if I could pack some of my old clothes and she took me to my bedroom. We crept up the stairs, avoiding the creaky steps, because Daddy was sleeping and he needed his rest. The room was the same as I'd left it, but it seemed smaller now and colder. She sat on my bed while I took everything I owned out of my few drawers and small wardrobe. I had a teddy that I used to sleep with and I packed him, too.

'You're even taller.'

I picked up some photographs on my bedside table of the family, Rose and other friends. I took them, too.

'And prettier, if that's possible,' she said.

I grabbed my shoes, bras, knickers, tops, jeans, skirts and two dresses.

'You're going to be fine, Catherine. You have my mother's strength in you.'

I reached into the top of my wardrobe and pulled out a little bottle of perfume my mammy bought me for my sixteenth birthday. I shook it and sprayed myself. I left behind schoolbooks and the dress my mother made that I wore to the dance. It hung alone in the wardrobe. She said nothing about that. She just sat on the bed, smoothing the blankets with her hand.

'Can I see Daddy?' I asked when I'd wrestled his old case closed.

'He can't be upset,' she said.

'I won't—'

'You will,' she said, and she sounded regretful. 'There's nothing you can do to change that now.'

She walked me to the front door and gave me a twenty-pound note from her pocket.

'I wish things were different,' she said as I took it.

'I had a baby girl, Mammy,' I said before she had time to close the door behind me. 'I called her Daisy.'

'I hope she finds happiness and I hope you do, too.'

It almost sounded like she meant it.

201

'Thanks for paying to get me out,' I said.

She looked at me quizzically, then shook her head, and I realised she hadn't, after all. I wondered what the hell was going on.

That was our goodbye, my mother's quizzical look and the shake of her head.

I walked back towards the road on the pathway that separated one field of pigs from another and halfway down, I heard my name.

'Catherine!'

I turned to see my brother Ronan. He was running towards me and my heart leaped. I leaped with it over the fence and into his arms. He was fifteen and as big as Mickey was the last time I saw him.

'I thought I'd never see you again,' he said.

He was warm and lovely. I hugged him and cried my eyes out because he was my brother and I would miss him.

'Just collecting a few things,' I said.

He immediately deflated. 'Oh, you're not home to stay then.'

Clearly, he wasn't aware of the judge's conditions.

'Can't,' I said, trying to smile. 'I have a big job lined up in Dublin. I'll be sending money home, Ronan, so if you don't want to stay here . . . If you don't want this life, come find me.'

'And what about Mammy and Daddy?'

'They'll be OK.'

He stared at me. 'You haven't seen him, have you?'

'She wouldn't let me.'

'I'm sorry, Catherine.'

'Me too, Ronan.'

Tears sprung into his eyes. 'You're going to be OK, aren't you?'

'I'll be fine,' I said. 'And you'll be fine. Tell Tim Catherine loves him and misses him, and I love and miss you, too.'

He hugged me tight and then I let him go. I didn't look back as I walked away from the farm. It was the last time I ever stepped foot in the place.

Chapter Fifteen

Janet

JANET HAD KNOWN SHE WAS pregnant even before she took the test. She'd made sure she took aspirin every morning as soon as she and Jim began trying for a baby and she couldn't believe it had happened so quickly. She didn't feel joy at first. She just kept thinking about how Jim might be having it off with his receptionist. *The fucking cliché.* She felt numb. All the joy and elation she'd felt when she'd got pregnant previously was replaced by anxiety and fear. *What if. What if.* The what ifs consumed her.

What if he wanted to leave her? Could she be a single mother like Caroline? She wasn't so sure. She had been so broken and it had felt like the pieces were only just slotting back together. What if she broke again? Worse, what if she lost the baby and Jim wasn't there to pick her off the floor? She wasn't as strong as Caroline. She wasn't prepared to lose her man. *But what if I've lost him already?*

She felt bad that she'd told her friends from the group before she told Jim. She felt bad about that, as though she had cheated on him somehow. Like he was cheating on her? Now the baby was real, now that she'd been to the doctor and everything, she had to make a decision.

Who do you want to be, Janet? What kind of marriage do you want to have? What kind of father for your child?

She was asleep when Jim came home after his night at the pub and he was gone when she woke the following morning. She decided her stalking days were over, handed back the rental car and threw her mum's old wig in the black wheelie bin. First things first, she needed to speak to Jim. She needed to find out what was going on with Tina Rossi and tell him she was pregnant. She wasn't looking forward to it. She wasn't looking forward to the heparin injections she'd need, either. They were so sore, like nasty bee stings. They used to make her cry. It took a lot more than that now.

She went to her GP and filled in a prescription for the drug, then she went home and injected herself in the bathroom. Then she vacuumed and cleaned the whole house, did a weekly shop and tried to kill the time.

Jim didn't arrive home until after eight. She'd cooked a spaghetti bolognaise and as soon as he'd showered, they sat down for dinner. Jim wolfed into it and Janet stared down at hers.

'This is a treat,' he said. 'You know I love your spag bol.'

'Jim?'

'Yeah?'

'What's going on with Tina Rossi?'

His mouth dropped open and some spaghetti fell out. 'Are you serious?' He seemed genuinely insulted.

'Just be honest. Is something going on?'

'Of course not. Jesus Christ, babe. What the fuck do you take me for?' He stopped eating. 'We're trying for a baby, for fuck's sake.' He stood up, moved over towards the bin and emptied the contents of his plate into it.

'I saw you.'

'Saw me what?'

'Talking to her.'

'She works for me!'

'She was in the pub.'

'You were watching me?'

'You were talking to her, holding her hand.'

'Jesus Christ, you were spying on me?'

'This isn't about what I did, it's about what you're doing.'

'I am working. I am building a business. I am doing my fucking best. What I am not doing is actively trying to blow up my marriage. Can you say the same?'

'I'm sorry,' she said, but he was out of the room and the hall door was slamming. 'And I'm pregnant.'

Even if he had been in the room, she spoke so quietly he would not have heard her.

Apples and Oranges

Catherine

I SAT ON THE BUS TO DUBLIN with the guts of thirty pounds in my pocket, a suitcase of my own clothes and a few mementos of my past. I didn't speak to anyone. The bus was only half full and I was way down the back on my own. I spent my time looking out of the window as I passed through small Irish towns that looked just as grey and desolate as my own.

I thought about Daisy and where she was and who was taking care of her. I talked to her in my head and I worried about what I would do next. How would I get her back, on my own, in a strange city with thirty pounds to my name? I needed to think about it and make a plan, but first I needed to find a place to stay.

I knew there were hostels by the bus station and if I stayed in one of them, I'd live a lot longer without a job than if I paid for a B & B. Besides, I was used to sleeping in dorms with strangers.

The cheapest place I found beat the institution by a long mile. People were friendly. The men were separated from the women. There were six to a room, but because it was winter, I rarely shared with more than three girls at any time and usually had a bunk bed to myself. I was careful with my money. I knew I needed to make it last.

I ate a piece of fruit for breakfast and drank soup for lunch in a small café nearby that gave soup to the homeless. I served soup for at least an hour every day to pay my way. Sometimes I lived on just that; I'd gotten used to the feeling of an empty stomach. Other days I'd cave and buy a bag of chips for my dinner.

Every day I'd walk the streets, in and out of every shop, asking for a job. I always got the same question: Do you have any retail experience? I'd tell them no but that I was a fast learner, and the door would close in my face.

I was there ten days and had walked every street in Dublin, when I turned a corner from Camden Street and I found myself on South Circular Road. I recognised it immediately – those red brick, two-storey over-basement houses. I put my hands to my stomach without thinking.

I thought about knocking on Justin's door – but then what? There was nothing to say. He'd done the worst thing he could have done. He had no conscience. He was father to a stolen child and he was glad. My parents needed his family's money and he didn't care.

So I stared at that stupid red door for a minute or two, and I was just about to walk away, when it opened. I ducked, but then I heard my name.

'Catherine?'

It was Auntie Martha. I stood up and she walked down the steps of her home.

I ran.

I ran all the way back down through Camden Street and then turned right and headed for Stephen's Green. I didn't stop until I found a bench by the duck pond, where I inhaled and exhaled to try to soothe my burning lungs.

I watched a mother and her toddler feed the ducks. He was determined but shaky on his feet. It made me anxious that he was so close to the water and then he leaned in. I jumped up and grabbed him – but he wasn't about to fall, after all, so I looked like a loonie or a kidnapper.

'Help!' the mother shouted, and I immediately let go.

'Oh God, I'm so sorry,' I said. 'I thought he was going to fall.'

She pulled him away from me and hugged him tight. 'You don't just grab other people's children,' she said.

'I know!' I said.

Then I was off and running again. I stopped halfway down Dawson Street with a pain in my side that matched the one in my heart.

You don't just grab other people's children! Really, tell that to the fucking nuns. Tell that to my parents, Auntie Fuckin' Martha and that prick of a judge. Tell it to Justin O'Halloran, the barefaced liar.

I was trying to think of other nasty things to say about him, because he was way more than a liar, he was the worst person in the world, but my thoughts were interrupted by the sight of a tall, handsome man in his late twenties with a moustache and long straight hair to his shoulders. He was standing just inside a funky hairdressers' window a little way away from me. I stopped, arrested by the sight of him and his shop.

Ireland was a grey and beige place in the seventies, but Viva Hair stood out, blasting colour, with its purple shop front and orange door, a lava lamp swirling in the window. Inside where he stood, the walls were pink and filled with framed posters of the bands of the day. He was smoking a cigarette. I couldn't take my eyes off the place. It was so colourful, bright and warm, and he was beautiful and enigmatic, and he smiled at me.

He walked outside. I stood rooted to the spot as he took my hair in his hand.

'Now that is hair I can work with,' he said. 'Such great texture. That's unusual in redheads; they can sometimes be a bit wiry.'

'Thanks,' I said, not really sure how much of a compliment that was.

'I'm looking for a model for a hair show. Are you interested?'

I stared at him in surprise. 'What would I have to do?'

'Just sit there while I do all the work.'

I looked around. In the shop window there was an advertisement for a receptionist.

'Gimme that job and you can do whatever you want to my hair.'

He laughed. 'How old are you?'

'Seventeen.'

'Shouldn't you be in school?'

'Maybe, but I'm not. I need a job and before you ask, I have no experience . . .'

He smiled.

'But I'm a fast learner.'

'Have you ever used a till?'

'Give me one day's trial,' I said.

'And you'll let me do whatever I want with your hair?'

'You can shave it off for all I care.'

He grinned and offered me his hand. 'My name is Tony.'

'I'm Catherine.'

We shook hands.

He stubbed out his cigarette and lit a fresh one, then opened the door to Viva Hair Studio, the grooviest hairdresser's in Dublin. I followed him inside.

The trial went brilliantly and Tony gave me the job before the day was out. My time with the nuns meant I wasn't lying when I said that I was a very fast learner. He took me into the tea room to discuss the terms of my employment and my salary. It wasn't much, but it was more money than I'd ever dreamed of. I started the next day.

At the end of the week when the shop was closed, he ordered in fish and chips for us both and started working on an up-style for his hair show.

'I'm thinking of doing something around a bird's nest.'

'Sounds shite,' I said, and he laughed at a culchie like me attempting Dublin slang.

'It's avant-garde.'

I didn't ask what that meant, because I'd a face full of chips, but he spelled it out anyway.

'Experimental, you know . . . ?' And suddenly he was imitating some leering old dear with his hand on his hip and a cigarette hanging out of his lip. 'See her, the young one with the bird's nest on her head . . .'

It made me laugh.

'Well, obviously, that suggests the young one's hair's a mess, but my bird's nest is going to be spectacular. We'll be the talk of the town.'

I didn't care either way. I'd only known him five days and I would have done anything he asked of me.

Working the reception in a hairdressing salon was more about people than taking appointments and ringing up the money. Of course that was important, too, but I was the first face all of the customers saw. I would meet and greet them. I tried to make sure I knew all the regulars' names, treating them like old friends, bringing them magazines and asking after the family. When I wasn't making small talk, I was making sure all of the girls had the right hair dye.

Viva Hair was one of the first salons ever in Dublin to serve tea to their customers. There wasn't a lot of coffee in Ireland in the seventies; it was tea and a few chocolate bourbons, and the ladies loved it. I made the teas and I was sent to buy the bourbons in bulk from a woman on a Thomas Street stall once a week.

When someone was off sick or the plumbing failed or anything at all out of the ordinary happened, I'd be the one moving schedules and calling plumbers. And if no one was around, I'd be taping leaks myself. I did it all except the hair and I loved it.

I worked all day, and two evenings a week, Tony and the team would practise their styles for his show. I was only one of three girls Viva Hair was presenting. Along with Tony's bird's nest, showstopper Amy – a hippy-looking girl from Galway with a tattoo of an exotic bird on her arm – was doing a dramatic cut on a girl with hair down to her waist. And Poor John (that's what his parents called him) – a Kerry guy with a lisp – was tasked with the wedding look, which was basically a plaited bun. They were all in their twenties. I was the youngest, but they never made me feel less than them.

There was something different about Tony. Not just the fact that he really took care of himself or he always looked good and smelled good. Not just that he could talk freely with the ladies about all sorts of things that mattered to them, unlike any man I'd ever known. No, I think the stark difference between Tony and other men was his empathy and kindness. He saw people's pain, no matter how hard they tried to hide it, and without ever asking why, he went about finding a way to heal it. I thought he was wonderful.

On the day of the hair show, I walked in on Tony and Poor John kissing the face off one another in the toilet down the back of the shop.

I got such a fright, I walked into the towel rack and ended up with a black eye. Tony was beside himself. He asked Amy to run to the butcher for a steak to slap on it and she was pissed off because she had her own prep to do, so he took off at high speed. Poor John was mortified.

'We've only been seeing each other for a few weeks.'

I was trying to take it all in. Poor John and Tony. Two men *kissing*! The concept seemed completely alien.

'Jesus, Poor John,' I said, 'are you sure you should be doing that?'

'I know, I shouldn't mix work and pleasure—'

'I mean, kissing men.'

He stared at me. 'Not you?'

'What do you mean?'

'You think it's wrong?'

'I don't think anything. I never knew it was a thing to think about at all.'

He could see I was shocked. 'Didn't your local priest teach you how wrong people like me and Tony are?'

'If he did, I wasn't listening – and anyway, what the fuck does he know about right and wrong?'

He smiled. 'Exactly.'

Tony arrived back with the steak and slapped it on my eye.

'This is a disaster,' he said.

I was sitting in the chair in front of the mirror and my eye was slightly swollen but already purple.

'I could do a dramatic eye,' Poor John said. He'd been messing around with make-up for a while.

'Christ. Right, do it. We have no choice.'

I was still a little shocked and suffering from a slight head injury, but we all packed up to go to the show anyway. It was in the large venue halfway across town. By the time we got there, I looked like I'd been in a fight. Backstage was buzzing and I didn't realise there would be a stage and a room full of people.

'All industry,' Tony said. 'This could be big for Viva. I don't want it to be just another salon. I want to be the best salon in town.'

Poor John was onstage first for the wedding category and his model, Tina, received a very enthusiastic response to his demo. Tony was pretty happy. Amy was unusually supportive.

'It's a fucking plait, but it's a nice fucking plait,' she said.

Poor John gave me his version of a smoky eye.

He turned the chair round so Tony could see me. 'Ta-da.'

'She looks like a panda.'

'She does, doesn't she?' Poor John said, not taking any offence.

Tony bought me a black slinky dress that he described as gothic. The nest was fake gold and he had fake blue-and-yellow speckled duck eggs interspersed with gold and silver ones stuck into it. In reality, they were painted hard-boiled eggs.

'What about an eye patch?' I said.

Tony looked at me. 'Seriously?'

'We could paint it blue speckled like one of the eggs – wouldn't that be avant-garde?'

Poor John and Tony looked at one another.

'I like it,' Poor John said, and Tony was already running over to Amy.

'Amy, get your coat on. I need duck-egg blue paint, some string and a cardboard . . . stat.'

'Do I look like the fucking Women's Institute?' she asked.

But Tony didn't care – he was shoving money in her pocket and telling her not to waste any time.

A few minutes later, she arrived back with the necessaries. The patch was made and I was brought out onstage by Tony, in my black gothic dress and bare feet, because with all the kissing and carry-on, Tony had forgotten his mother's lace-ups that he swore completed the look. My black eye was covered by a duck-egg blue cardboard eye patch.

My hair was down around my shoulders when the demonstration started and as Tony got to work, the judges whispered comments to one another and wrote things down.

Half an hour later, I was standing centre stage with my red hair tangled and entwined in a gold nest full of eggs. The crowd were on their feet. *People are insane.*

It was a triumph. A photographer took a photograph, and me and my bird's nest made the front cover of the hairdressing magazine and page 8 of the *Irish Press*. I felt more like a curiosity than a model, but people were telling me how beautiful and exotic I was, smiling and beaming at me. I was taken into strangers' open arms.

I didn't feel anything really, except glad that I hadn't let my friend down. I kept thinking about Daisy. *Where is she? Who is caring for her? Do they love her? Are they gentle? Are they kind? Does she miss me like I miss her?* I hoped not. I hoped that she didn't miss me at all; the pain was too hard to bear and I'd rather bear it alone. *I love you, Daisy. I will find you. I will get you back.*

Tony took us all out for a drink to celebrate and after a half a shandy, I just wanted my bed. Because it was late, he insisted on walking me home. When he saw I was living in a hostel, he was shocked.

'I didn't know.' He seemed ashamed.

'It's not bad. People come and go. The manager's from Cork. He's nice to me.'

'You'll come home with me.'

I stared at him. 'No.'

'I have a two-bed in Ranelagh.'

'You need your space,' I said.

'For all that queer stuff with Poor John, you mean?' He sounded upset.

'Queer? Is that what they call it?'

'That's what some people call it.'

'What else?'

'Poof, fairy, pansy, fag, queen.'

'Mean.'

'I like queen, but yeah, the rest is mean.' He smiled.

'What do you call it?' I asked.

'I'm a homosexual. I like men. That's it.'

'Oh.'

'I didn't mean to keep it a secret from you. I thought you'd just know.'

'Turns out I don't know much.'

'Yeah you do, I can tell. It's all there behind those sad eyes of yours.'

'I don't care if you're a queen,' I said, and he beamed at me.

'I do. I keep it a secret from others, Catherine, because I have to, not because I want to. Do you understand?'

'To keep you safe?' I said.

He nodded. 'Yeah.'

'I have a secret,' I said.

'You can trust me,' he said, and I believed him.

'They locked me away. I had a baby and they took her away,' I said, and I could tell he was as shocked as I was when I caught him kissing Poor John. 'They call me lots of names, too.'

Tony lit a cigarette. 'Get your stuff,' he said. 'You're coming home with me and that's final.'

We walked away from the hostel, Tony holding my case in one hand and linking me with the other, and me with a bird's nest on my head with a loose egg rattling around, wearing a black gothic dress and a pair of trainers. I asked him whether or not ladies were at the same thing together, kissing and stuff.

He laughed. 'Oh yeah, mad for it.'

'Makes sense,' I said.

We arrived back at his place a little after 10 p.m. It was a bachelor pad: small sitting room, tiny kitchen and a bathroom. It could do with some fresh paint, but it felt like a place I could call home.

He showed me into the box room. It had a single bed against the wall and the wardrobe was standalone and too big for the room, but there was no religious iconography and it had its own door, and that was enough. I found myself at home, with a room and a door that only locked from the inside. It was my choice whether to walk through it or lock it or leave it wide open.

Sitting on the bed alone, I cried salty tears, and not just because I finally had the privacy to do so unobserved, but also because I felt free.

Mammy's coming, Daisy. Do you hear me? Mammy's coming.

I sent my mother a letter that very week. I sent her back her twenty pounds and told her I had found my family. I was home now, and soon I would bring my daughter home, too. I wished her well and I said goodbye.

Chapter Sixteen

Caroline

CAROLINE GOT THE TEXT from Natalie: *Not pregnant. Devastated. Need a minute.* She figured she'd sent it to the others, too. She didn't want to push, to ask what she could do when there was nothing she could do. So she didn't ask. She knew what that felt like. *Please, please go away. In the words of Greta Garbo, I want to be alone.*

The urge to reach out to Natalie was strong, but what would she do? Ask the question everyone asked her: Are you OK? *Seriously?* She could text that everything would be OK, but she didn't know that. After ten minutes of typing, deleting and retyping, in the end she went with: *Be there when needed.* Natalie needed to wallow in it, and that was it. There was nothing that could be said.

Caroline knew Natalie was worried about her relationship too, and that Paul was an issue and it was all a shitshow. At least before, when Caroline had tried, Dave was there 100 per cent. They were in it together. Not like Linda. From the little that Natalie gave away, it didn't sound like Linda was completely on board.

Natalie didn't reply.

Caroline was in the office when the phone rang.

'Hello, Mrs Murphy?'

'It's Ms.'

'Apologies, Ms Murphy. I'm ringing on behalf of Lucy Belton's office. We have a cancellation for tomorrow, if you'd like to come in to have your laparoscopy. I know it's short notice.'

'Yes. Great. Absolutely,' Caroline said.

Caroline would have to move some work around. She got off the phone and knocked on Susan's office door, not waiting for her response before opening it. A pile of files was forming a wall around Susan's desk.

'I'm going to need a few days off,' she said.

Susan stood up, clearly not impressed. 'You're in the middle of a case.'

'I'm sorry, but it's important.'

'So is work.'

'I can push it for a week without anyone losing sleep,' she said, and she closed the door of Susan's office before she got a chance to reply.

Once, an action like that would have really worried her. *What have I done? My career! Am I crazy?* Now, she couldn't care less. *Do what you want. I don't care about this job anymore.* It was an awakening of sorts, just admitting to herself that she wasn't only bored of what she did or unmoved by it – she actually hated it. *Huh! When did that happen?* She'd never truly loved her work, but she'd liked a challenge, and once upon a time, her job was challenging. Once upon a time, it was her greatest challenge, but that was before she tried to start her own family. *I really hate my job! Fucking hell . . . Who knew?*

In truth, she'd only become a solicitor because she got the points in her Leaving Cert and her parents insisted she'd be mad to go to nursing school when she had enough points to study law.

'But I really want to be a nurse,' she'd argued.

'You put law down on your CEO form,' her father said.

'Yes, because you have to put more than one thing and I've a crush on Jimmy Smits on *LA Law*. I didn't think I'd get it!'

She didn't have enough points for medicine, so it was either law or nursing, and after several arguments, she 'chose' law. She didn't regret it. Not initially. She loved university and that was where she met Dave. She'd enjoyed her first few years in a small law office in town, finding her specialty in litigation. She enjoyed the cut and thrust of it. And then things changed and she changed, and arguing for a living didn't please her as it once had.

Caroline had often thought about what it would be like to be a nurse. She spent so much time around them, relying on their kindness and care. She valued that more than she valued a lot of things. She was a caring person, albeit a little less so with every year that passed. A job in the legal mire, dogfighting for scraps, and an adulthood filled with pain and loss had dulled her ability to care. She'd once got a kick out of helping people, putting others first, but these days she'd lost the habit of looking outwards.

The last ten years had focused her on herself and made her remiss about everyone else. She missed the old Caroline, the one who was free of the burden of 'me'. The one who would have showered her sisters with love and kindness at every new pregnancy, who would have been there for them and her nieces and nephews every step of the way.

She left the office and took the rest of the week off. Elizabeth would be fuming, but she didn't care. She briefly wondered if Susan and Elizabeth would begin plotting to oust her. *Maybe. Fuck it.* She had bigger fish to fry.

She ate a big meal at six o'clock, then snacked at 8 p.m. She couldn't eat past nine.

When Dave came home just after eleven, she was already in bed. She thought about mentioning that she had to have an endometrioma removed, but she figured it would just annoy him. *Cutting into yourself again? For what?* The truth was it was so big, she had no choice; it had to come out. She couldn't tell him that, though. It would only add to his argument that her body was a toxic waste ground from which nothing could survive.

She heard him singing to himself in the spare room. He'd been drinking. It was only a Tuesday.

Caroline was sitting in the hospital reception by seven thirty the next morning and processed by 8 a.m. She changed into a paper gown, putting on a dressing gown and slippers, and was waiting in the room just off the theatre by eight thirty. She was first in. She could hear the anaesthesiologist and nurse talking quietly among themselves. She sat on a hard bench and kept her legs tightly crossed, conscious that she had no knickers on. *The last thing I want is everyone talking about my clammy thighs – bloody mortifying.* Every now and then the heavy door would swing open and a member of the medical team would come or go. Some looked at her and offered a smile; others were busy, focused on anything but her.

She hadn't seen Dave before she left. He was sleeping off his drink the night before. She was glad. It made it easier to leave without him. This would be her first procedure alone. He had always been there to drive her there and to make a fuss. He always made a checklist to ensure they didn't forget anything. He'd be the last person she'd see before she walked to the theatre waiting room, and the first person she'd see when she opened her eyes. He'd drive her home in a pre-warmed car and cover her in a blanket. And he'd have a hot-water bottle ready to place by her side, in a bid to combat the onslaught of vicious cramps. He'd stop for takeaway coffees and a slice of coffee cake, her favourite cake in the world. He'd carry her inside their home and tuck her into bed. He'd kiss her on the forehead and he'd put on a box set. No comedy. Not after surgery. Something criminal. She'd loved crime after surgery.

Caroline blinked back tears. He was a good man and a great husband. She hated what she was doing to him.

So stop this.

I can't.

She was losing her grip and she hadn't even started on the hormones.

A nurse came to the door and called her in.

'Hello, Ms Murphy. It's go time.'

'Call me Caroline.'

'I'm Erica.'

'Hi, Erica.'

Erica made sure that Caroline got up onto the table safely. She took her slippers and dressing gown from her and placed them under the table. Caroline lay down.

'You've been here before, Caroline?'

'Many times.'

'So you know what to expect?'

'Yes,' Caroline said, and she was more nervous than she should be. Her hands were shaking and her teeth suddenly chattering.

'I'm sorry, this is unlike me . . .' She tried to clamp her teeth together, which only served to make her look like a mad woman.

'It's fine. It's cold in here,' Erica said. 'Everything is going to be fine.'

'Where's Lucy?'

'On her way. Don't worry. We won't get started without her.'

She nodded and hugged herself, waiting for the anaesthesiologist to loom above her. A man in his mid-fifties with thick glasses and a moustache appeared a minute or two later.

'I see you're a frequent flyer. How are the veins?'

'Shite.'

'Oh well, they haven't met me yet.'

She handed him her arm and faced the window. The room was a clean white box with boxed fluorescent lighting in the ceiling above her and below her it was laid with white conductive vinyl flooring. Three huge disk-shaped lights hung from thick heavy-duty hydraulic arms just above her and if she stretched her neck, she'd see the table with instruments that would cut into and carve her. Behind her was a computer and screen elevated and attached to another machine with tubes and wires emanating from it. The only piece of furniture was a press with glass doors, jam-packed with medicines of all shapes, sizes and colours. It looked strangely messy and out of place against the sterility of the rest of the room.

'There we go,' he said, and she looked to find a cannula inserted in her hand.

'Wow, you are good.'

He pretended to bow. 'Let's get ready to rumble,' he said, and she felt the anaesthetic course through her veins.

Her jaw relaxed and she felt warm. Her brain submerged in a soupy swamp and she was gone.

When Caroline woke up in a recovery room, she immediately felt pain. But it was bearable pain. She stared up at the ceiling made up of white Artex tiles sprinkled with thousands and thousands of tiny holes. *Why?* For a time, she tried to make sense of where she was and what was going on. Slowly, she remembered. *Ah. Surgery. Done. Yeah!* Her mouth was dry. She lay still, waiting for a nurse's head to pop above her.

'There you are,' the nurse said. 'How do you feel about some tea and toast?'

'Good.'

'Excellent, and then we'll get you on your feet.'

'Super.'

When the nurse was gone, Caroline lay alone again, wondering if she should just sit up. It felt nice on her back; her brain was still partially submerged in a swamp. *I'll just lie here.* She felt under her bed for her phone and pulled it out of her bag. *Ohhh, my phone.*

'There it is,' she said, and held it in her hand.

Then she was talking and then it was fuzzy and she fell asleep.

Caroline woke to see Ronnie sitting beside her, reading a newspaper.

'What are you doing here?' she asked, less alarmed than confused.

'You rang me and asked me to pick you up.'

'Oh my God! Seriously?'

'Jesus, did they drop you on your head?'

'No. No. I remember now. I'm so sorry. Thanks.'

Caroline was embarrassed. In her disorientated state, the only person she'd thought to call was a woman whose number she'd had on her phone less than a week.

'How did it go?' Ronnie asked.

'I don't know. I haven't seen anyone yet.'

'Well, you look like you've been dragged through hell by your hair.'

Caroline smiled. 'Exactly the look I was going for.'

'Well done. You never mentioned you were coming in. Thought it was months away.'

'Last-minute appointment.'

'You OK?'

'Don't know.'

The nurse arrived with tea and toast approximately an hour and half after she'd promised it.

'Your friend insisted on waiting with you,' she said.

She didn't sound too impressed.

'I wasn't taking no for an answer,' Ronnie said with great pride.

Caroline beamed at her.

The nurse put the tray on the side table and pushed a button to help Caroline sit up.

'Oh shit,' Caroline said.

'You are going to be sore. They did quite a job on you.'

'Right.'

She placed the tea and toast in front of Caroline.

'Any chance of a tea for me?' Ronnie asked.

'No,' the nurse said.

'Wow, that's hardcore.'

She shook her head and turned to Caroline. 'Eat and drink, then a walk and the loo. You know the drill.'

'When will Lucy be in?'

'As soon as she can.'

When she left, Caroline picked at her toast.

'Have the tea if you like,' she said to Ronnie.

'Nah, you drink up. Sounds like you've been through the wars.'

Sometime later, when Caroline had had her cannula removed, had peed on command and had taken a very slow walk down a very long corridor, Lucy Belton arrived.

'I'm sorry – you were asleep before I got into theatre.'

'It's fine. How did I do?'

Lucy looked from Caroline to Ronnie. 'Could we have a moment?'

Ronnie stood up. 'No problem. I'll be outside.'

She left the room and Lucy waited until the door was closed before turning back to Caroline.

'How are you feeling?' Lucy asked kindly, and Caroline knew something was wrong just by the tone of her voice, the tilt of her head, the look in her eyes.

'Just tell me.'

Lucy sat on the chair previously occupied by Ronnie and dragged it close to Caroline's bed.

'Your endometrioma was impressive to say the least. It required extensive excision.'

'OK, but now it's gone, right?'

Lucy nodded. 'Yes, it is. You're safe and you'll recover.'

Caroline felt tears building behind her eyes. 'But . . . ?' She croaked the word.

'But . . .' Lucy sighed. 'When we got in, the extent of the previous damage to the uterus became immediately obvious.'

'And? Please, just spit it out.'

'Caroline, because of the large number of adhesions, if you were to become pregnant, the likelihood of you sustaining and carrying a pregnancy to term would be nil. I'm so sorry.'

Tears began to pour down Caroline's face even before Lucy had finished the sentence.

'I cannot recommend continuing with IVF,' Lucy said, looking her right in the eyes.

'Nil?' Caroline repeated. She could feel panic rushing through her.

'That's my opinion,' Lucy said.

Caroline pulled herself together. *No. No. This is not the end.* 'Well, I don't care. It's worth trying.'

'I don't think that would be good for you,' Lucy said. 'As your doctor, I am advising you to step away.'

'No. No. No way. Absolutely not. I want to go again.' She was half shouting and half whining.

'Caroline, you'd be putting yourself in a potentially *very* dangerous situation.'

'I don't care.' She was shouting now. '*I don't care!*'

Lucy remained calm. 'I care. I will *not* proceed with another round of IVF, and your records will indicate the potential danger of any clinician doing so.'

'You can't.'

Lucy stood up. 'Caroline. Let it go.' She walked towards the door, turning to face Caroline before she left. 'Please, for your own sake. It's time.'

Lucy walked out of the room and Caroline felt like she couldn't breathe. *No. No. No. No. I can't. I can't let it go. Please. Help me.*

A few moments later, Ronnie stepped into the room. She looked shaken. Caroline didn't know if she'd heard or not, but one look at her was probably enough.

'Let's just get you home,' Ronnie said, and she helped to lift a hysterical Caroline out of the bed. 'Breathe.'

'I can't.'

'You can. Breathe.'

Caroline could barely speak through the tears and snot. Ronnie perched her on the edge of the bed and scrambled for her bag. She grabbed her wide-legged, soft, elastic-waisted jersey trousers and her soft jersey top. As she pulled them out, Caroline's knickers flew across the room.

'Shite. Sorry.'

Caroline barely noticed. She was too busy drowning in her own tears. Ronnie grabbed the roving knickers and handed them over.

'I can't bend down.'

'Maybe I'll call a nurse.'

'Just shove my feet through and drag them to my knees. I'll take it from there.'

Caroline was still crying a deluge as Ronnie did as directed. Caroline slowly and painfully stood. She leaned down, whimpering in pain, and pulled up her knickers. Ronnie put Caroline's feet through the trousers and heaved them up.

'There, that's the worst of it,' Caroline said, and fresh tears began to fall.

Ronnie helped Caroline to put her top on and then she was ready to leave.

The nurse arrived with a prescription for painkillers and some hospital pads. She didn't say much, or if she did, Caroline couldn't hear her through the buzzing in her ears. It was over. She had rubbish eggs. She had a husband who wouldn't give her his sperm and now she had a womb that was incapable of carrying a child.

Let it go.

All the images she ever had of carrying her own child, giving birth, nurturing, loving, holding, supporting, giving, receiving – they all faded away. A whole lifetime of firsts she'd fantasised about disappeared. First smile, first tooth, first step, first chuckle, first word, first day at school, first love, first heartbreak, first job. No feet on the stairs, no messing in the back seat of the car, no complaining when ordered to do homework or to take out the bins. No arguments, no fights, no screaming *I hate you!* No secrets, no gummy smiles, no tearful cuddles in the middle of the night. No clinging and I love yous. No tantrums in the supermarket. No incessant questions. No pointless stories that went on for days, no loud music, no friends with no homes to go to. No school runs, no Christmas surprises, no birthday chaos, no leaving home, no coming back, no mother of the bride or groom. No Mammy, Mam, Mum or Ma. No grandchildren.

And now, no Dave.

The hole in Caroline's heart that started with a pinprick so many years ago had grown so big, the hurt echoed. She had chosen the promise of a baby over the very real love of her life, and now it was over and she was alone.

Let it go.

Let what go? There's nothing left to hold on to.

Ronnie drove a bereft Caroline home, trying to be careful going over potholes and the many speed bumps that seemed to line the streets that led to Caroline's home. As she was helping her out of the car, Caroline whispered to Ronnie.

'If my husband arrives home, he doesn't know about the surgery.'

'That sounds messy,' Ronnie said with a sigh.

'Is anyone in that group in a stable relationship?'

'Loads, you just glomed on to the rejects,' she said.

'Story of my life,' Ronnie said and smiled.

She helped Caroline inside then took her upstairs and put her into bed. She boiled the kettle and filled a hot-water bottle, handing it to her, along with her meds, a glass of water and half a sandwich she took out of her bag.

'I'm fine, really.'

'I'm not leaving till you eat it,' Ronnie said.

She sat on the bed and Caroline couldn't help herself but ask. 'Why?'

'Why what?'

'Why did you join the group? Because you're not trying for a baby.'

'How do you know that?' Ronnie's eyes softened.

'I just do.'

Ronnie looked like she might get up and leave, but then she spoke quietly.

'When my parents died, I went looking for my birth parents,' she said.

'I didn't know you were adopted,' Caroline said.

'Me neither, till my teens. They sat me down one Sunday afternoon and told me. My mum cried the whole time.'

'Jesus,' Caroline said.

'I couldn't believe I was adopted. I didn't want to deal with it, so I packed it away and we never spoke about it again.'

'Christ! And your birth parents, have you ever tried to find them?' Caroline asked.

Ronnie stood up. 'Now that's a whole different story. You should rest.' She walked towards the door of Caroline's bedroom, then turned back. 'Caroline, do you love your husband?'

'Of course I do.'

'Mourn for the child you'll never have, because you can't fix your broken body. But you can fix your broken marriage.'

Ronnie left after that and Caroline thought about her words for a long time.

Paddy

Catherine

VIVA HAIR WAS ALWAYS a busy shop, growing more popular by the day. Our customers were anything from aged sixteen to sixty. The auld ones loved Tony because he could gossip with the best of them. The young ones loved him because he was so handsome. They were probably like me, thick enough not to know there was such a thing as homosexuality. He told me he was sure some of the older women suspected, but as long as he didn't speak about it, they were content.

In the two months I'd lived with Tony, I'd learned that love was love and sex was sex, whichever way you had it. He told me that the Church believed the sin was not in being gay but acting upon it. So basically, you could be who you were, you just couldn't *really* be who you were. It was bollocks. Being friends with Tony confirmed that God had no place in my world.

For the first time in my life, I felt I belonged somewhere. Not with people called decent who had hearts of stone, but with outsiders who embraced me as one of their own. Through my long discussions with Tony, I came to understand that relationships were complicated, that life was tough, that having someone to curl up with was as wonderful as I'd dreamed about. You just had to be careful about whom to trust. I'd failed at that once before and I was keen not to make that mistake again.

231

For Tony, the stakes were high; homosexuality was still a crime, punishable by a prison sentence. I remembered Sister Joanna: *Is this your first offence?* Tony knew a fella who'd been sent to prison after his father dobbed him in to the guards. It was all over the newspapers; he lost a good job, his flat, his family, and when he was released after six months, his life was ruined. He left for England. Tony met him in London once and he didn't say too much, only that he'd never be the same again. I knew what he felt like.

'You have to be careful about whom you share your secrets with,' he told me one day while we were painting the kitchen pale yellow.

I knew he was talking about Daisy.

I had bad dreams most nights. I dreamed about the institution, that I was falling from the attic window onto the cold stone yard far below. I always woke before I hit the ground, shaking and crying. The first time Tony heard me, he brought me tea and hugged me tight.

'You've got to fight those demons, Catherine.'

Sometimes I dreamed I was feeding Daisy. I'd look away for only a second and then she was gone, disappearing into thin air. I dreamed of Maria, crying and begging me to stay with her as the nuns held her down. 'Don't leave me, Katie. I'm scared, Katie.' Hearing that name, even in my dreams, brought it all back far too vividly. I dreamed of her broken on the cold stone yard, bleeding out. I saw her in a tiny coffin fit for a child. I woke up crying.

'You've gotta keep those secrets, Catherine,' Tony would say. 'And at the same time let go and move on.'

I told him I would. I'd let go of the pain the best I could – but I'd never let go of Daisy. I still planned to get her back, but I didn't tell Tony, because I knew it would upset him. He was a practical sort, not a dreamer like me. I didn't know how I was going to do it and resigned myself to the fact that I'd need money and security. I needed more than a receptionist's job in a hairdresser's and squatting in my boss's box room. I needed a career.

I asked Tony if I could train as a stylist.

'Do you want to be a stylist?'

'Very much.'

'You'll need to show some talent.'

'OK.'

'We'll see.'

I grinned.

'Don't grin at me. We'll see is not a yes.'

But it was a yes, and he started to train me on our own time a week later. Now I had a plan. I was going to become a proper stylist and make money. When I had enough of it, I was going to hire a solicitor and tell them I hadn't signed away my child. She was stolen. Then I would sue those nuns for custody and for anything I could squeeze out of them. I would get my girl back. It was only a matter of time.

The first time I met Tony's brother, Paddy, was when he came into the shop to formally invite Tony to their parents' thirtieth wedding anniversary. The door jangled open and I smiled, showing lots of teeth just like Tony asked me to.

'You have to make that customer feel like they are the only person in the world,' he'd say. 'Especially the fellas. Trust me, they love that.'

From the doorway, the man smiled back. He was tall, much taller than me, and blond with big blue eyes. He was so terribly handsome I felt myself blushing. Then he spoke and it was like a light went on. He held his hand out with a little envelope in it.

'Excuse me, miss, could you pass this on to Tony Mahon.'

'Come in,' I said.

'God no. If anyone saw me here . . .' He wiggled the card in his hand.

'And what's wrong with here?' I asked.

'Well, it's for ladies and for . . .' He looked over his shoulder. 'My university is just at the end of this street,' he said by way of explanation.

I ignored the mention of university because I wasn't impressed and instead I focused on the beginning of his sentence . . .

'For ladies and for what?' I asked.

'Well . . .' He looked around for someone invisible to dig him out of a very large hole of his own creation. He cleared his throat.

'Hello, brother,' Tony said, striding into reception with a big smile. He turned to me. 'Isn't he pretty?'

I made a face and Tony laughed. He took the invite. The pretty man seemed embarrassed.

'Sorry,' he said to me. 'My name is Patrick . . . Mahon . . . Tony's brother.'

'I'm not stupid,' I said.

Tony laughed again. 'She thinks you're a dick, Paddy.'

'Sounds like dick. Begins with a P,' I said, delighted with myself.

'Sorry,' Paddy said again, and then Tony followed him outside. They spoke for a minute in the street and then Paddy left.

When Tony returned to the shop, I pretended to be writing out an order for shampoo.

'Say what you have to say,' he said.

'I have nothing to say.'

'Except?'

'Except you didn't tell me you had a brother.'

'You didn't ask.'

'Are there any more of you?' I asked.

'Just a father and mother.'

'Are they pricks, too?' I said.

He chuckled to himself. 'Oh yeah.'

'Do they know your secret?' I asked.

'They don't want to.'

'Your brother knows.'

'Yeah,' Tony said. 'He does – but he doesn't want to, either.'

After that I saw Paddy a lot. He'd knock on the window as he passed and wave at me. At first I pretended not to notice him, but after a while it became difficult, especially when customers started pointing to the handsome man standing outside. Once I waved back, and then the next day he stepped into the shop, waving a white flag.

'What are you doing?' I asked.

'Starting again.'

'Why?'

He thought about it for a minute. 'You called me a dick beginning with P.'

'It felt right,' I said, and he laughed – a hearty laugh that made me blush.

'So . . . Can we start again?' he asked, and he was so beautiful to look at, and his smile was captivating and warm . . .

'OK,' I said cautiously.

'Great,' he said, and he looked genuinely pleased. 'I'm leaving now before I say something else to ruin this.' He was backing out of the door.

I giggled. I couldn't help myself.

'We're going to be friends, Catherine,' he said.

And then he was gone – but I didn't stop thinking about him for the rest of that day.

I think you'd like him, Daisy. He's sweet and he's funny and he's got kind eyes. What are kind eyes? It's hard to explain, kiddo, but you'll know them when you see them.

After that, Paddy called in once or twice a week. Tony was amused by his brother's visits, but he was also wary.

'Don't say too much to him, Catherine,' he said. 'He's a nice kid, but he's not one of us.'

Chapter Seventeen

Natalie

NATALIE WAS FORCED TO tell Linda over the phone that she wasn't pregnant. She didn't want to, but Linda kept ringing. Natalie asked her by text to come home, but Linda just kept ringing. She texted: *Just pick up the bloody phone.*

There was a long pause after Natalie spoke the word 'negative'. So long, in fact, that Natalie thought the call had dropped. She was home alone, rolled into a ball on her sofa with a face full of chocolate and mascara stains halfway down her cheek.

'Linda?'

'I'm here.'

'Well, don't you have anything to say?'

'They gave us the percentages. We knew it was a long shot.'

'That's it?'

'I don't know. What do you want me to say?'

'I'm devastated. Aren't you devastated?'

Linda swallowed hard. 'It's one try. People try for months and years. You and your group know that better than anyone.'

'You are talking stats and people and I'm talking us and our baby.'

'We don't have a baby, Natalie!'

'No, we don't! And don't you have a single feeling about that?'

She heard Linda sigh. 'We can have this conversation tonight. I have to go. I'm due in court.'

Natalie texted her new friends and then stayed curled into a ball for the rest of the day.

Natalie must have slept for some of the late afternoon, because she woke up to the sound of Linda opening the front door. She sat up and waited on the edge of the sofa to face her partner.

Linda had brought home flowers and a bottle of wine.

'Sorry,' she said. It was the first genuine and kind word she'd said since the insemination. 'You know how I get when I'm stressed.'

Natalie accepted the flowers. They were beautiful. Linda had probably paid a lot of money for them.

'I'll open the bottle,' Linda said.

'No.'

'Come on, you haven't touched a drink in two weeks.'

'I don't feel like it.'

'It's your favourite.'

'I don't want a drink, Linda.'

'So you're just going to wallow?'

'No, I just don't want to drink.'

'OK, more for me.'

Linda walked into the kitchen and Natalie followed in time to see her fill a big glass.

'What's going on with us?' Natalie asked.

'Please don't make a negative result about us,' Linda said. 'It's not the end of the world. You can try again.'

'You?' Natalie said. '*You* can try again? I thought *we* were trying?'

'You know what I mean.'

Natalie looked at her. 'Do you want to try again?'

'You're the one who wanted this, Natalie. I love you, so I support you.'

Then the doorbell rang. Linda left the kitchen to answer it and Natalie was left with her mouth wide open, gobsmacked.

Paul was the first through the door, then Linda and then Sylvia. Linda looked apologetic.

'I told Paul about the pregnancy test.'

Natalie looked nervously at Sylvia. She wasn't supposed to know and she didn't look happy.

'I mentioned it to Sylvia,' Paul said, and he had the good grace to appear uncharacteristically apologetic.

It was all getting too much for Natalie. She sat down heavily at the kitchen table while Linda introduced herself to Sylvia.

'Nice to meet you finally.'

'You too. I've heard so much.'

'Would you like tea – coffee, a glass of wine?'

'We're not staying,' Sylvia said, and she seemed less confident than she had the previous occasion Natalie met her. 'Look, there's no easy way of saying this, but Paul is out.'

'Out of what?' Linda said.

'This whole baby-making thing.'

Natalie was panicking. 'But he has a contract.'

'And he's fulfilled it.'

'But I'm not pregnant,' Natalie said.

Paul was shaking his head. 'I'm done.'

'But we agreed on at least two tries.'

'We only contracted for one,' Linda said.

'Well, why did we do that?'

'Because it was the right thing to do to give everyone a little space,' Linda said.

Natalie fumed. 'And whose idea was that?'

Why did I not check the contract myself? Why did I trust Linda with it?

Because I thought she was working for us! That's FUCKING why.

'Look, Paul and I are together now,' Sylvia said.

'Give it five minutes,' Natalie said.

'Go fuck yourself, Natalie.' Paul sounded hurt. 'You're always on your high horse around me, like I'm not good enough.'

'But apparently his sperm is?' Sylvia said.

'Fine. Go. It's for the best. And honestly, your sperm isn't good enough. So every cloud.' Natalie knew she was being a bitch, but she'd had enough.

Paul waved his finger at her. 'You're a cold bitch.'

Natalie shrugged. She was always her worst self around him and she knew it wasn't always his fault.

Sylvia shook her head. 'You know who you're not good enough for, Natalie? Linda.'

Natalie glared at her. 'You don't know Linda.'

'I know she's kinder than you,' she said, and she turned on her heel.

Paul was already halfway down the corridor, with Sylvia closely following and Linda apologising on Natalie's behalf.

'She didn't mean it, Paul. You know what she's like when she's upset.'

The door slammed. Natalie poured herself a large glass of wine and gulped it before Linda appeared.

'That was mean.'

'Was it?'

'He's my brother and I'm sick of you making him feel like shit.'

'But it's OK when you do it?'

'I love him.'

'Oh well, that's OK, then.' Natalie took another swig.

Linda sat down beside her at the table. She looked tired. 'I never wanted to be a mother,' she said. 'You know that.'

'But then you changed your mind,' Natalie said.

'No, you changed my mind. You pushed and you pushed and you told me that kids were non-negotiable, so if I wanted to be with you, I had no choice.'

'So you lied?' Natalie said, tears burning behind her eyeballs, bile scorching her throat.

'I tried.'

'Bullshit.' Natalie drank deeper.

Tears were sliding down Linda's face. 'I love you. I didn't want to lose you. I thought at least if I had some DNA in the mix, even if I didn't want it, I might love it.'

Natalie took a second to catch her breath. *It!*

'I love our lives, Natalie,' Linda said. 'During your insemination, I genuinely thought I was physically going to be sick. I know I wasn't there for you, but I was terrified. I didn't want you doing the test in front of me because if it was positive, you'd see . . . what I felt . . .'

It was a lot to take in. Natalie sat in silence, not meeting Linda's eye.

'And now that it's done, I don't want to do it again.'

'Well, Paul has seen to that,' Natalie muttered.

'Not with Paul and not with anyone. Natalie, I want you. I don't want kids. It's *my* non-negotiable now.' Linda was really crying now.

Natalie stopped to take a large glug of wine, blow her nose. She looked across at her partner.

Linda reached out her hand. 'Please.'

Natalie took Linda's hand in hers and she cupped it. She stood up and went round the table. She pulled her out of her chair and hugged her tight.

'I love you,' Natalie said, and Linda exhaled.

Natalie looked Linda in the eye and placed her palm on her cheek. Then she kissed her, long and deep. As she pulled away, Linda smiled through tears.

'I'll be out by the weekend,' Natalie said.

When Life Gets Messy

Catherine

PADDY CALLED IN A LOT after that. Tony didn't like it at first, but he warmed to his brother after a few months. Paddy was twenty-four and studying to be a doctor. He was working in hospitals by then but when he studied, he studied in the Trinity library.

'Have you ever been inside Trinity?' he asked, and I said no, I had no interest in the place.

'Why not? It's beautiful and it's just down the road!'

I didn't care how close it was. Justin studied law there, so I wouldn't be found dead in the place. When Paddy asked me to meet him for lunch on the grounds, I declined.

'What about when I'm working shifts in the hospital – will you visit me there?'

'No,' I said, and he didn't hide his disappointment. I felt a little queasy.

I want to, I really do, but I can't.

He asked me if I had a boyfriend. I told him I didn't.

'Can I visit you, then?' he asked, and my heartbeats quickened and I felt that familiar flutter of excitement. *Oh no.*

'You can visit me here anytime,' I said brightly.

He sighed and playfully shook his head. 'You just want me in here because it makes me nervous.'

I laughed. 'Well, it shouldn't,' I said. 'Nothing should if you want to be a decent doctor.'

'Well that shut me up,' he said.

He reached for my hand and when our flesh touched, my insides fizzed. I wanted to stay exactly like that and not move one inch. I wanted time to stop – but it didn't and I couldn't make that mistake again, so I pulled my hand away. He looked as pained as I felt when I did so.

'Sorry,' I said before I knew what I was saying.

He gulped. 'Don't be,' he said. 'See you soon.'

He was gone and my heart and stomach sank.

Never mind, Daisy. We can't be distracted. It has to be just you and me.

It was Poor John's birthday. Poor John liked a fuss on his birthday. I spent the previous evening hanging decorations and homemade banners with 'Happy Birthday' written all over them. And because he was a music geek, Tony thought it would be fun if we all dressed up as Poor John's favourite artists all day. Tony was Freddie Mercury in a skintight bodysuit. Poor John was David Bowie in a tight-fitting black suit, a dicky bow and a fedora. Amy shoved in a pair of false teeth and said she was Carly Simon, and Tony insisted I go as Karen Carpenter. All I needed was a pair of flares and a T-shirt, so I pretty much dressed as myself but with a flower in my hair.

We were booked solid that day. I still mostly took care of reception, but by then I had a few clients of my own and Tony had discovered I had a knack for blow-dries, especially the Farrah Fawcett look. I could flick with the best of them. Poor John was up to his eyes in up-styles and Amy had a queue a mile long. Tony had back-to-back appointments with models shooting for a winter catalogue in a studio just up the road. Poor John was running over two hours late.

I was handing out magazines to the girls who were patiently waiting, when she walked through the door. I didn't recognise her immediately. The phone was ringing and I acknowledged her with a smile as I answered the phone. I took appointment details from a regular for the following week, noting them in the book. Then I placed the phone on the hook and gave her my full attention.

'So sorry, what can I do for you?' I said.

And it was then that the penny dropped. It was Jen.

'My name is Jennifer Brown-Campbell. I have an appointment with John Foley for an up-style at 2 p.m.'

My mouth was dry. I couldn't speak. I think I flushed red, but I couldn't tell because my body felt numb from my head to my toes. She looked at me uncomfortably and we shared an awkward silence before I found my voice.

'Of course, let me see,' I said, looking at the appointment book. 'Yes, here you are. I am so sorry, but John is running very late today.' I pointed to three other ladies in front of her. 'Could I fit you in another day?'

'Absolutely not! I'm getting married in two weeks' time,' she said, and my heart nosedived into the pit of my stomach.

'Congratulations.'

'I don't need your congratulations, I need my appointment.'

'The wait will be over two hours,' I said, a little less friendly.

'This is a joke.'

'This is life,' I said. 'Sometimes it gets messy.'

She looked at me with narrowed eyes, just as Tony was escorting one of his models to the door.

'Are you in charge?' she asked.

Tony turned. 'Yes, I am. What can I do for you?'

'I have an appointment for a trial bridal up-style at two and I'm being told I have to wait over two hours.'

'I'm sorry, but . . .'

'I'm Jennifer Brown-Campbell,' she said, and Tony stopped speaking.

He smiled. 'Welcome to the shop, Miss Brown-Campbell,' he said, and I thought *what the fuck is this?* 'I'm really sorry, but the wait for John is unavoidable. If you'd like me to book you in for another day that suits you . . . ? In the meantime, the lovely Catherine here can do the best Farrah Fawcett blow-dry in the city and your hair is perfect for it.'

Oh Jesus, oh Jesus, oh Jesus.

'Fine,' she said, a little softened. 'I'm a big Farrah fan.'

'Isn't everyone?' Tony brought her over to the sink and he whispered in my ear. 'We need this one.'

Shit. Shit. Shit. Keep cool. Shit. Shit. Shit . . . Keep calm. This is for Tony and for Viva – and who is Jennifer Brown-Campbell and what makes her so fucking special?

I washed her hair. She relaxed back into the seat and as soon as she let herself go, I saw it – the familiar swelling of her stomach. *She's pregnant.* I thought I was going to be sick. I had no idea how far she was gone; she was tidy and the bump was small. It was the twelfth of October. My Daisy was nearly twelve months old.

I had to count to ten in my head to keep calm. My hands were shaking as I washed the soap out of her hair. I conditioned her for a long time, just trying to muster the courage to face her in a mirror.

'That's nice,' she purred.

Oh Jesus. Oh Jesus. Oh Jesus.

Eventually, I wrapped a towel round her head and showed her to the chair. She looked at me as I patted her hair dry.

'You look familiar.'

I stopped her in her tracks. 'Karen Carpenter,' I said, pointing to the others. 'And over there is Bowie, Freddie Mercury and Carly Simon. It's John's birthday, so we thought we'd have some fun . . . Would you like some cake?'

'No, thanks,' she said, still eyeing me up.

I was combing out her long blonde hair, when she looked up from her magazine and spoke to me again.

'I really do have a feeling we've met.'

'Sorry,' I said. 'Unless you've been in here before?'

'No, first time.'

I hunched. I counted on the fact that the last time she saw me, I was a good deal bigger, with a swollen face.

'Freaky,' she said, and returned to her magazine.

'I'm just going to put in some product to help lift it,' I said, and she nodded. 'So you're getting married?' I asked. I couldn't help myself.

'We're having the reception in The Shelbourne,' she said, suddenly smiling. 'It's my favourite hotel.'

It was only up the road, but I'd never been in it. It was too posh for the likes of me.

'Sounds amazing.'

'It will be,' she said. 'I'm marrying the man of my dreams.'

And my nightmares.

'Do you work?' I asked as I scrunched her hair with my fingers.

'No, I'm . . . I was . . . studying . . . Law in Trinity, but . . .' She stopped herself. 'You know, when you're in love.'

'Yeah,' I said as she briefly rested her hand on her stomach.

247

'It doesn't matter. I probably wouldn't have been that good anyway . . . A man's game and all that . . .'

We didn't speak after that. She just absent-mindedly glanced at her magazine as I blow-dried and flicked her hair. She was thrilled with the results.

'Oh, maybe I'll do it like this for my wedding,' she said.

'Are you wearing a veil?' I asked.

'White dress, veil, the lot.' She smiled.

She put her hand on her stomach, like she was guarding her secret from the world. I heard her stomach gurgle. People around her were munching on cake and sweets from bowls and she was starving herself, hoping her stomach wouldn't show.

I hate to tell you, it will.

'An up-style will work better with the veil,' I said. 'And John is the best in town.'

She smiled. 'You're probably right.'

'You could have it done for your honeymoon,' I said.

I don't know why I said it. I suppose I felt sorry for her. She seemed trapped – in a very different way to me, but trapped nevertheless.

'Oh, we're not going on honeymoon. Justin – that's my fiancé – he'll have exams soon enough and he needs to study.'

Justin needs to study. Of course. It's always about Justin.

The mention of his name made me feel nauseous. 'Oh well, another time,' I said, and I took her money and I made an appointment for her for three days' time.

Later, Tony explained that she was a socialite. A minister's daughter who could bring in a lot of quality clientele to the salon.

'We're already out the door with business,' I said. 'We can't keep up.'

'With those kinds of clients, we can move to a bigger location. I could build the business.'

I thought about whether or not to tell him who she was, but he was so happy, I didn't. I just planned to be out of the salon for her next appointment. I couldn't risk running into Justin; I couldn't risk being exposed.

It dawned on me later that night as I was tossing and turning in my bed that Daisy would have a sibling and probably not just one. Daisy looked just like her daddy. *Will Jennifer's child look like him, too, or will he or she favour Jen? Will he love that child? Will that baby remind him of the baby he gave to the nuns? Will Daisy's loss finally sicken and sadden him? Will he regret what he did to us? Will he do something about it?*

Oh! Daisy, I should never have trusted him. I should have run to anywhere but to his aunt's big red door.

Jen would probably end up a stay-at-home mother of four or five children while Justin did what he wanted and with whom he wanted. *What a prick.* I hated him with everything in me. He'd lied and cheated and impregnated two unmarried girls. I was glad he couldn't run away and dispose of Jennifer Brown-Campbell as he'd done with a pig farmer's daughter. I felt sorry for her. I'd lost my baby, and she'd lost her bright future.

Chapter Eighteen

Janet

JANET WAITED FOR JIM to come home, sitting on the stairs so that he couldn't just walk straight upstairs, shower, change and walk out. That's what he'd done the night before. He didn't even look at her. Tonight would be different. Tonight they would talk.

She'd injected her second injection at 7 p.m. and screamed a little, then she'd painted her nails black. She spent some time examining her black nails while sitting on the staircase. It was a bold colour and an even bolder choice, not really her at all.

She heard the key in the lock and Jim walked inside. He seemed surprised to see her sitting there.

'We need to talk.'

'I don't know what you want me to say.'

He looked tired and drawn and not the happy-go-lucky man she'd married at all.

'You don't need to say anything.'

'Oh, so you mean I need to listen?'

'For a minute, then you can have your say.'

'Fine. Can I eat dinner? I haven't eaten since breakfast.'

They walked into the kitchen. Janet pulled out a shepherd's pie from the oven, hot and gooey. It smelled like a little piece of heaven.

They ate for a while in silence, then Janet pulled something from her pocket.

'I found this,' she said, and she handed him the note.

He looked at it and he shook his head. 'What's that?'

'It's a note from Tina Rossi.'

'How do you know?'

'Because I rang the number, Jim.'

'Jesus! Is that a fucking kiss?' he said. 'I didn't see it, I swear!'

'So you're saying she slipped it in your very tight pockets?'

'Now you're just calling me fat.'

'Seriously, Jim.'

'I change my overalls twice, sometimes three times a day. They hang in the warehouse. You know that. I bring the extras home to be washed every Friday.'

He was right.

'So why the note?' she asked.

'I don't know. She's young. The kiss is out of order.'

'And you holding her hand?'

'Wha—?'

'In the local, the other night.'

'I didn't hold her hand – I touched her hand. She told me she'd broken up with her boyfriend and she was thinking about what she wanted to do next.'

'Well, there you go!' Janet said.

'What?'

'You're next, Jim!'

'Ah, will you stop. She mentioned going to Australia, for fuck's sake.'

'Unless you gave her a reason to stay,' Janet said.

He thought about that for a moment. 'Maybe . . . but I wouldn't. And I can't believe you'd think I would!'

'If you found this note in my pocket, what would you do?'

He couldn't answer that.

'Jim, she said you could talk to her anytime. What's that about?'

He looked down at his food. 'Look, I might have mentioned how bad things were when you weren't feeling yourself. The lads wouldn't understand. It was nice to have someone to talk to.'

'About our personal lives?'

'You have your group, Janet. I had no one.'

'What about your parents or your sister?'

'They were worried enough about you.' He was getting upset now. 'You want me to pile on?'

'Sorry,' Janet said.

'I was grieving, too. I thought we'd cracked it, babe. I thought I was going to be a dad – this time, I thought, this is it. We were going to walk into that room a couple and come out a family. We'd see our son or our little girl on the screen and I'd be holding your hand. And then there was nothing – only more pain and more loss. And you beside yourself. And everyone asking all the time, how is she? What can we do for her? And me not knowing how to answer. So yeah, I spoke to Tina, because she was the only one who asked how I was.'

'I asked,' Janet said quietly.

'You couldn't manage your own emotions, never mind mine.'

'It would have been nice to know I wasn't alone.'

'You knew that.'

'Did I?'

'You fell apart and I did my best not to.'

'You could have.'

'Bollocks, Janet.'

'I like to think that even on my darkest day, if I thought you needed me, I'd pull through for you.' She spoke even more quietly than normal.

He wiped a sly tear and wiped his nose with his hand. He sighed deeply and then grabbed her hand using the hand he'd just wiped his nose on. He held her hand in his damp one and she didn't care.

'I'll keep that in mind,' he said.

She smiled.

'So, I'll encourage Tina to go to Australia, then?' he said.

'I think that's one of your very best ideas.'

He laughed a little.

'And, Jim . . . ?'

'Yeah.'

'I'm twelve weeks pregnant.'

Jim held his wife's hands up to his face and he cried like a newborn baby.

One of Us

Catherine

A WEEK BEFORE MY EIGHTEENTH, we celebrated Tony's birthday with a party at the house.

'Can we celebrate it together – a joint bash, you and me?' he asked.

'No.'

'Why not?'

'I don't want to.'

'Why?'

'It doesn't feel right,' I said, thinking about my daughter, out there somewhere, without me.

'You're out of that place, Catherine. You're safe.'

'I know,' I said, and I hoped she was safe, too, but how could I know?

'You don't have to feel guilty, you know.'

But I did feel guilty. On my daughter's first birthday, I took to my bed, where I stayed in a tight ball and cried all day and well into the night. She was a year old and I wasn't there. Some other woman blew out her single candle. Some other woman kissed her face, held her, inhaled her scent. Some other woman heard her first word, witnessed her first steps. Could she speak yet? Did she say the word 'Mamma' to that other woman? I wanted that other woman to be kind, to give my child the love, comfort and joy she deserved, but I also hated her.

I miss you, Daisy. I will save all of my money and I will get all the right advice. I will find you. Until then, I have no time for birthdays.

I made Tony promise not to make a fuss. 'I don't do birthdays,' I said.

'OK.' He promised to say nothing. 'But secretly, this party is for you, too. Just between us.'

I laughed him off. 'Great.'

As Paddy had been hanging around the salon more and more, Tony felt like he needed to invite him. He didn't expect Paddy to say yes.

'I'd love to,' he said, and Tony's face fell.

'Well, it will be full of women and queens,' Tony said.

'I'd love to,' Paddy said again, and my heart leaped.

He's coming. Oh my . . . Stop it . . . Stop it, Catherine . . . Think about Daisy . . . Think about the future. Just us.

'Oh, for fuck's sake,' Tony said.

'Will there be a dress code?'

'Wear what you want,' Tony said, and he walked away.

'Brilliant,' Paddy said to me.

Tony was nervous. It was one thing his brother knowing what he was; it was another thing seeing it. He was adamant that we all had to be on our best behaviour when Paddy was around.

'You're the one who kisses fellas in the shop bathroom,' I said. 'I don't know why I'm being dragged into it.'

'All right, all right, I'm only saying – keep quiet about it. It's just going to be a nice evening of drinks and party food.'

'Tell that to Poor John.'

'He's been told.'

'And Amy?'

'Also told.'

'OK then. What about all of your other friends, the guys in leather and the ones with wigs who dance in high heels?'

'All warned.'

As excited as I was about the prospect of seeing Paddy after dark, Tony's angst upset me.

'Why is he coming if you can't be yourself around him?'

'Because he's my brother and he invited himself.'

'No he didn't, you invited him.'

'Because of you! I've had that shop five fucking years. He's never darkened the door until he met you, but now he practically lives in the place. I couldn't not ask him.'

'Well, that's not my fault.'

'I know, and it's nice to have him around, just not around *here.*'

Tony looked around at the house. We'd transformed it from a dull, lifeless bachelor pad to a bright and blingy one, repainting the walls and switching up the furniture. Although it wasn't a palace, it was a much warmer, cosier place than when I first arrived. I'd picked and placed the cushions he bought and I'd made him invest in frames for the piles of photographs he kept in boxes under the stairs. Soon, his white sitting room walls were peppered with photos of him and his friends, his mum and dad and Paddy.

He asked if I wanted to put up any photos, but who would I put up, anyway? The parents who sent me away? The boy who abandoned me? Or the daughter whose only image resided in my mind? I kept a small photo of Rose in my bedroom, away from view, and a few tiny black-and-white pictures of my brothers and me when we were small, which I kept between the pages of a book under my bed. I would have loved a photo of Maria and Marian, whatever their real names were. I looked out for them on the streets sometimes, knowing full well that those who made it out alive were probably all shipped off across the pond.

I often stared at the bedroom wall and I'd see my daughter's face as clearly as if she were immortalised in black-and-white photographic paper and surrounded by a silver frame. I'd spent so many hours staring into her face as I fed her that it etched into my brain. I'd lie in bed thinking about her and seeing her face, reaching out to touch it in my imagination.

I love you, Daisy. Don't be afraid. I will find you. I will get you back.

Tony bought me a dress for the party. He said it wasn't a birthday present. He said it was because I spent nothing on clothes and he didn't want me to embarrass him. I knew he was lying – well, mostly he was lying. The dress was red and short and with bell sleeves and a round neckline made of fine white lace. It was the most beautiful thing I'd ever seen. Expensive, too; it probably cost more than the contents of my entire wardrobe.

'Oh, Tony, it's too much.' I was so embarrassed, I blushed as red as the dress.

'You deserve a lot more,' he said, and then he held my chin so that I was staring up at him. 'Remember that.'

Then he threw a box of shoes on the bed. I opened them: black patent high-heeled shoes.

'Oh my!' I said, and he smiled. 'They're beautiful, but they're so tall. I'll break my neck.'

'You're beautiful,' he said. 'Now practise. I am not ending up in an emergency room on my birthday.'

I tried on the dress and shoes and stared at myself in the mirror. I looked like someone else. Someone better and brighter. Tears spilled from my eyes because as pretty and perfect as I looked, that desperate pregnant girl in a putrid-coloured corduroy dress looked back at me. *I love you, Daisy. I love you, Daisy. I love you, Daisy.*

The party started at 8 p.m. At 9 p.m., no one had arrived and Tony was still in the bath. I was sitting nervously, waiting for the doorbell to ring. It was my first ever party and I wasn't sure what to expect.

Amy banged on the door. She was already drunk. She pushed up the stairs and before I could stop her, she was sitting on the floor of Tony's bathroom while he was lying in a bubble bath. I wasn't sure what to do, but Tony wasn't in the slightest bit put out, so we shared some of Amy's beers and laughed together about stories of Tony and his wild friends. I relaxed. *It's going to be OK.*

I had to tell myself that a lot.

Tony shooed us out of the bathroom when he was ready to get out of the bath. Amy stumbled out and I was following, when he called me.

'Happy Birthday,' he whispered.

'Shut up,' I said.

'In a week, you'll be eighteen. You're free, little girl.'

'Free to do what?'

'Everything,' he said, and he shooed me out of the door. 'Go. I need to make myself beautiful.'

'You are beautiful,' I said, and I meant it.

Half an hour later, Tony swanned down the stairs in a pair of tight jeans that graduated into massive flares and the tightest white vest top he could find. His hair was in a bun and his moustache groomed to perfection. He looked handsome – and also, now that I knew, he looked really, really gay.

'I thought you were playing it straight?' Amy said.

'This is straight.'

'If you say so, Doris Day.'

'If Freddie can get away with it, I can,' he said.

Poor John was second through the door with a tray full of booze, followed by a guy called Jerry who lived in leather pants and often wore a jacket but otherwise remained bare-chested.

'Party!' Poor John shouted as he rocked through the door, confused to be greeted by only three of us.

Tony wasn't worried. 'They'll be here,' he said, lighting up a joint.

'Are you sure you want to do that in front of your brother?'

He shrugged. 'Drugs are for everyone,' he said, and Amy grabbed the joint from him and took a long drag.

She offered it to me, but I was scared of what it could do to me, so I said, 'Later,' then I pretended I needed to do something in the kitchen.

The clock hit ten and two hours after the party was supposed to start, everyone arrived and the place was packed to the rafters with all sorts. The music was turned up and the house was filled with talk and laughter. I kept myself busy, serving drinks and cleaning up spills, watching Tony (under his instruction) to make sure he didn't get carried away. It was nice, watching everyone let go and have fun, but I felt outside of that world – of any world, really. It all seemed so surreal.

And then the door opened and Tony turned to see Paddy enter. He was holding a bottle of red wine and he waved it and smiled at Tony.

'Happy Birthday, brother.'

Tony hugged him tightly. 'It's good to see you,' he said, and with a lot of drink in him and at least two joints, he really meant it.

Paddy was wearing a pair of jeans and a V-neck knitted jumper. He was fresh out of the shower and he smelled of sandalwood. Maybe I'd one too many beers, but I was mesmerised. Tony was handsome, but Paddy . . . well, Paddy was something

else entirely. His pale blond hair was still damp and his blue eyes
looker bluer than ever before. I noticed how chiselled his face
was and he seemed different, lighter and brighter.

Stay away from him, Catherine. Stay well away. You can't be
trusted.

I poured him a drink and I let them catch up. Poor John was
quietly trying to talk down a very stoned Michael, who had a
wig on sideways and was trying to shove on a pair of heels to
dance to a Supremes number.

'Not tonight, Michael.'

'It's a fucking party!'

'For Tony.'

'Fine, for Tony, but can I at least sing "Over the Rainbow" at
the end of the night? It's my showstopper.'

It was boiling. There were about 150 people in a house barely
built for four. I poured myself half a glass of beer and topped it
up with white lemonade, then went outside into the yard and
sat at the little table Tony had picked up at a flea market down
town. I was sipping away and watching the stars in the sky, when
I heard a cough. I turned to see Paddy, waving that silly sweet
wave of his. Inside, Leonard Cohen was singing about his great
love, Marianne.

'Mind if I join you?'

No, yes, please do, but shit, no . . . I can't . . . Oh God, you
smell so good. Maybe just for a minute.

I pulled out the second chair. He sat.

'A bit crazy in there,' he said.

'A lot of people all right,' I replied before biting the inside of
my cheeks.

Don't touch him. Don't touch him. Just do not touch him.

'One of the blokes is singing "My Way" and dancing in a bra
and knickers,' he said.

Shit. I was supposed to be managing the chaos but I couldn't move.

'Tony has friends from all walks of life,' I said. 'He's an artist.'

'Is he?'

'Yeah, he's one of the best hairdressers in Dublin.' I couldn't help sounding proud.

'And what walk of life are you from?' Paddy asked.

He asked me personal questions all the time, but I always managed to bat them away.

'Tell me something, anything at all. Please.'

I shook my head and I smiled the way I always smiled when I avoided answering him. 'There's nothing to tell.'

He wasn't letting go this time. 'Where are you from?'

'I come from a pig farm in a small town outside Cork city.'

He laughed. 'I can't imagine you on a pig farm.'

'Well, that's me.'

'How did you end up with this lot?'

'What do you mean?'

'You are different from them, that's all.'

'No, I'm not. I'm exactly like them.' I stood up.

He grabbed my hand and I felt the electricity pass between us. I wanted to kiss him, but I couldn't let him see that. Instead, I pulled back from him.

'I didn't mean to insult you.'

His pained expression hurt.

'You didn't,' I said. 'But you insulted them and they're my friends.'

'I'm sorry. Tony's my brother.'

'Yes, he is.'

'Whatever I say now, I'll sound like a prick.'

I stepped away from him. 'If everyone was like those people in there, the world would be a much kinder place.'

I walked inside to the smoke, music, joy and laughter. Tony had drunk a little too much wine and he had forgotten all about his brother. He called me over and asked me if I was having a good time.

'Brilliant,' I lied.

'I wish you didn't always look so sad.' He drew an invisible tear on my cheek with his finger. I smiled brightly to please him and he kissed me on my forehead. Then over my head, he saw Paddy enter the room.

'I should get going,' Paddy said.

'I'm glad you came.' Tony smiled. He looked around at all of his friends having the time of their lives, then back at his brother. 'This is me, Paddy.'

'I know,' Paddy said. 'And it's OK.'

'And Mam and Dad?'

He shook his head. 'It would kill them, Tony.'

'Well, thanks for coming, Paddy.' He offered his brother his hand.

Paddy pushed it away and moved in for a hug. 'Happy birthday, brother,' he said before he turned to me. 'I'm sorry if I offended you.' He pushed through the crowd, now singing a horrible rendition of 'Ain't No Mountain High Enough'.

When the front door closed behind him, Tony looked from the door to me. 'He's a nice man, Catherine, but he'll never be one of us.'

'I know,' I said, and I felt a skewer pierce my heart. *Just you and me, Daisy.*

When I went to bed an hour later, the party was still going strong, everyone taking turns to sing and tell jokes, the filthier the better. I lay in the dark listening to them for the longest time and I talked to Daisy in my head for a while, but I couldn't get Paddy out of my mind. The way he looked at me. The way his touch felt. *Is this your first offence?* I kept hearing those words in my head, followed by Tony's warning. *He's not one of us.*

I needed to focus and keep saving if I was going to hire a solicitor to get my girl. I couldn't be distracted. I couldn't share my secret – not with Paddy, not with anyone. *He's not one of us.* That, and my downstairs area, had never been the same since Daisy's birth. It felt all wrong. I probably wasn't even fit for a man.

And still I couldn't stop thinking about him.

No. No. No. Catherine. No.

One week later, on the day of my eighteenth birthday, a large bouquet of the most beautiful flowers arrived at the salon with my name on them.

'Did you do this?' I squealed to Tony.

He looked genuinely confused. 'No.' He put up his hands. 'Just the dress and shoes, I swear.'

I opened the card. They were from Paddy.

Happy birthday, Catherine.
Please forgive me. You can be whoever you want.
Love Paddy.

Chapter Nineteen

Caroline

CAROLINE DIDN'T LEAVE HER ROOM for three days. By the third day, Dave started to worry. He stood outside the bedroom door, knocking lightly. She slept mostly; she didn't crave any kind of food at all. She sipped from a bottle of water and took her meds on an empty stomach. She was bleeding heavily, so the only time she stepped out of her bed was to sit under a shower, letting the water pour over her while cupping her hands over her small wet bandage to protect the wound from the thumping water. Her stomach was swollen with gas and pain seared through her shoulder from the build-up of trapped air. The doctors blew her up to be able to do their work in minutes, but it wasn't so quick to dissipate. It would have helped if she'd walked around more, but she didn't have the mental strength to move. She just wanted to sleep.

Dave's continuous knocking kept stopping her.

'Hello?'

'It's Dave.'

'Come in,' she said at last.

He walked in and immediately she was conscious of how dark and disarrayed the room was. Clothes flung everywhere, a pile of pyjamas and nighties overflowing from the washing basket, drugs on her locker. There was probably a stale smell, too. She hadn't considered opening the window.

'You OK?' he asked.

'Yeah. Fine. Thanks.'

'What's going on?' He sounded concerned.

He opened the curtains, letting in so much light that she sought refuge under the covers. He opened the window to let in air.

'Nothing.'

He looked at the meds and the plasters on her locker. He examined her pallor and he picked up a pink nightdress to inspect the telltale reddish-brown stains of iodine.

'You had surgery,' he said.

She nodded.

'Are you OK?'

She wanted to cry. She nodded.

'Good,' he said. 'I just need to get some clothes.'

He made his way to the walk-in-wardrobe. They'd converted the second largest spare room and a generous en suite once they agreed to stop IVF.

'I mean, who needs three spare rooms, love?'

No one does.

It had been completed two years before, and it was a real point of pride and joy for Caroline for at least five minutes. Then the fleeting feeling passed. It was lovely, but it would be lovelier with a cot, a changing table and a mobile made up of stars.

He was faffing about for a few minutes, huffing and puffing.

'What are you looking for?'

'I can never find anything here, it's too big.'

'What are you looking for?'

'My black suit.'

Dave hadn't worn a suit since he left the bank. The gas company IT section were a younger and cooler demographic, who just about carried off smart casual.

She crawled out of bed, putting pressure on her stomach incision as she walked across the room. 'It's in with the others in your occasional wardrobe.' She opened one of six doors on his side of the wardrobe. 'Remember?' she said, pointing to a row of suits.

'Thanks.' He watched her move away stiffly. 'You look skinny.'

'Don't worry; it won't last long. Where are you going?' she asked as she settled back into bed.

'Out.'

'To an interview, a wake or a wedding?'

'On a date,' he said.

She nearly fell out of the bed with the fright. 'A date?'

He appeared from the wardrobe. 'One of the lads in work set me up with a friend of his.'

Caroline refocused. 'A date with a woman.'

'Well I'm not gay, am I?'

'Now?'

'Well, my wife is trying to get pregnant with someone else, so if not now, then when?'

'That's not what this is.'

'Yes it is,' he said, and he left the room, suit, shirt and shoes in hand.

'No one wears a suit on a date, Dave,' she shouted through the closed door.

'How would you know?' he shouted back.

She would have cried if she had any tears left in her.

She couldn't stay home after he left the house. There was a meeting on, but she couldn't face it. She liked Janet, and she was happy for her, she was, and she knew Jim and her were in a mess, but she just didn't want to see her. She showered for the second time that day, pulled on some clothes. Then she got in the car and drove to her parents' house.

She pulled up outside the large dormer bungalow she'd grown up in with her parents and her sisters. She was the eldest, then

Lisa. Michelle was the baby. The garden was overgrown. Her parents were never ones to care particularly for a garden. She'd often suggested they pave the whole thing.

'Why would we? There's plenty of room for two cars as it stands and so what if it's messy? It's wild. Some of us like wild.'

Caroline had a key, but she rattled the knocker. The bell had been broken since 1987. She heard her mother call to her father.

'Would you get the door, Denis?'

'I'm in the bog!'

'Ah, for God's sake, when are you not in it!'

She opened the door and smiled on seeing her daughter. 'There she is . . .' She kissed her face before turning her head towards the toilet door, second on the left. 'It's your eldest!' she shouted. 'Come in, love. Have some tea. You look peaky. Your lady bits at you again?'

'Yeah.'

'Ah! Sorry, my darling.'

She felt like crying again. 'It's OK.'

'And how's Dave? It feels like a lifetime ago since I saw you.'

'It's been a while all right. We've been so busy with work.'

'I know. I understand. How's Bruno?'

Well, that did it. Suddenly, Caroline was in floods of tears again.

'He died, Mam.'

'Oh my darling, I am so sorry.' She turned to the bathroom. 'Denis, will you ever finish your bloody business and get out of the bathroom, your daughter needs you!'

'It's all right, Mam.'

'No. It's not. I know what he meant to you.' She looked to the sky. 'RIP, Bruno. You were loved and cherished and I thank you for minding my little girl.'

'Thanks, Mam,' she said, and then they were hugging. Her stomach hurt and her wound pinched, but it was worth it.

'I'll ring Dave.'

'No, don't, Mam.'

'Why not?' she asked, putting on the kettle.

She was just about to shout at Caroline's father about whether he wanted tea or not, when Caroline spoke again.

'I think we're splitting up,' she said, and her mother nearly dropped the kettle.

'Ah, no! Ah no! Denis, *would you ever . . .*'

Caroline's dad walked in, newspaper in hand. 'There she is . . .' he said with his arms wide open.

'Caroline and Dave are splitting up!' her mother cried.

'Ah no, but sure, why?' he said, stepping back a little.

Caroline blinked back tears. 'I wanted to do another round of IVF. He didn't want to.'

Denis sat heavily into the chair. Her mother sat beside him and they faced their daughter, all thought of tea forgotten.

'You've been through so much,' she said.

'I know.'

'And you're splitting up because he doesn't want another round of IVF?' Denis asked.

'No, because I wanted to go ahead and do it without him.'

'Well, as far as I know, he's quite important to the process.'

'You can buy sperm now, Dad.'

'Ah stop! Sure, what in the name of God would you be doing that for?'

'To have a baby.'

'Ah, Caroline, what are you thinking?' her mother said.

'That I destroyed my marriage.'

'And a baby?' her dad asked.

'There is none. There'll never be one. My womb can't carry a child.' She spoke flatly. She was numb to it now.

'And Dave can't forgive you?' her mother said.

'Dave doesn't know.'

'So tell him!' Denis said.

'He's on a date.'

'Ah stop!'

'So, wait till he comes home and tell him then,' her mother said.

'Tell him what? Tell him I can't carry a child so he's my second choice?'

'Well, don't put it that way, Caroline!'

'I need to just think for a while, Mam.'

'Well, don't think too long,' she said, and after that, she got up slowly and started peeling spuds. 'Let me feed you bacon and cabbage, your favourite.'

It was never her favourite, but after three days of starving, suddenly the smell of salty bacon was tempting.

'How's Michelle?' she asked, and her mother froze. 'I know she's pregnant again, Mam.'

She turned to her daughter. 'Please don't make a fuss again, Caroline.'

'Of course I won't.'

She felt terrible. *I'm a terrible human being.*

After dinner, her father took her to his shed out the back. He liked to paint there, mostly seascapes and the odd landscape. He unveiled his latest piece of work; it was similar to the last three, but different, too.

'I like it.'

He sat down on a stool and he pointed to a chair. She sat.

'We should never have made you study law.'

'What?'

'I know you always wanted to be a mother. I remember you obsessed with your dolls from the age of dot.'

'Don't know what that has to do with law, Dad.'

'You had a baby doll. The bloody thing looked so real, you nearly gave poor Mrs Harris a heart attack when you dropped it and picked it up by the arm.'

She remembered. Mrs Harris was asthmatic. She had to have three puffs of her inhaler to steady her nerves. Caroline had rustled through her bag for it and administered it. She had felt so grown up and helpful.

'You would have made a lovely mother, Caroline, and Dave a good father. Your child would have been one of the lucky ones, but it wasn't to be, and in the absence of having something else to focus on, you've lost your way.'

'I like law.'

'No, you tolerate it,' he said.

Not anymore, she thought.

'It's good money,' Caroline said.

'It is, and a younger me cared about that stuff. Coming out of a recession and raising three girls on a taxi man's salary.'

'We did fine, Dad.'

'Doesn't mean I didn't make mistakes. But, Caroline, you should have been a nurse. If you weren't talking, feeding or changing that baby doll, you were bandaging your teddies, your grandparents and even the postman.'

She laughed at the memory. She had a bandage for every occasion.

'That was a long time ago and a very different me.'

'A girl who wasn't driven by the things she couldn't have and who delighted in the things she did.'

Caroline sighed. 'I've a lot of people to apologise to.'

'Take my apology first.'

She smiled at him. 'Thanks, Dad.'

'How's Bruno?' he asked just as she stood to leave.

'He died, Daddy.'

'Ah no! It was time, though, wasn't it, my girl?'

She nodded. 'Yeah.'

'Everything has its time,' he said, and she wiped away a tiny stray tear.

He pulled out a painting from behind a sheet and held it up. It was a picture of Bruno.

'Now, I'm not brilliant at dogs, but I worked really hard.'

'Oh, Dad, it's amazing.'

'I think I got his eyes right.'

'They're perfect.'

'They're a bit like the sea.'

'They're exactly like the sea,' she said, and she sniffed and hugged the painting. 'I love it. Thanks so much.'

'And I love you. Don't be such a stranger.'

'OK.'

She drove home with a full stomach and a warm heart, with the painting of Bruno in the front seat of the car. She parked the car and walked up the stairs to the bedroom, placing the painting on the dresser opposite the bed.

'There you are,' she said to her beloved dog.

She turned out the light so that she could pretend to go to sleep, when in actual fact she was never more awake in her life. She heard the ping of the phone. *Maybe it's Dave and he needs rescuing.* She turned on the light and sat up to read the text.

It was her dad:

Find your passion again, my girl. It will save you. I promise.
Love, Dad.

A Dick with a P

Catherine

IDIDN'T SEE PADDY IN THE weeks that followed my birthday. He was focused on his final year studies and although he'd sent those lovely flowers, after a while I figured he'd given up on me. Every day of his absence felt like a year and, despite trying not to, I ached for him. Part of me was relieved, the other part devastated by the loss of him. I didn't have a right to be. I knew that. I hadn't given him any real reason to think I was interested. I might have even been unkind. After all, he had tried his best.

I refocused on my work and on saving up. All of my money went into a tin that was covered in daisies. *I'm going to get you back, Daisy. We're going to be a family.* I didn't need distraction, but that didn't mean I didn't dream about Paddy day and night. It didn't mean I didn't spend time staring out of that window of Viva watching every passer-by. It just meant that my priority was to get my daughter back.

Tony became my inspiration. If he could survive and thrive in this terrible world, I could, too. He'd suffered relentless bullying at school and left just aged sixteen. After much consternation, his parents agreed to send him to hairdressing school. His father was a gynaecologist and his mother an academic who worked out of Trinity College, so to have a hairdresser for a son was a kick in the nuts. At least that's what Tony said. He worked in a hairdressing chain till he was twenty-five, and then opened his own salon using money he inherited from his grandfather. He planned on opening more and creating a chain of his own. He was a talented hairdresser with a head for figures and he'd built a successful business.

Paddy was following in his father's footsteps. He was the good son. Tony tried to pretend it didn't matter to him, but I knew it did. Tony's achievements were never celebrated, his success never recognised. He bought his own house while he was still working as a stylist, when he was only twenty-three. He got a mortgage on his own and he scrimped and saved, renting out the spare bedroom until he was in a position to afford the payments alone. He was out in the world, forging his own path since he was a teenager, while his brother, the golden boy, at twenty-four had never earned a pound in his life and was still living at home. Tony didn't care that Paddy was the favourite; he just wished his parents cared about him at all. I knew how he felt.

One month after my birthday, I woke to pounding on the front door. I heard Tony's feet thudding on the stairs and jumped out of bed, grabbing my dressing gown. I threw it round my shoulders and as I made my way out onto the landing, I heard Tony's voice.

'God Almighty, Paddy, what happened to you?'

I was down the stairs before I knew it and staring at Paddy. He was bleeding from his nose.

'A punch.' His left eye was swelling.

'Why?'

'Does it matter?' he said.

Tony turned to me. 'It's OK, Catherine, go back to bed.'

'No, don't. Stay. Please stay,' Paddy said.

I pulled my dressing gown on and buttoned it up.

'What happened?' I asked.

'I'm a dick with a capital P,' he said.

I couldn't help it. I smiled.

'I'm sorry about what I said at the party,' he said to me.

'It's OK.'

'What did you say?' Tony asked. He was assessing the damage to Paddy's nose by squeezing it.

'Ouch!'

'It's definitely not broken,' Tony said before turning to me. 'Catherine, hold his nose and his head back. I'll look for something to stem the blood.'

I swapped places with him. I placed my fingers gently on the bridge of Paddy's nose and with the other hand, I cradled the back of his neck. He moaned a little and placed his hand gently on my hip. *Oh God. Don't, Catherine. No.* But I couldn't help it; even with a swollen eye and bloodstained face, his touch lit me up. At the same time, I remembered the cold whipping my legs, the smell of the priest cycling his bike, the grotto lying ahead, the bang of the heavy door, the cold tiles under my bleeding feet. *Please, Catherine. You can't ever be Katie again.*

Tony was clattering around in the kitchen. 'I can't find any fucking cloths.'

'What are you thinking?' Paddy said to me, and our eyes locked.

'You don't want to know.'

'I do.'

'I'm thinking, how did a good boy like you end up in a fight?'

'It wasn't much of a fight,' he said.

'Do we even have kitchen roll?' Tony shouted from the kitchen.

'We ran out earlier. Just grab a tea towel.'

'Oh no. I love those tea towels.'

'Oh, for God's sake, Tony, the blood will wash off.'

274

I could feel Paddy's hand on my hip, his touch sending shock waves through my entire body. I needed to pull away, fast, but I couldn't seem to move.

'Trust me, I've been punched enough to know. The blood never disappears entirely,' Tony said.

He entered the room holding up a bag of peas in one hand and a tea towel and an apron in the other. He looked pointedly at his brother and at the hand rested above my hip. I let go of the bridge of Paddy's nose and we swapped places again. As soon as my hip was free of his hand, I felt cold, like I was missing something. Tony placed the towel against his brother's nose and the bag of frozen peas on his eye.

'How does that feel?'

'Terrible,' Paddy said.

'Yeah, well, it will pass,' Tony said.

'How many times have you been punched?' Paddy asked.

'Too many to count,' Tony said.

'Because of what you are?'

'Yes,' Tony said evenly.

Paddy took the bag of peas from his eye. 'At the party . . . I told Catherine I didn't think she was one of you.' He had the decency to looked shameful about it.

Tony pulled away, but Paddy grabbed his arm. 'I don't know why I said it.'

'You said it because you believe it,' Tony said.

'You're different, Tony, but that's OK, because so is she.' He looked across at me. 'And that's what I love about her.'

My knees almost buckled.

'But I was wrong, so fixed it. I told everyone my brother was a queer and that I think it's groovy.' The word groovy didn't sound right coming out of Paddy's mouth.

'You did *what*?' Tony said.

275

'I don't want to be one of them,' Paddy said. 'I'd rather be one of you.'

'You are a fucking idiot,' Tony said.

'Yeah, I worked that out as I was hitting the ground.'

'You have no idea what it means to be one of us,' Tony said.

'I'm sorry.' Paddy looked like he was about to cry.

Tony softened. 'Don't be. I'm glad you don't.' He turned to me. 'He can sleep on the sofa,' he said, and he walked up the stairs.

'I'm trying, Catherine,' Paddy said.

'I know, but maybe you should start by not calling your brother a queer,' I said gently.

I knew he was doing his best and I felt bad for him out there with all those cold, ordinary people. Then there was the fact that he said he loved me. Tony and I had chosen to ignore it in the moment, but it was out there.

Tony and Paddy were very different, but I could see the similarities between them. Paddy wasn't as open or empathetic as his brother, but then he was a white male from a good family and had never been given the opportunity to learn from pain, exclusion, intolerance, hate or cruelty, so how could he be? He didn't have any secrets. He had nothing to hide. The world embraced him and it was designed for his success.

The world had not embraced me.

'You should sleep,' I said, and I moved to get some blankets from the hot press, but then Paddy was holding my hand and looking at me with his blue eyes.

'What are you hiding, Catherine?'

'Does it matter?' I asked, and I think I stammered a little, because all I could do was feel his touch and hear his words: *and that's what I love about her . . .*

So he thought he loved me? I'd heard that before. That was how the nightmare started.

Is this your first offence?

'Only if it matters to you,' he said, and I wanted to believe him, that who I was and what I'd done and what had been done to me didn't matter. But it did.

He kissed me then, and I couldn't help it: I kissed him back and he wrapped his arms around me. I sunk into him and it felt so good and I didn't want it to stop – but there she was, Sister Buckaroo, staring me down with contempt. *Is this your first offence?*

I pushed him away.

'No,' I said regretfully and he said he was terribly sorry and explained that he'd been drinking, as though he was mentioning it for the first time.

'You should sleep,' I said, and I threw the bedclothes on the sofa and ran up the stairs.

I lay in bed worrying about what it all meant, feeling sick inside.

I knew Paddy was as lonely as I was, lonelier really. I knew from Tony what kind of house he lived in. Tony's parents were introverts, lost in their own work and not particularly family orientated. They both had studies where they would disappear into for hours on end. Paddy was thirteen when Tony packed his bags and moved into a student hostel in town. He wasn't as introverted or academic as his parents but he wasn't an extrovert either. He liked studying and working in the hospital. His parents were so absent it almost felt like he had the place to himself. He didn't mind being alone most of the time. He liked it. I liked that about him; I liked being alone too. The institutions had not just taught me self-reliance, they had isolated me from others and from the world, so that even amongst the noise and chaos of Tony's life, I was always apart from it. I was alone, like Paddy.

But in Paddy I had someone to be alone with. It was all so confusing. I wondered what he expected of me, and worried about that. I couldn't make another mistake. I had to be strong for Daisy. I had a plan that I needed to stick to.

I didn't sleep a wink that night.

Chapter Twenty

Natalie

LINDA BEGGED NATALIE TO STAY, but she couldn't. There was nothing really left to say. They wanted very different lives and no one was to blame, it just was what it was. She would miss Linda more than she thought she could ever miss anyone or anything, but she knew she could never trust her again. What if Natalie really had become pregnant with Linda's brother's baby? What if Linda still felt the same? What if she was left alone while her partner remained torn? Linda had lied to Natalie, to Paul and probably even to herself. It had been a lucky escape.

Natalie blamed herself too. *What was I thinking? Why didn't I see? What did I nearly do?*

She and Linda were wrong for one another. She should have admitted that instead of papering the cracks, just hoping against hope that love would be enough. Sometimes it's not. She knew that now. And as much as she had mourned the baby that never was, she was relieved. It wasn't right and it never would be and finally she was rid of stupid bloody *Paul.*

They shared one last night together. Linda cried through most of it, but they toasted one another's health.

'I wish you love,' Natalie said.

'I wish you a different kind of love,' Linda said.

They drank and they kissed and they had sex and they cried, then they drank some more.

The next morning Linda left the house before Natalie woke. She found a note on her pillow:

I can't watch you go.

Natalie packed up everything she owned. In truth it didn't amount to much more than three cases, a backpack and an overflowing handbag. All the furniture was Linda's; in fact, looking around, she realised everything in the house was Linda's. She booked into a hotel near her office, left her bags there and went to work.

She didn't talk to anyone. She just lost herself in numbers. She felt safe and comfortable there, only breaking for lunch. She was a creature of habit, always eating lunch in the same spot just four doors down from the office, sometimes with workmates and sometimes alone. The coffee shop was busy that day, but she managed to grab a stool at the long counter that ran the length of the glass window looking out onto the canal. She was sitting in front of an uneaten chicken sandwich, staring into the middle distance, when she spotted Paul approach.

He barrelled through the narrow shop to grab a stool beside her, drinking a takeaway coffee from another establishment. If anyone noticed, they didn't say. He wanted her to know that he was sorry about everything.

'It's not your fault,' Natalie said. 'It's mine and Linda's. I'm sorry we dragged you into our mess.' She meant it.

'I'm not. You forced me to make an effort. You gave me focus, something to do. It was nice feeling needed, if not wanted . . .' He laughed easily.

She got up to leave. 'I'm sorry I made you feel that way. I can be a real bitch.'

'And I can be a fucking dick,' he said and she laughed.

He followed her out the door.

'I'm glad you're happy, Paul.'

'Look,' he said as they walked towards her office, 'I know my sister and I know she's not maternal. She was wrong to hide it but she just wanted to make you happy.'

'Did you know how she felt?' Natalie asked.

Paul shrugged. 'I guessed when she didn't attend the insemination. I was more excited about it than she was.'

'Is that why you wouldn't do it again?'

He nodded. 'She's my sister and she was miserable.'

'How's it going with Sylvia?'

'It's early days, but I really like her. Honestly, if I have a kid, I think I'd like it to be with her.'

'Wow, I really like this Paul. I might even miss him.'

'Don't worry, I'll be a tit again in five minutes.'

They hugged in front of Natalie's shiny four-storey block of offices. She thought about phoning Linda to tell her of the peace brokered between her and Paul, but she didn't. She had to get used to not sharing her life with Linda anymore.

Linda was busy fighting her case, fighting for other people's families. They were the ones who needed her. Natalie would miss her spirit, her care, her concern for those whom few others bothered with. She'd even miss the low moods brought on by mourning the loss and losses of strangers. She'd just miss Linda.

Natalie went back into her office and worked till seven. She picked up her phone and saw a message from Ronnie: *Caroline's womb is super fucked. Poor thing is devastated. Hope you are OK. See you at the meeting?*

Shit!

The meeting was at eight, and it was that or sit in a shitty Travelodge all evening.

It had already started when Natalie made it in. Sheena made a face and tapped her watch. Ronnie and Janet had kept a seat for her and waved her over. Caroline was nowhere in sight. A new woman Natalie hadn't seen before was talking about her experience of fertility drugs. Normally, Natalie would have given this woman her full attention, but tonight she was only interested in news of Caroline.

She sat down beside Ronnie. 'What happened?' she whispered.

'She took a cancellation appointment to get rid of the endometrioma. It was massive; her womb's in shreds.'

'Shit,' Natalie said.

'Anything you'd like to share with the group, Natalie?' Sheena asked, raising her eyebrows.

'No thanks.'

'Sure?'

'I'm fine. Thank you.'

Sheena nodded to the other woman to speak.

Natalie leaned in to Janet. 'You OK?'

'I'm fine. Jim didn't cheat. He was just sad and needed someone to talk to.'

'Sure?'

'I'm positive. Seriously. It's all good.'

Natalie smiled at her. 'One out of three.'

'And you?' Ronnie asked, and tears welled in Natalie's eyes.

'It's all gone to shit.'

'I'm sorry, Natalie. Vicky here is trying to talk,' Sheena said.

'I'm so sorry, Vicky.'

'No, really, it's fine, I'm done,' Vicky said, and the room fell silent.

All of a sudden, Natalie was aware that everyone was staring at her. *What the hell am I doing here? I don't even have a relationship, never mind trying for a child.*

'Me too,' Natalie said, and she stood up and walked across the floor.

Sheena called after her. 'Natalie? For God's sake. Please?'

'I don't belong here anymore.'

Natalie kept walking. The cold air smacked her in the face. She barely had time to recover, when Ronnie and Janet were by her side.

'What happened?' Janet asked.

'I left Linda.'

'Wow!' Ronnie said. 'What the hell is wrong with you people?'

'Turns out she didn't want a baby, after all.'

'Oh,' Janet said.

'Yeah.'

'Not a massive surprise though, is it?' Ronnie said.

'No,' Natalie said. 'I suppose it isn't. Please, for fuck's sake, change the subject.'

Ronnie sighed. 'It's been a pretty shit week all round, really.'

'Except for Janet,' Natalie said. 'I'm really happy for you, Janet.'

'Don't be, not yet – not for a long time.'

The women nodded.

'How's Caroline?'

'Terrible,' Ronnie said.

'Should we visit her?' Janet asked.

'No. She'll come round when she's ready.'

'She's right,' Natalie said. 'Look, I should go.'

'Where are you staying?' Ronnie asked.

'A Travelodge.'

'Bollocks to that,' Ronnie said.

'What?'

'You'll stay with me.'

'No. I couldn't.'

'We're friends, aren't we?'

'Yeah, but . . .'

'I have a spare bedroom, parking and I'm a stone's throw from the M50.'

Natalie didn't know what to think. Everything was happening so fast.

I don't even know you. Not really.

'Don't worry, I'm not a psycho. Besides, you can't live in a Travelodge, for fuck's sake,' Ronnie said.

Natalie nodded slowly. 'I'll start looking for a place tomorrow,' she said.

'Good. Let's get your stuff,' Ronnie said.

So that was what they did.

The Baby, Imelda

Catherine

O N THURSDAYS THE SALON was open till 8 p.m. so that all of the ladies could get their hair done in time for the week-end. After that, we cleaned up and were usually ready to leave just after nine. By then, I was a full-time stylist – still in training, but I didn't have to answer the phones anymore. Tony hired a Sligo girl called Rachel. She had a Mohawk, a ring in her nose and wore nothing but denim. She was sweet and liked to laugh. I liked her.

I was brushing my client's hair from the floor, when Paddy appeared behind me.

'Tony said you can leave – if you want to, that is?'

Tony and I hadn't discussed Paddy's declaration of love. I couldn't bring myself to talk about it and all he said to me the following morning was, 'Be careful, Catherine.' I told him I would be.

When I turned, Paddy was holding out my jacket for me. It had been two weeks since the kiss and I'd missed him. I put down the brush and he smiled. As he helped me put on my jacket, I brushed against him and my insides fluttered and burned. Once again, I had to tell myself *no*.

It didn't take much to dampen down my desire. I'd just pic-ture the bull priest and I'd feel the cold on my bare feet and that crossbar. I'd picture Buckaroo, *Is this your first offence? Katie.*

10078. I'd picture my escape and my recapture and I'd feel my heart break. The stone on the walls, the smell of wax on wood, the click-clack on the tiles, the steel bed, the rough blankets, those terrible three dresses, the pain, the swelling, the cruel birth, my little girl being torn away.

It didn't take much to harden my resolve, but all the love and lust and fear I felt when Paddy touched my hand made my head spin. I wanted to tell him to leave the salon and never come back. I wanted him to know that I was broken and that he should stay away from me. But I couldn't say those words – they stuck in my chest. So I clung on to his hand and we left the salon. We walked down Dawson Street towards Trinity College.

'Please let me show you Trinity,' he said. 'My student card will no longer grant me access come September.' He sounded sad.

'OK.'

I knew the chances of meeting Justin were slim, particularly at this time of night, and anyway, I was done running. When we walked onto the grounds, they were lit up. Although there was a lot of grey stone, it wasn't sinister at all. Instead, the place was warm and inviting and filled with young people buzzing about. There was an energy about the place that I couldn't quite understand, but it felt good.

He took me to the pub and we sat in a dark corner under an archway. I sipped on a shandy and he talked to me about the hospital, the patients and all the carry-on there. The life-and-death stuff was fascinating – the politics of it all, not so much. I talked about the salon and all of our clients. We talked about music, but he really didn't know very much on that score. I talked about the films that I'd go and see on a Saturday afternoon, but he often worked shifts on Saturdays, so he didn't have much time for films.

'You're beautiful,' he said out of nowhere.

'Stop it.'

'And I like that you know what you want.'

He didn't know what I wanted. He didn't know me at all. How could he?

'You know what you want,' I said. 'You'll have your medical degree.'

'I was told what I want. It's different.'

'But you like what you do.'

'I'm lucky it's working out. That is, if I don't fail.'

'You won't,' I said. I knew from Tony that Paddy had received top marks throughout his medical training. His graduation was a formality.

I thought about Justin and how stressed he was over a simple Leaving Cert. *Loser*.

'I like that you're independent,' he said. 'You don't need anyone.'

'I'd be lost without your brother.'

'And I like that you're loyal to him.'

'He's loyal to me.'

'I like that you say what you think and you don't tell lies.'

That hurt. I did tell lies. I lied every day.

'I'm going to graduate in September. I want you to be there and to meet my parents.'

'I can't, Paddy,' I said.

'Please, Catherine, just give me a chance.'

'It's not you.'

'Please, don't . . .'

He reached out for me and I shifted away. His touch was like a magnet. If I got too close . . .

'I can't be your girlfriend,' I blurted.

'Why not? You like me. I know you do. I can feel it. I know it.' He looked pained.

'Why isn't friendship enough?'

'Don't you want someone in your life?' he asked, and he was so handsome and so sweet and not full of shit like Justin. He was honest and straightforward and when he looked at me, my heart raced and my palms sweated.

'Some day,' I said, but I knew his patience was fading. I needed to get out of here or maybe I'd never leave. I stood up. 'I have to go.'

Always running, Catherine.

He stood. 'Catherine, please.'

I grabbed my jacket. I made my way through the busy pub in the dark, people bumping into me and me into them. I just needed them all to move and move fast before my legs gave way. I burst out into the warm evening and I stopped to take a breath, but Paddy was behind me.

'Catherine.'

I turned round.

'I love you,' he said, and I couldn't bear it.

'You don't know me, Paddy.'

'I don't know information about you because you won't share it – but I know you.'

I wanted to run, but surrounded by all that grey stone, standing on a cobblestone yard, I suddenly felt faint. He didn't have to catch me, but all of a sudden he was by my side and together we were navigating our way through the Trinity arch and onto College Green.

'Can't you trust me, Catherine?' he asked.

I shook my head. *He's not one of us.*

'I don't want to see you anymore, Paddy,' I told him.

He looked like he might cry.

'I wish you the best and I know you'll have a lovely life. You deserve it,' I said.

And then I stood at my bus stop and I watched him pass by.

Paddy didn't call into the shop after that. I didn't talk to Tony about it and he didn't ask. I felt broken and so very alone. I missed him as I showered and I missed him staring into my cup of tea. I missed him on the bus into town and I missed him while I was cutting hair. I missed him when I talked about the weather and I missed him when Poor John and Tony broke up because Poor John was sleeping with another man. I missed him when Tony took to his bed for a week, when I took him food and tissues and listened to him cry. I missed him when Poor John handed in his notice and left, and I missed him when Mrs Justin O'Halloran walked into the shop with a pram and her baby inside it.

She had been in twice since the wedding; Tony had cut her hair both times but he could barely fit in his clients who actually made appointments, never mind interviewing for replacement staff and recovering from a broken heart. Amy was up to her eyes, so I was all they had to offer her.

'You gave me the Farrah,' she said.

'Did I? I do a lot of those.' I tried to play it cool, but inside I was raging.

She sat down in the seat and she pushed the pram with one hand while I examined her hair.

'Just a trim?' I asked.

'No, I want a change. Something different. You know?'

'I think a bob would suit you.' I placed my hands on her hair to show her how it would frame her delicate face.

She smiled. 'Yes, that sounds perfect.'

I tried not to look at the baby. I couldn't bear it. *Stay strong. Stay strong. Stay strong. Oh, Daisy, help me.* I needed to focus on something other than her child or my child, because my nerves were burning and my head was buzzing. It felt like my Daisy was being ripped away all over again.

I focused on Paddy as I stared at her pretty blonde hair. I wanted to cry on his shoulder. I wanted to tell him everything. I wanted him to know me and all that I'd been through. I wanted him to know Daisy. I wanted to say her name out loud.

Jen peeped into the pram and sighed. 'Asleep! Finally,' she said, and she stopped pushing the pram. 'She's been grizzly all day.'

She! A girl like my girl. *Oh, Daisy, where are you?*

'How old is she?' I asked, attempting to unclench my jaw as I spoke.

'Nearly two months,' she said. 'The image of her father, all that black hair.'

Daisy looked like him, too. What do you look like now, Daisy? Would I know you? Would you know me?

'She's beautiful,' I said. 'What's her name?'

'Imelda, after her grandmother – her father's mother. I wasn't exactly happy initially, but it's grown on me and she idolises her.'

Does she? What a bitch.

I tried to change the subject. 'I think you said you were doing law?'

'You have a good memory.'

'I was impressed, is all. Not many girls I know get to study law,' I said, and I was lying, but I was also telling the truth.

'I dropped out after the baby. It was the right thing to do.'

'Do you miss it?'

'Yeah, I really do . . . Thanks for asking.' She seemed sad.

'Still, it must be nice to be a mother.' I gulped back my own tears. *Don't break. Don't break. Don't break.*

'It is.' She hesitated. 'But the truth is, she wasn't planned. I would have liked to have waited, but you know . . .'

I nodded. *I do.*

'I'm being too personal,' she said. She seemed suddenly embarrassed.

'Don't be silly. You know what they say about hairdressers – we're fifty per cent stylists, fifty per cent agony aunts.' I forced a chuckle, but it came out more like a cough.

She asked me if I was OK and I nodded.

'I don't get out much – you know, with the baby.'

'Would you like a cup of tea? And maybe some bourbons?'

'God, I'd love that.'

After that, I calmed myself down and we talked about general things, staying away from the personal.

When the bob was done, she grinned. 'It'll be so much easier to manage,' she said.

It really suited her. She was very pretty and she was nice for a posh girl. I prayed the child wouldn't wake. I couldn't watch her hold it; I knew that much. I was quick – at least as quick as I could be while doing a decent job. Tony checked it before she stood up.

'Beautiful,' he said.

I walked her to the reception and Rachel took her money. She beckoned me before she left.

'This is for you,' she said, and she handed me two pound notes. 'Take it. I love my hair. Thanks.'

It was when she moved towards the door that I saw Justin through the window. He was ashen-faced. He was still handsome, but he was nothing on Paddy. I didn't give him a moment to register any feeling; I just walked into the back with his two pounds in my pocket.

I don't know what lies he told his wife that day, but I never saw either of them again.

Chapter Twenty-One

Janet

R ONNIE INVITED THE WOMEN over for coffee the next morning via text. Caroline declined the invite, but Ronnie wasn't having any of it. She told Janet to pick her up anyway.

Janet pulled up outside her house and honked the horn. When Caroline didn't appear, she got out of the car and rang the bell. Then she rang it again and again and she knocked and then she phoned Caroline. She could hear the phone ringing through the open upstairs window. She stood back and shouted in her loudest voice.

'I'm not leaving here without you.'

Caroline appeared in the window. 'For fuck's sake,' was all she said.

Fifteen minutes later, she was dressed and slowly making her way to the car. Caroline made it clear she didn't want to talk, so Janet whacked up the radio and just drove.

Ronnie's apartment was a new build just off a roundabout and four minutes from the airport. The building was imposing, not exactly pretty, but every apartment had a good-sized balcony; some overlooked the roundabout, but others more fortunate had a view into the distance of green fields, although the grounds immediately underneath were a wasteland. There was another block half built and the area was still a large building site. The communal areas were kept well and the lift was nice and big. There were lots of windows, which was nice aside from the stupid view of the roundabout. *I mean, who builds overlooking a roundabout!*

It was much better inside than out. Ronnie's apartment was huge. That was a surprise. It was furnished with expensive furniture and the walls were alive with photo after photo telling a story of a life filled with adventure and love. The biggest photo was one over the fireplace; it was of Ronnie dressed in her pilot's uniform, with her arms around her parents. Ronnie's head was thrown back, laughing, her dad's mouth wide open and smiling, her mother wiping away a happy tear.

Janet was drawn to that photo. She just stood looking at it, taking it all in. She patted her stomach.

'Wow, this is stunning,' Caroline said, looking around.

'The view of the wasteland is shit, but apparently they have a plan to get it sorted in the next few years.' Ronnie called out for Natalie.

She emerged from her room a minute or two later, eyes puffy from crying. She hugged Caroline. 'I'm so sorry, Caroline.'

'I'm sorry, too,' Caroline said.

Ronnie and Janet stood back, allowing the two women some space. Then Ronnie made coffee and they sat at her dining table, looking out over the wasteland, drinking coffee. Janet had a glass of water. She wasn't drinking any stimulants because of the baby. She didn't want to make a big deal of it in front of Caroline and Natalie; she felt awkward, no longer a part of the club. They didn't try to make her feel like that, but that hug between Natalie and Caroline was heartfelt. She had barely got a mumble out of her the whole way there.

'Do you have any sisters or brothers?' Caroline asked, focusing on the many photos of Ronnie with different people all over the world.

'Only child,' Ronnie said. 'Mum and Dad's pride and joy.'

She smiled as she said it, but sadness crept around the edges of her eyes. Janet noticed a look between Caroline and Ronnie. They knew something she didn't, but that was OK.

'Can I ask what happened?' Natalie said.

Janet noticed she and Caroline were holding hands.

'Mum had cancer and she fought for a long time. Dad lasted six months without her. His heart just gave up.'

'Oh God. I'm so sorry,' Janet said.

Caroline grabbed Ronnie's hand. Now, the three of them were holding hands. No one offered Janet a hand. She just kept hers firmly on her stomach.

She felt like the odd man out. She was once a part of their club, but now her pregnancy had nullified her membership. She'd seen it before with other women who had once been a part of the group. As soon as they became pregnant, they were out. No one wanted to hear from them again. She was one of those women.

Janet wanted to go home. She wanted to eat dinner with Jim and seal their new start.

She got up to go to the bathroom, more because she wanted to give the others a minute alone than because she needed to pee.

When she saw the heavy bloodstains in her knickers, it was a shock.

Oh no!

She wiped herself: more fresh blood. *Oh God, no!* She pulled up her pants and didn't stop to wash her hands – instead, she was through the door, out into the hallway and into the sitting room within seconds. She was already crying.

'I'm losing the baby.'

Caroline, Natalie and Ronnie stood in unison. They were on top of her within seconds.

'Calm down,' Caroline said gently. 'Nice and easy does it.'

Breathing was becoming an issue. 'I can't. I can't calm down.'

'Yes, you can,' said Natalie. 'We're going to the hospital. I'm driving. Let's go.'

Natalie led the way with Janet following, Caroline and Ronnie bringing up the rear. Natalie sat Janet in the front seat of her car while the other two got in the back. She started to drive and just as she exited the apartment grounds, dark clouds rolled in and seemed to merge to create a blanket of darkness. They hadn't even hit the roundabout before the skies opened and rain bounced down on the bonnet.

Janet cried into her hands as Natalie navigated her way through traffic, her windscreen wipers going ninety to the dozen, just giving her flashes of pictures of what lay ahead of them.

'Pull over!' Caroline said. 'You can't see two feet in front of you.'

'No way.'

'Drive in the bus lane,' Ronnie shouted.

'You'll get fined,' Caroline said.

Natalie pulled into it. 'I don't give a shit.'

'Good for you,' Ronnie said.

Janet just cried silently.

Natalie spotted the garda car up ahead just as they passed the Church of the Holy Child. She overtook two cars in what Ronnie described as a rock-solid move. Then she drove up his arse and beeped him out of the way, which no one in the car thought a good idea.

'I can't be arrested!' Janet cried.

The garda car stopped and a guard who was about six foot four and built like a brick stormed towards Natalie, who rolled down the window and was instantly soaked.

'My friend is miscarrying. Help us get to the Rotunda Hospital. Please.'

He looked in at the fragile, frightened Janet who was sobbing at the mention of the word 'miscarrying'. Then he nodded. 'We'll have you there in a jiffy, love. You hang in there.'

Within seconds, his sirens pealed and the cars parted as he cleared the roads until they hit the hospital. Ronnie and Caroline took Janet by the arm, leaving Natalie to park and to thank the guard.

They're holding my hand now. I'm one of the gang again. Oh no, I don't want to be.

Please don't die.

At reception, Janet explained who she was and asked for her consultant.

'Aidan Greene – he knows me well. It's happened before.'

The nurse guided her into a wheelchair. 'Aidan's at a delivery, but we'll get you in to see one of his team.' She patted her on the shoulder. 'You're here now,' she said, and she wheeled her away from her friends.

'Jim! Jim needs to know!' Janet shouted after them. 'I left my phone in the car. The code is 550055 and you'll find him under Smookey Poo.'

It was something they used to call one another in the early years; they grew out of it, but the legacy remained on her phone. At any other time, it would have been embarrassing, but she barely registered it.

The nurse wheeled her straight into radiology and she ended up in the same room she'd been in a year before with Derek. Janet was shaking like a leaf, hugging herself, unable to stop. *Don't die, please don't die.* Her breathing was rapid and shallow.

'It's my fault. I didn't take the heparin for the first twelve weeks. I didn't know. I should have known. It's my fault.' She was crying again.

The nurse said something kind and then there was someone else in the room and she was talking to that person instead. Janet could hear those around her speak, but their voices were distant and imperceptible. She could see figures moving in a blur around her. She was underwater, gasping for air.

It was the nurse who finally pulled her out of it. One minute she was drowning and the next she was holding a woman's hand. She could see her and hear her and she was telling her, 'We've got you.' Janet lay on the table and she felt the nurse hitch up her jumper and roll down her trousers.

The jelly hit her stomach and the cold sent chills up her spine and a shock wave through the top of her head. She could feel a headache form behind her left eye and as the radiographer pulled the monitor close to him and into her eyeline, she squeezed her eyes shut.

'Janet?'

'Yes.'

'Look. Come on, open your eyes. Meet your baby.'

What?

She opened her eyes and there on the screen in front of her was an actual foetus, with a head and a nose, a mouth, a big old curvy stomach and something that looked like a foot.

'Perfect,' he said, rolling his probe around her stomach.

'Perfect?' she repeated. She sat up and stared at it.

'Everything is developing as normal.'

She couldn't believe her eyes. 'But the blood?'

'Lots of women spot.'

'But there's so much.'

'I see from your notes you need heparin. You're on Fragmin – two subcutaneous injections daily?'

'Yes.'

'That would do it. The heparin thins the blood, so bleeding is not uncommon.' He snapped off his gloves. 'You're fine and baby is fine.' He smiled at her. 'Things are looking good.'

She was immediately hit by such a wave of joy that it almost washed her away. The baby was fine. Everything was fine.

Then she thought about Jim and how he'd missed it. 'Any chance of a photo?'

'No problem.'

Janet floated out of the radiography department with feet light as a feather. She found Jim and her friends in the waiting room on the ground floor.

Jim stood up, ashen-faced. 'Babe, I'm so sorry.'

She held up the picture. 'I'm fine, Jim. We're both fine!'

He walked to her and snapped the photo out of her hands. 'Oh,' he said, and his nose was red and his eyes were teeming like the rain outside. 'Oh, look. Hello.' He turned to the others to show them the picture. 'Did ya see, ladies? That's our baby.'

He was hugging Janet and he couldn't seem to stop crying. Despite her happiness, for a brief moment Janet thought about Caroline and Natalie and any pain her baby would cause them. She heard Ronnie in her head. *One out of three . . .*

'I'm sorry,' she heard herself say.

'For what?' Caroline said.

'I'm no longer in the club.'

Natalie looked at her. 'Is that what you think?'

'I don't want to be a reminder of . . . I don't want to hurt you.' She was looking at Caroline, but she was talking to all three of them.

Caroline moved slowly towards her and put her arms around her. 'You could never hurt me,' she said, and she was crying, too. 'I'm happy for you.'

'Me too,' Natalie said, and Ronnie chimed in, too.

Janet suddenly found herself in the centre of a large hug.

Jim went off to bring the car round, still crying with joy. Caroline, Natalie and Ronnie waited with Janet under the porch, watching the rain.

'We should celebrate,' Natalie said. 'Let's go to lunch sometime or something equally ordinary.'

'Good idea,' said Ronnie. 'But let's not do ordinary. How about the Aran?'

'For lunch?' Caroline said. 'It's well over 100 miles away, never mind the fact that it's a bloody island.'

'So I'll fly us. We'll be there in an hour.'

Natalie stared at her. 'Seriously?'

'I love the Aran Islands,' Janet said. 'Haven't been there in years.'

'So, let's do it,' Caroline said. 'Might be nice to escape for a day.'

'It'll have to be Friday,' Ronnie said. 'I'm working at the weekend.'

'I'm easy,' Janet said.

Caroline was still off work for another few days and Natalie said she could get a day off.

'Is flying OK for the baby?' Janet asked.

'Perfectly safe,' Ronnie said.

'OK then.' She grinned and clapped her hands. 'We're going on a road trip.' She put her hands on her stomach and grinned. *Stay with me now, baby.*

Jim pulled the car round and Janet got in and waved to her friends. They watched her drive off with her husband.

'I'm so happy, babe,' Jim blubbered, and as she squeezed his free hand, she realised she was crying, too.

I Love Paddy Mahon

Catherine

TONY AND I WERE BOTH in a funk. As angry and disappointed as he was in Poor John, he missed him, too. I was scared that in losing Paddy, I'd lost my one chance of happiness. I was sick of lying on my bed staring at the ceiling and wondering where my daughter was, and what Paddy was doing and with whom.

Tony was in the bath when I banged on the door.

'Come in,' he said, and I walked in to find him surrounded by bubbles, candles ablaze and Leonard Cohen's 'Chelsea Hotel' playing on a stereo. I could always tell Tony's mood by which Leonard Cohen album he was listening to and which song he'd rewind over and over. 'Chelsea Hotel' was a bad sign.

I slumped onto the floor with a mug of tea. We didn't speak. Instead, we listened to Leonard singing about fleeting love, absorbing the words that flowed from him. He was singing about needing someone and at the same time not needing them. I knew how he felt and I wanted to sob but I didn't. Instead, I interrupted Leonard's lyrical lies to himself.

'Have you seen Paddy?' I asked.

'He's fine.'

'Does he miss me?'

'You know he does.'

'I miss him,' I said.

'I told you to be careful.'

300

'I was.'

'Not of him,' he said, and I hung my head.

I'm sorry.

'I want him back,' I said.

'You're either in or you're out, Catherine.'

'What if I'm in?' I asked.

I wasn't letting go of Daisy; I just needed to know.

'Well then, you have to tell him about what happened to you.'

'But you said . . .'

'That was before.'

'Before what?'

'Before he was one of us. Besides, don't mind what I said. Sometimes you keep your secret and sometimes you just have to tell the truth and hope for the best.'

'What if I can't?' I said.

Tony looked at me. 'What have you got to lose?'

I thought about it. *Nothing.* I lost everything when I lost Daisy. I had nothing left to lose.

'Look, Catherine, I would have spent the rest of my life pretending to my brother that I was someone else if he'd let me. I know it's hard for him to understand, but now he takes me for who I am and I think he might do the same for you.'

'And if he doesn't?'

'Then you move on to someone who will,' he said. He sank lower into the bath so his shoulders were no longer on show. 'Wouldn't it be nice to live in a world with no more secrets?'

I nodded. It seemed impossible. Leonard was singing 'Lover, Lover, Lover' by now. He was singing about his fear and cowardice and shame and begging his lover to come back to him – it felt like he was singing directly to me.

'Everything changes, Catherine. That's how we move on.'

I stood up to leave. 'Tony?'

His eyes were closed like he was drifting away. 'Yeah?'

'My baby – her name is Daisy. I'm going to tell your brother everything and then I'm going to find her.'

His eyes popped open and he sat up, but I was already closing the door behind me.

I'd never been to Tony and Paddy's parents' house before. It was a house on a hill overlooking Dublin Bay. You could tell by the interior that they had money and at the same time that they didn't care about money or aesthetics of any kind. It was a house built of books and not much else. The floors were made of wood; any wall space not inhabited by books was wallpapered in a fading art deco black-and-red shell-like image that seemed to run throughout the downstairs area. The furniture seemed to be antique but uncared for. The place felt more like a dusty old library than a home.

I sat in the front room across from Paddy's parents. Tony had told me so much about them, but still they were a surprise to me. They were plain people. I'd expected them to be bookish, but because of their two beautiful boys, I'd also expected at least one of them to be handsome. They weren't. Margaret Mahon wore her hair short and a pair of round glasses perched on the end of her nose. Richard Mahon was mostly bald on top; he wore a thick knitted cardigan with a belt, and his glasses hung from a cord around his neck.

Paddy wasn't home. He'd taken on an extra shift but he'd be home soon, they told me. They were adamant that I wait. I was a curiosity to them, a glimpse into the outside world; at least, that's how it felt. I really didn't know what to say. It was very awkward and tense, but they had insisted.

So we sat in the front room, waiting for Paddy to return. A whole two hours passed, mostly spent in silence. They didn't seem uncomfortable at all. When they did speak to me, it was to ask questions.

'Patrick never mentioned your age?' Richard said.

Paddy never mentioned my age because he had never mentioned me at all.

'I'm eighteen,' I said.

'Patrick is twenty-four,' Margaret said.

'I'll be nineteen in December.'

'He'll be twenty-five in November,' she replied.

'And where did you say you go to school?' Richard asked.

I didn't say I'd gone to school anywhere. 'I don't go to school. I work for Tony.'

'Tony?' Margaret said.

'Your son, Tony.'

'Anthony? You work for Anthony?' She seemed very surprised at the mention of his name.

I nodded. I'd never heard Tony called Anthony before.

'In that salon?' Richard asked.

'Yes.' *Where else?* For academics, they didn't seem that sharp to me at all.

'Isn't that nice,' Margaret said, but her face suggested otherwise. 'And you and Patrick are . . . ?'

'Friends,' I said, but then I couldn't help myself. 'But he told me he loves me . . . twice . . .'

We all stopped talking after that.

It was just after 8 p.m. when Paddy walked inside the front door. Margaret called him to the front room. He was clearly surprised to see me and I wondered if he'd be angry, the way Justin was if I did anything that was in any way my own idea. He wasn't. He beamed.

'Hello,' he said.

'Hello,' I said.

He turned to his parents. 'This is my friend, Catherine.'

'Yes, we know,' Margaret said. 'Apparently, you love her.'

'I do,' Paddy said, without so much as a flinch.

'She's eighteen,' Margaret said.

'I know.' I saw him swallow. 'Did she mention if she loved me?' he asked.

'No, and we didn't ask,' Richard said, and then both of his parents' necks snapped round and they were staring me down. I didn't know where to put myself or what to say. I'd practised the conversation on the bus the whole way here and it had never gone in that direction or even close to it. I certainly hadn't expected his parents to be in the room.

I stood up. 'I do,' I said.

'Are you sure?' Paddy said. It seemed for him it was as though his parents weren't there at all.

'I am,' I said, still painfully aware of their gaping mouths and uncomfortable shuffling.

'How come?' he asked, and he had good reason to. I hadn't given him much indication of my love to date.

I needed to be honest, not just with Paddy, but with myself.

'Because I had a hole in me when we met and when I lost you, it doubled in size.'

He grinned and hugged himself and sighed. Then he crossed the room, passing his parents' open mouths. He took me in his arms and he kissed me and I melted. It was very romantic, aside from the gaping spectators.

'Ah, now really, Patrick, a little decorum wouldn't go astray,' his father said.

Paddy grinned at me. 'Let's go,' he said.

'What about dinner?' his mother said.

'We're having fish and chips by the pier, Mother. They're Catherine's favourite.'

He took me by the hand and we headed for the door.

'They are my favourite,' I said as we left, and I was so proud to have someone in my life who knew that little fact and cared about it.

I felt lighter than I had in a long time, but as soon as the front door closed behind us and the cold air hit my face, I remembered why I'd knocked on his door in the first place . . . Daisy. I had to tell him and I knew that it would change everything.

We took our fish and chips to a bench overlooking the sea and we snuggled together as we ate. He told me how much he'd missed me and I told him how much I'd missed him. He told me in a few years he'd be a consultant but in the meantime, his wages were enough to get us a nice house somewhere in town.

'For us,' he said.

My joy began to ebb away. 'I can't live with you.'

'Why not? You live with Tony.'

'It's not the same and you know it.'

'As soon as I'm a consultant, we'll get married,' he said.

'I've heard that before,' I said.

He looked around at me, frowning. 'Why?'

'You asked me once what I was hiding . . . Do you remember?' I asked.

He nodded. 'It's why you have a hole in you.'

'Yes.'

'What happened to you, Catherine?'

'I had a baby,' I said, and after keeping it pent up for so long, the words just fell out of my mouth.

He stared straight ahead. We both remained silent while he absorbed that information.

'When?' he asked.

'The twenty-sixth of October, 1976,' I said, and such a short time had passed between then and now, but it felt like a lifetime.

It was a lifetime. It was Daisy's lifetime.

'In one of those places?' he asked, and he still couldn't bring himself to look at me.

'Yeah.'

'Did they hurt you?'

It was an unexpected question. I later found out that he had treated some girls from 'those places' in the emergency department.

'Yeah,' I said. 'They did. In every way possible.'

Tears spilled from my eyes and suddenly I was back in that place. Sister Mary Frances' knuckles were shoved into my back and she was calling me names. I could smell the place, a mixture of floor polish, incense and musty fear. I could feel the chill in the room where I cried myself to sleep and the rough texture of the blanket that scraped my skin. And I could hear Maria crying. *No. No. No.*

'I had a girl,' I said. 'I called her Daisy.'

'Where is she now?' he asked, and his voice was so low it was almost a whisper.

'They stole her,' I said.

That's when he looked at me.

'She wasn't theirs to give away,' I said, and my shoulders fell and I sobbed as a little girl.

He took my hand in his. 'Who is the father?' he asked.

'A boy who said he loved me and that he'd marry me,' I said, and my nose started to run, so Paddy handed me his pristine pocket handkerchief with his initials embroidered into it. I blew my nose. 'I'll wash it,' I said, shoving it up my sleeve.

'What do you want to do, Catherine?'

'I want to get her back.'

'Did you sign anything?'

'No.'

'One question.'

I gulped.

'Do you really love me?' he asked.

'I do. I really do. I was just scared. I am scared.'

And I did and I was. Despite the damage those nuns had done, I knew I loved him. I wasn't a silly girl anymore. I knew what was real now.

He sat back and thought about everything that had been said. I waited for judgment and he squeezed my hand.

'I'll walk you to the bus,' he said, and my heart sank.

Oh no.

We walked in step, holding hands, and in silence. Everything around us sounded so loud. The hum of the engines of passing cars and the screeching of the brakes on a double-decker bus. The voices of children ringing out as they laughed and chatted and spun their bike wheels, chasing one another in and out of light traffics.

I desperately tried to think of something to say, but nothing came to mind. He was lost in his own thoughts. I doubt he heard or saw anything going on around him.

Had his love turned so quickly to hate or disdain? If so, it wasn't love. I had learned that the hard way. Did he think I was a whore now? Fallen and filthy?

As I got onto the bus, he told me he'd be in touch. Then the bus pulled off and I cried all the way home.

Tony was waiting in the kitchen. He offered me tea from the pot. He saw the tracks of mascara on my face and handed me a ginger nut biscuit.

'I'm sorry,' he said.

I ate the biscuit in one go and wiped my nose.

Tony poured me a cup of tea. 'It's his loss.'

'It's my loss,' I said.

'Do you know what I did when Poor John slept with someone else?'

'You sulked and treated him like shit in the shop?'

'Aside from that.'

'No.'

'I went out and I flirted and I had fun.'

He seemed to forget that he'd also taken to his bed, refused to eat and listened to Leonard Cohen full blast all day and all night.

'Yeah, well, your kind of fun doesn't get you pregnant and locked up.'

'No, but my kind of fun can get me beaten to death or locked up. So I win.'

I even chuckled a little at that thought, though our circumstances seemed grim and my heart was an open sore.

'Let's go dancing this weekend,' he said.

But I didn't want to dance. I wanted to disappear.

'I just want to hide in my room and cry,' I told him.

'OK, that's fine, but you have to eat.'

I promised I would, then I grabbed the packet of ginger biscuits and took them with me as I walked up the stairs two at a time.

'And not just ginger bloody biscuits!' he shouted, but I was already in my room, face down on my bed and bawling like a newborn baby.

Where are you, Daisy? I wish you were here. I wish I could hold you and touch you and kiss your little face. I wish I could feel your weight on my shoulder or in my arms as you suckle. If I close my eyes and cup my hands, I can feel the warmth of your head in my hands or trace the wrinkles in your neck. I can feel your fingers tighten around mine. I am so tired, Daisy, but I won't give up. I may lose everything and everyone else, but I will get you back, I swear.

I couldn't sleep that night. I just lay awake in the dark re-living my time with Paddy and trying my best to make sense of his reaction. The hole in me was bigger than ever and I felt so stupid and naïve.

It was Monday morning and just after eleven when the door-bell rang. The salon was closed Sunday and Monday and I'd spent all of Sunday in bed with half a packet of ginger biscuits and a record player, Tony's Leonard Cohen collection playing on repeat. I hadn't washed, so my face was still stained with mascara and blotchy from salty tears.

I heard the doorbell but ignored it, burying my head under the pillow. A minute later, Tony was standing over me.

'Catherine?'

'What?'

'It's Paddy. He's here.'

I lifted the pillow. 'What does he want?'

'You.'

'What?'

'Just go,' he said.

I stood up and looked in the mirror. 'Oh God!'

'Go.'

I tried to flatten my hair, clean my face and wipe my nose all at the same time. It failed to improve the situation. Paddy was standing at the bottom of the stairs.

'Are you all right?' he said. He seemed shocked by my state.

'No. I'm heartbroken,' I wailed. *Stupid fucking question.*

He seemed genuinely confused. 'Why?'

'Because you don't want me anymore,' I cried.

'I didn't say that. When did I say that?'

'You didn't say anything at all.'

'I told you I needed to think about things, that's all.'

'Oh yeah? And what conclusion have you reached?' I shouted, letting my frustration out.

And then Paddy took out a box from his pocket and opened it to reveal a ring with a small solitaire diamond.

'We'll get married,' he said, 'and then we'll get Daisy back.'

Chapter Twenty-Two

Caroline

CAROLINE TOOK A TAXI HOME from the hospital on a high. It was the first time in a long time she'd been happy to see anyone else pregnant. The look of sheer bliss on Janet's face when she returned to the waiting area holding a photo of her baby was something Caroline would never forget. Jim's utter and complete collapse into a blubbering wreck was, weirdly, a joy to behold. It was a privilege to be a part of it.

She felt bad about suspecting Jim and stalking him on and off for a week. He seemed like a warm, kind, straightforward man. Like her Dave. *They'd get on.* She wanted to roll back time to before their beloved dog died, to before she'd told him he wasn't enough. *I'm a bloody fool.* She knew time travel wasn't possible, but maybe if she tried really hard to win him back, he'd stay. It was worth a try at the very least.

He was there when she got home. She parked the car and ran inside; the rain was still pelting, but it wasn't as bad as the hellscape they'd travelled through to get Janet to hospital.

Dave was cooking at the stove.

'Can we talk?'

'I'm going out.'

'With that woman?'

'No.'

'With another one?'

'Does it matter?'

'Yeah, of course it matters. You're my husband.' She tried to mask the tears in her voice.

'Doesn't feel like it,' he said.

'You did that,' she mumbled.

'No, Caroline, you did it. We got off the baby train three years ago and there was no way I could get back on it now, but you didn't care.'

She sat down at the table, facing him. He kept his back to her at the stove.

'I'm off it too, for good this time.'

'How come?'

'I can't carry children. Too much damage has been done.'

He nodded to himself. He kept stirring. 'Then I'm sorry for you.'

That was a surprise. She expected something more.

'That's it?' she asked.

'What do you want me to say?'

'I don't know.'

That you forgive me. That you love me. That we can be together again. Anything but I'm fucking sorry for you.

He turned the gas off, plated his dinner and sat up on the counter to eat.

'You won't even sit with me?'

'There's nothing left to say.'

She stood up and walked over to the island, pulling out a stool then gently easing herself onto it.

'Of course there is. For God's sake, Dave.'

'Nothing's changed, Caroline.'

'Didn't you hear me? I can't have a child!'

'You couldn't have a child before. It didn't stop you.'

'It's different now. Before there was hope.'

'No there wasn't, Caroline. You just wouldn't listen.'

'What does it matter? I'm listening now!'

'It matters because I didn't matter. It matters because you've finally accepted you can't have children, it doesn't mean you won't crave and yearn for them. It just means you're going to carry on obsessing. Nothing will ever be right and everything we do will be laced in sadness and bitterness. I want more. I *deserve* more.'

She stared at him. Part of her knew he was right. Not having a family had coloured everything for the past decade. Why would that change now? Just because she had managed a smile and a warm feeling for a pregnant woman didn't chase away the darkness and the demons in her head.

'You do matter,' she said. 'You have always mattered.'

'Not enough, Caroline. The truth is, I'll never be enough.'

'I'll try. Please, Dave.'

'You shouldn't have to try, Caroline.' He got off the stool and picked up his plate.

She followed him to the door.

'This can't be it,' she said in a pleading tone as he closed the door on her.

She stood in a daze. *What have I done?*

Then she dragged herself up the stairs. She walked into her en suite and started to run a bath. She stripped off as the steam filled the room and once it was full, she slipped in and submerged to her shoulders. *I think he's really leaving me,* she said to herself, and she wept for the man she loved and the life that was never quite good enough.

As she lay in the bath, she wondered if she'd made the wrong choices. If they had sucked it up and started the adoption process years ago, she could be a mother now. Maybe she'd be a happier, warmer woman. Maybe she'd be doing something she loved for

313

a living and talking to her poor sister, whose only sin was having a baby. Maybe she wouldn't have been so focused on her pain and her needs and her wants and her desires . . . Maybe she'd think about someone else, anyone else, everyone else . . . It was nice, surrendering to Janet's joy. Feeling happiness for someone else felt good.

What now?

She was lying in bubbles, just simmering, when she heard the car start outside. She wanted to jump up and run into the street. She wanted to beg Dave to stay and give them another chance, but he was right. He had asked her if he was enough and she had told him he wasn't.

There was no coming back from that.

The next morning, in the office, Caroline popped her head round Susan's door. Susan was leaning on the window, looking out.

'Don't jump,' Caroline said.

Susan turned to face her. 'I won't if you won't.'

'I'm taking Friday off.'

'Of course you are.'

'The case is in hand. Nothing's happening until next Thursday.'

'And you're all over it.'

'I am. We'll win and we'll win big.'

'And in the meantime . . . ?'

'I'm spending the day with friends.'

'That doesn't sound like you.'

'No, it's not like me at all.'

'You know, I think you're the best solicitor we have.' Susan moved over to her desk and sat. She pointed to a battered green leather chair. 'Sit.'

Caroline sat.

'I know you're not looking to go anywhere else.'

'You've been doing your homework.'

'I don't want to lose you and I definitely can't afford to oppose you.'

'That's a big compliment.'

'*Are* we losing you?' she asked.

Caroline shook her head. 'I don't know. I look at my life and the next twenty years and I don't know where I belong.'

'You belong here with us.'

'Maybe. I just need to get my head on straight. Work some things out.'

'So spend a day with your friends. Get your head on straight.'

Caroline worked for the rest of the day. She left at six and drove home through dense traffic, listening to the radio with Susan's words ringing in her ears. *You belong here with us.* But Susan was wrong. Caroline didn't belong there. She wasn't sure she belonged anywhere.

She met Dave in the kitchen. He was brushing the floor. She dropped her bag on the table.

'What's going on?'

'We need to clean the place a bit.'

'Who's coming over?'

'An estate agent. Tomorrow.'

This revelation nearly floored her. 'You're serious.'

He nodded. 'We just need to know what our options are, that's all.' He looked as sad as she felt.

'OK, you're right. Good idea,' she said as brightly as her broken heart would allow.

She grabbed her car keys and she walked out of the door. She sat in her car, turned on the engine and drove. She kept on driving until she found a lonely spot – a field surrounded by fields. She parked the car on the verge and gingerly climbed the fence. Then she walked and walked before stopping. She looked up towards the sky and screamed until her voice and knees gave way.

What have I done?

Let Her Rip. Let Her Tear

Catherine

AFTER MUCH CONSIDERATION, discussion and debate, I invited my mother to my wedding by letter. She declined the invitation but told me that she was very happy for me and that she wished me well. It hurt, but my family's absence was the least of the cruelty I'd endured. I packed away the pain. Paddy was enough for me and Tony was already my family.

Their parents weren't immediately on board with the wedding, but when Paddy explained we were getting married no matter what they did or said, they caved. I wasn't particularly sure they liked me, but then again, I wasn't sure if they liked their sons, either. They were terribly polite, but at the same time they said exactly how they felt and what they thought, no matter how outrageous it seemed to others, all the while being terribly practical. They weren't emotional people. It made it easy and at the same time difficult to be around them.

They insisted on dinner after the wedding.

'You surely can't expect us to come into town for a ceremony and not eat?' Margaret said.

We were thinking of just hiring a car and slipping off to Galway for our honeymoon straight afterwards.

'Your mother's right,' Richard said. 'If you have no friends, the least you can do is feed the few people who do turn up.'

Paddy conceded. Tony was pissed off.

'Brilliant, the perfect opportunity for them to ask me again if I have a woman in my life.'

I was looking forward to the day, but I was also scared witless. We hadn't had sex. Paddy said he wanted to wait, which I knew was a generous lie. He had been with girls before and he was in a position to access contraception, but he didn't push. He knew what I'd been through. We talked about it and I was so embarrassed, I hid my face behind a tea towel while I explained that I was worried about my downstairs being messed up by the nuns. *Let her rip, let her tear . . . Maybe she'll think twice the next time she contemplates tempting a man.* I told him what the doctor had said when he sewed me up. *This was totally avoidable. I am sick of coming to this place and fixing up girls who should have been cared for properly.* Although I'd been in a haze of pain and blood loss, I remembered those words verbatim.

Paddy pulled at the tea towel I was shielding my shame with. 'We'll fix it. We will fix it all.'

He took me to the Rotunda Hospital to see a gynaecologist, who a friend from medical school had highly recommended. I didn't want to go. I was panic-stricken, but he gently persisted, making a valiant attempt to assuage my fears. I sat in the waiting room shaking like a leaf while he held me tight and spoke to me about all the things we would do and the places we would go. I'd never even been on a plane.

'You are going to love Paris, Catherine. We'll go there in our first year of marriage, I promise.'

I knew nothing of Paris. All I saw was the door leading to a room where my knickers would come off and my legs would be spread and a man I didn't know would do things to me. I felt sick.

Then it happened. A woman passed by in that familiar black habit and robes. I didn't see her face, it was concealed by a veil, but I screamed my bloody head off and tried to make a break for it.

Paddy held me close to him and whispered in my ear, 'She doesn't work here. This is a national hospital, government-funded, not a private charitable institution. I checked. I don't know what she's doing here, but this is not the Catholic Church and that woman will not be going next to or near you. Do you hear me?'

It was hard to hear him over all the crying I was doing, but eventually I quietened down, burrowing my head into his chest. *Oh no. Oh no. Oh no. Don't be scared, Katie . . . No, I'm not her. I'm Catherine. My name is Catherine.* I was in such a panic for a second, I forgot my own fucking name. That's what they did to us. I thought I was OK, but with the sight of a nun's habit, I was back in that place, lost, helpless, a number, a skivvy, a sinful girl. A living incubator for a decent woman, a slave whose baby would be sold on the block.

Paddy pulled my face away from his chest. 'Breathe, Catherine.'

I think I might have been going slightly blue.

'In and out, in and out,' he said, and those words seemed to lock me back in that place.

I breathed in and out. I wanted to scream at him to stop talking, but I couldn't. I felt like I was dying. I focused on the wall.

'Catherine?' he said, and I could hear the anxiety in his voice.

Then he ran out of the room and left me there like a wet rag, panting feverishly and staring at the wall. *Are you there, Charles?* I asked. I had a pain in my chest and I felt dizzy and weak. *Charles? It's me, Catherine. I know how rough they were, how unkind. I know you suffered unspeakably. It was right there in front of us, but we chose not to see it. People do that, Charles. They choose not to see what is uncomfortable or talk about what is unspeakable. I'm sorry I was a part of it, but no more. If I don't fucking die in a gynaecologist's office, I promise to open my eyes to it all and I'll speak about it, too. I couldn't save you and I couldn't save me, but I'll save someone. I promise you that.*

Paddy returned with an oxygen tank on wheels and placed a mask on my face. He instructed me to breathe slowly while he rubbed my back.

'It's just a panic attack.'

A nurse hovered beside him. 'I really do need to take that back to delivery, Dr Mahon. The water baby's heart rate is up and down like a yoyo.'

I pulled the oxygen mask from my face. 'I'm OK,' I said, and my head was swimming, but at least I could breathe.

The nurse nodded, took the tank and left.

'We can just go, if you want to,' Paddy said.

But I wanted to get it over with. I needed to know what damage they'd done to me.

The room was small and the window was high up on the wall, just below the ceiling, so although light streamed in, it was impossible to see outside, except for the tiniest hint of white clouds. I was lying with my legs spread and a strange man in his mid-sixties between them. I let myself drift and my mind moved outside my body and that room to another place, safe and warm.

I was in a rocking chair with Daisy in my arms, only a few days old. I could feel her weight in the crook of my arm and the softness of her head, her silky, wispy black hair. I could feel her fingers grip mine and the kick of her feet. I could feel her stretch and arch her back as her eyes blinked at me and the corner of her mouth curled upwards.

The doctor stood up. He told me I could get dressed and he pulled the curtains around me. I quickly put on my knickers, flattened down my dress and made sure my hair was in place.

I waited a second or two for the high colour on my cheeks to recede. I heard the door open and footsteps then the scraping of steel from the legs of a chair against the hard black-and-white tiled floor.

I opened the curtain to reveal Paddy sitting opposite the doctor. A chair had been placed beside him. I hadn't expected him to be inside the room and it came as a shock.

As I sat down, the old doctor looked towards Paddy and shook his hand.

'Nice to meet you, Dr Mahon.'

'Likewise,' Paddy said.

'Well, you're in luck,' he said, and he was talking to Paddy, not to me. 'There was significant tearing and trauma and there is scar tissue, but someone made a good job of rescuing the area.'

My face reddened. It was as though I wasn't in the room.

'What about muscle damage or pelvic organ prolapse?' Paddy asked. He didn't seem to notice my rage.

'No signs. She was young enough to recover.' He didn't even glance in my direction.

'That's good news,' Paddy said, and I wanted to scream, shout, kick the door down.

Instead, I stood up silently. I walked to the door and swung it open.

'Catherine?' Paddy sounded confused.

I slammed the door behind me and I walked and then ran out of that place.

I was halfway down Parnell Street when Paddy caught up to me, red-faced and breathless.

'What happened in there?'

'He spoke to you about me and my private parts,' I shouted at him.

He tried to grab me to him, but I pulled away.

'You talked to him as though I wasn't even there.'

'I didn't mean anything. It was just doctor to doctor.'

'Bollocks. This is my body. I fucking own it – not those fucking nuns and not you.' I turned on my heel.

'I'm sorry. You're right. I was wrong. I see it. I'm so sorry,' he said, and I knew he meant it.

I stopped dead on the street, allowing him to catch up to me.

'If I'm in the room, act like it,' I said.

He nodded. 'I will never do that to you again. I swear to God,' he pleaded.

'You'd better not,' I said.

'Yes, my love.' He placed his arm around mine and together we walked through the city.

That was how I came to find out that my downstairs area hadn't been destroyed. The appointment took place two months before the wedding, but even in the knowledge that I wasn't broken, I still wanted to be married. Not just because I didn't feel safe, but also because I was terrified of having sex. The longer I could put it off, the better.

I spent a lot of time thinking about that. *What will it feel like now? Can I relax? Is it even possible, knowing what I know and having come through the hell I've come through?* I'd turn to jelly whenever Paddy touched me, but even the smallest hint of pleasure was laced with guilt. I desperately wanted to be Paddy Mahon's wife and I hoped being Mrs Mahon would change how I felt about myself as a woman. *Will I be decent then? Will the shame dissipate as soon as a gold band is placed on my finger? Will a man by my side make the world think me worthy of my girl?*

The night before our wedding, Tony, Paddy and I enjoyed a quiet candlelit dinner in the house. Tony raised a glass to his brother.

'You're one of us now, Paddy,' he said, grabbing my hand and squeezing it tightly before kissing it. 'Isn't that right, Catherine?'

I smiled widely and nodded to my future husband.

Tony wasn't losing me to the other side; the other side was losing Paddy. We were not normal. We would never be normal and I was OK with that. I don't know why tears fell, but they did. I'd come a long way from the pig farmer's girl and the Pitiful Whore, but I had a way to go.

Soon, Daisy. Soon.

On my wedding day, I was filled with both excitement and trepidation. I hadn't slept a wink; my stomach was in knots and my heart beat so fast it felt like it was going to pop out of my chest.

Tony gave me away, his hand in mine as we walked down the aisle to where Paddy stood, beaming. His parents were not so happy. His mother looked uncomfortable and his dad carried a blank almost bored look. But I didn't care. I just focused on Paddy.

We said our 'I dos' and signed a register and everything was a blur. After the service, we went for dinner in The Shelbourne. A table for five. I wore a pretty pale pink silk dress to the knee; it didn't look or feel like a wedding dress, but it was special.

I had never been in The Shelbourne Hotel before. We were in a corner booth in the restaurant. I thought about Jen and how pretty she would have looked on her wedding day. I pictured her in the glamorous ballroom. I didn't think about Justin anymore; I couldn't bear to. I only thought about her and how she was doing and if she was well and happy. I hoped she was. I looked at my new husband sitting beside me and I knew I was happy. I was happy but also scared. We were man and wife and later that night, we would share a bed. My stomach was in a heap. *Oh no.* As lovely as the food was, I couldn't eat a thing.

'You're not eating,' Richard said. 'Do you not enjoy a good steak?'

'I've never had one before.'

That shocked him.

'I've had every part of a pig, though,' I said, and Tony and Paddy grinned at one another.

'That sounds horrific, dear,' Margaret said.

'Does it?' I said, examining the bloody slab of cow on my plate.

'Can I ask what the plan is now that you are married?' Richard asked.

'Against our better judgment,' Margaret added.

'I'm moving into Tony's box room with my wife until we secure a rental close by.'

'Close by the hospital?'

'No,' I said. 'Close to Tony.'

'You want to be close to Anthony?' Margaret said. 'I don't understand.'

'But you can afford to rent in a far better area than Anthony,' Richard said.

'No offence taken,' Tony said.

'And no offence meant. But, darling, you are a hairdresser and Patrick is a heart surgeon.'

'Still in training,' Paddy mumbled.

'I want to live near Tony,' I said, 'because he's my best friend and my boss. He may not be a heart surgeon, but he is my family.'

'Oh,' Richard said.

He sounded like he wasn't quite sure what I was on about, but Tony hugged me to him and kissed me on my forehead.

'It would be nice if you had a family of your own, Anthony,' Margaret said.

Tony shrugged. 'Yes, it would.'

'Anyone we should know about?' Richard said.

'Hopefully out of their teens,' Margaret mumbled.

'It's our wedding day,' Paddy said. 'Do we really need to hound Tony today? If he wants you to meet someone, he will introduce you. In the meantime, best to keep out of it.'

Tony clapped his hands together and laughed. 'I second that.'

'Fine,' Margaret said. 'Do as you wish, but don't come crying to us when it all goes to hell in a handbasket.'

This struck a chord with Richard and he recited a poem, 'The History of Popery', written in 1682 about going to hell in a handbasket and dead fanatical dogs. It wasn't your usual wedding celebration, but I loved it anyway. It was right for us. I just needed to get my nerves under control and not ruin things. *Come on, Catherine. It's going to be OK,* I told myself, but my stomach had other ideas.

Chapter Twenty-Three

Natalie

NATALIE RETURNED FROM THE HOSPITAL and holed up in Ronnie's spare bedroom, where she promptly fell asleep and dreamed in bright colours – but when she woke up, she felt numb. She stared at the ceiling and the wall, and out of the window and at the foot of the bed and then the wall again. And after crying and biting her nails and cursing when she drew blood. After thinking about the past, ruminating on her own liability for the failure of her relationship, meditating on change and deliberating on how to move forwards. And all this after hiding under a pillow and banging her closed fist on a soft mattress. Picturing Linda's face, her eyes, her nose, her mouth, her breasts, her legs, her everything. Missing all of it as though she were missing a part of herself. After all of that, once the apartment front door had shut, leaving her alone, she finally got up.

She walked into the living area and the light streamed in from the big window, temporarily blinding her. She wandered towards the kitchen units, spotting the coffee machine on the counter. She started opening and closing presses in quick succession in a bid to find coffee pods. She did find them, and beside them, to the back of the press, was a book. She pulled it out; it wasn't thick and the cover was just a photo of a young girl sitting on a gate. She read the back of the jacket. It was self-published. She flicked through it and it bore the raggedness of a book that was well read. She made the coffee and, trying to escape herself, she sat on Ronnie's sofa, drank coffee and started to read.

She didn't hear Ronnie come in – she heard her shouting before she saw her. Ronnie was red in the face. She grabbed the book and tore it out of Natalie's hands, hugging it to her, barely able to get the words out. She looked like a different person.

'What the hell . . . ? Who the fuck do you . . . ? This is mine . . . Personal to me . . .'

'I'm so sorry.' Natalie was utterly mortified. 'I had no idea.'

'You don't just take things that aren't yours,' Ronnie said, and she was crying now.

Natalie was so shocked. She wasn't sure what to say except how sorry she was. With the book in hand, Ronnie stormed out of the apartment. Natalie heard the front door slamming.

What the fuck was that?

She rose from the sofa and looked around. She felt so lost, sad and so utterly alien. She just stood there and cried.

When she was done with crying, Natalie got dressed and left the apartment. She drove into town and walked into the first estate agent she found. She spoke to a pleasant woman, who introduced herself as Samantha. She took a seat and explained that she was looking for a home to buy. Samantha asked her where she'd like to live.

Natalie wasn't sure.

'OK, well, a house or an apartment? We focus on the South-side and the city.'

Natalie wasn't sure about that, either.

'Well, what's your budget?'

Natalie didn't know. Samantha started to look at her as though she were deranged.

'I'm sorry, I don't mean to waste your time. It's just that I had a home till yesterday and now I don't, so it's all a bit new.'

She must have looked wretched, because Samantha took pity on her.

'Why don't I get us a coffee and we can start narrowing things down a little?'

Natalie spent the next hour and a half with Samantha and when she left, she had a clear plan for her immediate future. She was going to buy a three-bed house with a small garden and parking in a search area between Dublin 4 and Dublin 8, with a maximum budget of seven hundred and fifty grand. She had some savings, zero debt and a six-figure salary, so getting a mortgage approved wouldn't be an issue. Natalie wasn't a spender; she wasn't a mean person, but she wasn't dazzled by pretty things, either. Money never burned a hole in her pocket, so she had a decent enough deposit.

Samantha wanted to take her to a place that very evening, but Natalie was tired and just wanted to return to the bed in the box room and hide for a while. She agreed to start viewing homes next week.

Natalie walked out of the place feeling good. She was beginning again. A fresh start in a place that would be hers. It wasn't a relationship with a woman she loved and it wasn't motherhood, but it was something. There was a meeting on and if she hurried, she'd make it. She didn't want to go back to Ronnie's, so she hailed a cab and hoped Ronnie wouldn't show up.

Buckaroo

Catherine

WE STAYED IN A ROOM IN The Shelbourne that night. I
drank two glasses of red wine on an otherwise empty
stomach. It was a standard room but it was pretty and the bed
was big with soft sheets and fluffy pillows. I felt a little sick after
the wine. Margaret had ordered it for the table and I wanted her
to see me as a grown up, so I'd drank it, despite it tasting like
burned firewood.

I sat on the side of the bed and took a few deep breaths while
Paddy took off his shirt and trousers. I felt every part of me
tighten. *Oh no. Oh no. Don't make a fuss, Catherine.*

He looked at me doubled over at the side of the bed and
kneeled down in front of me. 'We don't have to do anything
tonight.'

I looked at him and he wiped away a stray tear from my eye.

'It's been a long day. Let's just lie in one another's arms and
sleep.'

I sighed a heavy sigh of relief. 'Thank you,' I said – and then
I threw up.

It wasn't pretty and he wanted to help, but I insisted on cleaning myself up.

Afterwards, when I'd scrubbed my teeth and my tongue and
gargled with water, I lay in bed beside him, his arms around me,

and he told me a story about the first time he saw me through the window of his brother's shop.

'I often passed before that day and I never stopped – I just glanced in to see if Tony was there and if he was happy. I missed him, but I didn't know what to say, so I walked on by. And then one day you were there, standing in the window, cleaning it with everything you had in you. The sunlight was in your hair and your eyes sparkled and you smiled at me. The very next day, I walked up to my brother's shop for the first time. You were the most beautiful thing I'd ever seen. Still are.'

And of course I didn't believe him, but I believed he believed it. I was glad I'd brought the two brothers together. Their relationship had grown since Paddy had first come into that shop and it would continue to grow, and that meant the world to me. I turned to face him and I asked if my breath smelled of wine or sick.

'Neither,' he said.

Then I kissed him and he kissed me back. And he touched the back of my neck and traced his fingers down my spine and *oh my God!* Everything inside me fluttered and fizzed and . . . *Oh no. Oh no . . . here comes the guilt and the fear . . .* And then I remembered something: I was loved and I was safe. Paddy and I were married – no one could hurt me now.

So I let go and neither of us got a wink of sleep that night. And God love the people in the room next door, because the headboard nearly went through the wall and around two thirty in the morning, Paddy let out a roar that would wake the dead.

We laughed and we cried and we had sex more times than felt possible. So much so that I was sore and he was raw and we both walked funny on the way to breakfast.

We'd used condoms. I didn't want another baby. I wanted Daisy. He understood that. I wasn't afraid of anything anymore.

As we ate breakfast in the dining room, we made plans to go back to the institution to face Sister Joanna and the others. Paddy wasn't unnerved by it at all.

'I think you'll be an amazing mother, Catherine.'

He was the first and only person to say that to me; even Tony had his doubts.

'What about the salon?' he had asked.

'I'll make it work.'

'How?'

'I'll work part-time.'

'But I need you full-time.'

'I'll make it work.'

Paddy didn't have a problem. 'We'll get help,' he said. 'Easy. I'd like more than two but less than five. How about you?'

'I used to want three, but now I'd be glad just to get Daisy back.'

'We will get her back, and three sounds like a perfect number.'

'Not too soon. I want some time with her.'

'Whatever you want, my love.'

It was all too good to be true. The pig farmer's daughter, the girl whose parents turned their backs on her, escaped the grasp of those nuns and landed on her feet, happily married to a good and decent man, and soon to be reunited with her stolen child. Paddy wasn't going to let them get away with it. He'd take them to court if he had to. I believed him.

How naïve we both were.

I didn't think about the people who had adopted my daughter. I didn't think about Daisy's new mum and dad. I made myself forget them.

We moved into a three-bed house four doors down from Tony. He encouraged us to buy, but Paddy had never lived outside his parents' posh suburban home and he wanted to see what living in town was like before committing. I didn't care. The rent was relatively low and though the place was in a state, I knew that with a little work we could make it beautiful and the perfect place for Daisy to come home to.

When we had time off, we pulled the terrible wallpaper off the walls and painted the place and freshened it right up. We painted the cabinets in the kitchen and tore up the mouldy carpet on the stairs. Tony helped. I painted the box room pink and hand drew daisies on the walls. I bought a cot in a second-hand shop; it was wooden and in perfect condition. I bought a mattress and pink blankets and a soft pillow with little bears embroidered on the edges.

We wrote to the institution to ask for a meeting. Our first request was denied, so we wrote again and again and again. Finally, three months after I was wed and a week after we'd completed the renovation of our rental home, we received a letter from Sister Joanna, offering us an appointment to meet her in her office the following Tuesday at 11 a.m.

Paddy took the day off. It was short notice and the consultant he worked under wasn't best pleased, but Paddy took the heat and we made our way from our new home to that place. He seemed nervous – unsure even. He'd been so positive up to this point, but now here we were, about to face the dragon.

He wanted to slay her for me, to be my hero, and I loved him for that. Before my marriage, I would have been so afraid of returning to the place that harmed me, but now, I was utterly changed. I was on my way to becoming a certified hairdresser and I was working in one of Dublin's top salons. I was the wife of a doctor, and I was ready to face that woman and get my baby back.

I sat next to Paddy on the train to Cork, with no fear of who would try to sit with us, no dread that I'd be hauled off. I was scared, though. How could I not be?

The taxi left us outside, refusing to drive up the avenue. I walked through those gates, leaning on Paddy as soon as I caught sight of the imposing stone building. The air seemed to change and become heavier, and the stone on the solid ground beneath me seemed to waver.

I held on to my husband's hand as tight as I could and he held on to mine. Together, we walked to the side door that was slightly ajar. They kept us away from the main entrance and any sight of the poor girls currently interned. I didn't falter or turn dizzy or weak-kneed when I saw Sister Joanna walking towards me. Instead, I stood taller. I could feel every inch of myself taking up space that had previously been denied me. If she noticed my silent protest, she didn't let on. Instead, she just smiled weakly and offered my husband her hand.

'I am Sister Joanna,' she said.

He shook her hand.

'Dr Patrick Mahon, Catherine's husband.'

She looked from him to me and nodded.

'Lovely to see you again, Catherine.' She said my name through gritted teeth. 'And what can we do for you?'

She walked ahead of us, making us follow her and maybe even speak to her back, but neither of us fell for it. We remained silent until we could see her face.

She didn't entertain us in her usual office; this was a different room at the edge of the property. The desk was empty except for one file with my name on it. There were two chairs in front of the desk. She sat and pointed to the chairs. I thought of all the many times when I was heavily pregnant or had just given birth that a seat was denied to me. I sat and faced her.

'We're here to get Daisy back,' I said.

'And who is Daisy?'

'Catherine's daughter, the child you took from her illegally,' Paddy said.

She turned to him, facing him down, her smile fading to nothing.

'Is that what she told you?'

'Yes, it is,' Paddy said, and he briefly looked to me.

'I told you I wouldn't sign those papers,' I said. 'I didn't sign them and you sold her anyway.'

'We don't sell babies. We give them to good homes.'

'Liar,' I said.

She opened the file and threw it across the desk. 'Maybe you didn't sign the papers. But then, Catherine, we didn't need *your* signature. You see, you were a minor at the time.'

I saw my mother's scribble immediately.

Oh no. Oh no. Oh no.

'Your mother knew what was good for you and she knew what was good for that child. She signed the papers and, on her instigation, the child's adoption was fast-tracked.' She turned the page. 'As you can see, Catherine, Judge O'Halloran signed off on it mere months later.'

I couldn't believe it. How had I not seen it coming?

I snapped the file out of her hands and scoured through it, leafing through page after page of information about me. I saw the name, Katie, and that stupid fucking number. I saw details of what was done to me and notes about my high blood pressure. I traced my finger on my mother's signature and clenched my jaw at the sight of the legal handiwork that prick O'Halloran presided over, ensuring his granddaughter would never be seen again.

Then I saw another name: Martha's. I quickly scanned the page as Sister Joanna tried to grab the file back. Martha O'Halloran, the judge's sister, Justin's aunt, the woman who had fed me chicken sandwiches and then returned me to the nuns – she had paid to free me. I would have been enslaved in that place had she not.

I didn't know what to do or what to think. The world seemed to swim around me. Paddy stood up and he dragged me to my feet.

'We'll see about this,' he said.

'There is nothing for you to do, Dr Mahon, except to move on with your lives.'

'You should be ashamed of yourself,' he said as she walked us to the door.

'Plenty of that to go around,' she said as she shut it behind us.

I was too stunned even to cry.

Chapter Twenty-Four

Janet

JANET ARRIVED AT THE MEETING EARLY. She felt strange about going now that she was pregnant but also compelled. *Please don't die.* She wasn't going to say anything to the group. She'd wait until she was fourteen, sixteen weeks, or just too big to hide it. She didn't have to decide. She knew Caroline, Ronnie and Natalie would keep her secret as long as she needed them to.

Sheena was setting up the chairs when she arrived. Janet automatically went over to the snacks area and started to fill the Burco with water. They talked idly about the weather.

Natalie was the first of her friends in. She looked a little grey.

'You OK?'

'Ronnie bit my head off.'

'Why?'

'I picked up a book!'

'What?' Janet asked, but by then the hall was filling up and Caroline was walking towards them.

She sat down beside them just as Ronnie entered the room. She waved to Ronnie and pointed to the chair next to hers. Janet watched Natalie redden slightly and squirm.

Ronnie didn't look like herself at all. Usually she was so tall and broad-shouldered, her eyes so bright, wearing a smile that came so easy. Usually she filled up space, but somehow she seemed smaller, fragile, unsure where to put herself. Caroline and Natalie shared a look of concern before Janet stood up and walked over to her.

'Are you OK?' she asked.

Ronnie shook her head. 'Not really.'

Sheena stood up and welcomed everyone to the meeting. The ladies all sat. Ronnie kept her head down. Sheena welcomed two new members to the group, neither of whom wished to talk.

'Anyone wish to say anything?' Sheena asked.

Mary put up her hand. 'I would.'

The room became still.

Mary beamed. 'I have news,' she said. 'Good news.'

She couldn't hide her joy. Janet knew she couldn't be pregnant; surely it was too soon after a negative IVF.

'We're giving up IVF,' Mary said.

'And that's good?' Sheena sounded a little confused.

'We're going to adopt,' Mary said. 'We're starting the process next week.'

'Good for you,' Sheena said.

Janet watched Caroline and Ronnie's eyes meet at the mention of adoption. *What's going on there, then?*

'You're sure?' Natalie said.

'Positive. There are so many kids in the world who need good homes.'

There was a moment's silence around the room and then Ronnie got to her feet.

'Can I speak?'

'Of course.'

'I was adopted,' she said. She swallowed hard. 'I was adopted and my parents were wonderful. I had a good, happy childhood. But, Mary, just make sure you do your research. Make sure your kid is coming from someone who doesn't want them.' She breathed in deeply. 'My birth mother, she didn't give me up. I was stolen from her.'

Natalie stared up at her. Her eyes were suddenly filled with tears. 'Catherine was your mother?'

'Who's Catherine?' Janet said, looking around.

'Well, clearly she's Ronnie's mother,' Mary muttered.

'Yeah, she's my birth mother.' Ronnie looked to Natalie. 'I don't know how far you read to in her book . . .'

'I got as far as her marrying Paddy and trying to get you back from the nuns,' Natalie said.

'Oh, the nuns . . .' Mary looked around. 'Of course . . . My own family have a history with them.'

'What happened?' Janet asked.

'She was young. She was put into one of those places where they punished young girls.'

'But you were happy?' Sheena said. 'You had good parents?'

'Yeah, I had parents I adored. They never knew what had happened, why I was there to be adopted. But I also had a mother who was devastated by my loss. A mother I never got to know.'

'How come?' Caroline said.

'She tried to find me, but the walls were up. By the time I tried to find her, it was too late.' A tear rolled down her face.

'She died?' Caroline said.

'Worse,' Ronnie said.

'What the fuck is worse than death?' Mary asked.

'Lots of things,' Ronnie said. She looked at Natalie and said softly, 'I'm sorry.'

'Don't be. I'm sorry.'

'Well, I don't know what to say,' Mary said. 'I thought I was coming in here with some good news.'

'You were, you have,' said Sheena. 'It's brilliant news and it's a different world now. You'll be a wonderful mother.'

Mary smiled. 'Yeah,' she said. 'I hope so.'

After the meeting, the four women exited the building together.

'Are you OK?' Caroline asked Ronnie.

'I'm fine. It's just a little raw, that's all.'

As Mary passed them, Ronnie ran up to her. 'Sorry, Mary. I shouldn't have made that meeting about me.'

'That's OK. You had a point.' She smiled. 'We'll do it the right way. I promise.'

'I know you will,' Ronnie said.

'Well, see ya ladies,' Mary said. She paused. 'This is probably my last meeting. It's been nice knowing you all.'

'Good luck,' said Janet.

Mary smiled and waved as she got into her car.

Ronnie turned to the others, brightening a little. 'I'll be fine. Are you all still on for our little island lunch?'

'Yes please!' Janet said, and the others all nodded.

Later, as Janet walked home, her thoughts drifted from lunch in Achill to the question: what is worse than death?

Martha

Catherine

I DON'T REMEMBER MUCH THE WEEK that followed our visit to the institution. I was frozen, like that first night in Cork, standing barefoot and bleeding on those intricate tiles, hunched over holding my stomach, petrified into position: *The Pitiful Whore.*

Paddy visited one solicitor and then another and another, and it soon became clear that there was nothing to be done. Daisy was gone and worse than that, there was no way of me finding her. All I could do was register, so that if she ever came looking for me, she could find me. Tony sat with me and watched me stare at the wall.

'You can have another baby,' he said, and I wanted to tear his pretty hair out of his head.

'I have a baby. Her name is Daisy and she is not fucking replaceable.'

'I know. I'm sorry. I didn't mean she was. Of course she's not, but she's gone, Catherine, and I just want you back. Paddy and I both do.'

Paddy didn't know what to do in those early days when depression took hold and I couldn't keep my head up. He was kind but also impatient.

'You need to be OK, Catherine. It's been a week. It's been two weeks. It's been three weeks . . .'

340

He didn't know how to fix me. Neither did I. I had no religion or church to turn to, no family, no friends except Tony – and I'd already threatened his life on more than one occasion. I was finally grieving for my child and it was overwhelming.

They took you. I'm not getting you back. I've lost you.

I lived in a fog. I couldn't eat or sleep or function in any real, meaningful way. I spent a month lying in my bed, staring at the wall. I didn't talk to Charles in my head or call to him. I didn't seek comfort or guidance in anyone, living or dead. I didn't want comfort – I didn't deserve it because I'd failed her.

The what ifs kept going round in my head, all the way back to the day my mother slapped me and I realised that I was pregnant. *What if I had slapped her back? What if I had packed my bags and left right then and there?* I wondered about the bull priest. *What if I made him crash his bike? What if I jumped off and ran for my life?* I thought about my biggest mistake, trusting Justin. *What if I'd escaped and moved to Dublin and met Tony before Daisy was born? Or not Tony but someone decent like him? What if I wasn't such a stupid, silly girl?*

It was in one of those daydreams that it dawned on me that Martha O'Halloran was the one who had paid for my release. *Why?* She was a stranger to me. *Why would she do that? Of all the people . . .* I didn't understand. Had someone asked her? Had Justin asked her? What would have happened if she had not? There was so much I needed to know. So much I would never know.

I wrote a letter to my mother on the day we returned from the meeting with Buckaroo. I told her I knew what she'd done and that I never wanted to see her again.

Her reply was four words:

I understand.
  Love,
  Mammy

I wanted to go down to that farmhouse and pull her eyes out of her head, but I knew that seeing her again would only sicken me more. I didn't need answers from her. I knew why she did what she did. She told me that day, on the farm. She'd been bought. And I knew why Judge O'Halloran did what he did. He was protecting his son by throwing me to the wolves. I wondered how he felt when news of Justin's second indiscretion came to light. Maybe he felt bad for what he'd done – but no, he wouldn't. He was probably delighted to have a minister's daughter in the family. The only piece of the puzzle that didn't fit was his sister paying for my release. Over and over again, I asked the wall, *why?*

Paddy was beside himself. 'Please come back to me, Catherine,' he kept saying. I wanted to, but I didn't know how. He took me to another one of his doctor friends, a head shrink who was about as useful as a bottomless bucket.

Tony sat with me and told me all the news from the salon while attempting to feed me biscuits and chocolate cake. I refused food. I was skin and bone and I felt like I was dying – and I wanted to. He pretended that things were better than they were and more hopeful because that was all he could do. No point in him screaming and crying 'Catherine, you're killing yourself.'

But he knew how bad things were and Paddy knew, too. Even the head shrink knew – not that he could solve it. No one could.

Daisy was gone for good. I would never know her. She would never know me.

So I stared at the wall and slept.

One day, Tony arrived with cake and refused to take no for an answer.

'I'm not leaving until you take at least one bite and a big bloody bite at that,' he said.

I stared at the cake. *I used to love chocolate cake . . .*

'Poor John is moving to London,' he said. He hadn't spoken about Poor John in a long time.

I'd always been fond of Poor John. I missed him in the salon. 'How do you know?' I asked.

Tony nearly fell off the side of the bed when I said that. It had been a while since I'd spoken.

'I ran into him,' Tony said.

He didn't say where. He never mentioned the places he went and I never asked.

'He hates the salon he's in . . . Full of auld ones looking for a blue rinse. I asked him back, but he said it wouldn't work. I don't know why – we're both over it.'

'You're not.'

'Bollocks.'

'You're not,' I said.

Tony sniffed and placed the plate down on his lap. 'I wanted him and he wanted everybody.'

'I'm sorry.'

'I thought he'd come back.'

'There's a lot of that going around.'

Tony looked round at me. 'I know me losing John and you losing Daisy isn't the same, but we have to keep fighting, right?'

'For what?' I asked. *What's left to fight for?*

'For happiness,' he said.

I thought about my mother, staring at the old photo of my smiling father and his smoking friends on the back of a trailer, bitterness etched into her face.

'Some people just don't get that lucky,' I said.

'That's why it's a fight, you feckin' eejit.'

I thought about what he said and I knew he was right, and I also knew I was lucky to have the life I had. I thought about the girls left behind in that place, about Martha O'Halloran. *Why?*

If I was never to know anything else, I needed to know that.

I waited until Paddy had gone to work and then I dragged myself out of bed. Slowly and painfully, I made my way to the bathroom, where I showered for the first time in days. I dressed myself and I noticed how thin I'd become. I was a shadow, just like the nuns wanted me to be. That hurt. *You did this to yourself,* I thought, looking at my gaunt reflection in the mirror.

I put on a little make-up and somehow it made me feel a little stronger, a little better. I put on an expensive coat that Paddy had bought me as a present and the handbag that cost more than a week's salary. The last time I'd spoken to Martha I had been dressed like a corduroy clown, bloated with child and desperate; now, I was dressed expensively, thin as a rake but still desperate.

A lot changes. A lot stays the same.

I rang her doorbell. I wasn't scared of bumping into Justin; I knew he'd have moved on as soon as he married. There was no way Jennifer was bringing a baby up in Auntie Martha's basement. No doubt they had a beautiful home in a leafy suburb while he still struggled to make his grades in university. I didn't care. I wasn't here about Justin O'Halloran.

She opened the door and as soon as she saw me, she grabbed my hand and held it. Tears filled her eyes.

'I hoped I'd see you again,' she said, and the door swung open and she let me in.

I followed her to the kitchen.

344

'Are you hungry?'

'No.'

'You haven't a pick on you. Please let me give you something. I have lovely tomato soup, made fresh, and brown bread . . . Please.'

I nodded. 'OK.'

'Sit,' Martha said, pointing to the small table against the wall.

I sat. She flicked on the gas flame under a large pot.

'I always make too much. It's just me, you see.'

'Why did you help me?' I asked her.

She sat and clasped her hands together, knotting her fingers. I could see the tension in them.

'Justin rang his father to ask his advice. I told him not to, but he was adamant he couldn't conceal the truth from him. My brother, Jeffery, took it from there.'

'Why didn't you tell me? I could have run.'

Martha sighed. 'I never married. This was our parents' home. There were only two of us, Jeffery and me. He got a job in a prestigious firm in Cork straight out of university. Then he met Imelda and he made his life there. I stayed here. I've only ever been away from this house once, for eight months in 1951.'

The soup was bubbling in the pot; she stood up to stir it.

The penny dropped. She was just like me.

'You were in one of those places,' I said.

'I was in the same place,' she said, lowering the heat. She turned to face me. 'I lost my little girl, too.'

I felt tears in my eyes. 'Then you should have known better.'

'I have a roof over my head because my brother agreed not to sell the house from under me, but he reminds me often that his goodwill has limitations.'

'You have a job – you could buy your own house.'

'It's not that simple,' she said. 'Life just isn't that simple.'

She tasted the soup and poured some into a bowl for me. Then she cut some bread and returned to the table with the soup and the slices. She took the butter out of the cupboard and then grabbed a knife and a spoon, placing them in front of me. I stared down at the soup. She placed a swirl of cream on top.

'Eat it while it's hot.'

I took a spoonful and it was hot, a little too hot, but it was also tasty. I felt the heat roll down my throat.

She moved to walk away again. 'I'll get you a glass of water.'

'No. Please. Sit. Talk to me.'

She sat. 'What do you want to know?'

'Do you know O'Halloran is paying my parents to keep me away?'

'Yes.'

'Do you know he had my mother sign my baby away and he used his influence to hasten the adoption?'

'Yes.'

'Do you know where she is?'

'No. I'm sorry. I don't.'

'Did they even care where they put her?' I asked.

'I know she's with a good family. My brother's pride would prevent anything less.'

'Are you sure?'

'I'm absolutely positive.'

'Do you think your brother knows where they put her?' I asked.

'No.'

I tried to hold back my tears. 'Where did your child go?'

'America,' she said, and she welled up. 'At least that's what I suppose. A lot of babies went to America back then.'

'I'm sorry,' I said.

'Thank you.'

'You never married?'

'No. They left me with some medical problems that I didn't think it would be fair to burden any man with.'

'Oh.'

'And you? Are you all right, Catherine?'

'I thought I was,' I said. 'But then I thought I'd get my girl back.'

'You have to let go,' Martha said gently.

'I've heard that before.' I remembered my old friend Marian from the nun's greenhouse saying something similar. 'What if I can't?'

'Then you run the risk of letting them ruin your entire life.' A tear escaped.

'Is that what they did to you?' I asked.

'It's what I did to myself.'

I looked at her. 'Thank you for releasing me,' I said, and my gratitude was sincere.

'It was the least I could do. I'm a coward, Catherine, but you . . . You're a fighter. Remember that.'

I finished up all of Martha's soup and I even ate a slice of brown bread with butter. When I was leaving, I hugged her tight and whispered in her ear, 'There's still time.'

She seemed older but she must have only been in her mid to late forties. There was still time.

She smiled and nodded.

I arrived home after Paddy. He was beside himself.

'I thought you'd done something terrible,' he said as I walked into his arms.

'I'm done with all that now, Paddy.'

'You're back?' he asked, and he sounded almost afraid.

'I'm getting there,' I said.

Four months later, I found out I was pregnant. I was happy and of course I was sad. I knew the baby would never replace my Daisy. This was another child, totally different; this child would not live inside a desperate young girl, or be pulled away halfway through a feed, left to cry alone until a stranger picked her up. This child would be born to a loving mother and a father. This child would be safe.

I didn't want to call him or her kiddo; that term of endearment belonged to Daisy. Cuddles was the word I used.

'Hey, Cuddles, try not to make me too sick today; I've got four cuts and a colour coming through this door.'

'Cuddles, ignore your uncle Tony. I do *not* look like a beached whale.'

'Cuddles, can you feel your daddy's arms around you? Wait till you see him – he's so handsome.'

'If he's a boy, he won't care,' Paddy said.

'If he's a boy like Tony, he'll be impressed,' I said, and Paddy laughed.

Chapter Twenty-Five

Friday the Thirteenth – Morning

THE SKY WAS A PRETTY LIGHT blue and although it was cold outside, there wasn't a hint of a cloud in the sky. Caroline had thought about cancelling the trip to the Aran Islands – after all, she was still grieving. But time and time again, she talked herself back into it. *It will be good for me. It's something different. It's an experience.* On the flip side, she really hated 'experiences'. She was shit sick of them. How many experiences can one woman have? All the experiences in the world couldn't fill the baby-shaped hole in her life.

But flying to the Aran Islands with Ronnie and the girls was better than watching Dave guide an estate agent around their home, so on the morning of Friday the thirteenth, she woke up, showered, ate a light breakfast and was about to get into her car, when the estate agent rolled up in his silver BMW. She glimpsed through the window and with a silver jacket and waistcoat and slicked-back hair, the word 'prick' immediately sprang to mind. *Don't be unkind, Caroline.* She was making an effort to be a better person. She had good days and bad.

He stepped out of the car, brushing himself down.

'You Caroline?' he said.

'Yes.'

'Going somewhere?'

'Yes.' She got into her car.

'It's Friday the thirteenth – unlucky for some, wha'? Mind yourself out there.' He tapped the top of her roof as she drove off.

Caroline wasn't a suspicious person; the date had barely registered with her at all. She had never been a nervous flyer and now that she had finally mentally committed to the outing, she was looking forward to it. *A change is as good as a rest.* Despite layering her face in make-up and concealer, her eyes were puffy. She'd cried herself to sleep, not because she couldn't have a child or that she was jealous of her friend's pregnancy; her tears were reserved for her aching heart. Dave couldn't forgive her because Dave knew she was broken and there was nothing that would fix her. She didn't resent him for that. She pitied him for having wasted so many years on her.

I'm sorry you weren't enough, Dave.

She didn't want to give up, but deep down she knew it was kinder to let him go. She'd hurt the man she loved enough. *It's done, Caroline.*

Janet didn't sleep much the previous night. She was looking forward to their day out, but she was also busy daydreaming of and talking to her baby. Every once in a while she slipped up and begged her child to stay with her and not die, but mostly she kept things positive. She talked about their future together and all the things the world had to offer. 'I know it can be hard sometimes, baby, but it's worth it. Trust me,' she'd said, and then she rolled over and kissed her sleeping husband and made plans.

She woke up early and checked out four CVs of girls looking to take over on the reception desk of her husband's business. Tina had handed in her notice when Jim made it clear that theirs was a working relationship only. She had plans to travel and left on good terms, according to Jim. Janet didn't question it.

She was just glad she was gone. Once the CVs were vetted, she placed her two top picks on the kitchen counter and waited for the girls.

Caroline picked her up and, in the car as they drove, Janet mentioned the date to Caroline as a joke. 'Friday thirteenth, unlucky for some . . .'

'So I've heard,' Caroline said.

'I hope Ronnie is a decent pilot,' Janet said. 'I haven't come this far to die in a plane crash on a bloody unlucky day.'

'Friday the thirteenth on your gravestone just feels like a piss-take.'

Janet laughed.

'I think we'll be fine,' Caroline said as she drove into the car park beneath Ronnie's building. Ronnie and Natalie were waiting. Everyone had gone to the trouble of dressing up and Janet briefly thought about how lovely Ronnie would look in vintage. It was the first time she'd thought about vintage clothes for a while.

Caroline rolled down the window.

'It's a beautiful day for flying, ladies,' Ronnie said before directing Caroline into a parking space.

Once parked, they exited the car and Ronnie and Natalie led the way towards Ronnie's Range Rover.

'Wow, nice car,' Janet said.

'It's big for one,' Ronnie said. 'An impulse buy. I'm more of a sports car person.'

'Next time,' Janet said, and Ronnie nodded, but for a moment the mood dipped. She wasn't the only one who noticed it.

'Get in,' Ronnie said, opening the passenger door for Caroline.

She helped Caroline in. She was still sore, although a lot more nimble than previously. Natalie and Janet climbed into the back, then Ronnie turned on the engine.

'Let's do this,' she said, and Janet felt her insides fizz as they drove onto the motorway. *We're going into the sky, baby.*

Natalie watched the world go by from the back seat. She and Ronnie had enjoyed a drink together the previous night. Ronnie had apologised for her outburst once again, but there was really no need. Natalie couldn't imagine how painful Ronnie's past had been. Catherine sounded like an incredible woman from what she'd read and she couldn't imagine what it would feel like for Ronnie to read of her birth mother's misery.

Ronnie told her that she'd met Catherine's husband and children and her best friend, Tony. 'They were nice,' she said. 'Tony won't stop calling me.' She feigned annoyance, but she smiled when she said it. She didn't mention Catherine and Natalie didn't ask. She'd pried enough.

In the car, Ronnie played chart hits loudly and the women talked about all kinds of things. Natalie noticed how happy Janet looked. Of course she was still nervous of losing her child, but she seemed more secure and confident. Maybe it was just in Natalie's head, but her voice seemed a little louder. The women laughed and Caroline even sang along to a Cher track. Natalie missed Linda and her old life, but her friendship with these women was proving to be a very soft landing.

She leaned back and smiled to herself. *It's going to be a good day.*

She's Not Daisy

Catherine

THE BABY CAME ON THE twelfth day of June. My blood pressure wasn't an issue during the entire pregnancy, probably owing to the fact that I wasn't being worked to the bone and terrified for my life. I worked in the salon until the last week, when I was just too tired. I was home and lying on our new sofa when I felt the first cramp. I knew I was in labour, but I also knew I had lots of time, so I got up, showered, painted my nails and fixed my hair. I took out the nightdresses that I had packed a month earlier and re-ironed them. I checked the baby bag, twice, to ensure I had everything noted on the list. I put on some perfume and a smart maternity dress that was just plain black jersey that fell over my bump and to my feet. I put on my gold sandals and a full face of make-up.

Then I phoned Paddy and told him that I needed to go to the hospital.

'I'm coming. *I'm coming*!' He dropped the phone.

I sat on my new sofa and cried with every labour pain. Not because it hurt, but because I was so emotional and so utterly terrified. I was shaking like a leaf and battling the urge to run. I couldn't understand it. *Stop it, Catherine. This is a good day. Don't ruin it.* Inside me, Daisy had been safe. But once she was born, I lost all control. What if that happened again? I knew it was completely different, and yet the fear and dread that washed over me was incapacitating. *What if the baby is sick? What if the baby fails to thrive? What if the baby doesn't make it out alive?*

I knew that they couldn't or wouldn't take Cuddles from me, but what if I just wasn't meant to be a mother? What if I wasn't fit, just like those nuns had told me. What if they cursed me? What if I could only be an incubator and never a mother to my own child? I had to talk to myself, to calm down. *Cop the fuck on, Catherine.*

I saw the car pull up outside and I pinched myself hard. 'Stop this, now,' I said aloud. 'This is different.'

I wiped away my tears just as Paddy burst through the door. Before he left work, he'd stopped in the gift shop at his hospital to buy two balloons: one for a boy and the other for a girl.

'We're having a baby!' he shouted, and he was so excited, but I was shaken to my core.

Seeing me in such a state took some wind from his sails. He took me in his arms and lifted me from the sofa.

'It's going to be OK, my love,' he said. He kissed the top of my head. 'It's going to be better than OK.'

The voices screaming 'What if . . .' inside my mind quietened a little as we made our way outside and towards the car. I breathed in the fresh air. *You see, Catherine, it's different already. You can breathe.*

This birth was different from Daisy's in every way possible. A kind-faced midwife greeted us at the door and took us into a private room that my husband had paid for. She explained what was about to happen and we both listened politely, then she told me to say goodbye to Paddy and that he'd see me soon.

'Don't worry. I'll be here,' she said, then turned to Paddy. 'Your wife is in good hands.'

He was sent away. Lots of men went to the pub, but he went to the salon and drank tea while Tony made a huge fuss of him, telling every client who walked through the door what was happening. Meanwhile, I was in a pretty nightgown on a comfortable bed, with a lovely nurse called Fidelma by my side. I was having contractions and she was coaching me, and she was so gentle when she examined me. I didn't cry once, but I kept saying thank you.

'Don't be silly, that's what I'm here for,' she said, as though her kindness meant nothing.

I gave birth to a little girl at two minutes past ten that evening. I had no stitches and she was placed in my arms within minutes of her birth.

'Isn't she beautiful?' I heard the doctor say. And my first thought was: *Wow! She is definitely not Daisy.* And of course I knew she wasn't Daisy, but seeing her with her red hair, pale skin and her little chubby cheeks in such contrast to her sister, it somehow shocked me. Just as beautiful, just as loved, but entirely different. Even the way she felt in my arms – her weight distribution, the way she suckled, the way she moved and cried and kicked. *You are not her. You are you. Hello you.*

Paddy wasn't allowed in until the next morning due to two drunk fathers kicking off and the matron shutting the ward down. I spent the night with her in my arms just staring at her.

'You should put her in the cot and get some sleep.'

'No, thanks.'

'You must be exhausted.'

'I'm fine.'

I didn't want to let her go and I couldn't allow her out of my sight. *What if* . . .

Paddy arrived just after 8 a.m. with a large bunch of flowers and the pink balloon, a box of chocolates, a bottle of champagne and a huge cuddly toy. 'For Cuddles.' He dropped everything on the bed and moved over to have a look at her, stroking her face with his finger.

'She has your hair,' he marvelled.

'And your chin,' I said.

'And your dimple.'

'And I think she'll have your eyes,' I said, and I raised her up to him. 'Hold her.'

It was my first time letting her go. He took her in his arms.

'Oh my God, I'm done for,' he said. 'My two beautiful redheads.'

I watched him hold her and love her and then I looked around the room at the balloon, the chocolates, the champagne and flowers and the beautiful big fluffy bear. I remembered the steel cot, the broken locker and the carbolic soap in that place. I remembered the pain and sense of helplessness when I woke in that cold room, and now here I was, in another room, in another world, with my husband and daughter. I was twenty years old and a mother of two.

We called her Jessica and I didn't change the nursery, so she slept in a pink room and surrounded by daisies. It was both difficult and comforting.

I haven't let you go, Daisy. Never will. I love you. I miss you. I hope you are happy. I'll be waiting for you.

I qualified as a stylist a few months before Jess was born and I went back to work when she was six months old. We bought the house we rented because we were content there. Tony was close by and it just worked for us. Jess was with a childminder four days a week and then a year later, I got pregnant again and it just didn't make sense to work after I had twin boys. They were a huge surprise and a lot of work. We called them Philip after Paddy and Tony's granddad, and Richard after their dad. They were a funny pair; happy in one another's company and as loud as they were sweet. I spent a few years up to my eyes in nappies, navigating my way through tantrums.

I was happy, but I never forgot my Daisy. I saw her in my other children, in their cries, in their laughs, in everything they did and said. She was always with me and she always will be.

Chapter Twenty-Six

Friday the Thirteenth – Afternoon

THE PLANE WAS A FOUR-SEATER single prop Cessna 172, painted in blinding white, with a navy and grey wave on its side.

'There she is,' Ronnie said as they walked up to it.

Caroline's stomach flipped. Unusually, she felt a surge of abject nervousness. *Weird! I like flying.*

Stepping onto this plane was not the same as a regular Boeing; the Cessna reminded her of something straight out of a world war. Her legs turned to jelly as they approached. *What the hell is wrong with you, Caroline?*

She looked to Janet, who was clapping her hands together with childlike glee. 'Oh my God! This is so cool.' She was rustling around in her handbag. 'Damn it, I forgot my camera. It's on the bloody kitchen counter.'

So, she's all right, then, Caroline thought, looking towards Natalie, who was striding ahead with a confidence that suggested boarding a tiny little plane was as natural as sitting in a Fiat 500.

As she did so, she fished into her pocket and pulled out a camera. 'I brought one. It's a disposable I picked up at a wedding. Took a few of the strangers at my table while I was pissed, but plenty of film left.'

Janet clapped her hands together again. Caroline felt slightly faint. Ronnie noticed her colour fade.

'You OK?' she asked, and Caroline tried to laugh it off.

'Just finding my sea legs.'

Natalie and Janet looked her way.

'You didn't mention you were a bad flyer,' Natalie said.

'I'm not, not usually,' Caroline said.

She'd flown on small planes in the middle of nowhere before, because Dave didn't think a holiday was a holiday unless you were knee deep in piranha-infested water in the middle of the Amazon or on a remote island with just a tent and a piece of flint – but those plans were bigger than Ronnie's sparkly new one. It was like stepping into a flying car and cars don't fly. Caroline felt herself slowing down.

Ronnie stopped and placed her hands on Caroline's shoulders. 'Everything will be fine. We are going to celebrate Janet's pregnancy in a really cool little spot I know and love on the Aran Islands. We are going to have a really lovely day. Nod if you understand me.'

Caroline nodded.

'You're up front with me,' Ronnie said, pushing her forwards and towards the right-hand side of the plane.

Ah crap. But Caroline didn't argue owing to her tongue being stuck to the roof of her mouth. Ronnie helped her to strap in. Janet sat in directly behind Ronnie, and Natalie piled behind Caroline.

Natalie squeezed Caroline's shoulder. 'This is going to be great,' she said before winding the dial on the plastic disposable camera back. She took a photo from the window looking out onto the tarmac. Her face fell a little. 'I wish Linda could be here,' she said.

Janet turned to face her. 'Linda wasn't the woman for you,' she said. 'You'll find someone who wants what you want, and you'll have your family and life will be good again,' Janet said with an authority and assuredness that sounded like she was some kind of oracle.

Natalie just smiled.

Caroline sat frozen to the spot, watching Ronnie carry out her checks. It was disconcerting to say the least. She was used to being at the back of the plane with her head stuck in a magazine, waiting for drinks to be served. *Calm down, Caroline. Do not mess this day up*. She looked up into the clear blue sky and it was such a calm day. *Just chill . . .*

And then they were moving, hurtling down the runway at a speed of knots. Her eyes were glued to Ronnie's hands gripping the steering wheel, which looked more like a gaming device than a grown-up and proper navigating tool.

Caroline blew out excess air that had magically accrued in her lungs and before she could even blink, they were climbing. Over the buzzing that was now playing in her ears, she could hear Ronnie's voice. 'Gone out on the west, departure at 1,000 feet.'

After passing Maynooth, they continued climbing. Caroline could see the dial – 1,500 feet and still climbing – and her head and neck felt heavy. Natalie was oohing and ahhing and winding back the plastic camera, clicking photos, asking everyone to turn to her and say 'cheese'.

Caroline couldn't move her neck. It seemed stuck – but Ronnie who was flying the flipping plane turned 360 degrees and grinned. She even gave the thumbs up. Natalie pressed the button then she turned round and winked at Caroline.

'If you let go of the steering wheel one more time, I will punch you in the face,' Caroline said.

Ronnie laughed, choosing to ignore the threat of violence. 'It's not exactly called a steering wheel.'

'I don't give a shit what it's called. You know what I'm saying,' Caroline said, and Ronnie chuckled before threatening to raise her hands.

'Look, no hands!'

'Not funny,' Caroline said, but Natalie and Janet were laughing. They were having a ball.

'It's so beautiful,' Janet kept saying. 'Feels like we're just cruising through a piece of heaven.'

'I love being up here on days like this,' Ronnie said, and despite her anxiety, Caroline could see how happy and relaxed her new friend was.

This is exactly where she belongs, up here in the clouds and looking down on the world. She looked different, like a weight had lifted and she was free. *I envy you, Ronnie.*

Janet and Natalie talked about the restaurant they were going to and what they would eat and whether or not one alcoholic drink was appropriate for Janet to drink.

'Absolutely not,' Janet said in mock horror.

'Ah, go on,' Natalie said. 'Have a shandy.'

'Better yet, have a Bellini,' Ronnie said.

'I just really fancy a Cidona,' Janet said. 'I've been craving one all day.'

'Well, unless this is a time machine taking us back to 1986, you'll be out of luck,' Natalie said.

'You're doing great,' Ronnie said to Caroline.

She was focused on the sky in front of them. 'I feel better.'

'The colour is returning to your cheeks.' And then Ronnie turned left, and Caroline's stomach hit the floor. *How long more?*

'What would you do if you weren't a pilot?' Natalie asked Ronnie, and Caroline registered pain flitting across Ronnie's face.

'I couldn't think of a worse life than a life in which I couldn't fly.'

'I can see that,' Janet said. 'It's a privilege to be up here.'

Ronnie nodded and smiled, but Caroline could have sworn she saw tears filling her eyes.

They had taken off from the Weston Airport in Celbridge and flown over Maynooth before following the motorway. They were flying at 3,000 feet over Enfield, when air traffic control made contact with the plane. Initially, Caroline didn't pay too much attention, because Janet and Natalie were singing Joni Mitchell's 'Both Sides, Now' from the album *Clouds*.

But then the voice on the radio was talking and Ronnie's expression changed ever so slightly, although it was noticeable to the hyper-engaged Caroline.

'The pilot seems to be heading back to the field on a solo . . . not on radio contact.'

Caroline observed Ronnie looking out of the side windows as though she were about to use a roundabout. The girls were still singing poorly. Caroline followed Ronnie's eyeline. *Nothing to see but sky.* Again, the voice spluttered through the radio.

'Advise that the plane is now at your three o'clock opposite direction, not in radio contact.'

Ronnie's back was arched; she was focused now, and on alert. *What? What's wrong?*

The next thing Caroline knew, she could feel the whole plane tumbling in the air and the girls stopped singing. In an instant, the momentary silence was replaced with an almighty bang. No one spoke. No one had time to breathe, let alone speak, as Caroline felt the plane stopping dead in the air.

Oh God. I'm going to die today. Dave! Oh no, Dave.

She must have turned to look out of the window, because suddenly she could see the top of a wing cutting right through her horizon as they started to spin to the left. She could see the other plane below her. Some of the wing was missing and it was spinning so fast, it was just a metal blur. *I'm so sorry, Dave. You were the love of my life. I'm such a fucking idiot. I love you. Goodbye.*

Janet held on to her stomach and her unborn with both hands and breathlessly watched the plane below them spinning and tumbling to the ground. She started to say 'Please don't die, please don't die,' to her baby and to herself and to the others. 'Please don't die.'

Natalie was stunned, still hugging her plastic camera, eyes wide open and staring ahead.

'Please don't die,' Janet shouted again.

And in that moment, as the ground was fast approaching, Ronnie recovered from the spin and restarted her engine in one slick move, as though she had been waiting for exactly the right second to deliver them from impending death.

As the plane limped along, Janet stared out of her window, to see the other plane crashing into the ground below. *Please don't die.*

There was no sound; they were too far away to hear the impact. There was no inferno or dreaded blackened smoke. All Janet could see was a white plume rising back up and into the sky. *Oh my God. He died.* She refocused on Ronnie, who was struggling to keep the plane in the air. Beside her, Caroline seemed catatonic.

Air traffic control was still going.

'Mayday, Mayday, Mayday, Golf, Romeo, Oscar, November, November.'

'Go ahead, November, November . . .'

'Just been in a mid-air collision. The other aircraft is down. Position two miles south of Enfield,' Ronnie said.

Suddenly, Natalie was screaming. Janet grabbed her hand and squeezed it tight.

Ronnie was calm. 'Natalie, stop it. We will be OK, but not if you give the pilot a fucking migraine.'

Natalie stopped screaming.

Air traffic were talking on the radio. 'Rescue services – position two miles north of Enfield.'

'Negative, negative – two miles south of Enfield,' Ronnie said, and she was holding the plane steady, but it was taking everything she had in her.

Janet closed her eyes and thought about her husband and the children she'd lost. She held on to the baby in her belly with one hand and Natalie with the other. *I'm not ready to die. We're not ready.*

Natalie didn't realise that Janet was holding her hand until she looked down. She was numb, mentally and physically. She'd just witnessed a man die. She was braced for impact and it took her a moment or two to realise their plane was still in the air. Ronnie was back in control. How much longer could she keep them alive? Ten minutes, five? *I wish it had worked out, Linda. I'm sorry. Take care of her, Paul. She needs you. Sorry, Mam and Dad. I can't fucking believe this is the way I'm going to go.*

'Caroline, put your hands on the control,' Ronnie said, and Caroline turned to face her, white as a sheet and trembling.

'What?'

'Caroline, I need you to put your hands on the controls and when I ask you to turn to the left, exactly like you would a steering wheel, just turn to the left slow and steady. And when I ask you to push forwards, just push forwards.'

'I can't.'

'Caroline, the controls are semi-jammed and I need you to help me land this plane.'

'Absolutely not.'

'Just help her land the fucking plane, Caroline,' Janet roared, and it shook Caroline out of her daze and into action.

She grabbed on.

'OK. OK. OK.'

'No one's going to die today. Not in this plane,' Ronnie said.

And with Caroline's help, she began to turn the plane around.

'Are we going to try to land in one of those fields?' Natalie heard herself saying, but her voice sounded like it was coming from the other side of a dense fog.

'We have a damaged engine. If we put it in a field on soft ground, the plane could flip and burst into flames.'

'Oh God,' she heard Janet say. 'Not today, not today.'

'We have a damaged engine, but there's enough there to get us back.' Ronnie's voice was calm and cool.

Natalie started praying then. She wasn't really much of a God-botherer, but if you're not going to pray following a mid-air collision, when are you? She was halfway through the Our Father, when she heard Ronnie say to air traffic control that she wanted to keep it tight.

'Don't want a long flight over residential areas.'

'So, if we go down, we don't take too many others with us,' Caroline said. She was flying the plane with Ronnie now.

Ronnie nodded. 'But we're not going down. You're a natural,' she said, and Caroline laughed hysterically. She was crying too, but she nodded her agreement.

'No one's going to die today, not on this plane,' she mimicked Ronnie, who smiled.

'That's right.'

And then Natalie saw the airstrip and the lights flashing and the rescue services waiting. She felt Janet's hand in hers and she held her breath as she braced herself for a hard landing. As

Ronnie shouted clear orders to Caroline, she heard Janet whisper to her baby, 'Don't die, please don't die.'

And she felt the bang, bump and shudder of the wheels as they tore along the ground. She could smell the burning and hear the sparks and then all of a sudden, they landed. The propeller came to a dead stop as Ronnie shut down the engine and all went quiet for one moment before the sirens blared as the white, red and blue lights sped towards them.

'Are we alive?' Natalie said, looking to Janet, who instantly looked down at her stomach before reaching Natalie's gaze. 'We're alive,' she said.

Ronnie and Caroline were staring at one another.

'We did it,' Caroline said.

'We did,' Ronnie said, and they were hugging and laughing and crying and it was all so overwhelming, Natalie's head buzzed. Her heart beat so fast and her hands trembled.

We're alive.

They climbed out of the plane and into the arms of people waiting to rush them to ambulances, to take them to the nearest hospital for check-ups, but there was nothing wrong. No one had banged a head, scratched themselves or even lost a nail.

Ronnie had saved them. Ronnie and Caroline together had saved them. It was a miracle.

Hello, Catherine

Catherine

THE YEARS PASSED QUICKLY WHEN the kids were young. Jess was four and the twins had just turned three. I was back in the salon part-time and planned to go back full-time as soon as the kids were all in school. It was a bright spring morning when my doorbell rang, and I answered it with a toddler in my arms and Jess hanging on to my leg, demanding cheese. I didn't recognise him for a second, but then he nodded and offered me that shy smile.

'Ronan!' I said, looking my brother up and down. I nearly dropped the kids.

'Hello, Catherine,' he said.

'Come in, come in.'

I was so happy to see him. I put the kids on the play mat on the floor and hugged him tight.

'All these yours, Catherine?' he asked, looking around at the three kids.

'Yes. I'm afraid they are.' I laughed lightly.

'And you, Ronan? How are you?' I pointed to the sofa and made him sit.

He sat, cap in hand. 'I'm fine,' he said.

'Would you like a cup of tea? Something to eat?'

'No. I can't stay long.'

'But you just arrived.'

'I know, but the pigs won't feed themselves.'

'You didn't leave?'

'It's my home.'

'And Tim?'

'He's there, too.'

'So he'll feed them.'

'I have to get back. Mammy doesn't like it if I leave her too long.'

I ignored the mention of her name. 'And Mickey?' I said to change the subject.

'He never did come home. He sends a letter now and then.'

'He was never happy there,' I said.

'I know.'

'And you, Ronan, are you happy there?'

'I am, Catherine.'

'Then I'm happy for you.'

He stood up and picked up a framed photograph of Paddy, the kids and me. 'What about you?' he asked.

'I'm as happy as I can be,' I said. 'And that's a lot happier than I thought I'd ever be.'

He placed the photo back down on the fireplace and he sat once more, twisting his cap in his hands.

'I have some news, Catherine.'

'Daddy's dead?' I asked in a matter-of-fact way. It seemed the most obvious reason for him coming to see me.

He nodded his confirmation. I felt nothing. He and Mammy died for me the day I found out they signed my baby away.

'But it's more than that.' He looked nervous. Tiny beads of sweat formed about his lip. He seemed unsteady. *Oh no.*

I steeled myself. 'OK.'

'He had a disease.'

'I guessed.'

'It's a bad one.'

'OK.' I was starting to feel very uneasy.

'They call it Huntington's.'

'Never heard of it,' I said quickly and defensively, although I had no idea what I was defending.

'They say it's genetic – that if a parent has it, then the kids might have it, too.'

'But his parents were fine,' I said.

'They died in their late thirties before symptoms had a chance to show themselves.'

'Was that what happened to Charles?' I asked.

'No.' He shook his head. 'That was something else. This only happens when you're older.'

'How old?'

'Dad was diagnosed in his early forties.'

'What did it do to him?' I asked, and I felt a pain pierce my heart.

'It stole him away, Catherine. Little by little, piece by piece, until it killed him.'

My spine stiffened and my eyes softened. 'Was it a hard death?'

'It was a harder life. Death was a mercy,' he said, and he couldn't meet my eye.

'Is that what lies ahead for us, Ronan?' I whispered.

'I hope not, Catherine, but it's best you know about it.'

He left shortly after that.

I watched for Paddy to return home and met him at the front door. 'What do you know about Huntington's?' I asked him.

'I know it's horrific,' he said. 'Why do you ask?'

'It killed my father,' I said, and I watched the colour drain from his face.

And then I was in his arms and he was repeating the words, 'It won't be you, it won't be us.'

I wanted to believe him, but somewhere inside me, another bomb went off.

Chapter Twenty-Seven

Friday the Thirteenth – Evening

CAROLINE SAT ON THE EDGE of the gurney, waiting for the doctor to give her the all-clear. She rang Dave as soon as she got off the plane. She told him that she'd been in a plane crash but that she was fine, and once he ascertained her location, he hung up. It only seemed like minutes before the blue paper curtain moved and there he was, standing in front of her.

Dave.

She smiled at him. 'I missed you,' she said, and then she was in his arms and they were hugging and tears ran down her face.

He pulled back and looked at her, examining every inch of her. 'Are you OK?'

'I'm fine. We're all fine.'

'You were in a mid-air collision, Caroline.'

'I know. I helped Ronnie land the plane,' she said in a voice that suggested she couldn't quite believe it herself.

'You could have died.' He sounded as bewildered as she felt.

'Someone did die, Dave. A young cadet. He lost his way and found us.'

'I'm so sorry,' he said, wiping away a stray tear tumbling down her cheek.

'I survived, Dave.'

'Yeah.' He laughed nervously. 'You did.'

She grabbed his hand, holding it in hers and examining it. His wedding ring was still on his finger. She looked up at him.

'I thought I was going to die,' Caroline said, 'and all I saw or thought about or cared about was you. You were the person I spent my last moments with. Just you. It's always been you, Dave.'

'It didn't feel like it,' he said quietly, tears gathering in his eyes.

'I know, and that's my fault. All this time I've been waiting for the miracle – I thought that it would be a baby, but it's not. It was never a baby. It's here and now, me and you. It's surviving a mid-air collision. It's a second chance.'

'At what?'

'Life. Our lives.'

'And the hole inside you has miraculously disappeared?'

'I used to wonder what was the point in me. Now I know.'

'Are you sure you didn't hit your head?' Dave asked, and she grinned.

'I'm never going to be a mother,' she said, smiling. 'That ship has sailed.' She was laughing now. 'I'm free.'

She laughed and laughed and Dave started to look around for a doctor, but then she stopped and tears glistened in her eyes.

'I thought I was going to die and I realised as the plane was hurtling towards the ground that I was lucky and so very stupid . . .' She bit her lip. 'When Ronnie told me to take the controls, I did it to get back to you.'

Dave broke into a big smile before he exhaled. 'My girl is back,' he said with his arms in the air, and then they hugged and stayed in one another's arms until a nurse interrupted them with the offer of some tea and toast.

When Janet was scanned, she got to see her baby again.

'Snug as a bug in a rug,' Jim said, standing beside her, holding her hand, afraid to let go.

'We're fine, Jim.' She was staring at her little one.

'Fine? You've just survived a plane crash. Not many get to say that, babe,' he said.

'I know and it's weird, but I knew as long as I survived, the baby would, too. I'm not scared anymore, Jim.'

'Of course not, Janet, you're bleedin' invincible.'

She laughed as she got off the table. 'They'll be making movies about us,' she said.

'One day,' he said.

And then she stopped and thought about the young fella who had died. 'He was only twenty, Jim.'

'I know, babe. And I'm sorry, but I'm just really glad he didn't take my whole world with him.'

They walked out into the hallway arm in arm.

Natalie was treated for mild shock. Ronnie sat with her.

'Are you OK?' Natalie asked for the tenth time in the space of half an hour.

'I'm all good,' Ronnie said.

'I'm OK, too.'

'I know.'

'When can we go home?' Natalie asked.

'Soon.'

'You saved us.'

'I had help.'

'You saved us,' Natalie said again.

They sat in silence for a while.

'What's worse than death?' Natalie said out of nowhere.

'What?'

'You said your birth mother wasn't dead, it was worse than death. I wasn't going to ask, but we just survived a plane crash together, so . . .'

Ronnie shuffled in the chair. 'She has Huntington's. Do you know what that is?'

'It's a rare hereditary disease. It causes the breakdown of nerve cells in the brain, causing movement issues and cognitive and psychiatric disorders.' Natalie rattled it off verbatim the way she did all the other information stored in her brain, like she was at a pub quiz. It was a moment before she realised she was talking about Ronnie's mother.

'That's right,' Ronnie said.

'Oh no,' whispered Natalie. 'Hereditary.'

Ronnie looked at her and nodded.

'What's inherited?' Caroline asked as she walked towards them. 'Dave's just getting the car.' She stopped in her tracks, obviously sensing the weight between them. 'What is it?'

'I recently discovered I have the gene for Huntington's disease,' Ronnie said.

Natalie could see Caroline's face dropping. It was clear she knew exactly what that meant.

'It's not that you can't have kids,' she said. 'It's that you won't.'

Ronnie nodded. 'Yes.'

'And there's no escape?' Caroline asked.

'No. It's just a waiting game.'

'I'm so sorry.'

'Thank you,' Ronnie said, and she looked between her two friends. 'I'm sorry I barged into your group. I just wanted to be anonymous. I couldn't face a Huntington's group. I couldn't look at what lay ahead, you know? I didn't want anyone in my real life to know.'

Natalie understood why Ronnie didn't want to tell anyone in her life. Flying was her reason for being. When she got too sick to fly . . . *Poor Ronnie.*

Janet appeared with Jim by her side. 'The baby is fine. Better than fine. Baby has grown,' she said.

The women clapped and cheered.

'I'm really glad I met you all,' Ronnie said. 'Before today, I had considered suicide.'

'Jesus! What in the name of God did I miss?' Janet said.

'We'll catch you up,' Natalie whispered.

Ronnie was on a roll. 'But today we experienced a miracle. We're alive and maybe, just maybe, if I get one miracle, why not two?' She grinned. 'I have time – and I don't know about you ladies, but I'm going to make the most of it.'

'I'm entering the lotto,' Caroline said.

'Me too,' Natalie said.

'I wish I knew what was going on,' Janet said, but she smiled anyway.

That night, Natalie and Ronnie were chauffeured home. They sat together in the back of the car, listening to the sounds of life around them.

'What now?' Natalie asked out of nowhere.

'Now I fight,' Ronnie said. 'Just like my mother.'

Natalie put her arm around her and Ronnie snuggled in.

'I'm not a lesbian,' she said with a smile in her voice.

Natalie laughed. 'You're not my type even if you were.'

'Bollocks, I'm a ride,' Ronnie said, and the two women laughed till they cried.

Time to Let Go

Catherine

PADDY AND I HAD OVER twenty good years together. After some time out, I returned to the salon and together, Tony and I worked in the shop, making it one of the most sought-after in Dublin. I loved my job and I loved my kids. I loved my husband. It was a good life.

And then I turned forty, and soon after that my limbs stopped fully co-operating. I was clumsy and half the time, I couldn't remember my own name. I felt profoundly sad again. The diagnosis came quickly after that and the chorea. I could no longer control my own body. As a doctor's wife, I've been afforded the best possible care and drugs, but it doesn't matter, this disease destroys. It's impossible to abate. I can feel myself disappearing, little by little and piece by piece, just like my brother had said.

Soon, I won't be able to do anything for myself. My ability to think is impaired and my body will give up. I won't be able to communicate. I will be a prisoner locked inside myself. Sometimes I will recognise my loved ones and find comfort in their care, and other times I won't. I will be somewhere else, lost in the madness of my own diseased mind, unaware of anything bar a fixed spot on a wall.

I'm tired of being scared. I've given in to it now.

The medication helps to manage my mood; it relaxes me and makes surrender a little easier. I'm not always myself, but I'm still here somewhere beneath the rubble.

Before my symptoms appeared and when the kids were old enough, I started working with a group to highlight the sins of the Church. My aim was to demand justice for the terrible things done to the girls and women whose lives and babies were stolen in those criminal institutions they called mother-and-baby homes. I can't do that anymore, but before this disease gets the best of me, I've asked Paddy, my love, to type these words and to tell this story.

I wanted people to know what was done here – how much criminality, cruelty and unnecessary suffering occurred in plain sight. I wanted to fight for the women and children who were never given a chance, like my little friend Maria. I have much to tell and little time to tell it. Someday soon, I'll be too far gone, so Paddy is helping me to express all the things I need to say to those who hurt me, and to those who have been hurt.

So here it goes . . .

To the nuns, priests and orders whose mortal sins committed in the name of Jesus Christ went unpunished, to the government that co-sponsored the discrimination, torture, theft and murder of unmarried mothers and their children, to the society that turned a blind eye to the suffering of our most vulnerable citizens – the shame you piled on us young women of Ireland is now yours to bear for eternity. We were not the problem. You were.

To the good men in my life, my beloved Paddy and my best friend, Tony, take care of each other. I know you will. I've been so lucky to have you both to save me. Thank you for loving me and for giving me this family.

To my kids, Jessica, Philip and Richard, you know your mammy loves you and you know what lies ahead. Don't feel bad. Remember me laughing and hugging you tight. You've taken the genetic test and you've all won the lottery. I can die knowing I didn't pass this terrible disease on to you – and I cannot tell you the immense joy and relief that brings me.

To my daughter, Daisy, as ever, I worry about you. I hope someday soon you'll find me before I disappear. It seems too cruel, but then life is cruel, so I need to tell you now, while I still can, how much I love you. I carried you with me and I carry you still. You are my miracle and you always will be. I can't tell you whether to get tested or not. That is up to you. Know that I would die a thousand times to save you.

It's time for me to let go.

Your mammy.

Chapter Twenty-Eight

Caroline

CAROLINE HANDED IN HER NOTICE the day after the crash, but two months later, she was back in a solicitor's office – the office of Justin O'Halloran of O'Halloran, Browne & Jarvis. Ronnie sat next to her, calm, collected and almost detached from it all. It was an ambush. He didn't know who Ronnie was or why Caroline had requested the meeting. He'd heard of Caroline and assumed it was work-related, not personal in nature. He'd welcomed them into his office and asked the ladies to sit down. He was still handsome, just a little worn, his black hair peppered with grey and his curls all but gone. He still had those eyes, Ronnie's eyes. He looked into them and smiled.

'So, what can I do for you?'

'I'd like some money,' Ronnie said.

'Excuse me?'

'My client, Ronnie, is in fact your daughter, originally named Daisy,' said Caroline. 'Ronnie would like some money.'

He looked from Caroline to Ronnie, the truth dawning. Then he pushed back his chair and took a deep breath. He remained silent for a moment. Neither woman spoke, allowing time to soak in the information.

When he spoke, his voice was soft. 'I had imagined this day, many times over, and never like this.' He stood up and went to the window. 'You're bribing me. You do know that's illegal?'

'Absolutely not,' Caroline said. 'Ronnie has grounds to sue the nuns who held her mother against her will, and who sold Ronnie off without her birth mother's consent. She has grounds to attach your father to the complaint, as he acted illegally in the matter.'

'He did no such thing.'

'*He* engaged in bribery,' Caroline said. 'He bribed Catherine's parents to sign Ronnie's adoption papers and then he bribed them to banish her from her hometown. He used his money and their dependence on charity to rip Catherine from her family and Ronnie from hers – and, as you pointed out a few seconds ago, bribery is illegal.'

'He's a sick old man.'

'And I don't give a shit,' Caroline said.

'What do you want?' He turned to face his daughter. There was no edge in his voice. He asked as if he genuinely really wanted to know.

'I have money put away,' Ronnie said. 'A lot of it. My parents were wealthy and I've earned my own money, and I'll continue to do so for as long I can. I've lived a good life. But I have the Huntington's gene, like my mother has and like my grandfather had . . .'

'Oh God, no,' he said.

'It will kill me,' said Ronnie, 'but until it makes me sick, I want to live. I want to go to places where the people are worse off than me and I want to help them. I want to spend my money doing that. I don't want to have to worry that by the time I need help, it will all be gone . . .'

'And Catherine?' He sounded heartbroken.

Bloody cheek of him, Caroline thought.

'She's at the end stage.'

'Did you get to meet her before . . . ?'

'No.'

'I'm so sorry,' he said, and Caroline could see him visibly crumble.

Ronnie seemed to steel herself.

Caroline held her breath. 'There is a clinic in Zurich that specialises in the care that I will one day need. I want to go there and, if necessary, I want you to agree to pay for it.'

It was a lot to take in. He was crying even as he turned away from her. 'I'm so sorry,' he said. 'I'm so terribly sorry.'

'I don't want your pity.'

'No, of course not.' He reached for a tissue and blew his nose. 'You're just like your mother.'

'You really didn't know her,' Ronnie said.

'No, I suppose I didn't.' When he turned round, his nose was red and his hand shook a little as he spoke. 'I was a bullied, frightened, stupid, selfish boy and I am sorry. I acted like a bully, too. I know that. I gave her up when I should have protected her and you. I stood by as they drove her away.

'I was glad I hadn't let the side down and relieved the problem was taken care of. But now . . . If somebody did to my girls what I did to your mother, well . . .' He shook his head in shame. 'I will pay you anything you want for as long as you want, and not because you hired the Rottweiler who is Caroline Murphy but because I am so terribly, terribly sorry. I owe you and it is the very least I can do.'

Ronnie hadn't expected that. Neither had Caroline. She'd read Catherine's story in preparation for the meeting and he seemed like such a prick in the book.

'Thanks,' Ronnie said, and it was the first time she seemed vulnerable, moved even.

'Whatever I have to sign, I'll sign it. I can set up an account and give you access to it.'

'We'll handle the details another day,' Caroline said. She was kinder now, feeling a little overwhelmed by his genuine heartfelt admission and apology. *If only the religious orders were capable of that.*

They moved to stand.

'Please, wait,' he said. 'Can't we . . . talk?' He picked up a photo on his desk. 'This is my wife, Jen, and these are my two girls, Mellie and Sue. They are not far behind you in age. They would love to meet you.'

'They know about me?'

'Oh yes, they know. I've been waiting a long time for a knock on my door.'

'I don't know . . .' Ronnie glanced at Caroline. 'I've a lot on.'

'I understand, saving the world. No better woman, I've no doubt, but if you are ever in town, we would all be very happy to see you. I know I don't have a right to, but I would like to know you.'

'I'll keep that in mind,' Ronnie said, and all three stood up as he walked them to the door of his large office.

'It was so lovely to meet you, Ronnie,' he said, and he looked like he wanted to say more, but his emotions got the best of him, so much so that Caroline wanted to take him in her arms and hug him right then and there. Instead, she nodded.

She and Ronnie didn't utter a word in the lift or in the lobby of the large office block, or even in the car park or in the car. Not until they were a safe distance from the entire complex and driving on open road.

'That was not what I expected,' Caroline said, and when she looked over at Ronnie, she was silently crying.

'Me neither,' she said.

'How do you feel?'

'Like I'm flying.'

It was the best day of legal work Caroline ever did. And the last.

Epilogue

January 2020

IN THE TEN YEARS SINCE Ronnie had left the country to save
the world, Caroline had often received postcards from her,
giving her small insight into the life of an aid worker. During
that time, Caroline had gone to nursing school. She'd aced her
exams and specialised in midwifery; she was now working out
of the National Maternity Hospital. During that time, she also
repaired her relationship with Michelle and Lisa, and she and
Dave became Tommy's favourite aunt and uncle, mostly because
they spent a shit ton of money on him.

Unlike her friend, she hadn't gone on to rescue orphans, feed
the starving or set up safe havens for the hunted. She helped
women to bring life into the world, and she loved every second
of it. The joy experienced by new parents was like a drug. Even
when a tragedy occurred and her heart broke, it was an honour
to be there to care for each and every family. The ten years since
leaving law had been the best and happiest years of her life. Her
health had improved, her flare-ups were less and even when she
was in pain – maybe because of it – she was brilliant at her job.

Caroline had remained friends with Natalie and Janet throughout the years, attending every christening and birthday, and
always on hand for Christmas jaunts. Janet went on to have two
kids, one boy and a girl. The girl was a mini Janet with a way
louder voice. Natalie had three. After her and Linda's split, she'd

decided to try for children on her own and had two – a little boy named Barry and a girl called Justine. She swore she was done after that, but then she met Tess and they decided to go again. It was Tess who gave birth to their third child, another girl, little Ellie, with a huge head and the biggest smile on Planet Earth. They had got married two years ago in a large ceremony in a hotel in Dublin, with their three kids in attendance. Janet's were there, too, and Caroline had never enjoyed a wedding so much. It was the very best kind of mayhem.

The call came on a Saturday afternoon. Caroline was only just out of bed, having worked a busy nightshift. Her mobile phone was still in her bag, but she fumbled for it anyway. She didn't recognise the number.

'Hello?'

'Is this Caroline Murphy?'

'Yes.'

'My name is Maja. I am ringing from Zurich.'

Caroline's heart skipped a beat.

'I am ringing to let you know that your friend, Ronnie, died at five o'clock this morning. It was a peaceful passing. She wanted you and your friends to know that she carried you with her and she carries you still. It was time for her to let go.'

Tears gathered in Caroline's eyes. 'Was she alone?' she asked.

'No. I was with her when she went. I held her hand and read from her mother's book,' Maja said. 'That always made her calm.'

'Thank you for phoning.'

When Caroline hung up, she cried tears of sadness and joy and hope. She walked into her garden and looked up into the sky and beyond and called out to her friend, 'Goodbye, Ronnie, we loved you. We always will.'

Dave came out of the house, snacking on a teacake. When he saw her, his face fell.

'What's the matter?'

'Ronnie died this morning,' Caroline said.

Dave reached out to her and she leaned on his shoulder. 'I'm so sorry.'

She tried to smile. 'She knew it was coming and she'd lived a good life,' Caroline said. 'A full and beautiful life.'

And then she wrapped herself around her husband and gave thanks for her own full and beautiful life.

Acknowledgements

To my agent Sheila Crowley, you are brilliant not just as an agent but also as an advisor and editor. I am so lucky to have you and we're only getting started. To Emily Harris, Sheila's right-hand woman, thanks so much for always being there and I'm looking forward to us all meeting again when this pandemic has passed.

To everyone at Bonnier: Kate Parkin, for all your support since day one, to Margaret Stead, Clare Kelly, Felice McKeown, Katie Lumsden – you have all been incredible, whether it's editorially or social media or PR, I couldn't have asked for more passion, enthusiasm or support.

To Sarah Bauer, my editor and the genius behind the title *Waiting for the Miracle*, you are a star. This has been such a weird year and so we've only met on Zoom. This too shall pass, and I can't wait to give you a big hug. In fact, I can't wait to give you all big hugs. Roll on the vaccines, roll on re-opening, roll on the *Miracle*, roll on life.

To Simon Hess, Declan Heeny and Helen McKean in Gill Hess, I could not ask for a more supportive team on the ground in Ireland. You've been amazing, and I'm so grateful for your dedication and sheer determination.

Terri Harrison, you are such an incredible woman. When I conceived the character of Catherine, I knew exactly who she was and where I wanted her to go, but I needed to find someone who could bring me inside those hellish mother and baby institutions. I scoured the internet and you leaped out at me. It was a privilege talking to you, not just because of what you went through, having your beloved baby stolen, but also because of the way you've lived your life since. You've waged a battle against those who hurt so many while helping to care for those they hurt. Thank you for telling your story and adding reality and colour to mine. Thank you for being strong, brilliant and kind.

To all the ladies who have experienced difficulty getting or staying pregnant, I want to say a massive thank you for talking to me and being so open and frank. It meant the world and not just because you were helping me with a book, but it was just so lovely to feel part of a community. Infertility can be very lonely and so being able to talk with others who understand and identify was a joy. Emma Reardon, Carol Hess, Elaine Geraghty, Andrea Hayes – you are legends, and thank you. I spoke to so many women, and if I've left your name out I am deeply sorry and still very grateful. Ellen Battles, you were so incredibly helpful with the medicine and especially with Janet's journey. Thank you again.

Chief Pilot Aidan Murray, I cannot thank you enough for allowing me to fictionalise your very real experience of surviving a mid-air collision. It is an extraordinary tale of courage and ability and not just a great story but incredibly inspiring. I also want to thank you for an unforgettable experience in a simulator; it was the first and last experience I'll ever have landing a plane, and I'm good with that.

As ever, to my family and friends – we've come through a difficult 2020 and no doubt 2021 will be more of the same. You've kept me sane through a pandemic and I'm so lucky to be able to say that despite it all we've laughed most days.

To Donal, my husband and the love of my life, we've been through the wars trying to start a family of our own, and it wasn't to be but that's OK, because I have you and you have me and we have dogs. We are where we are because of all we've been through and I wouldn't change a thing.

Reading Group Questions

1. How do Catherine and Caroline's plotlines complement each other?

2. Did you know much about mother and baby institutions before you read this book? What did you learn?

3. How does this novel explore motherhood, both the experience of it and the yearning for it?

4. What do you think the significance of the title is?

5. *Waiting for the Miracle* has a big cast of characters. Do you have a favourite, and why?

6. What did you make of Justin? Did seeing him from Caroline's perspective as well as Catherine's change your opinion of him?

7. Ronnie is a bit of a mystery. How well did you feel you knew her by the end of the novel?

8. Caroline and Catherine's lives are partly very different because of the eras they are living in. How does the novel look at changes in Ireland over the last fifty years? Do you think it would be a very different story if it were set elsewhere?

9. This novel is both sad and funny. How do those elements of the book work together for you?

10. Friendship is at the heart of this novel. How do their close friendships help Catherine and Caroline get through difficult times?

11. Tony and Catherine share a strong connection. Why do you think this is? Does this affect their friendship, and did their connection feel real to you?

12. Were you pleased with how things ended with Caroline and Dave? Did you expect that?

13. Caroline changes career at the end of the novel. If you'd been through what she has, do you think you'd be able to do her new job?

If you enjoyed *Waiting for the Miracle*,
you'll love

Anna McPartlin

The bestselling author of *The Last Days of Rabbit Hayes*

Below the Big Blue Sky

'Hilarious and relatable!' Lucy Porter